THE

EIGHTH HOUSE

Dreena Whiteley

For my brother John Whiteley

UK

Marcia had been intrigued by the urgency she had heard in the woman's voice. The woman was her next client and she had only succeeded in squeezing her into a one-hour slot after a last-minute cancellation. Of course, at that moment, Marcia had no idea of the impact that this woman would have on her life as she walked through the door. The attractive dark-haired woman's attire and large diamond ring told of wealth and privilege. This wasn't her typical type of client. Marcia returned her smile, noting a certain ruthlessness in the woman's dark brown eyes. She knew nothing of this woman except that she had said her name was Suzette. She neither knew nor cared if the name was real. It would not be entirely truthful to say that Marcia loved her work; she had started doing it out of necessity to provide a comfortable lifestyle for her and her son. For some unknown reason, this woman was making her uncomfortable enough to want to get the meeting swiftly out of the way.

"You came highly recommended," the woman said.

Marcia smiled briefly, not wanting to engage in light conversation but only to do what she was paid to do. Marcia looked up from the desk, holding Suzette's eyes. She could feel the woman's tension as she began to reveal the insight that the cards were providing as she laid them out. She approached the subject tactfully.

"There may be something of a criminal nature in which you have dealings … I would advise you to heed a warning – and it is of the utmost urgency." Marcia saw a flicker of uneasiness in Suzette's eyes, but she remained impassive as she continued.

Suzette leaned back in her chair, watching Marcia intently. "May I ask you what situation this might be connected to?" she asked.

Marcia sensed that the woman was testing her and that she was aware of what Marcia might reveal. Tapping her finger on the card of the scales of justice, Marcia held nothing back.

"The law will make its presence known … I also see the skull and crossbones representing Customs and Excise." Marcia glanced towards her client, observing her demeanour change and her face drain of colour.

"In what regard?" Suzette asked, alarmed.

Marcia raised an eyebrow and continued, "Hidden money … financial dealings … illegal substances … narcotics."

Suzette was now anxious, pushing her for more detail. "Do you have any idea when this situation will …"

Marcia interjected, "The number twelve will be significant," she said, concluding the appointment. Suzette's face had become an inscrutable mask as she reached for her bag and paid Marcia her fee.

Marcia was not an unattractive woman. She knew that her slim, curvy figure suited bright, close-fitting clothes, and she had spent her life keeping fit and well, swimming, meditating and eating healthy, wholesome food. She wore her hair short and swept back off her face. The fashionable vibrant red colour complimented her skin tone and she could go without makeup, as her facial bone structure was perfect.

But it was not just Marcia's positive outlook and physical well-being that sustained her. From a young age, Marcia had been highly intuitive, with a powerful psychic ability that was both a blessing and a curse. One of her earliest prophetic dreams was as disturbing as it was real. Growing up, her closest friend Angela had been as dear to her as a sister, but the girls went their separate ways after they left school, as so often happens. Unexpectedly, a few years later they had bumped into one another and had excitedly caught up from where they had left off. That night, back at home, Marcia dreamt of Angela. Tears ran down her cheeks as she cried out to Angela, who did not reply, leaving her with an overwhelming sense of sadness. The tragic call came the following morning. Angela had taken her own life in the night. This was not an isolated incident, many more followed. Unable to understand, and anxious to make sense of it, Marcia visited a famous medium, who told her she had a rare gift and to use it wisely. Under his tutelage, she honed her tarot card reading to perfection. This gift provided her with a way to earn a living and keep her head above water.

Marcia's mental health was important to her, as throughout her life she had many hardships. The tragic death of her parents in a car crash, at the age of fourteen and being sent to live with her mother's half-sister Gaynor who, out of duty rather than love, took her into her household but made it clear she wasn't wanted.

When Marcia was sixteen, she had met a good-looking young man who was a mechanic. His name was Andrew Anderson. They had met at a local dance and Andrew asked her to meet him again. Within a couple of months, she found herself pregnant. A thrilled Andrew asked for her hand in marriage, much to Gaynor's delight. Marcia accepted and they married a few months later, just before Reuben was born. Marcia and Andrew rented a one-bedroom flat and Andrew worked every spare hour for their future. Marcia took to motherhood and when Reuben was two years old, they decided that they would like to expand their family, but for five years of trying, it didn't happen. Andrew at this time began to suffer from persistent headaches, which he said was most probably from the fumes at the garage. A few days later, after he returned home late from working on a private job, Marcia had run him a bath. Within ten minutes of Andrew getting into the bath, Marcia, who had just put Reuben to bed and was preparing Andrew's evening meal, was suddenly filled with a feeling of dread that she didn't understand. She decided to look in on her husband. Her blood-curdling screams resounded around the small flat as she tried to lift him from the water. The coroner's verdict three months later was that a brain tumour had killed him. She became a widow at the age of twenty-four. She found herself the sole provider of her baby son, and she devoted her life to him.

She and Reuben were very close; however, as he grew older, things began to change. Marcia constantly fought against what every fibre of her being was telling her: that her son was getting deeper and deeper into the dark world of drugs. She sensed that it could only end in disaster. His handsome film star looks, his olive skin and raven black hair gave away nothing of the turbulence that raged in his mind. Marcia knew that the death of his father must have contributed. She consulted the tarot cards hoping that there was light at the end of the tunnel in this disturbing chapter in her son's life. The Grim Reaper and Tower were always next to or above one another; both tarot cards indicated darkness looming over his life, and the two cards filled her with dread.

Reuben's eighteenth birthday arrived and he had decided to fulfil his dream of backpacking around Asia for three weeks. Marcia's heart sank, given that she knew of the darkness that surrounded him and the necessity for him to guard against danger. He had given her a wry smile as he closed the car door and turned towards the airport entrance. Marcia pulled the car out to join the traffic leaving the airport, for the return journey home. She couldn't shake off the overwhelming sensation that she would never see her son again, and tears streamed down her face. The three weeks that Reuben was away in Asia seemed like a lifetime to her as she marked off each day on the calendar.

Finally, on 14 March, Reuben was due home. As she crossed out the date on the calendar, the phone rang in the lounge. Surely now she would hear his voice and learn that he was back safe in the UK, bringing relief from the three weeks of fear that had gripped her since his departure. She answered the phone and through a daze listened to Reuben telling her that two kilos of heroin had been found in his rucksack and that he would not be returning home for the foreseeable future. Marcia, still gripping the receiver, felt dizzy, and she found herself sinking to her knees and sobbing. Reuben's words barely registered. "I am eighteen, Mum, don't worry. I'm responsible for my actions." Marcia was beside herself.

Three weeks later, her son was mysteriously released from prison. Reuben had rung Marcia telling her that he was being relocated; no one would know his identity. He had been given an ultimatum: going to prison for a period of five to ten years or giving the names up of the men behind the drug deal, which had resulted in him settling for the latter and thus regaining his liberty. Freedom came at a price, however. There would always be the possibility that one day the accused would come after him if they discovered his whereabouts. It was a secret that Marcia would have to take to her grave, as his life depended upon it.

Living in the shadow of this situation day after day, Marcia went to bed each night feeling mentally exhausted. At times, as she meditated – a vision of her son and his surroundings filled her mind. Marcia felt as if she could reach out and touch him. Only by keeping herself busy could she gain any peace of mind. When she wasn't giving tarot readings, she swam, practised yoga or went for long walks to fill her days. She had few friends and had steered clear of serious relationships after her husband's untimely death. She couldn't envisage her situation changing any time soon. It was a constant battle for her to maintain the façade of normality and mask her inner turmoil. She preferred to keep herself to herself – that way no one pried or asked questions, and she could fool herself that life was okay. Her heightened senses enhanced her intuitive abilities, which became stronger as time passed, and she gained a reputation as a powerful psychic, one who was incredibly accurate.

She had promised herself a holiday so she could relax and recharge her batteries, but as the winds of change began to blow, they conspired to alter Marcia's destiny, leading her down the very path that she had tried to avoid, changing her world to an extent that she could never have imagined.

Marcia walked to the kitchen and having poured herself a large glass of wine, she opened her laptop to browse the holidays in Mexico that she had been looking at earlier. Breaking her reverie, her phone rang. The number was unfamiliar; she was going to ignore the call. Two weeks of pure luxury and relaxation beckoned. Okay, she had paid more than she had planned, but the gorgeous location and the hotel's tropical views had persuaded her to indulge. This was a well-earned holiday, and nothing was going to stop her from going. The phone stopped ringing and the answer machine kicked in.

The voice, tinged with urgency and begging her to call back, was Suzette's.

"I had a reading from you two weeks ago and I need to speak with you urgently."

When Marcia called back, the phone rang only twice before it was picked up.

"I *need* to see you, Marcia, as soon as possible," Suzette stammered.

"I am very sorry, Suzette, but I am planning on going on holiday to Mexico shortly, so if you would like to ring at a later date…"

Suzette pleaded with her, "I won't take up too much of your time, a couple of hours … I live a few miles from you … I need you to visit me."

Marcia was frustrated as Suzette hurriedly insisted that her driver would collect her and return her home. "My husband will more than treble your fee for the inconvenience."

Marcia hesitated, she could use the extra cash, but her time *was* limited.

"If you make it around six pm tomorrow evening, I can tie up some loose ends. But I can only spare a couple of hours," she advised.

Suzette expressed her gratitude.

Marcia's intercom sounded. She glanced at the clock – 6 pm. Her mind had been working overtime since speaking to Suzette. Something was going on, though she could not quite put her finger on it.

Marcia walked toward the Mercedes. The driver smiled weakly without speaking as he opened the car door for her. Everything seemed surreal as they drove through the traffic, though no words were exchanged on the journey. Marcia felt a rising sense of unease as the car turned off the main road and escaped into the countryside. All around her were centuries-old farms and villages. Vast woodlands filled the landscape. She was surprised by the splendour as the car turned into a long tarmac drive, lined with lampposts. Marcia took in the tennis court and a treehouse. The large house was the type she had only seen in magazines. The car stopped in front of a flight of steps. Suzette, looking glamorous and suited to wealth, came to the door as Marcia approached. Marcia sensed a shift of power because Suzette was on her own turf. Suzette was making small talk as she waltzed through the house, which was filled with expensive furnishings. Marcia could see from the lounge windows a large swimming pool surrounded by sun loungers. The grounds beyond were enclosed by a wall. This place, Marcia thought, must be worth a small fortune.

As if reading her thoughts, Suzette said, "This house isn't ours, including the furnishings. It's rented from one of Max's friends whose wife died and he couldn't face living here anymore." He lives in the Caribbean and travels with his schooner, island hopping. Fortunately, we do not own this property, as it would be confiscated."

Marcia wasn't interested. All she wanted to do was conduct the reading and leave so she could get ready for her holiday. Taking the seat Suzette proffered, she sat opposite her at the long refectory table.

"Please don't feel uncomfortable, Marcia. Make yourself at home," Suzette said.

She offered a glass of wine, which Marcia declined, as she didn't drink while she was working.

"I must tell you the good news first," Suzette said as she sat back in her chair and crossed her legs. Her eyes never left Marcia's.

Marcia felt an element of deviousness as Suzette smiled. Here was a woman who would use anyone to gain what she wanted. Her eyes gave it away, Marcia noted.

"Firstly, I would like to thank you for the accurate reading. You certainly have a special gift," Suzette said leaning forwards, "And, one, I might add, that you could use to everyone's advantage."

Marcia felt on edge as Suzette continued.

"In a few minutes, my husband will phone. He wishes to speak to you."

Marcia didn't respond.

"Don't feel alarmed. The outcome of this phone call could change your life beyond your wildest dreams."

As Suzette finished speaking, her mobile phone rang. She answered it and walked out of the room. She returned as quickly, calling for Marcia to follow her. "My husband, Max, would like to speak with you," Suzette smiled, handing her the phone. She left the room and closed the door.

The charming voice on the other end of the phone was not something Marcia had expected. Her mind drifted back to Suzette's earlier tarot reading when she recalled her suspicions that the pair of them were involved in narcotics. The house, rented or otherwise, meant big money. Max Greenaway, Suzette's husband, was still on the phone thanking her for Suzette's previous tarot reading prediction.

"Even though I am now residing under her Majesty's pleasure," Max laughed, "Please let me explain a few things to you." "Please do not worry. I have made enquiries about you and discovered the problem your son Reuben Anderson

11

encountered with the law regarding bringing narcotics into the country from his trip to Asia. Please don't concern yourself about how I discovered about him, because I'm a man who knows many influential people. Believe me when I say that his hiding place will remain secret. In return, all I ask is that you will work as my adviser. It will be extremely beneficial to you. I can be a very generous man, he added."

Marcia's mind raced, shocked, as he mentioned her son. She pulled up a chair and sat at the table, her hands trembling as he told her, "You have two days to make your decision. Hopefully, Marcia, you are wise enough to make the right one."

Her throat constricted. Trying to keep her voice calm, Marcia told him she would give it some thought.

"Goodbye," he said abruptly, ending the call.

Suzette opened the door, and taking Marcia's hand, told her not to worry. "Let's go out on the terrace and have some wine. I can explain a few things to you." Suzette picked up a bottle of wine and two glasses as Marcia followed like a lamb to slaughter, walking out into the cool evening air.

"I know what my husband has asked, Marcia. He told me earlier, and although you may think at the moment that you are being pressured, I can assure you, I will help you through this. We can work together."

Marcia took a seat at the garden table. She felt she needed the wine to help steady her nerves and she reached for the glass.

"We are going to need one another Marcia, we are both in a desperate situation, but with your gift of foresight and my knowledge of what Max's world is like, we can become allies." Marcia tried to register what she was implying, gulping a mouthful of wine as Suzette continued. "There is something else I want to add before you make a decision. If you work for

12

Max, I will need you to withhold certain things from him. It would be best for you and me."

Marcia felt as if she had lead in her stomach as Suzette revealed her plan. "Max is astute and didn't survive by being stupid, although he didn't believe me about your warning, until the police raid on that date, but then he learnt too late. It opened his eyes after that as he realised what an asset you would be to him, even though he is in prison. It was my fault that I had told him your name, not realising he would make enquiries about you and unearth the problem you face with your son. But let's put that to one side and talk about you and me. I can run his business from the outside, but I am not going to be his puppet. I need you to assist me, Marcia."

Marcia's incredulous look brought a conspiratorial smile to Suzette's face. "There are certain things that we women must keep from our men, and this situation will give me an opportunity that I never thought would arise. Max is an influential man and he has eyes and ears everywhere, but he wouldn't have you on his side if he knew you and I had joined up. Please give it some serious thought, Marcia. I have seen the way you live, please don't think I'm being a snob, but I know how both of us could have a life of luxury," Suzette said.

Marcia had drunk half of the wine in her glass and had regained her confidence. "Suzette, material things are not as important to me as they obviously are to you." She glanced at the diamonds on Suzette's fingers. "I am also going on holiday to Mexico in two days, so I can't make a decision just yet." Marcia knew she was playing for time, but she needed to get her head around what Max and Suzette were proposing.

"If you decide to help me and give advice to Max, then the holiday will have to be cancelled, but you will be reimbursed," Suzette added.

Marcia didn't reply. She couldn't wait to get away from there. She told Suzette she wanted to go home. Suzette made the call for the driver to collect her.

"Mikey is one of Max's most trusted friends. Loyalty is high on my husband's list," Suzette said. After placing the phone down, she continued, "I know you may think I'm being hypocritical by asking you to be duplicitous with my husband, but it is a necessity. I am tired of living like a prisoner and tired of my husband's controlling ways when I can now be free," Suzette confided.

Marcia didn't respond.

That night Marcia cried herself to sleep. She knew she had no other option but to work for the pair of them if she were to keep her son safe. Marcia was aware that Suzette had tried to sugar coat the situation with the promise of a luxurious lifestyle if she helped her. But it all came down to blackmail. These were powerful people, steeped in the world of drugs, and there was no escape for her. Marcia knew the path she must take.

The following day, Marcia reluctantly cancelled the holiday. "Unforeseen circumstances," she told the woman on the phone. She had laughed out loud, as she put the phone down; it was either that or cry at the way her life was going.

Marcia waited for the telephone call that would alter her life. It was now Friday, and just after six in the evening, and her nerves had been on edge all day. The shrill ring of her phone seemed to fill the apartment making her jump with alarm.

It was Max. "Have you made your decision, Marcia?" he said flatly.

"Yes," she replied quietly. "I will do it."

"Thrilled to have you on board. You won't regret it, and the secret about your son stays with me," Max reassured her. "My wife will ring you later."

Suzette rang that night. "Have you thought about my proposal, Marcia?"

"I do hope you realise, Suzette, what you are getting us into, like you told me, your husband is astute and for me to try to keep him from discovering whatever it is that you have in mind, could be dangerous because of the circles he mixes in, as I clearly saw in the tarot cards from the first reading I did for you."

Suzette reassured her, "We can pull it off and I'll go into more detail next time I see you." She told her that Mikey would be picking her up the following evening, and there was one more thing: "Max and I will require your services at random times. You will need to be on call and flexible with your time, so it would be best if you do not take on any more clients." It was a directive more than a request. Marcia stayed silent.

On arrival the following evening, Suzette eagerly took hold of Marcia's arm, guiding her into the lounge. "I'm so pleased you have decided to come on board with me Marcia. I'm sure we are going to have a long friendship." She didn't pause for breath, "Marcia, if you see anything in my husband's reading about me, I want you to keep it to yourself. We cannot have anything that will upset him, can we?"

Marcia's heart sank and she thought it could not get any worse. She felt certain that Suzette was withholding something. "Are you telling me to double-cross your husband?" she asked incredulously.

"No, please," Suzette replied, "Don't think of it like that. All I require is for you to use your words in such a way that he will be satisfied and it will enable us to move forward without his knowledge. Max, will be behind bars for a few years. I will conduct his business with your help, but there are certain things I don't want him to know." Suzette said conspiratorially. "You are safe, so don't worry about a thing … later this afternoon, I would like you to give me a reading before my husband speaks to you."

Marcia had never been in a situation where she had to play one person against another, and she realised what a dangerous game she had agreed to take part in.

Suzette made lunch; Marcia declined the wine, as she wanted a clear head. Suzette changed the subject and talked about the garden, the house and how she swam in the pool regularly.

"Do you swim, Marcia?"

Marcia smiled, "Yes regularly."

"You may use the pool whenever you wish," Suzette offered. "As I said to you earlier, I have a feeling that a new friendship will emerge now that everything is out in the open." Marcia thanked Suzette for the offer, without any intention of taking her up on it, and as for the friendship, she would rather have become pals with a cobra. Suzette was on her second glass of wine as she reached out to touch Marcia's hand.

"The world I live in with my husband … it's different from the one that you're used to. Whatever your principles, please put them to one side. My husband and his associates are not people to mess with. They have no scruples, especially when it comes to disloyalty, so please bear that in mind, Marcia. I know you have the ability to outsmart Max. I wouldn't have involved you if I thought differently, Marcia."

Marcia felt panic rising in her chest. "You have asked me to withhold anything I see in the reading about you from your husband, and now you tell me how he feels about betrayal."

Suzette smiled thinly.

"I have a feeling that you are far too clever for him, with the gift you possess, and you are eloquent. Concentrate on Max's business and everyone will be fine. When you are ready, we can go inside and you can give me a reading."

Marcia followed Suzette into the house. Once they were seated, Marcia took out her tarot cards and passed them to Suzette, who by now knew the routine.

Marcia began to lay each of the twenty-two major arcana cards on the table. "I can see a man coming into your life, on an emotional level. You must be careful of him and a woman who will betray you."

Suzette interrupted, "Can you describe the man?"

"Yes," Marcia replied. After giving his description she went on to say that Suzette would regularly travel to meet him. "He is not far from here and I feel that you will have a clandestine relationship with him very soon." Marcia actually sensed that this guy was already on the scene, but she kept it to herself. "There are three men that you must be on guard with and one of them is your husband." Suzette shook her head as Marcia continued, "I think that your husband knows more than you realise, therefore please don't underestimate him."

Suzette intercepted, "Are you saying that I am going to have an affair?"

"Yes, you are," Marcia replied flatly.

"Who is the woman you speak of?" Suzette asked.

"I feel that she is connected to this man and that there is a child involved in this relationship," Marcia answered. She felt Suzette was withholding something about this situation. Marcia told her that she would take a journey overseas shortly and would eventually relocate to distant shores. "There are big changes in your life and you will eventually end up having the last laugh."

Once the reading had finished, Suzette was thrilled. "I know that I have to be wary of Max, but the other two men you spoke of are of no importance to me."

Marcia was aware that Suzette hadn't taken on board her warnings. She found that was the way with many clients – they only listened to what they wanted to hear, and Suzette wasn't going to be any different.

"There is someone whom I am attracted to that fits the description, but that is all it is … an attraction."

"It won't stay that way, and my advice to you is not to get involved with him, as he will betray you," Marcia replied.

Suzette gave a small laugh. "It does seem intriguing, and if anything that you have predicted occurs, I will certainly keep you informed." Suzette rose from her seat and thanked Marcia. "Max will be phoning in half an hour to speak to you, so please keep in mind our agreement."

Marcia smiled thinly, following her out of the room.

Minutes later, Suzette's phone rang. She answered, and then passed the phone to Marcia, hastily retreating from the room.

Max didn't beat around the bush. "Now to get down to business. How do we do this?" he queried.

"I am going to shuffle the tarot cards," Marcia replied. "Tell me when you feel ready."

She shuffled the cards for a few minutes. When he said to stop, Marcia began to lay the cards out on the table. Voices and impressions came thick and fast into her mind. Marcia took control.

"I feel a Spanish and Irish connection that will bring disruption into your life. Your world is going to be transformed by an unexpected twist of circumstances and the legal system will connect it." Marcia paused; she felt apprehensive because of Suzette's deception.

"This is rather confusing. I can understand the link to Spain, but can you be more specific?" Max asked.

Marcia explained that his life would become cloaked in secrecy. "You are going to have an opportunity to regain your freedom, but it comes at a price."

"Regain my freedom…," he repeated.

Marcia sensed that Max would lose out on a business deal, but she stayed quiet about that, as she didn't know if it would involve Suzette or not. Whatever was going to happen with Max, she knew he was going to do things in secret. "There is going to be a legal formality that you will agree to, and when this situation arises you can take it as a sign that your life will become transformed."

She stated that was the only information she was getting from the reading.

Max was silent for a moment. Then he said, "Well, it sounds intriguing and you have certainly given me something to think about." He thanked her and said he would speak to her again soon.

Marcia left the room and joined Suzette, who was seated at the breakfast bar. "Everything fine with my husband?" Suzette queried.

Marcia felt mentally drained as she repeated what she told Max. "Suzette you must tread carefully because I feel that Max can't be trusted."

Suzette waved Marcia's concerns away and passed her an envelope. "I have given you some extra money for helping me." Taking Marcia's hand in hers, she smiled. "Don't look so worried," she reassured her. "I can handle Max, as long as you keep him happy with your predictions. You may not be used to this sort of thing, but I will help you by giving you an insight into how Max's mind works, so just leave that to me."

Mikey drove Marcia home in silence. She sensed that the driver took in far more than he let on. On the journey home, she reflected on the irony of the situation. It was ironic that although her son Reuben's life had been turned upside down because of narcotics, and she herself had never touched them, she now found herself in the employ of a drugs baron. Her mind drifted, wondering where destiny would lead her.

The following morning, Marcia was awoken by her mobile phone ringing. Suzette's number flashed across the screen and she felt apprehensive answering it as it was so early. She braced herself, hoping that there wasn't a problem, and she answered the call.

Suzette apologised for disturbing her. "It's imperative that I see you. I will explain when you get here. Can you be at my place in two hours?" She didn't wait for an answer. "I will send Mikey to collect you."

"Okay," Marcia replied sleepily. She dragged herself out of bed and jumped in the shower. The past few weeks had been emotionally draining, and the lack of sleep was telling on her. She skipped breakfast.

Upon arrival at the imposing entry gates, Mikey pressed the buzzer to be let in. As soon as the gates opened, he sped through and continued down the long drive. By the time they reached the house, Suzette was standing by the front door, fear registering on her face. Suzette thanked Mikey as he nodded to her and took his leave in silence.

"Please," she said, with a sense of urgency, "Come in and I will tell you what has happened." Suzette shut the front door behind her and they went into the lounge.

"Whatever is the matter?" Marcia asked, "You are making me feel nervous."

"Max wants to question you, but I needed to speak with you first." Marcia saw that Suzette seemed uneasy.

"I have a confession. I have been seeing one of my husband's contacts over the past week. I met up with Gary twice, but as we were leaving the hotel where we stayed overnight, a woman saw us." She wrung her hands as she spoke.

Marcia couldn't believe the woman's audacity. She slumped on the settee as Suzette paced the room.

"I didn't know her, and she didn't know me, but she knew him. She is Gary's girlfriend's close friend. The look the woman gave me was venomous, so I tried to make it appear as if we were not together."

Suzette sat on the arm of a large, comfortable-looking chair. "I knew that she saw Gary put his hand on my back as we were coming out of the entrance doors. Gary told me when I spoke to him later that the woman would tell his Mrs what she had seen, "Gary phoned me to say that Kathy had ripped into him and said she would make enquiries as to the woman he was with. Her friend had sent her a photograph of Gary and me that she had discreetly taken on her mobile."

Marcia listened, gobsmacked at her revelation. More so because he was a close friend of Suzette's husband. Marcia had previously predicted that Suzette would start seeing someone else but she had not been aware of who with.

"Max has grilled me about this, but I denied it and explained that I had booked the room in the hotel for a spa evening with a friend, and it was a coincidence that Gary was in the hotel that night too." Suzette continued, "Gary had made a reservation separately, just to be on the safe side."

Suzette confided that her marriage had been unhappy for the past couple of years. "Max is a controlling man. I've felt suffocated, as he wants to know my every movement. Things came to a head when Gary visited our house recently to see how I was doing while Max was in prison. We had a couple of drinks and one thing led to another, and now this, but don't tell me to stop seeing him, as I can't, and Gary feels the same way as I do."

Marcia shook her head in exasperation.

"Please, don't involve me in this, Suzette. You know the position I'm in and the danger I face."

"There will be no threat if you play your cards right," Suzette said earnestly. "Max won't be able to find out, and if my life goes according to plan, with your help, you will benefit far more if you side with me rather than with my husband."

Marcia knew that she was between the devil and the deep blue sea. She resigned herself to going along with Suzette.

After Suzette had explained in detail about her life, Marcia began to feel compassion for her. She had had a difficult upbringing, and she had endured a lot of strife with Max. Suzette said that now she had Marcia and Gary as allies she planned to leave Max.

"Don't you think it's a bit early to be making plans with this man?" Marcia asked.

"I know it's complicated, Marcia, and you think it's a whirlwind romance, but I have known Gary for a long time. I desperately need a tarot card reading, Marcia," Suzette pleaded.

Before doing the reading, Marcia needed to clear her mind, which had been swamped and clouded by Suzette's affair with Max's associate. She went into the garden to meditate for fifteen minutes. When she returned, her mind purified, she found that Suzette had shuffled the pack. Marcia mentally switched off all outside influences as she began to lay each card out.

"I see obstacles that lay in wait for you with this man, Suzette. Also, I see a warning about a man linked to your husband, a close associate. I feel it could be Mikey."

"You are wrong about Mikey. You must be confusing him with someone else," Suzette insisted, as she looked at the cards spread across the table, anxiety registering on her face. She asked if this new relationship would work out in the long term.

Marcia didn't understand Suzette's refusal to listen to her previous counsel. Marcia had already told her about the man's impending betrayal. Marcia shook her head. "He is not the one for you. He is disloyal, as I told you before, Suzette. However, there is a new love moving into your destiny, a good man who will appreciate you, but you haven't met him yet. Distant shores will have an impact on your life with him for the good. So please be patient, Suzette, and wait for the tide to turn in your favour."

Suzette looked crestfallen. "I have no more patience, I've put up with Max far too long, and now with him out of the way in prison I'm going to continue to see Gary."

Marcia knew her advice was wasted, as Suzette wasn't listening to her. Upon gathering the cards and putting them away, she looked into Suzette's eyes and told her, "You are not only taking undue risks, but you are also playing with my life, my world has been turned…"

Suzette interrupted. "Max will be ringing shortly and when he does, act normal, give him the guidance he needs with his business. Any questions about me, well you know how to play it." With that, the phone rang. Suzette answered and passing it to Marcia, she left the room.

"Hi," said Max.

Before Marcia could reply he told her there was something he wanted to be clarified. "It is of a somewhat personal nature and all I require is a yes or no answer."

Marcia picked up the cards and began to shuffle. She did not fully let herself tune in to the cards as she normally would. This way she was in better control of what she would say. Her stomach lurched as she laid each card on the table.

Marcia composed herself as Max's chilling voice asked if there was anything to concern him about in his marriage. Marcia felt a trickle of fear run up her spine as she glanced at the layout.

"No," she lied.

"Are you absolutely sure?"

Marcia picked up a threatening undertone. Reassuring Max that all was well, she fought to sound positive. He thanked her for putting his mind at rest, his tone became lighter as he told her that being behind bars could play havoc with one's mind.

Marcia asked him if there was anything else he wanted to discuss. Max told her that he would speak with her in a couple of days.

Marcia couldn't get off the phone quick enough. She couldn't believe the line she had crossed by lying to Max about Suzette. She remained seated for a few moments, trying to get her head around the situation. Her hands were shaking as the door opened and Suzette popped her head in. Seeing that she was off the phone, Suzette raised an eyebrow.

"Well, don't leave me in suspense, what did Max say?"

"He asked me twice if there was anything to worry about in his marriage and I told him that all was fine," Marcia replied.

"Was he satisfied with what you told him?"

"As far as I could tell he was satisfied with my answer, but I sensed he was only testing me," Marcia sighed wearily.

Suzette grinned happily, as she stood up and clapped her hands.

"Brilliant, like I said that you and I will make a great team, Marcia. Max is suspicious natured. He only trusts Mikey. Suzette took her hand, pulling her to her feet.

"Max will phone me later, before they are locked up for the night, and I will smooth things over with him, so cheer up and let's go and have some wine to celebrate."

Marcia agreed to one glass of wine. She felt she needed something to calm the feeling of trepidation. Although she sensed that Suzette was conniving, she couldn't help warming to her. Marcia knew Suzette was treading on thin ice with her husband. Marcia's perception told her that Max was streets ahead of his wife when it came to strategy. When Marcia finished her glass of wine, she made her excuses, feigning tiredness. She felt she needed her own space and to get away from the deception.

Suzette spoke to her on the phone the following evening and told her that Max was fine. She had smoothed things over with her husband and asked Marcia if she could pay her a visit in two days' time.

Forty-eight hours later, just as she arrived at Suzette's house, Suzette informed Marcia that her lover Gary, his girlfriend *and* their child would be visiting later that day. Marcia froze. Suzette, watching Marcia's reaction reassured her that she was okay with it. "Gary had explained to Kathy that he had bumped into me at the hotel and said that it was pure coincidence that we were at the same place that night. Gary had told Kathy that I needed a friend, and for her to give me a call, which she did. I was prepared, as Gary had pre-warned me, so I had to play the charming hostess and invite them to stay the night. Kathy asked Gary to drive down later once his business was concluded." Suzette said it like it was an everyday occurrence to invite your lover, his girlfriend and their child to stay overnight at her home.

The more Marcia heard about Gary the less she trusted him. "I know it's up to you what you do, but please be careful, I feel this woman is far shrewder than you think," she counselled.

"Please don't worry," Suzette responded. "I want you to stay here until early evening, meet them, and tell me what you pick up."

"Who are you going to say I am?" Marcia asked.

"An old friend of mine," Suzette replied, "One, that gave me a tarot reading a long time ago and that we have always kept in contact."

"Do you think it's wise to tell them that?" Marcia wasn't looking forward to being in their company.

"Yes, I do, it will keep them both on their toes," Suzette laughed. Marcia knew that Suzette had some nerve, but this took the biscuit. Suzette went over the story of how they had met. Marcia knew she was getting deeper and deeper into this shady life, and it was getting scarier by the day.

They heard the buzz of the front gates. Suzette answered the intercom and let them in. "Okay," she said, "Just relax."

As Suzette opened the door, a dark-haired woman walked in holding the hand of a small, blond boy who looked to be about four to five years old. The poor lad seemed timid and subdued. She was not an attractive woman physically, but she had a strong presence and Marcia didn't like the energy she was giving off. Here was a woman who would fight tooth and nail for what she wanted.

Then, through the door bounced a short, slim man, radiating confidence, with a welcoming smile that lit up his face. "Hi ladies, how is everybody?" He fleetingly caught Marcia's eye then looked at Suzette.

Marcia thought it must be his extrovert personality rather than his looks that attracted Suzette. She sensed he was a charmer. During Suzette's introductions, Marcia noticed that the woman's focus was on her alone. She moved across to where Marcia was sitting on the settee.

"I am not moving from my spot," she asserted, "Mystics hold a great fascination for me." Gary glanced over briefly, and Marcia caught a hint of amusement in his eyes.

26

"Please, let me get you a drink. Your son must be hungry and thirsty after the journey," Suzette said.

Marcia thought Suzette and Gary's body language belied that there was something between them.

"We stopped off at a café on the way down," Kathy replied reassuringly, "Bradley and I are fine. What about you Gary?"

"I'm cool. If you don't mind, Suzette, I will wander around your beautiful grounds," he said, looking out of the window.

Marcia caught the inconspicuous look they gave one another. The flush on Suzette's face was a giveaway. She wondered if Kathy picked up on it.

"Take Bradley with you and leave us girls so that we can get to know one another," Kathy said, as Gary and her young son went out of the door. "Men, in general, don't believe in any type of 'mumbo jumbo'. They think it's all a load of crap – fortune telling, tarot cards and the like, but I love it." Kathy said, turning to look at Suzette,

"How fascinating to have such a powerful friend, Suzette, one to warn you of impending problems." Marcia sensed that Kathy didn't believe what Gary had told her about the chance meeting in the hotel with Suzette. Once more, Kathy's attention was back on Marcia.

"I do hope you can stay for a while. I would love it if you could give me a reading," Kathy said.

Suzette interrupted, "I am sorry Kathy, but Marcia has an appointment this evening so she can't stay too long."

Marcia understood that was her cue.

"Yes, I have an appointment with a regular client. I am sorry, but I must leave soon, otherwise, I will be late."

"Surely," Kathy said, "if I make it worth your while, you could come up with some excuse and re-arrange another time with this client?"

"Like I said," Marcia replied, "This is someone who uses my services regularly and I cannot let anyone down. Perhaps the next time we meet."

A look of irritation flickered across Kathy's face. Marcia thought that this woman was used to having what she wanted and she wasn't going to give up easily. Kathy, however, changed her tactic and turned on the charm.

"Maybe I can book an appointment with you the next time we are down this way?"

"Of course," Marcia replied, never intending to give this woman a reading. If she could avoid it at all costs, she would. The situation was bad enough as it was without having to deal with Kathy as well.

Marcia made her apologies and rose to leave. "Please give my regards to Gary. I must go now. The traffic will be horrendous and I can't be late for my appointment."

Suzette saw Marcia to her car, kissed her on the cheek and said, "I will ring you very soon."

Suzette rang Marcia the very next day. "They have left," she said, "What did you think about Kathy?"

Marcia explained exactly what she had sensed and advised Suzette, "She believes that something is going on with you and Gary, so be very careful."

"Well," said Suzette, "I believe in the old saying about keeping your friends close and your enemies closer. Kathy had too much to drink last night and she was constantly berating Gary, much to his annoyance. To be honest, I think she has a drinking problem," Suzette said. "Today we went out for lunch and Kathy drank a whole bottle of wine and started nagging at Gary again … and I felt sorry for her little boy, bless him, he was quiet most of the time. Do you think you could come over Monday lunchtime as I need to talk to you, also Max will be ringing later that day and he has asked to speak with you too?"

"Okay," Marcia replied and put the phone down.

Marcia arrived at Suzette's at noon. "Max is setting up a deal with Gary and I am going to oversee it. I have also planned to meet Gary in a couple of days to spend the night with him at a hotel. Don't worry, Marcia, I always text him on his other phone, which he uses for private calls, to confirm the time of our meeting. Kathy doesn't know this phone exists."

Suzette also told her that when Marcia had spoken to Gary, he'd felt uncomfortable in her presence. "He told me that it was your penetrating dark eyes that made him feel as if you could see through him."

"Well, if he has nothing to hide, Suzie, then I would say he hasn't anything to worry about," Marcia replied, shortly. She went on to say, "I can understand you falling for him. He has an outgoing personality." But what Marcia did not say was that she felt he couldn't be trusted. There was something about him that made her slightly uneasy. Marcia knew that no matter what she said to Suzette, she was too wrapped up in Gary to take any notice. Over coffee, Marcia was just beginning to unwind when Suzette released another bombshell.

"I am going to work alongside Gary against Max. Gary told me he could get a far better deal. I know you must think that I am treacherous, Marcia, but I want to be with Gary no matter what, and he is planning to take over from Max and we will run the business side of things together. Please give me a quick reading. Tune in for me," she said.

Marcia couldn't believe what she was hearing. "Listen to me!" she said harshly. The tone Marcia was using was stern and authoritative, "I am in enough of a mess and now you are going to scheme behind your husband's back with the man who is supposedly your husband's friend? Do you have a death wish? I don't know much about the criminal world, but as you told me in the beginning, disloyalty is one thing to be afraid of and I am stuck in the middle of all this."

"I know what you are saying is right, but if all goes according to plan, I will be financially independent. I need you to listen to me, as I have a proposition for you, Marcia. I am going to Spain next week and I want you to come with me."

"Why on earth do you need me to come with you?" Marcia was flabbergasted by her request.

"I am going to meet up with Gary before the trip to Spain. Max and Gary have associates out there. A big deal with them is in the offing and I need to know who I can trust."

Marcia was mortified. She felt that this was like living a bad dream. Marcia was becoming more immersed in their criminal activity, and she couldn't see a way out.

Suzette gave her some insight into Max's finances. "Marcia, I know where Max has stashed a great deal of money, which I intend to have for myself, and it will allow me to break away from him."

Marcia's jaw dropped. "Suzette, I don't know if Gary has turned your mind, or what planet you are on, but to steal your husband's money would be disastrous for us. Max would never let you get away with it, so how can you think of doing such a thing?"

Suzette poured herself some wine, offering a glass to Marcia, who shook her head. "I have a foolproof plan that I know Max will fall for. If I didn't have faith in what I'm going to do, I wouldn't attempt it."

Marcia held her head in her hands. "I will guide you as much as possible, but all I ask of you is when I give you warnings, you must pay heed to them."

Suzette reassured her. "I promise you I won't go against anything you advise me, and we will have a lovely life once everything is settled."

Marcia thought Suzette was insane. She might as well be playing Russian roulette.

Marcia spent all that week advising Suzette, coupled with phone consultations with Max. She managed to fit in a couple of swim and sauna sessions at her local health club. Then at the end of the week, she was packed and on her way to Suzette's, where she would be staying overnight. They would then leave early the following morning to go to Spain. Suzette had asked her driver Mikey to take them to the airport.

Mikey dropped them off at the airport the next morning. He'd hardly said a word, but Marcia sensed he was taking on board everything they were talking about, and she noticed him glancing periodically in the rear view mirror. Although Marcia liked his energy, there was something about him that she didn't trust, and she instinctively was careful what she said to Suzette.

At the airport, the two women had a quick look at the duty free shop. Suzette wanted a bottle of her favourite Chanel perfume, and she encouraged Marcia to pick out something for herself.

Marcia declined.

"Don't be silly, Max is paying for all this, so grab some of your favourite perfume." Suzette ignored Marcia's refusal and purchased two bottles. She gave one to Marcia. The two women boarded the plane for Alicante. Suzette was telling her about the people whose villa they were staying at in Altea, but Marcia was only half listening as the aircraft began to move along the runway. She glanced out of the window, and as the plane began to rise into the clouds above Gatwick airport, she realised how surreal her situation was.

Spain

As they walked out into the Spanish sunshine, Suzette's phone rang. It was Max's cousin Jimmy Grant's wife, Joyce, who they would be staying with. She had called to say that she would be meeting them at the airport. Suzette had filled Marcia in on all the details on the flight over – about Jimmy Grant's reputation as a womaniser, and that he was a powerful man in the drug world. Marcia didn't really want to hear about the crazy things her new hosts got up to. She was finding it hard enough to deal with Max and Suzette's shenanigans. But against her better judgement, she couldn't help but warm to the bubbly blonde woman who welcomed them. Marcia guessed that she might be in her late fifties, but she had a youthful energy. Joyce introduced herself to Marcia and hugged both women, then she opened the boot of her car and helped them put their cases in.

Suzette said, "I know that you believe in star signs, well you will enjoy talking to your visitor as Marcia is a psychic medium who does tarot card readings."

Joyce took her eyes off the road and turned around, beaming at Marcia in the back seat. A car horn honked as Joyce swerved and put her hand up in apology to the offended driver.

Looking in the rear view mirror, Joyce said, "You will go down a storm with my friends out here. We all love tarot readings and read our horoscopes in the newspaper. Do you mind if I tell them you are here? … They will pay you good money."

"Well," Marcia replied hesitantly, looking at Suzette.

"Of course she will," Suzette interrupted and laughed, "Let us get business sorted first and then we can make arrangements for Marcia to read for your friends." By now, the car was making its way up a steep hill, and Joyce pointed out a stunning villa at the top.

"Welcome to my home," Joyce said, as they drove through large, ornate gates and stopped outside Joyce's magnificent villa. Marcia got out of the car and looked out at an incredible view of the bay in the distance. The scenery was breathtaking.

A man called out as he walked down the steps in their direction,

"Come on you women, get out of this heat and I'll pour you a drink."

Joyce laughed, turning to Marcia. "This is my husband, meet my Jimmy."

On introduction, Marcia was struck by the intensity of Jimmy Grant's piercing blue eyes. He reminded her of the actor Ben Kingsley. He exuded an aura of power that Marcia found intimidating, although he was extremely friendly, hugging Suzette and then putting his arm around Marcia's shoulder. "Welcome to our home," he said, taking their cases.

As the two women walked out onto the terrace after being shown to their rooms. Jimmy waved them towards him as he sat at the garden table. He turned his attention to Marcia. "I have been told that you delve into all that mystic stuff and to be honest, I have never believed in all that psychic crap, but I have it on good authority from Max that you have made an impression on him. I believe that the proof is in the pudding, and if certain people say you are sound, then I'll abide by that."

Marcia felt uneasy and wondered how much Jimmy Grant knew about her. She smiled at Jimmy and said, "May I ask if you are a Scorpio sun sign?" Jimmy shook his head and laughed, and confirmed that he was.

"How can you tell?" he asked.

"Your piercing blue eyes … and I can sense your intensity."

"Mental," Jimmy replied, "…and intriguing, he rose from the chair. "I will leave you ladies for a while as I have a few phone calls to make."

The women lay on sun loungers under large umbrellas around the pool on the sunny patio. Marcia was taking in the scenery and half listening to Joyce and Suzette chatting away about the latest fashion and local gossip, which held no interest for Marcia at all. She liked clothes and shoes, but fashion designers were way beyond her finances. These women were out of her league as far as wealth. Marcia felt that under different circumstances she could get used to living out here in the sunshine, instead of the constant gloom of England. Jimmy appeared at the poolside and asked Suzette if he could have a word with her in private.

Joyce immediately got up from her sun lounger and moved closer to Marcia saying, "Go on you two," waving off Suzette and Jimmy. "Sort out whatever you need to do because Marcia and I are going to get to know each other."

Once they were alone, Joyce asked Marcia about her psychic gift. "I am fascinated by anything to do with the afterlife. Can you tell me how you first realised you were psychic?" she asked.

Marcia told her how she had been having visions and hearing voices from a young age. Marcia opened up to Joyce, telling her about the people who had come to her for advice over the years. She went on to explain how she became interested in astrology. "It became a fascination for me. I was taught by an expert in astrology, and from there I devoured works by an American astrologer. Once I became proficient, I used a combination of the tarot cards and the astrological cycles. I find it hard to explain, but it is as if someone else takes over when I'm conducting a reading. I hear voices and sense impressions when I look at the cards, but I also randomly say things that turn out to be predictive. I learnt yoga and meditation, which helps me to control my mind."

"How fascinating to be able to see into the future," Joyce said, staring at Marcia in wide-eyed awe.

"It is a very interesting vocation, but it's not always such a good thing to be able to predict events, Joyce. We would all like to be told that there is a light at the end of the tunnel but, unfortunately, it isn't always the case. From my point of view when a client wants to know if a lover or husband is deceiving them, or if their current relationship work out, and I can 'see' the deception or an imminent breakup, it can be a curse to 'know'. It puts me in a very difficult position." Marcia could see that she had struck a chord, as Joyce's smile left her face. She sat up and faced Marcia.

"Please, Marcia, may I book in a reading with you tomorrow morning, after you have had a good night's sleep? Tonight, Jimmy has booked our favourite restaurant at the marina, where you will meet many of our friends. Once they know what you do they will all be clamouring for your attention."

"Of course," Marcia replied, "There will be no problem in giving you a tarot reading." Marcia sensed something was troubling Joyce, even though she remained cheery. Marcia was looking forward to getting to know her even better, as she was taken with her.

Joyce told her she had one daughter who was at university in the UK studying law. Joyce laughed and said, "My daughter Sara gets her brains from her father, but she looks very much like me. Only her vivid blue eyes are from Jimmy." She went on to say how much she missed her, even though they spoke regularly. Joyce exclaimed in an excited, girly way, which made Marcia like her more, "Sara is coming home soon for two weeks and she is bringing her boyfriend with her. She usually keeps her love life private, even though I know she has had a few boyfriends in the past. But this lad seems to have made an impression on her. I do hope Jimmy takes to him, as Sara is his world, and I wouldn't like to be in the poor lad's shoes if he upsets him."

Joyce went into the villa to prepare lunch. Marcia sat deep in thought, considering the recent changes in her life. A feeling of sadness tore at her heart as she thought of Reuben and wondered what he might be doing at that moment. Returning to the here and now, Marcia thought about the lifestyle Joyce and Jimmy were living in Spain, and the illegal activities she knew they were steeped in, and it frightened her.

Joyce appeared on the terrace alongside Suzette and Jimmy and announced, "Okay, now we can have lunch."

Jimmy made his apologies as he had business to attend to and said that he would see them later.

The afternoon saw the women swimming, talking and laughing, as Joyce entertained them with stories of the ex-pat experiences she had been party to in the past. Joyce seemed to love everyone. She had a naivety about her that added to her charm. "You must visit us again soon," Joyce said to Marcia, "I would love you to meet Sara. Please come back in two weeks. I want you to give me your opinion about this new guy in Sara's life."

Suzette spoke for them both, "Of course, I will arrange things back home and we will come out for a few days, won't we, Marcia?"

Marcia knew it was a directive and not a query. She agreed, knowing she didn't have any choice in the matter.

That evening, the three women and Jimmy drove down to the marina to meet their friends at the restaurant. As they entered the busy eatery, the maître d' spoke to Jimmy with a reverence that made Marcia realise exactly how high Jimmy's status was. Men stood up to shake his hand and he was offered a seat at the head of the largest table. The women at the table all looked so glamorous, wearing expensive jewellery and dressed with low necklines and short hems, which was in vogue with the people they mixed with. Marcia thought it looked like a scene from a Hollywood movie. Suzette, Marcia and Joyce sat at the far end of the table, away from Jimmy.

Before Jimmy sat down, he spoke. "Please let me introduce you to Marcia. She is a friend of Suzie's from the UK. This lovely lady has a powerful gift," he said, "She is psychic, and I can vouch for her. I have it from a credible source that this lady is the real deal."

By now, all eyes were on Marcia and the women around the table all stared at her, excited at the news.

Joyce said, "Okay girls, any of you who want a psychic reading will need to ring me in the morning and I will arrange a time for you with Marcia." All but one of the women talked excitedly about booking a reading. A very attractive blonde young woman stated in a very loud voice that she thought it was all rubbish and that she did not believe in it.

Jimmy spoke over the top of the woman. "Eve, please keep your opinions to yourself. Let us have a sociable evening and make sure things stay pleasant."

Throughout the evening, Marcia tuned in to whoever was speaking. They all seemed pleasant enough in their way, however, the one who gained Marcia's attention was Eve, the psychic cynic. Marcia assumed that Eve was in her early thirties. She was extremely glamorous, with a stunning figure. She had long blonde hair and almond brown eyes. It was not just her looks that Marcia took note of. She sensed something else was going on with her, and it wasn't until later in the evening, once the wine had been flowing, that she realised what it was. From where Marcia was sitting, although Eve appeared to be keeping a low profile, she had noticed her turn to Jimmy several times throughout the meal and whisper to him. He always responded with a soft smile as he held her eyes. Marcia's radar homed in. Her senses were telling her that the pair were emotionally linked. Marcia's attention was drawn to Eve's dinner date, and she noticed that whenever he got up from the table, he would put his hands on Eve's shoulder. Both Eve and her partner seemed to be holding court with Jimmy more than anyone else. Marcia discreetly studied the man as he leaned back in the chair to the left of Jimmy. She thought he was strikingly handsome. His coal black hair, streaked with grey, gave him a look of attractive maturity. As she watched, she heard him speak to the man opposite him. His Irish accent was so appealing that Marcia felt drawn to him. He suddenly turned his head to look in her direction. She flushed as his dark brown eyes held hers. She caught the hint of a smile, and then he resumed his conversation. Much to Marcia's surprise, she found herself attracted to him. She silently reminded herself that he was in a relationship and linked to Jimmy Grant's nefarious world.

Marcia got up and headed to the ladies' room. As she pushed the door open, she felt someone behind her. Joyce tapped her shoulder and put her finger to her lips. She then tried all the cubicle doors to make sure that they were all unoccupied.

"Well, what do you think of our friends?" she asked, leaning against a washbasin.

"They all seem fine, a nice friendly bunch of women," Marcia replied.

"What about Eve, don't you think she is stunning?" Joyce questioned.

"Absolutely," replied Marcia, without adding anything else.

"She is a man-eater, who doesn't deserve the decent man she has got. Let me tell you, Marcia, Eamon's wife is not satisfied with him being Jimmy's right-hand man. Her aspirations are to get to the top of the tree." Joyce seethed. Marcia knew that Joyce had been drinking, but was taken aback by her verbal attack. Marcia didn't know what to say as Joyce continued.

"I liked her when she first came onto the scene, but there was something that I didn't trust about her. Eamon, her husband, is a great guy, loyal to the bone to Jimmy, and I tolerated Eve because of that." Joyce rambled on, the wine loosening her tongue, "That little lady might take me for a fool but believe me, Marcia, many things I may be, but a fool is not one of them."

Marcia put a comforting arm around her. "I have no idea about anyone else out here, but I know you are not foolish. You are a lovely woman. Please don't upset yourself,

Joyce." Marcia sensed that Joyce knew far more than she was revealing.

"I am sorry, Marcia, whatever must you think of me? But that woman pushes me to my limits with her falsity."

"Joyce, I have to use the loo, otherwise I will burst." Marcia crossed her legs and both women laughed.

Once seated back at the table Marcia noticed Eve's husband was watching her. She inadvertently caught his eye and he held her gaze. He smiled, showing beautiful white teeth. She returned the smile and inexplicably felt butterflies in her stomach. *Whatever is going on with me?* she thought. She had not felt this attracted to a man for years.

At the end of the evening, everyone wished each other goodnight, all the women except Eve said they would ring in the morning to arrange for Marcia to give them a reading. The men, irrespective of the amount of alcohol they had consumed, all drove their cars home. They knew they wouldn't be bothered by the police, even though Spain's law had a zero-tolerance attitude to drink driving.

Arriving back at the villa, Jimmy bid them goodnight. Suzette followed suit and went to her room. When they were alone, Joyce hugged Marcia and thanked her for listening to her earlier. "Anytime, Joyce. If you feel you want to let off steam, I am a good listener, but you will have to excuse me now as I feel tired and need to get a good night's sleep. It appears there will be quite a few women that want a reading tomorrow, and I will have to be up early."

After Marcia showered and slipped on a camisole, she got into bed. Her thoughts turned to Suzette, whose quietness throughout the evening made her wonder why the usually talkative woman, who always takes over the conversation, had been subdued. Marcia wondered if it might have something to do with Gary or with the talk she'd had with Jimmy earlier. In the short time she had known Suzette, Marcia realised that she was a woman who would jump in where angels fear to tread and prayed that Suzette hadn't got them involved in anything else.

Marcia slept late the next morning, awaking to the sound of Joyce and Suzette's laughter coming from the terrace. It was 10.30 and she couldn't believe how long she had slept.

"Come on sleepyhead," called Joyce, "it's lovely out here. We've waited for you to wake before cooking breakfast."

Marcia apologised as she yawned and rubbed her eyes.

"Please don't apologise, you needed the rest. I'll start breakfast now; help yourself to coffee and juice." Joyce went into the kitchen and Marcia joined Suzette at the garden table.

"You don't seem yourself, is anything wrong, Suzie?" Marcia asked, "I noticed you were a bit quiet last night."

"I am fine," she replied, "There are just a few things to sort out when I get home, that's all. You seem to have been a big hit out here with the women, Marcia. They are all buzzing with excitement about their readings today."

"Except for Eve," Marcia replied.

"Don't pay any heed to her. She is someone to be watched. That girl has an agenda, according to Joyce," Suzie said.

Marcia stayed silent.

"After breakfast, and when you've got yourself ready, Joyce wants you to read her cards. I don't need to remind you to be careful and not to reveal anything you see in the cards that would upset anyone, especially Jimmy."

Marcia nodded in agreement.

Joyce's cheerful voice called out, "Breakfast will be ready in ten minutes girls." She came out with the full works: scrambled eggs, bacon, tomatoes, sausages and beans. Marcia had told Joyce that she didn't eat meat, so she cooked her a

Spanish omelette especially. "Come on girls, eat up, you will need this to revive you after all the drink last night, well except you, Marcia, I noticed you only had a couple."

"I don't drink very much, as I need a clear mind," Marcia laughed, "Otherwise I wouldn't be able to get much work done."

Marcia noticed there was no sign of Jimmy, and as if Joyce had read her mind, she said, "Jimmy won't be back until this evening as he has to attend to business." Once breakfast was over, Suzette and Marcia helped to clear up and then headed back to their rooms to shower.

"As soon as I have got myself ready, I will do your reading, Joyce," Marcia said.

Joyce replied that she was excited and couldn't wait.

Marcia and Joyce sat opposite one another in a quiet room at the back of the villa. Passing the tarot cards to Joyce, Marcia explained that she had to first shuffle the cards. Once Joyce shuffled the cards and handed them back, Marcia began to lay each one out on the table. As she put the fourth card down, a feeling of pain and loss overwhelmed her. She felt uneasy but composed herself and calmly began. "Joyce, your life is going to be transformed within a year and you will pull up your roots to live overseas. Your daughter will spread her wings, but you will be far happier than you have been in a long time." Marcia hesitated not knowing whether to give the warning that her daughter must be careful of a man that she is emotionally involved with, but she decided to keep it from Joyce for now.

Joyce paled as she interrupted. "What on earth do you mean, Marcia?" she asked alarmed.

"Please don't worry, you both will be fine, but I want to speak about you now, Joyce. I can see in the tarot cards that you have been going through emotional turmoil."

Marcia felt as if she had to guard every word she said.

"You are right, I have Marcia," tears began to trickle down Joyce's face.

Marcia automatically reached across and placed her hands over Joyce's.

"Jimmy is having an affair with Eamon's wife, Eve, and it's not just a feeling, Marcia. It's something I discovered."

Marcia wasn't shocked, but she didn't respond.

"Can you please look at the cards and tell me what you see?" Joyce pleaded.

"Tell me why you think Jimmy and Eve are having an affair," Marcia asked, gently.

Joyce wiped her tears and sat back in her chair. "A few weeks ago I found a diamond stud earring on the floor of Jimmy's car, under the back seat. I had been clothes shopping and was using his car. As I placed the shopping bags on the back seat, the large diamond stud caught my eye and I immediately knew that it belonged to Eve O'Donally. You see, Marcia, Eamon had bought the diamond earrings along with a matching necklace, as an anniversary gift for her. He had shown them to me before he gave them to her. A while later he told me he had been annoyed that Eve had managed to lose one. And I have it tucked away. That is my evidence, Marcia."

Marcia tried to pacify Joyce. "All I am going to say to you is these big changes that you and your daughter will undergo will see you happy, so, dry your tears and please believe what I am telling you."

Joyce stood up and hugged Marcia, "I don't know why, but I do believe in what you are saying to me."

Marcia spoke again, soothingly. "Just sit back and let everything unfold and stop your worrying. Come on, let's get some sun. Suzie and I will be returning to England in the morning and I still have readings to do for all of your friends this afternoon and I would like to have a good swim and chill out for a while."

"I feel we have become firm friends, Marcia. I like you and you are welcome to stay at my home whenever you wish," Joyce said, smiling warmly.

Marcia thanked her and they joined Suzette at the poolside.

"Is everything okay, Joyce?" Suzette asked as they approached.

"I feel far better now than I did before my reading, Suzie. Marcia has a wonderful gift, and her insight is spot on." Joyce smiled.

The women swam and sunbathed while Marcia regaled with stories of the many situations she'd found herself in as a result of her mediumship talents. Joyce was enthralled by everything Marcia had to say.

Marcia felt concerned about Joyce's revelations. She knew by what Suzette had told her that Jimmy was a player, but she didn't know if Joyce was jumping to conclusions about the diamond earring she found in Jimmy's car. She didn't want to get involved, as she already had enough to contend with, without having to experience the wrath of Jimmy Grant. At around two in the afternoon, the buzzer from the gates sounded and Joyce got up to let the women in. She opened the door to four women who looked just as glitzy as they did the night before. "Okay girls, I have the room ready, Marcia will be a few minutes. Who wants to go first?" Joyce announced, seeming more upbeat than she had earlier.

"Me!" said Cindy, before the others had time to answer; "As you know girls, I am a Leo and I always like to be first," chuckled Joyce's best friend. The other women went outside to join Suzette, and Joyce showed Cindy into the room where

Marcia was waiting. She and Joyce had been close for many years, and they would do anything for one another.

Marcia began the reading as she normally would, asking Cindy to shuffle the cards, and then laying them out on the table, "There is going to be an ending through death that you will not be upset about. You are going to be very happy in your future and you will work in some kind of creative role and then later in the entertainment world."

Cindy was shocked. "Do you mean someone close to me will die?" she asked.

"This death will bring about big changes in your life and I see you helping someone that is connected to this situation, but you won't be saddened by this passing." Cindy pursed her lips, shaking her head. "If it doesn't affect me, I can cope with that."

Marcia said, "I know you are no stranger to sadness. I can see that you have had a great loss in your life already … I also feel that Joyce is going to leave Spain … not yet, but within a year she will move to another country and I feel it will be the USA. But you will have a new lease of life that brings you joy."

Cindy sat back. "Wow," you are right about a loss in my past. My husband died a painful death from cancer. He was my childhood sweetheart. It was a devastating loss, but life moves on. I had a wonderful husband and have two beautiful children. Rhys adored them they were his world; can you see if they are going to be okay and that nothing is going to hurt them?" Cindy asked.

Marcia reassured her that her family would be fine. She looked at the card of Jupiter, which represents travel and overseas connections and asked Cindy if her children were abroad now. Cindy gasped at Marcia's accuracy, as both her children were travelling at present, and she didn't think it likely that they would be living back at home anytime soon.

Marcia grinned, then announced, "Cindy you are going to have a dark-haired man come into your life that you will have a strong emotional bond with and who will bring you contentment."

Cindy laughed, as she stood up. "Great, that's enough for me to get on with. I cannot wait to meet this tasty man and get my leg over," she chuckled.

"On your way out can you ask your next friend to come in?" Marcia said, as Cindy left to join Joyce on the terrace. As the afternoon wore on, even though Marcia was feeling mentally drained, all the women seemed pleased with what she had told them, and as she finished, she was looking forward to joining the others outside in the sunshine to recharge her batteries.

The women sat talking around the pool, keen to know more about Marcia's abilities. They were a nice bunch, Marcia thought, especially Cindy. She could understand why Joyce felt so close to her. Both women had warm personalities.

Jimmy returned around six that evening and asked if they'd all had a good day and whether they'd like to go out. They agreed to stay in and enjoy a takeaway Indian meal from Jimmy's favourite restaurant. Suzette, who still didn't seem her usual self, made her excuses, explaining that she was suffering from a migraine and she got up to go to her room.

Marcia noticed the look Jimmy gave Suzette as she left the room. He said, "Something playing on your mind Suzie, you seem rather preoccupied?"

"Too much sun and wine," she replied. "I will be alright in an hour or so, Jimmy."

The evening went well. The food arrived around 9 pm, and Suzette, feeling refreshed, had joined them and seemed to be back to her usual self.

Jimmy took over the conversation. He focused on Marcia and told her, "Joyce and my daughter have brought so much happiness into my life. If anyone upsets my Sara, they had better emigrate or they won't live to tell the tale."

Marcia heard the intense passion in his voice and thought that he must be very possessive of his daughter and woe betide anyone who hurt her. Jimmy and Joyce said their goodnights and retired to their bedroom after the meal. Suzette and Marcia had to leave early in the morning, and it was Joyce who was going to drive them to the airport. Jimmy had previously told the women that he would be gone early as he had a busy day ahead of him and he looked forward to them returning soon.

The next morning, Joyce drove them to the airport and walked with them to the terminal. She hugged them goodbye and handed Marcia an envelope. "I collected the money from the girls for their tarot readings … and I've put something in there from me too."

Marcia tried to refuse Joyce's money. But Joyce insisted. Marcia reluctantly accepted the money and thanked Joyce again for everything. Suzette told Joyce that although they were both sad to part, they would definitely see each other again in a couple of weeks.

UK

Mikey collected Suzette and Marcia from the airport, and on the drive home, he expertly wove in and out of the traffic, which was always a nightmare on the run from Gatwick. Suzette had spoken to Marcia briefly on the plane about a business situation that she was involved in, although she had only given her an outline of it. Marcia hadn't been in the least bit interested. Suzette already had her involved up to her eyebrows. Marcia felt as if she were a pawn in a chess game and she couldn't tell who would come out as the winner. She sensed that something was brewing amongst Suzette's associates in Spain, and she didn't want to be involved in the fallout.

When Marcia put the key in her front door, she felt relieved to be back home in England. Her apartment was her haven, away from the crazy world she'd found herself involved in. She put her case in the bedroom and sat on her bed, opening the envelope that Joyce had handed her. To her amazement, there were 500 euros and a note that read, "Thank you for all your help. I can't wait for you to return, see you soon."

Marcia was looking forward to a quiet couple of days, as Suzette said she'd ring her in 48 hours after she'd had a meeting with Gary. Suzette was also waiting to be granted a prison visiting order so she could visit her husband Max.

Marcia had booked herself in for a relaxing massage and facial the following day and was looking forward to having the day to herself. She'd also decided to have her eyebrows dyed, something she had wanted to do for a while, and with Joyce's generosity, she could now afford to. She had it on good authority from the other women at the health club that she belonged to, that there was a talented beautician who did amazing work, so she'd been quick to book her. Marcia entered the beauty salon with butterflies in her stomach. She was trying to justify to herself the reasons behind her wish for a transformation. Gina, the beautician, introduced herself and put Marcia at her ease right away, chatting about her life while she got to work on Marcia's new look. "Let me get a mirror and I will show you the results," Gina said.

Marcia looked at her reflection and was thrilled. "What an amazing difference it has made!" Marcia said.

"If you don't mind me saying so," Gina enthused, "you are an attractive lady who hasn't really made the most of it. I have some free time between my next appointments, if you allow me; I can give you a few easy makeup tips that will enhance your features."

Marcia willingly agreed and relaxed totally under Gina's masterful brushstrokes and expertise. The transformation was brilliant. She felt like a new woman and Gina ensured Marcia that she would be capable, after a little practice, of obtaining the same results herself. Marcia felt so uplifted that decided to buy some new dresses to go with her new look. She found a couple of dresses that she liked, but when she saw the price tags, she changed her mind and splashed out on just one.

As Marcia pulled up outside her home, her mobile rang and Suzette's name came up on the screen. She seemed to be on top form. "I need you to come to see me tonight. Please stay over, as I want you to come with me on a short journey tomorrow. It's important to me and I will appreciate it, Marcia," Suzette said.

Marcia reluctantly agreed to be there in the next couple of hours. She felt like a puppet on a string. But even Suzette's demands couldn't dampen her high spirits. On arrival, Suzette showed her to the guest bedroom and said, "Come into the kitchen when you're ready, as I am preparing something for us for supper." Suzette was so preoccupied with whatever was going on in her own life, that she hadn't even noticed Marcia's new look until they sat facing one another at the kitchen table.

"Wow, what have you been up to?" Suzette asked Marcia, "You look great."

Marcia explained how the young beautician had dyed and reshaped her eyebrows, and had given her a makeover. She told Suzette that she had treated herself to a new dress from the money she had earned in Spain.

Suzette told her she would not have to worry about money anymore. "You and I are going to go shopping next week, and you can have the works – shoes, dresses, bags, and I'm talking top designer," Suzette exclaimed.

"Look Suzie, I know you are generous, but that's a bit over the top, don't you think?"

"Oh, don't you worry. You will earn it Marcia, and while we have a glass of wine, I will explain how."

Suzette explained the plan she had in mind. "I am going to tell Max that there has been another raid at the house and that they had found the large amount of money that was buried under the garden shed."

Marcia was stunned. "You are joking! Suzie, please don't be foolish. You will invite more trouble by telling lies. Max will never fall for that in a million years."

Suzette laughed, "Yes, Max will, because you are going to back me up. Now listen, I will tell him the police brought dogs in and found the money and I was arrested and then later cleared of any involvement."

"Is this what you were scheming about in Spain, Suzette? I thought you were up to something, but I never thought it would be something like this." Marcia felt drained.

"Don't worry about a thing, Marcia. If we are to make our new business successful, which I plan to start when we get to Spain, I am left with no option other than to take the money," Suzette said.

"I don't want any involvement in this," Marcia said, "He will kill us." She couldn't believe Suzette could take things this far; it was bad enough that she was sleeping with Max's associate.

"Listen to me, Marcia. I am going to put a stop to Max. He's using an illegal mobile phone to call us all the time from prison. I'm going to make an anonymous call to the prison and report the phone, which will ensure that it will be discovered in a search and will prevent him from making contact for a while. Max can't stop me from leaving him. Please believe me, Marcia. Tomorrow I am going to meet Gary, he is booked into the same hotel as us and I need you to cover for me as we are going to sort out a business situation, and also to have a bit of fun."

"So, you want me with you for two nights?" Marcia asked.

"Well, actually, it will be three," Suzette said, "I need you with me because Max will want to speak with you at some point, as it won't take him long to replace the confiscated mobile and I will need to concentrate on moving the money. You will be driving me to a secret location to hide the money. I have everything planned out." She went on to say that her cousin Colin, who had a smallholding in the countryside would hide the money for her. "Max won't suspect anything, as I rarely speak of him, but my cousin is trustworthy."

Marcia picked at the meal that Suzette had prepared for them, feeling sick to her stomach. At about ten that night she went to her room, feigning tiredness. She needed time on her own to sort her head out. She lay awake for hours worrying about what would happen if Max discovered Suzette's deceit. Did she honestly think he would believe her about the police raid? Surely, Suzette couldn't think Max was that stupid. Playing with fire was an understatement, Marcia thought. She only managed a few hours' sleep that night as the situation continued to play out over and over in her mind.

By one pm the following day, Marcia and Suzette had checked in to the plush spa hotel. Opulence was an understatement, Marcia thought, as she sat on the four-poster bed looking out at the amazing views of the countryside.

"Okay, let us go out for a couple of hours," Suzette said, "I need to speak with my cousin who only lives half an hour away."

Marcia, under Suzette's direction, drove to their destination. The smallholding was set back in about two acres of land. Upon arrival, Colin and his wife welcomed Marcia like a long-lost family member. They were typical country folk. Marcia thought they were a homely couple. The cottage was messy, with boots and rabbit nets in the hall, but it was cosy, and the aroma of homemade bread was making Marcia's mouth water.

"Come on girls," Colin's wife Madge said, "sit yourself down and I will give you some decent home cooking as the pair of you look like you need a bit of weight on you."

Suzette refused as she said she needed to talk with Colin. They disappeared out to the back of the house, while Marcia tucked into the freshly baked bread and strong cheese, washed down with a mug of coffee. Marcia could see Suzette and Colin through the kitchen window, deep in conversation, walking around the grounds. Madge, who hadn't stopped talking since they arrived, was asking Marcia a million questions. She said they rarely had company, as their only son lived in New Zealand with their two grandchildren, and even if they could afford the cost of the flight, they couldn't leave the farm because of their animals. Marcia thought that Madge was one of the nicest women she had ever met. It was obvious that she was starved of female company. She said she had no friends and invited Marcia and Suzette to come back any time.

Suzette and Colin returned from their talk and Madge insisted that Suzette eat something before they go. As they said their goodbyes, promising to return very soon, Colin and Madge hugged them both and told them to stay safe. On the return journey, Suzette told Marcia that the following week they were going to take the money to Colin and that he would hide it. Madge didn't know of any of the goings-on she said, and the less she knew the better. Suzette said her money would be safe with him and that no one would suspect his involvement.

Back at the hotel, Suzette went upstairs to see Gary. Marcia was aware of what sort of entertainment Gary and Suzette were indulging in, but she was grateful for the time on her own, which she spent by trying all the spa treatments. Suzette told her to book whatever she wanted and to bill it to her room.

Suzette woke Marcia up around six-thirty the next morning telling her that they would be leaving in an hour. She was almost drunk with excitement. Her mood was catching, and Marcia laughed as Suzette provided her with all the intimate details of her and Gary's night together. Marcia couldn't help but giggle at some of the things she told her. Suzette was like a teenager in love.

"Please tread carefully Suzie ... don't let everything run away with you," Marcia tried to warn her.

"Today will be the day that I am going to set the wheels in motion and this will be the beginning of the end of my relationship with Max."

"I feel scared for you, Suzette. You are playing a dangerous game and I feel there will be repercussions from Max."

Suzette brushed off the warning. "Let us not think about it for the moment. I have promised you a shopping trip so let's not waste any more time." she smiled.

The two of them hit the shops, purchasing shoes and dresses by designers that Marcia had only seen in magazines. They each bought a beautiful Coco Chanel bag, all at Suzette's expense. Marcia was hesitant after Suzette treated her to the first dress. The price of the Alexander McQueen made her baulk.

"I told you I would look after you, Marcia, so take what I offer you and remember that there is plenty more to come," Suzette reassured her.

Arriving back at Suzette's, the women kicked off their shoes, and Suzette poured them each a glass of wine. She told Marcia that Max would be phoning and to just act calm. He would be questioning her, she said, about a deal that was supposed to happen next week. Suzette had set the deal up with Gary. All Marcia had to do was confirm that everything would be fine.

Marcia started to get anxious, "We will both be okay, so get yourself together. He will be phoning in a minute."

Marcia gulped from her wine glass and began to inhale deeply and rhythmically to compose herself.

The phone rang and Suzette gave Marcia the nod. She picked up the phone, walking from the lounge to the kitchen. After ten minutes or so, Suzette returned and passed Marcia the phone. Marcia was now in full control of her emotions and calmly took the receiver from Suzette.

Max asked how she was and then said he wanted a reading. He wasted no time in asking Marcia for advice regarding a couple of business situations.

"I want to know if I can trust putting so much money into these particular deals," he said.

Marcia then explained to him that she would shuffle the tarot cards and ask him to tell her when to stop. As she was looking at the cards, Marcia was fighting with herself as to what she should say. She gave him the go ahead on the business deal but warned him that someone in the prison couldn't be trusted and she went on to describe him.

He was silent for a moment. "Fine," was the only reply.

Marcia then told him, "Do not worry if you see yourself back to square one, as there is a planet going retrograde, and in layman's terms this means there can be a period of disruption of about six weeks. But, if you pay heed to whom you are divulging your plans to, you will be all right. He thanked her and hung up. Marcia was shaking as she returned to Suzette in the kitchen. She relayed word for word what she had told Max.

"Relax," Suzette said, "You have covered our backs."

"What do you mean?" Marcia asked, feeling the anxiety rising.

"Just wait and see," Suzette told her.

"I am finding all this to be mentally draining. I have to concentrate on using double meanings when dealing with your husband, knowing that you are deceiving him."

Suzette placed her hand on Marcia's arm. "I know what I am doing. I have dealt with criminals throughout my marriage to Max. I am going to turn the tables on him, Marcia. This is all new to you, from what you have told me about your early life. You haven't had it easy and I am going to ensure that you and I succeed."

Marcia sighed wearily, "I have brought a book with me so I'm going to get into bed and read."

As Marcia lay in bed that night, she prayed that Max believed Suzette, but she didn't hold out much hope. How could a woman such as Suzette, who was trying to fight her corner against hardened criminals, imagine that they would tolerate her duplicity.

The following morning, Suzette appeared excited, as Marcia came into the kitchen. "I have received a message from one of Max's contacts. His prison cell had been turned over and the mobile phone had been discovered, resulting in Max being shipped out to another prison which is hours away from here. Then I am told that my prison visiting order had been cancelled." she beamed triumphantly.

She discussed the recent events with Marcia, who expressed her concerns and told her so. "Marcia go home and get away from all of this for a while and I will contact you later," Suzette said. "I'm going to get in touch with Gary to tell him the news." Suzette helped her carry her shopping bags to the car. "Drive carefully and have a relaxing evening," she said.

"Relaxing evening?" Marcia mused to herself on the drive home. She thought Suzette must be joking, everything was blowing up ... Max would become suspicious pretty quickly once Suzette reveals that the police have been to her home with a detection dog and discovered the money. She felt as if she was walking on a knife edge.

Two days later Marcia returned to stay overnight at Suzette's as she said she needed to discuss things with her. "I have given Gary a consignment of drugs that had been hidden before the police raid, thanks to the warning you gave us, Marcia. The sale of the drugs will give Max and Gary £250,000 each. Gary is going to make the contact, complete the deal and collect the money the following week," Suzette said to Marcia over a glass of wine.

Marcia implored her to listen to common sense. "I am telling you that the situation will go dramatically wrong. Max is no fool and you won't outfox him. Gary will betray you and Max over this deal, Suzette. Gary is having a clandestine affair with you, so why do you think that if he could betray Max by sleeping with his wife, that he could be trusted with so much money."

Suzette wouldn't have any of it. She was adamant that Marcia was wrong about Gary.

Two days later, Marcia found herself back at Suzette's after Suzette called her saying she couldn't discuss her concerns over the phone. Marcia had found herself slowly becoming fond of Suzette, even though she felt exasperated by her refusal to listen. Her generosity towards Marcia was beyond anything that she had ever encountered. She was even beginning to enjoy the profound conversations with her too. That tough outer veneer that Suzette projected hid an unhappy and vulnerable interior that made Marcia empathise with her over the months she had known her. But as much as she had become fond of Suzette, Marcia knew she couldn't afford to drop her guard. Because at the end of the day, her son's welfare was at stake. Thinking of Reuben always gave her a physical ache that nothing could relieve.

Suzette looked worried as she opened the door to Marcia and hurried her inside. "Gary rang me to say that his contact had declared the cocaine wasn't pure and, as a consequence, he couldn't get anywhere near the amount of money that had been agreed, so he is now waiting to hear what is going to happen."

Marcia's alarm bells began to ring immediately. She sensed that this was the beginning of the scam that Gary was going to pull on Max, but she knew that Suzette believed every word that Gary was telling her, and that it would be useless to say anything.

"Max has another phone coming in a few days via a contact within the prison. He also has an associate on the outside who informs me of events. Plans have now changed," Suzette revealed. "I am going to take the money to Colin tomorrow and then I will make an appointment with my private doctor and feign a nervous breakdown. He will give me a prescription for tablets and then I'll tell Max that the stress is having a detrimental effect upon me."

"When I tell him that the police came with a sniffer dog and found the money, it will be even more convincing." Suzette saw the incredulous look on Marcia's face. "Come on, don't worry, I can deal with him. He will be more concerned about my mental welfare, trust me, he loves me and will believe anything I tell him."

Marcia couldn't believe Suzette's naivety.

When the time came for Suzette to execute her plan, she asked Marcia to stay over again for a couple of days to help support her. The money was now hidden at Colin's and the doctor had prescribed her Diazepam. She was now waiting for a phone call from Max. Suzette knew that Max would be desperately trying to arrange a visiting order for her, and with the number of inside contacts Max had, that would be sooner rather than later. "I have no intention of paying Max a visit yet, and when the time comes, I am simply going to say that I am too unwell to travel."

Marcia braced herself for the onslaught. Max phoned the following day and went ballistic when Suzette told him that the police and the sniffer dog had turned the place over and discovered the hidden money under the garden shed and that she had been arrested and held in custody for hours. She said she had been released on police bail, pending enquiries.

"Did the police give you a receipt for the money?" Max shouted over the phone. Suzette confirmed that they had, but that the whole experience had shaken her to the core and consequently she was feeling at rock bottom. She said she had been to visit a doctor who, alarmed by her mental state, prescribed her anti-depressants to help her cope. Suzette told Marcia that Max's anger had turned to shock and sympathy at the realisation that she was in such a vulnerable state over the recent events. Her acting, she said, had been very convincing, and he was so genuinely concerned about her welfare that he hadn't asked if Marcia would give him a reading.

"How on earth are you going to come up with a plausible excuse for not being able to produce a receipt for the money?" Marcia asked.

"I'll cross that bridge when I come to it, Max is more concerned about me, and I will lead him to believe that the anti-depressants are affecting my memory and I cannot remember where I've put it," Suzette replied.

"Well, let's hope he believes you," Marcia said, shaking her head.

"I am going to tell Gary that the police raid was a put-up job because he will be worried about me."

Marcia couldn't believe what she was hearing. "Suzette, please, take my advice and just tell Gary exactly what you told Max. I know you have feelings for him but the less people know about it the better." Eventually, she brought Suzette over to her way of thinking. Suzette phoned Gary and relayed the events of the police raid. He asked if she wanted him to come to see her, but he would bring Kathy to make it look as if they were both there to provide moral support. Suzette told him that the last thing she needed was to see Kathy. She said she had her friend Marcia staying with her and she would ring him if there were any further problems.

Marcia had got the gist of the telephone conversation and sighed with relief at Suzette's refusal. "Stay away from him, at least for a while Suzette, until this blows over with Max. Because how am I going to explain that I didn't forewarn him that there was going to be another police raid."

Marcia was grateful to return home finally. She went straight to her health club and enjoyed a relaxing time swimming and chilling out in the sauna. It was her treat to herself after all of the stress. She knew the monthly membership fee to the exclusive club was expensive but the outdoor swimming pool was the only luxury that she hadn't denied herself for years. Marcia hadn't felt so relaxed in a while after the massage she had splashed out on at the club. She intended to read a book that evening, but as she came through her front door, she could hear her mobile phone ringing inside of her bag. By the time she was able to dig the phone out of her bag and answer, she had missed the call. She listened to the message that Suzette left. She sounded frantic so Marcia called right back.

"Marcia, I have rung Gary's private phone numerous times and haven't had any reply."

"I'll be right over," Marcia told her. She quickly put a few things in her overnight bag and drove straight there.

Over a glass of wine, Marcia was trying desperately to calm Suzette down. No sooner had she said, "I'm sure there's a reasonable explanation why he isn't answering his phone." Suzette's mobile rang with an unknown number.

Suzette tentatively answered. It was Kathy. Suzette pressed the loud speaker so Marcia could hear. "Hello, Suzette. I found your telephone number on a piece of paper in a pair of Gary's jeans." Marcia and Suzette exchanged surprised glances. "I have no idea how he would have my…" Kathy interjected. "Gary told me that Max's home was raided again and he asked me if we should visit you."

"Yes, I'd forgotten that I told Gary, as I was concerned that the police might come calling. To be honest with you, Kathy, my nerves are shot to ribbons and I have been pre-scribed tranquillisers and they have addled my brain." Suzette grimaced in Marcia's direction.

"I don't know what is going on but I have had two thuggish looking men at my door asking for Gary and they demanded I tell them his whereabouts. I never know where or who he is with and I told them so. These men are after him, as one of them said Gary had been a naughty boy, and that they would come back if they couldn't find him. If he makes contact I will let you know, Suzette, and I'm sorry that I have laid my worries at your door when you have enough on your plate." Suzette switched the call off.

"What is happening, Marcia, for these men to come after Gary?"

"Suzette, you are going to be in so much trouble if you don't steer clear of Gary, not only with Max but there are others involved, as you have just heard that woman of his tell you."

"Max is phoning tonight he has another mobile phone." Suzette topped her wine up but Marcia declined more. "He wants to speak to you, Marcia, so just be careful what you say to him … I don't know if he is suspicious or not."

When the call came in, Marcia sensed Max's indifference to her. She knew it would take some persuasion to win back his confidence. "Why did you tell me that everything would be alright when everything has gone wrong? Are you playing games with me, because if you are then you are a very foolish woman?" Although Max unnerved her, Marcia hoped she could sway him.

"Max, I informed you that situations could invariably go wrong for six weeks. But after that, you can move forward. I will tell you, as I have told many others in the past, if you pay heed to my warnings, you will be successful. But if you choose to trust people who will betray you, then I'm afraid it is not my fault but yours." Marcia heard Max suck air through his teeth.

"I did tell you that you are not to worry if things went wrong because they would right themselves within six weeks. Did I not?" Marcia stood her ground.

Max didn't reply, and he ended the call.

....

Max lay deep in thought on the bunk in his cell waiting for news. It came through as a thumbs up on his smartphone screen. He was very pleased with the outcome. He deleted the messages, switched off the phone and put it away in its hiding place. An afternoon nap was on the agenda and tomorrow he would be seeing Suzie. As he drifted off to sleep, visions of his beautiful wife swam before him. His passion for her was as all-consuming, as it always had been. He loved her more than anything and when he got word that Gary Wiley was making a play for her, along with trying to double-cross him, that had been the last nail in his coffin.

Max's associates reported to him how they had soon found Gary lying low in a small village in the West Country. It seemed he'd booked into a bed and breakfast under an assumed name and was planning to stay for a few days until he was ready to leave for a new life in Thailand. He was sitting in the snug area of the local pub, relaxing, enjoying the quiet, and sipping his glass of lager before turning in for the night, when Max's henchmen found him. They had searched him and his room and recuperated the money. They also found the plane ticket to Thailand that he had on him. Then they took Gary Wiley on a country ride and repaid him by smashing his kneecaps with a hammer.

. . . .

Marcia was with Suzette when Kathy phoned with the devastating news about Gary. She could see the shock on Suzette's face and was trying to make sense of what was being said. She heard Suzette say, "If you need anything at all, all you have to do is call me, Kathy."

"What is it?" Marcia asked, concerned.

Suzette's tears flowed as she told Marcia that Gary was lying crippled in a West Country hospital with smashed kneecaps.

"I can't believe all this is happening. Why would anyone inflict such traumatic injuries on Gary? What has he done to deserve such life-changing damage? Kathy told me that his knee bones are shattered beyond repair and that she must be prepared that he may never be able to walk again." Marcia tried to comfort Suzette as she sobbed.

Marcia's intuition informed her that Max was behind it, but she decided to keep it to herself.

"Dry your tears and please listen to me, Suzette," she said, "I could see in your tarot reading that Gary was going to deceive you and would leave you high and dry. I am warning you, Suzette, don't put a foot wrong, as we are both in great danger. You are visiting Max tomorrow and I want you to look your best for him, so get a good night's sleep, get your finery on tomorrow, and face him, without letting him see that you are bothered about what's gone on. Gary's fate is sealed. If he survives this ordeal, let Kathy have him. You can start a new chapter in your life."

Marcia had talked to Suzette for hours the previous evening about what she was faced with, and she felt she finally had got through to her.

Kathy called the following morning after visiting Gary in the hospital to say that she had found a flight ticket to Thailand in Gary's personal effects. Kathy told Suzette that she would devote her life to care for Gary, as he was permanently crippled.

Around one-thirty pm they reached their destination. Marcia was relieved that Suzette had regained her self-assured persona. She dropped Suzette off in the prison visitors' car park. Marcia said she would find a local café and wait to hear from Suzette when her visit with Max was over.

. . . .

As Suzette entered the prison's visiting room, she momentarily felt a nervous flutter as she took a seat. Composing herself, she beamed a smile at Max as he came through the door flanked by prison warders. Max sat at the table opposite Suzette and briefly kissed her, placing his hands in hers. Suzette knew that holding hands wasn't allowed, and she was aware that visiting could be revoked. Suzette noticed that the guard who was watching them gave Max an imperceptible nod. She knew that Max must have a connection with him. Max's eyes were devouring her. Suzette knew that Max took in everything. As he searched her eyes, she smiled reassuringly. She told him how much she was missing him and that she had spent sleepless nights trying to cope with the thought of being without him. Suzette said her nervousness was causing panic attacks, "You have always taken care of everything, Max. How will I be able to cope on my own?" she said dejectedly.

"I may be behind bars," he stated firmly, "but I can assure you, Suzie, that I am sorting everything out to ensure that everything runs smooth with no outside interference."

Suzette knew by Max's tone, which was laced with a hint of warning, that he was at the helm. Suzette's whole being told her that Max had someone on the outside who was passing him information. When he told her to be a good girl, although he spoke in a light-hearted manner, Suzette sensed it was loaded. She played up the nervous act and to convince him she even squeezed out a few tears. Suzette knew her husband well enough to know that it would touch him. She could see that Max was perturbed by her mental anguish. Trying to console her, he told her to get away somewhere for a few days. "Take Marcia with you and recharge your batteries," he encouraged her.

Later that day, Suzette contacted Joyce and told her that she would definitely be coming out to Spain again for a week and that she would be bringing Marcia along. Joyce was thrilled.

"As soon as you book your flights, email me the details and I will be waiting for you in the usual place outside the airport," Joyce said. She was pleased that Marcia could make it too, what with her daughter Sara coming over with the new man in her life. "I want Sara to have a tarot reading and I hope that Marcia will be able to tell, one way or another, whether this new guy is the right one for my daughter."

The days flew by as the women shopped for more clothes at Suzette's insistence. Marcia's life had taken on a new meaning and she secretly felt at times that she was enjoying it.

. . . .

On the way to the airport, Mikey was his usual quiet self. Marcia could see that he was observing them as she caught his fleeting look in the rear view mirror. She suddenly knew that there was more to Mikey than met the eye, which filled her with dread.

She mentioned it to Suzette as soon as they were out of his earshot. Suzette dismissed her concern. "You can trust him with your life, he's had Max's back for many years and he would lay his life down for him."

"I'm sorry, but I have a gut feeling about this and I am never wrong!" Marcia replied adamantly.

"Please stop worrying about Mikey. He is an old friend who wouldn't harm me or Max," Suzette laughed. "This is one time you are wrong – now come on. Our plane will be taking off in a couple of hours and I want to purchase some bottles of Krug champagne for Jimmy at the duty free."

. . . .

"Everything now appears as it should be," Mikey passed this information on while he was on the phone to Max, glancing at the retreating backs of the two women as they moved towards the airport doors. He was well aware that Suzette had been led astray by that prick Gary Wiley. He had been keeping an eye on Wiley for Max, as he oversaw everything for him while he was away. Mikey had feelers out everywhere. He knew that Suzette trusted him, by the way that she spoke freely in the car. That was how he picked up on what was going on, and he'd been quick in getting word to Max. He didn't know for certain if something had happened between Suzette and that scumbag Wiley, but in their world, you didn't need certainty to do something about it. Mikey had put Max in the picture about Wiley, informing him that when he had spoken to a few contacts, he didn't like what he was told – that Wiley had pulled a stroke with one of the East Sussex boys. Mikey had put two and two together, concluding that he thought because Max was facing a long stretch behind bars, the arrogant little prick assumed that he was now the King Pin. Upon Max's orders, Mikey ensured Wiley got what he deserved. Mikey's thoughts turned to Marcia. He sensed that she was batting on Suzette's side, which he'd picked up from their late camaraderie. He was unsure about her. He would keep his ear to the ground, as he knew before long all would become clear to him. He wasn't one to let anything slip under his radar. He was aware that Marcia was on the payroll. Max had informed him that she was a useful contact and that given her gifts of foresight, Max hoped to be alerted of any future trouble. Mikey found it difficult to believe that Max had let an outsider into the fold, but if the boss waswith it then he would go along with it too. Max had told him that Marcia was an astounding psychic and that she'd warned him about the impending raid, even getting the date of it correct. For a time, Mikey had thought that his old mate had totally lost it … *a bleeding psychic?* Still, he supposed it was a sign of the times. He thought about Marcia. There was something spooky about her. She had the most intense dark brown eyes he'd ever encountered on a woman – she was mesmerising and enigmatic. He thought that she was attractive and he'd noticed the recent changes in her clothes and a flattering new hairstyle. In fact, her whole look seemed transformed. She had gone more upmarket. Mikey felt Suzette had something to do with it. He knew that Max had said he'd put Marcia on a good retainer, but the clothes she was now parading in told its own tale. Mikey knew the clothes by the particular designer that Suzette favoured. Still, let the two women have some fun, as long as they toe the line. Otherwise, he would ensure the pair of them would pay the price.

Mikey was fond of Suzette, but he wasn't a fool. *When the cat's away the mice will play,* he thought of the adage. Let's hope for everyone's sake that it won't apply to the boss's wife. Mikey began to cough uncontrollably. He felt he couldn't get his breath, and indicating, he pulled onto the M3 hard shoulder. The reoccurring cough had been bothering him lately. He felt as if he was coming down with something for a few weeks now and the hack had been getting more persistent. He would use his old mum's method and buy some Vicks rub. "That will sort it out," he muttered to himself.

Spain

Joyce Grant picked the women up from Alicante airport. Marcia was pleased to see Joyce again. As Marcia and Suzette got into her car, Joyce complimented them, "You girls look amazing, there will be a few heads turning." Marcia smiled to herself at Joyce's exuberant mood. She thought that Joyce deserved the happiness that her daughter Sara's visit was bringing her. Marcia knew Joyce adored her daughter. one could get a word in as Joyce spilled forth her excitement about the forthcoming party that was planned for her daughter. "Sara will be arriving in the morning. I can't wait to see her, although I'm a bit nervous about Sara's boyfriend Matt, who will be coming with her. Knowing Jimmy, the lad will be in for a grilling. But to be honest with you girls, Matt will be leaving after a couple of days, as Sara said he was going to Edinburgh to visit his ailing grandmother. I feel I need to inform Jimmy that Matt is of Scottish heritage because when he discovers it, I know that he's not going to be very happy. Jimmy told me he had a run-in way back with a 'face' that ran a gang in Scotland. Jimmy had been double-crossed by him and there'd been a blood bath, with Jimmy coming off the loser, although the Scotsman had been left with a permanent reminder. Jimmy said he had slashed his face from below the cheekbone to the corner of his mouth."

Suzette said nothing. She glanced at Marcia, who went pale at the descriptive violence, as Joyce relayed the story. "My Jimmy vowed never to have any dealings with anyone north of the UK border again. He tarred everyone with the same brush," Joyce added. "I pray that this boy won't stay long in Sara's life, for both of their sakes, although Sara does seem full of the lad whenever we speak about him on the phone. I'm hoping, Marcia, that you will be able to throw some light on the situation." She smiled wistfully into the rear view mirror at Marcia. "The last thing I want is for Jimmy to cause any upset with Sara. Although Jimmy worships her, his hatred of the Scottish would override his feelings for her – I know him," she said with finality. The more Marcia heard about Jimmy Grant the more apprehensive she felt about being in the man's company. The thought of him slashing someone's face with a knife horrified her. *What is Suzette getting me into?* she thought, as Joyce pulled up at her villa.

Jimmy and his right-hand man Eamon were out on the terrace, sitting at the garden table in the shade of the canopy, deep in conversation. When the women came through the doors, both men looked up and smiled. They stood up to welcome them and Marcia's heart skipped a beat as Eamon placed his hand on her arm. His touch felt like an electric shock. He kissed her on the cheek and she took in the fragrance of his aftershave. Marcia thought he was even more handsome than when she had last seen him. His nearness unsettled her and she struggled to compose herself. *What is going on with me? I haven't ever felt this attracted to a man before.* Eamon momentarily held Marcia's eyes, as he complimented her. His Irish brogue melted her and she lowered her eyes coyly, as she thanked him. Jimmy put his arm around both women and welcomed them back. Suzette gave Jimmy the two bottles of his favourite Krug champagne and he smiled, thanking her for the gift, saying that she sure knew the way to his heart.

Jimmy turned to Marcia. "I know you have only just arrived, but once you have settled in, I would like a private word with you in my office, Marcia. Let's say in an hour if that's okay?" He didn't wait for her to reply.

Eamon said his goodbyes and told them he would see them all the following evening. Marcia felt perturbed by Jimmy's request and wondered why he wanted to speak to her privately.

Joyce showed Marcia to her room, where she quickly showered after unpacking, putting on a soft blue Chanel shift dress with a pair of sandals. She looked at her reflection in the mirror and was pleased by what she saw. Suzette had purchased Marcia numerous clothes and shoes and had given her dresses from her vast wardrobe. Suzette's generosity seemingly knew no bounds.

Marcia came out onto the terrace to where Jimmy was waiting, "Wow, look at you Marcia! Things must be looking up, you look amazing," he said, giving her the once-over. Marcia flushed under his gaze.

"We must find a decent man for you, as Joyce tells me you are on your own."

Marcia smiled, without answering him.

Jimmy led Marcia to his office. He locked the door and proffered a chair. He sat opposite her at the magnificent desk that seemed to fill the room with its presence. Marcia thought of how power suited him. He leaned back in his chair and his eyes bore into her. She found him intimidating.

"Your presence the last time you were here caused a bit of a stir among the women. Word has got back to me that you have said one or two things that have made some people a little bit uneasy," he stated, leaning towards her, placing his muscular forearms on the desk. He held her gaze, his undertone threatening.

"I am unsure about this psychic stuff that you do, even though your work, if I may call it that, comes highly recommended. You certainly intrigue me, Marcia, but I hope that you don't cause any unrest in my camp."

"Jimmy, may I just tell you, I am not here to cause trouble, and if I see anything during the psychic readings that shouldn't be revealed, I will avoid it. I am professional and eloquent, whereby I can put the situation in a context that will not be disconcerting," she reassured.

He smiled as he sat back, studying her. His demeanour changed to one of appraisal. "What an interesting woman you are, Marcia, and if I might add, one that I feel should not be underestimated. Looks and brains are a rarity," he added, "which I admire in a woman."

Marcia didn't respond. Her control gave nothing away. He slowly rose from his chair and walked towards her.

"Thank you for our talk, Marcia. It was a pleasure. Maybe we can continue our discussion some other time soon. I have to leave you women, as I have work to do, but enjoy the sunshine and please feel at home."

They joined Joyce and Suzette on the terrace. Jimmy bent down to kiss both women and told them that he would catch up later. Joyce poured Marcia a glass of wine, which was much needed after the conversation she'd just had with Jimmy. Although she didn't show it, Marcia was shaken by his warning and knew she had to be extra careful in what she said, especially with Joyce. Putting everything to one side, she asked Joyce to tell her all the exciting details about the forthcoming party. Joyce didn't need to be asked twice, as she spoke of all the people that were invited and the stories that went with them. It seemed to Marcia that their circle was a who's who in the criminal world. Suzette was laughing with Joyce and joined in adding stories about situations that she had been involved in in the past with Max. Marcia realised what a sheltered life she lived in comparison. Suzette seemed to have perked up. Marcia knew how much Suzette had been rocked by what had happened to Gary. Even after the betrayal, Marcia knew that Suzette still had feelings for him. *Time will alter that,* Marcia thought. Time, she knew was the greatest healer. She momentarily thought about her son and wondered where he was. She glanced out at the sea in the distance and sent a silent prayer to him.

. . . .

Jimmy was in his office at his haulage company, waiting for a lorry driver that was due in from a return trip across the continent from the UK. This trip was going to be a particularly important consignment that would set Jimmy up with a new outlet. Alan Baxter, the lorry driver, had done a couple of dummy runs and all had gone well. He had worked for Jimmy's firm for a couple of years and proven himself trustworthy. He didn't live in Spain – his base was a few miles from the docks where he worked in the past as a stevedore. He had been approached by one of Jimmy's men and asked if he wanted to earn some extra money on the side. Jimmy knew the man was kosher.

Jimmy checked his watch. He felt uneasy when he realised that Alan was two hours late. His mobile rang – the call had a UK code. Jimmy knew that for this man to ring him, the news couldn't be good. And he was right. Alan Baxter had been pulled in by Customs and Excise as his lorry went over the weigh bridge. The caller reassured Jimmy that Alan wouldn't sing. Jimmy Grant sat alone in his office trying to figure out what had gone wrong. Alan had sailed through twice previously. He couldn't put a finger on it, but his gut feeling was telling him that there was a canary amongst them. He was hell-bent on finding out who it was, and he knew the person who would be able to help him.

Jimmy would be losing a great deal of money due to the cocaine shipment being discovered at the port in the south of England, as well as a reliable lorry driver in Alan Baxter.

He was pleased to see his daughter Sara and welcomed her new boyfriend, although the lad didn't hold any interest for him. His mind was elsewhere with the thought of the vengeance he would wreak on the person who leaked the information about the shipment.

. . . .

The party was a success – the caterers had overlooked nothing, the food was amazing and Marcia had never seen anything like it. Joyce walked amongst the guests beaming with pleasure as she played the hostess and showed off her beautiful daughter. Marcia immediately took a liking to Sara and her young man, Matt. She observed Jimmy and thought that he seemed troubled, even though he had been friendly and smiling throughout the day. Marcia noticed at one stage that Jimmy and Eamon had disappeared into Jimmy's office. Marcia had been observing Eve throughout the evening and sensed that something was shifting between her and Jimmy. Jimmy tended to ignore her. Marcia was intrigued as she saw Eve's eyes constantly glancing towards Jimmy's office. Marcia thought that Eve appeared uneasy. She caught sight of Suzette with a man who was paying her a lot of attention throughout the evening. He was a tall, heavily built man with silver-grey hair. Marcia thought perhaps this attractive man could take Suzette's mind off her recent upset with Gary.

Marcia walked towards them and Suzette introduced him. "Greg," she smiled gaily, "This is my dear friend, Marcia." Greg put his shovel-like hand out and kissed Marcia on the cheek. She thought how well they suited one another.

"I am a lucky man to have the company of two very attractive women." He said looking at Suzette as he spoke.

Marcia thought that he was probably in his early fifties. She looked into his warm, hazel-coloured eyes and saw a strong character. She could tell he was a man of authority. Marcia could understand Suzette's attraction to him.

"I hope you like Altea, Marcia, as I would hate for you not to return. I have been trying to convince Suzette that this is the place to live for the weather and the scenery."

Marcia smiled to herself knowing he was directing his questions at Suzette and not her.

He told Marcia that he was a good friend of Jimmy's and that their friendship spanned many years. He informed the women that since his wife died two years previously, he had thrown himself into his construction company. "It must be fate that I accepted this invitation, otherwise I would have missed you two attractive ladies," he said, glancing at Suzette, "…and I am pleased that I came."

Marcia noticed that Suzette was hanging onto Greg's every word and she could tell that something was going to happen between them.

Marcia said goodnight, telling them that it was way past her bedtime. She found Joyce, and thanked her for a wonderful evening and retired to her bedroom.

There is so much going on here, she thought as she drifted off to sleep. Her mind turned to Eamon. Once more, she had seen him watching her and her heart started to flutter as she relived her conflicted feelings about him. She was certainly attracted to him, but she was unsure as to why he was giving her so much attention. He was a married man. There was no mistake as to what type of people were gathered at the party. They looked more suited to the mafia, she mused to herself. Each woman was as glamorous as the next, with diamonds that put Marcia's recently purchased jewellery in the shade. She felt out of place amongst the richly dressed women, even though the black dress she wore had cost Suzette over £3000. She couldn't even begin to count how much money Suzette had spent on her. Marcia didn't want to think about the money that Suzette had stashed away or the consequences if Max discovered the truth about the deception.

Jimmy had got word back to Max about the problem with the lorry shipment. Jimmy and Max were distant cousins and had previous dealings with one another. Jimmy informed Max that his men should keep their ears to the ground. Max felt that the leak had most likely come from Jimmy's neck of the woods and that he should sort it. Max advised that Jimmy should speak with Suzette's friend, Marcia, who might be able to throw some light on the situation. Jimmy had given it a lot of thought, as he wasn't sure if he believed in that kind of thing, but he finally decided to ask Marcia for a reading.

. . . .

Later the following day, Marcia found herself sitting opposite Jimmy, reading his cards. She had been surprised by his request given their previous conversation in his office, and she felt apprehensive about what the cards might reveal. Marcia asked him to shuffle, and explained that if there were any questions he'd need to wait until the reading was completed. Marcia cleared her mind and began to lay out each card.

"You are surrounded by deception and there is someone who is out to bring you down. I feel you are closely connected and they want revenge." Marcia hesitated, looking into Jimmy's eyes. "This is a female that you had an emotional attachment with and you must be careful of who you trust." Marcia continued, "There is a warning for you to be on guard with the sea, as danger lurks there for you."

You could have heard a pin drop, so intently was Jimmy listening to Marcia.

"There is financial loss with your business and if you aren't careful the next one would see you facing an exceedingly difficult situation."

Jimmy shifted in his seat and Marcia could see that he was feeling distinctly uneasy. "Can you give me as much information as possible as to how this woman is going to deceive me?"

Marcia looked down at the cards and tapped the tarot card next to the card of Pisces. "I can see that she is a networker, young, not over the age of forty, with long fair hair and I feel that she is in your circle of friends. There is a cloak of secrecy around this woman. The only way I can liken her is to an ice maiden, one who commands attention, and if she doesn't get her way, she will cause disruption."

"Okay," Jimmy said flatly, "that's fine, thank you for your help, Marcia. Can you tell Joyce I will be joining you all soon once I have sorted out one or two things?"

As Marcia closed the door, Jimmy locked it and moved towards his desk. Leaning against it, he pondered Marcia's incredible ability. He thought she couldn't have known any of the information she had seen in those cards of hers. He looked out at the magnificent Mediterranean Sea view and contemplated all that Marcia had told him. She had described Eve O'Donally. About a week ago, he had stopped answering her calls and he felt sure that she had lost interest in him as he had her. Surely, he mused she wouldn't be foolish enough to play games with him, but what puzzled him was how on earth could Eve know what had been planned with the shipment. Marcia had spoken of his recent financial business loss and warned him of future trouble if he wasn't careful. A creeping realisation came over him, and with that, he picked up his phone.

. . . .

Jimmy had spoken to Eamon about the situation with the cocaine shipment and who'd known about the drugs run to the UK with Alan Baxter. Eamon had sheepishly told him about Eve overhearing their conversation, how she'd walked into Eamon's office while he was talking about the port. He said he always locked the door but had somehow forgotten that time. "There is nothing to worry about with Eve. She's grand," Eamon reassured. Jimmy had known immediately that Eve was the informer, and without pausing for thought, he'd put his plan into action and sent two of his henchmen to orchestrate "an accident".

The women were in total shock when Joyce said that Jimmy had phoned her to say that he had received a call from Eamon about Eve. The Guardia Civil had come to Eamon's home to inform him that the Mercedes that was registered in his name had been involved in an accident; the female identified as dead at the scene was his wife, Yvonne O'Donally. The officer said that by the impact to the metal rail, she must have taken the bend at great speed, giving her zero chance of surviving the 60-metre drop. Eamon was asked to come to the morgue to identify Eve.

Jimmy said Eamon was grief stricken, blaming himself for letting her use the powerful car. Joyce rang Cindy to tell her the news and she rushed over to see her immediately. Although Eve wasn't flavour of the month with the women, she had still been part of their circle as Eamon's wife and everyone was in shock.

Upon Jimmy's return, he agreed it was a tragedy, but Marcia observed that Jimmy wasn't overly bothered. She picked up on an icy detachment when he spoke of her, and he appeared more interested in speaking with Marcia, asking her to step into his office. There was something in his manner that told her that Jimmy was pleased that Eve was no longer on the scene. It was a feeling she couldn't put her finger on. He praised Marcia's intuitive abilities and for the help she had given him. He didn't reveal the exact reason why, but Marcia knew she had gone up a notch in Jimmy's books. "You have been spot on with that reading you gave me." There wasn't any compassion for Eamon in Jimmy's conversation. Marcia took note that it was all about Jimmy, who said he fully realised how advantageous her "gift" could be for him. He added that he was going to give her a bonus as she got up to leave his office.

Marcia flatly refused. He raised his hand to stop her. Opening the desk drawer, he passed Marcia a sealed envelope. Marcia, hesitating, looked at him shaking her head.

"Take it," he commanded. His tone brooked no argument. Marcia had a feeling that there was something underhand about Eve's accident. It was something that she'd picked up on while Jimmy spoke, but she decided to put it to the back of her mind. Marcia knew that the people she was dealing with were a dangerous bunch, and whatever went on in their world, it had nothing to do with her.

Cindy, Joyce and Marcia were sitting on the terrace discussing the report of Eve's demise – which declared it as an accidental death, and they discussed the effect it must be having on Eamon – when Sara and Matt came through the doors. Marcia thought Sara was a very attractive young woman and the young man with her was her absolute match. The couple looked like they'd stepped off a catwalk and their personas blended well, although Sara was as charming and friendly as her mother, her blue eyes showed passion and intensity like her father. Sara appeared self-assured, as someone who was used to getting her own way. Joyce had told Marcia that Sara could wrap Jimmy around her little finger. Matt, Marcia thought, didn't exhibit the same level of intensity as Sara did, or her drive. He appeared a much gentler soul, but despite this, they complemented one another. *They have a similar relationship to Joyce and Jimmy,* Marcia mused. *Definitely wedding bells for these two,* she predicted silently.

Suzette looked glamorous. Marcia could see that she had gone the extra mile with her mode of attire and makeup. Marcia was intrigued when she declared that she wanted to browse the shops, refusing Joyce's offer to join her. "If you don't mind, I am going to have a bit of alone time for a few hours. Life has been demanding lately and I want to clear my head."

Joyce smiled cheerily she knew that Suzette was familiar with the area, as she had visited many times before. "To be honest, Suzie, I do feel rather tired. I only asked because I didn't want you to go alone, but what with the party and all the planning, I will just lay in the sun." Joyce glanced at her daughter and Matt, wondering when Jimmy would get around to having a private chat with him. Jimmy had been so preoccupied of late with his business, but Matt was leaving Spain tomorrow and she knew Jimmy would speak to him before he left. One thing Joyce knew about her husband was that he wouldn't ever leave anything unfinished.

The meeting between Jimmy and Matt took place that afternoon. Jimmy had swaggered in, in a commanding way that Marcia had come to be familiar with, asking Matt if he would like to be shown around the area. He told the women that he wanted to spend some time with Matt man-to-man so he could get to know his daughter's boyfriend – he wanted to show Matt a boat he was interested in buying.

....

At first, Jimmy kept it light, asking Matt about his ambitions in life. Matt informed him that he was aiming to open a restaurant with a potential business partner, Louis, who lived in the US. Matt said that he had struck up a relationship with him a few years back when they'd met at university. Matt said his friend Louis' family-owned restaurants in New York and they were going to help him with the legalities of attaining a green card to enable them to live in America.

Jimmy nodded his approval. "It looks as if you have big ambitions. I'm impressed." Jimmy pulled into the parking area at the marina and was about to get out of the car when he asked Matt, "What did you say your surname was again?"

"I didn't," Matt replied, "but it's Bennett, although my birth certificate states MacDonald, which is my father's name. However, I don't use it."

Jimmy froze. "Come again?" he said in a distinctly icy voice. "Repeat what you just told me." Jimmy continued, "What's with the Scottish connection?"

Matt revealed that his father, who now lived in Edinburgh, originally came from the poor area known as the Gorbals on the south bank of the River Clyde. "My mother divorced my dad years ago when we moved to London."

For once in Jimmy's life, he was gobsmacked. *This lad must be related to that Scottish bastard Mac,* he thought. Trying to compose himself as he walked along the pontoon against the backdrop of the stunning yachts bobbing against their moorings, Jimmy didn't give them so much as a glance as his mind worked overtime. He was finding it extremely difficult to contain his rising anger. "What type of business did your father run?" Jimmy grimaced. He was almost a hundred per cent certain that Matt's father was the same man who had wiped him out of business many years ago.

Matt confessed that he hated his father and was no longer in touch with him, and the only family member he was in contact with was his adored grandmother who lived in Edinburgh. He went on, "My dad was a real rough diamond years ago, and he was hated by many. He was some sort of a gang boss and he terrorised the local community."

Jimmy's blood boiled over. This confirmed his suspicions. *Here I am with this boy … parading him around like a*

fucking peacock with my Sara looking to get serious with him.
Well, it isn't happening. No way will I have him or any other
bastard connecting that lot in Scotland to my family. He has
to go, Jimmy fumed to himself. Pointing Matt in the direction
of the yacht they supposedly had come to look at, he briefly
picked out its finer points. There was no way he could concentrate on frigging boats now. "Okay," he stated, cutting it short,
"we will make a move back and get out of this heat." Matt was
disappointed that they weren't going to get a tour of the luxury
vessel, but he realised that a black mood had descended over
Jimmy for some reason, and he wisely kept his mouth shut and
followed him back to the car.

. . . .

Sara and Joyce were beaming at Jimmy when he returned to
the villa. Sara spoke first, "Daddy, I have some news for you.
You are going to be a granddad, and once the baby is born and
everything is arranged, we will be moving to America."

Although Joyce had been upset when Sara disclosed
earlier that she would be living across the pond, she felt happier
when Sara explained that her mother could frequently come to
stay with them. "We were going to tell you later this evening,
but I couldn't wait!" She threw her arms around her father's
neck and kissed him on the cheek.

Joyce saw the look on Jimmy's face. She could see
that he was fighting to contain his hidden anger. He made
a show of congratulating the couple before excusing himself,
explaining that he had a few phone calls to make. Worried,
Joyce rose from where she was sitting next to Marcia in the
sun by the pool, and followed him into his office and closed
the door. Jimmy sat stony-faced with his head in his hands.

Joyce walked round to him and placed her hands on his shoulders, asking him what was wrong. Jimmy couldn't find the words to express his anger at what he had found out about Matt's family. He turned to face her without speaking, as Joyce continued, "Jimmy we are going to be grandparents, and you should be as thrilled as I am. Whatever is bothering you?"

Jimmy stood up, moving to stand by the window, looking out at his favourite view. He told Joyce what Matt had revealed about who his father was. Joyce sighed as she waited for him to finish. She knew she would have to handle this very delicately. "It's not the boy's fault who his father is. Please, Jimmy, can't you put your anger aside and think of Sara's happiness?"

Joyce told him how much Sara loved Matt and how ecstatic they were about the pregnancy. She was overjoyed at Sara's news and thought Jimmy would feel the same way. He had always been a difficult man, but surely the fact he was going to become a grandfather would have made him happy.

Joyce might have known it was too good to be true. Only her Sara could fall in love with the son of Jimmy's arch enemy. She looked into Jimmy's tired eyes, and realising how much he had aged of late, she almost felt sorry for him. But she pulled herself up with a jolt. Jimmy had been the cause of most of her anguish over the years, due to his wandering eye. She had pondered at times, whether it was out of habit that she was still with him. He'd had numerous affairs over the years, but the one that had hurt her the most was his affair with Eve. He not only betrayed her but also Eamon, his right-hand man, who knew nothing about it. She had lost any feelings of love she had had for Jimmy a long time ago. *What sort of man does the dirty on not only his wife but also his most trusted friend?* she thought.

However, she was wary of Jimmy's temper and she trod carefully. "Please, Jimmy, don't say a word about it." Joyce feared that they would lose Sara and their new grandchild if Jimmy drove them away. "Matt is a nice lad, Jimmy, and he has had no contact with his father since he was a child."

"Sara has made her bed and she can lie in it. We'll wipe our hands of her," he scoffed. Stunned by his words, Joyce walked dejectedly from his office, knowing Jimmy wouldn't tolerate any connection with his old adversary. With a heavy heart, she re-joined her daughter on the terrace.

. . . .

Suzette drove to the top of the steep hill, following the sat-nav coordinates that she'd been given. She finally took a left turn by a restaurant she recognised as one she and Max had eaten at when visiting Jimmy and Joyce previously. Within a few minutes, she had reached her destination – a stunning villa with breathtaking views. Greg walked down the steps to greet her as she pulled up outside the gates.

"You are a vision of beauty," Greg said, unabashed, taking Suzette by the hand and leading her inside.

Suzette fell into Greg's embrace, unashamedly. She had felt starved of affection since being so let down by Gary. She melted against Greg's strong, wide chest, enclosed in his bear-like arms. Greg tilted her head gently back and kissed her lightly, then taking her by the hand, led her through what was clearly the master bedroom onto the huge balcony. A bottle of chilled wine and two glasses awaited them. The view of Mascarat beach in the distance, with its crystal clear waters took her breath away. The visual beauty of the area was extraordinary and the tropical garden below completed the picture. She heard Greg pouring the wine behind her and he offered her a glass, looking directly into her eyes. She knew they both felt that destiny had played a role in their meeting. As Suzette spoke once again of her joyless marriage to Max, she revealed that in her desperation she had foolishly succumbed to another man's charms, who, like Max, had used her. "I know it's disloyal, but Max treats me as a possession. I don't know what it is to be cared for. I'll never be able to get away from him as he wields so much power."

He turned round, putting his arms around her, motioning towards the ornate bed at the far end of the room. Looking into her eyes lovingly, he whispered, "You don't have to stay with him, Suzette.

"I'd like nothing more than to leave him, Greg," she answered breathily. They began tearing each other's clothes off and were naked before they'd even reached the bed. Afterwards, Suzette lay in Greg's arms, in the afterglow of their recent lovemaking.

"I have a proposition for you," Greg murmured into her hair. "I want you to come and live with me out here in Spain. I will look after you. Don't worry, Suzette."

Looking up at him with tears in her eyes, Suzette answered, "There's nothing I'd like more, Greg, but I'm too frightened. I know Max will send people after us when he finds out."

Greg smiled reassuringly. "If you want me in your life, I will sort it out. I can assure you that I'm more than capable of dealing with the likes of Max." Greg sat up and swung his legs out of bed. Suzette watched him adoringly as he crossed the room and fetched the now warm bottle and glasses from the balcony. "A toast then," he grinned, "to our new life together."

Suzette thought she had never seen a more magnificent sight than Greg, standing naked before her with his arms outstretched, holding aloft the bottle and glasses. "Come back to bed," she said, huskily. Max was all but forgotten in the flush of her new found love.

. . . .

After Suzette had returned, she sat down with Joyce, Marcia and Cindy at the poolside. Joyce told her that Jimmy had gone out and that Sara and Matt had retired for a siesta. Marcia immediately noticed the change in Suzette – the spring in her step and a radiant look. She noticed an inner glow that wasn't there before Suzette had left. It was patently obvious to Marcia that Suzette hadn't gone shopping. She thought it was more likely that she'd had a rendezvous with the man she had met last night. Marcia had felt like a wallflower the night before. The spark between Greg and Suzette had been ignited last night at the party and she had no desire to interrupt. She had been amazed that no one else had noticed their intimacy. She could see that Suzette was overflowing with a new found happiness. Clearly, she had put Gary's betrayal behind her.

Joyce spoke excitedly of her coming grandchild and Sara's forthcoming marriage plans, which were to be in six weeks' time. Joyce said she was going to throw the biggest and most luxurious wedding reception ever. Cindy, being an organiser par excellence had already taken over from Joyce and the women were excitedly discussing their plans. Cindy had made a list of all the names of the business contacts she knew Joyce would need to make this the wedding of the year. Marcia could see that Suzette was a million miles away, although she was obviously pretending to be listening. Marcia wanted to speak to her but knew it would be difficult to have a private talk with Suzette with Joyce and Cindy within earshot. One thing Marcia had come to recognise about her friend in the short time she had known her was that Suzette acted impulsively and she had a sinking feeling that Suzette may have jumped out of the frying pan into the fire. She could only hope her new man was worth getting burnt for.

Marcia asked Suzette if she would like to swim with her, and Suzette's eager response told Marcia she was excited and desperate to talk to her alone. Suzette went off to change and Marcia powered through her laps, knowing she wouldn't get much swimming done after Suzette joined her in the water. She sensed she had plenty to tell her. She completed twenty laps by the time Suzette arrived and Marcia indicated that they wade to the far end of the pool where they started doing some gentle exercising. She knew that their aqua aerobics wouldn't arouse Cindy and Joyce's suspicions, but it allowed her and Suzette to talk without being overheard. Suzette was gushing about Greg. She was on cloud nine as she spoke of the wonderful time she had spent with him, telling Marcia every intimate detail. Marcia was pleased that her friend had had such an enjoyable time with her new love interest, but when Suzette announced that she would be relocating to Spain permanently and insisted that Marcia must come too, Marcia looked at her in surprise thinking she may be rushing into things. However, she knew she had no choice but to go along with her. Her head was spinning at the sheer speed with which everything was changing in her life, but she could scarcely believe that Suzette would think it would be that easy to get rid of Max. She knew Max would stop at nothing to hunt them down. Suzette was obviously not thinking straight but it would be pointless for Marcia to try to talk sense into her at this moment in time. She was obviously infatuated with Greg and Marcia knew that as generous as Suzette was, her ruthless streak would override any reasonable argument from her. She couldn't believe Suzette's naiveté; did she honestly think that Max would let her get away from him? She most probably would seek his revenge on not only his wife but also her.

Matt flew to Scotland the following day and a tearful Sara joined her mother and Cindy on a pre-wedding shopping spree – just the thing to cheer her up after Matt's departure. Suzette and Marcia had stayed behind, as they wanted to catch up on some sunbathing before they faced the bleak weather back in England in a couple of days.

Jimmy strolled across the terrace. "Marcia may I speak with you in my office?" he asked, smiling.

Marcia threw her yellow sundress on over her swim-suit and followed him inside. As they stepped inside the villa, he told her to get her cards, as he had a few questions he needed answers to. Marcia entered his office, whereby Jimmy locked the door. Although she momentarily felt uncomfortable, she composed herself as she sat facing him. Marcia began the reading by warning him once more about a business deal that he would be involved in within the next few days. "I see the skull and cross bones, indicating Customs and Excise, the ocean, a ship and disaster for you if you are not careful. Heed my advice and beware of danger concerning this over the next few days." She fleetingly held his eyes, and then looked back at the cards, as she informed Jimmy that he would lose out financially and that he would find himself facing danger. Jimmy nodded, pressing his lips together without commenting. Rising from behind the desk, he thanked her.

"Please continue to enjoy this beautiful weather while you can," he smiled, as Marcia packed the cards away without saying anything. She was relieved to get away from the proximity of his energy that always seemed to unnerve her.

. . . .

Max had sent word from the UK about a big consignment of cocaine that would be coming in from Turkey on a fishing trawler. The offer to come in on the deal with Max had been tempting, as the street value was over twenty million sterling. Something was telling him to be cautious and seek Marcia's advice before he committed himself, however. With her warning ringing in his ears, Jimmy had made a call to decline the narcotics offer and sat back to see what would transpire. It didn't take long. Later that day, Jimmy found out that the trawler boat entering the channel at Teignmouth in the UK had been boarded by armed officials. Jimmy was informed that the captain and crew were arrested. Once threatened with an exceptionally long prison sentence, the chief officer had no doubts it wouldn't take too long before the trawler captain would give up the name of his contact. Jimmy had been told via his contacts that Max could be facing a further prison sentence since he had been named for importing class A drugs. Jimmy, breathing a sigh of relief at his narrow escape, decided he had to have Marcia on his payroll.

. . . .

That evening, Marcia had been contacted by Jimmy again. She felt apprehensive as to why he wanted to speak to her so soon after his tarot reading. He didn't waste any time on pleasantries. Passing her an envelope, Jimmy told her it was a thank you for her previous advice. Marcia could feel by the weight of the envelope that it had to be a large amount of cash. Alarmed, she tried to hand the money back, explaining that the gift was too generous. Although Marcia had been given the go-ahead by

Max to give advice through her tarot card readings within his circle in Spain, Marcia felt that this wouldn't be the only time that Jimmy would ask for her services. Whatever had occurred from her previous predictions for Jimmy to be so generous, Marcia had no idea, but she sensed that Jimmy intended to use her for his own gains, which made her feel decidedly uncomfortable. Marcia froze as he informed her that he needed her by his side.

"You are invaluable to me. Take the money ... it's peanuts compared to what you have saved me," he smiled.

With a heavy heart, Marcia realised that there was going to be no escaping the fact that she would need to take up residence in Spain. Her mind was in turmoil as she walked back out into the sunshine through the terrace doors, wishing she had never set foot in Spain. She knew that she was going to face the unbearably heavy burden of being forced to work for Max, Suzette and now Jimmy. All of them were only out for themselves. It appeared to be the norm in this criminal dog-eat-dog world and she was in the middle of it all. She was impatient to pack and so pleased that there was only one day left of their stay in Spain. She was certainly in no rush to hurry back.

Suddenly Eamon's voice broke through her thoughts and she noticed him sitting at the far end of the terrace under the sunshade with a bottle of water in his hand, speaking to Suzette. Her heart skipped a beat. He looked drawn and unshaven. She could see by his appearance that Eve's death had knocked him sideways. He was deep in conversation with Suzette. At that moment, Marcia decided to return inside, hopefully unnoticed, but Suzette spotted her and summoned her over. As she approached the table, Eamon stood up, smiling warmly, his dark eyes gazing into hers with an intensity that made Marcia blush. His welcome greeting belied the fact that he was struggling emotionally, He looked to her as if he hadn't slept for days, yet she still thought he was probably one of the most handsome men she had ever seen. Marcia demurely sat down, wrestling with the feelings she experienced every time she saw Eamon. He never failed to set her heart fluttering and she momentarily felt guilty. She desperately hoped he hadn't noticed the effect he had on her.

However, Eamon clearly had other things on his mind as he excused himself after asking if Jimmy was in his office, saying that he needed to speak with him. Suzette remarked to Marcia that her heart went out to him, as she could see he was devastated by the tragedy, even though he hadn't said so. He doesn't wear his heart on his sleeve," Suzette announced. "But I know Eve's death has taken its toll on him."

"Poor man," Marcia breathed. She couldn't trust herself to say more.

. . . .

Eamon was facing an inner battle of a different sort. While he was in his and Eve's bedroom, not long after the accident, he absent-mindedly opened her chest of drawers. He didn't know what had made him do it, but curiosity had overcome him, and discovering Eve's locked jewellery box at the bottom of her lingerie drawer, he was intrigued, as he knew she wasn't security conscious. She had always left her valuable diamonds on the dresser. He had never known her to put them under lock and key. It was something he had berated her about regularly. It was more than curiosity now that had him rummaging for the key to the jewellery box, but after a few minutes, he ran out of patience, strode to the kitchen, went to the cutlery drawer, and taking a knife, placed the box upon the kitchen island and forcibly broke the lock.

It hadn't been the jewellery he had bought her over the years inside that took his interest – it was a small book. Realising it was a diary, which he was unaware that she had kept, part of him was reluctant to discover what secrets it would reveal. He pulled up a chair and sat down. Upon opening the diary he began to read the first entry, his mind started reeling at what Eve had been up to behind his back. Eamon felt as if he had been slammed in the face as he read the intimate details of Eve and Jimmy Grant's affair.

Three pages in he threw the book across the room in disgust, icy anger building up. He opened a bottle of wine; the first glass he downed did nothing to quell his ire. Pouring another, he sank it back. Glaring at the diary where it lay, he retrieved it, and slumping back into the chair, he forced himself to read every entry. His hatred for Eve and Jimmy Grant took over from the previous grief he'd felt by her death. It was all in there: when the affair began; where they met up at different hideaways; Eve's obsession with Jimmy and her plans to eventually replace Joyce. In the latter pages, Eve had written of Jimmy's casual dismissal of her and her resultant anger. Her final entry consisted of a threat, which she stated bold and clear, that she was intending to take her revenge on Jimmy. She had something on him that would see him being locked up, and by the time he was released he would be so old, no other woman would want him.

Eamon was stunned by the implications that she would inform on Jimmy, because if Eve had carried out her threat, Eamon being his right-hand man, would have been brought down with him. His devastation over Eve's death was rapidly turning to loathing for her and that bastard Jimmy Grant. He knew he was a womaniser and he wouldn't have trusted him with any female that took his fancy, but Eamon had foolishly trusted Eve. He laughed wryly at his own stupidity. He had loved her, been one hundred percent loyal to Jimmy, and the pair of them had played him.

Eamon decided to play the heartbroken husband and keep his new found knowledge to himself until he felt the time was right. There would be a payback, and Jimmy Grant would pay the price, big style, but not yet.

Eamon's mind churned as he knocked on Jimmy's door. He had patience and he told himself he would wait, no matter how long it took. He swallowed hard and pushed away the sick feeling in the pit of his stomach when he heard the door being unlocked from the other side. Jimmy welcomed him and putting his arm around Eamon's shoulder, he spoke to him of the upcoming funeral. "We will give Eve the best send-off ever," Jimmy said, "No expense spared as I will foot the bill. There's no need for you to worry about anything. Everything will be taken care of and once this is all over, I want to speak to you about a plan that will put us right up there on the map."

Eamon had let Jimmy do all the talking, not trusting himself to even disagree with the funeral plans. If he had his way, the conniving bitch would have been dumped at the nearest refuse tip. Jimmy walked Eamon to the door and, as he went to open it, he revealed that he now had someone new on the payroll.

Eamon was surprised by Jimmy letting someone new into their circle. It was so unlike him. Eamon spoke for the first time since entering Jimmy's office, "Who is he?" he frowned.

"Not a he, *a she*," Jimmy replied. "Suzette's friend Marcia. She is worth her weight in gold. No one will be able to get past her insight," he declared, laughing. "Believe me, she will be a total asset to the firm."

Eamon gave a slow nod without replying. This was unsettling news. The few moments he had spent with Marcia earlier had only increased his attraction to her and now. He had heard the women talk of Marcia's power, of her second sight and her tarot reading accuracy. Unlike most of the men, this was something Eamon had grown up with in Ireland. His maternal grandmother, mother and aunt, all had had the gift. People would come from far and wide to ask for advice, a spell or a good luck charm, and it was something he was wary of. Marcia intrigued him – he'd be a liar if he didn't admit that she often popped into his mind since the first day he'd set eyes on her. He thought Marcia had that indefinable something that men found irresistible. When she had sat with him and Suzette on the terrace earlier and had kept her eyes lowered, he was overcome by his feelings of protection towards her. If he hadn't got up when he did, he wouldn't have been responsible for his actions, so strong was his attraction to her.

. . . .

Suzette and Marcia had been lying by the pool in the glorious sunshine, discussing Eve's death and the effect it was having on Eamon. Their idle chat had also strayed towards thoughts of Sara and Joyce's happiness, given the impending wedding celebrations and baby plans. Suzette brought the subject up again about her and Greg. "I know we have only just met, and you must think I am being foolish, but we both feel the same about one another, and I must see him one more time before we go back to the UK."

"Suzie," Marcia began, "My heart goes out to you, but how on earth are you ever going to have any kind of life with this man with Max on your trail? How am I ever going to get it through to you, the danger you are putting us both in with this ridiculous plan of yours?" She knew her friend wasn't listening and Marcia felt mentally drained.

Suzette then asked her if she would cover for her so that she could call Greg and see if they could meet up before leaving the next day. Before Marcia could even answer, Suzette had phoned Greg, and then telephoned a taxi, as Joyce was out in her car. Marcia realised Greg had asked Suzette to come over right away and she prayed that the women didn't return before Suzette got back from Greg's, as she knew she wouldn't be able to explain her absence.

. . . .

Greg was overjoyed that Suzette could get away for a couple of hours, upon receiving her call, he immediately changed his plans and arranged to meet her back at his villa. Greg was one of the largest contractors in the building business on the Costa Blanca and although he long since left Jimmy and his shady past behind, he kept in contact with him. He had gone straight years back but he and Jimmy had a past, strengthened, when through a stroke of good fortune, Greg had obtained a contract via Jimmy's associate who had gained planning to build a big new shopping complex.

Jimmy had used his influence to sway the man to use Greg's small building company, which had put Greg right up there with the big boys financially. Although Jimmy never discussed what was going on with his life, the two men would often sit over a beer and reminisce. There was a strong bond between them, and Greg felt he owed it to Jimmy. He knew it was underhanded of him seeing Suzette, Max Greenaway's wife, who was Jimmy's distant relative. Greg and Jimmy had come from Hackney in the northeast of London and their mothers had been childhood friends they had a long history together.

Greg knew what he was getting into where Suzette was concerned and thought that he would need to explain the situation about Suzette's unhappy marriage to Max, and he hoped that when the time came, that Jimmy would understand. Greg knew there wasn't any love lost on Jimmy's part with his cousin, so he felt certain he was on safe ground. Greg was in far too deep with Suzette already – so little time had passed since they had been in each other's arms, but he was aching for her return. Max was of no consequence to him. He had reassured Suzette over and over, that no matter what it entailed, he would overcome any obstacles they faced.

. . . .

Suzette and Marcia sat back in their seats on the plane with a glass of wine each. Suzette had talked of nothing except the new love in her life. She told Marcia she was confident that Greg would sort everything out, and come what may, they would be together.

Exasperated, Marcia tried to convince her that it was sheer folly. "Aren't you forgetting one thing?" Marcia asked her, "What about Max? He may be behind bars, but he still has so much sway. You don't seem to comprehend that he could hurt you if you take such dramatic steps, and I cannot foresee him letting you get away with it. Not to mention, you're also involving me and risking my son's life."

"You worry too much, Marcia" Suzette retorted.

Marcia finally realised that she was wasting her breath, as Suzette ignored her pleas and changed the subject to the big wedding in six weeks' time. Joyce and Cindy, in typical fashion, had taken Sara to a top designer for a fitting of her wedding dress and had taken command of every detail. Sara would be four and a half months pregnant by the wedding date and the designer had allowed for the slight expected expansion. No expense would be spared, and everybody who was anybody would be attending this glorious affair. Although Marcia was trying to come to terms with what lay ahead for herself, by the time the stewardess had poured them both another wine, she couldn't help but be caught up in the excitement of the upcoming grand affair.

Suzette said excitedly, "We both require stunning outfits and one of the first things we are going to do when we get back is go on a glorious shopping spree. I'll make you look like a million dollars, Marcia. I am going to ensure you get a man in your life when we begin our new lives in Spain. I'm not going to see a good-looking woman like you go to waste when there are so many handsome men out there."

The last thing Marcia wanted was a man from the criminal circle that all those men seemed embroiled in. Although there was one in particular who may have tempted her to the dark side, she mused. She couldn't deny that Eamon invaded her mind often, when she was least expecting it. She was thankful that she was putting time and distance between them, as surely she could now get him out of her system. He was an added complication she didn't need. She knew full well that had the opportunity arisen she would have been very tempted by him. She wasn't naïve enough to think that there wasn't an attraction between them, it was palpable and she was certain he felt it too. It was pure animal magnetism, like nothing she'd ever experienced before. She would have to bring all her determination and inner resolve to the fore to get that damned man out of her mind.

UK

Max was taken aback when the prison warder opened his cell door to inform him he had two visitors. Max immediately recognised the two men as plain clothes police officers. No wonder his refusal for a visit had been totally ignored by the prison warder. Max sighed and composed himself. They greeted him as if they were old friends and both proffered their hands. Max had had enough dealings with the law to know that this wasn't a social visit. The questioning by the older officer began pleasantly enough, but Max's continual denial of his involvement in the Turkish drug shipment only served to irritate both officers. Even after several hours of grilling, he would still not admit to having any knowledge or involvement. Although Max's name had been given up by the fishing trawler captain, Max stood his ground. Upon being asked how this man could have pulled his name out of a hat, Max declared that he was being set up, and for them to prove he was involved. The officers sneered at that, informing him that they would soon be back, and if he didn't confess, he should make himself comfortable in his prison cell, as he would have a much longer extension to his stay. They assured Max that they had a reliable source who would give evidence against him.

Back in his cell, he mulled it over in his mind. He was confident that they had nothing on him. His trusted circle was deliberately small and the Turkish skipper had come highly recommended, however, a seed of doubt was beginning to grow. He could trust his cousin and business associate, Jimmy, with his life – but why then did Jimmy decline the deal? It had been a closely guarded secret and they would have stood to earn plenty from it. It didn't make sense. There was only one conclusion – someone must be feeding Jimmy information. Max felt he was sitting on a powder keg waiting to explode.

. . . .

The women had only been back in the UK a few hours when Suzette received a phone call from Max telling her about the police visit and how he felt that someone was trying to stitch him up. He arranged for Marcia to give him a reading later that evening. Both women were unnerved by the news and Marcia's stress levels went through the roof. This whirlwind life that she was caught up in was putting the fear of God in her, and she didn't know which way to turn. Confiding in Suzette, she spoke again of her fears for her son's safety as she realised that each and every one in this frightening game was out to obliterate each other.

Max, in her estimation, was one of the big players and she knew that she'd have to convince him that she was protecting him from impending trouble. Marcia was aware that it would be far from easy, not only did she have to juggle Suzette's plans for the pair of them to live in Spain; she was now expected to keep Max on an even keel, not to mention now being in Jimmy's employ as well. She felt sick to her stomach. Did Suzette honestly think that although they both would have Greg's protection that it would be enough to prevent Max's contacts from getting to them?

"I know you are an intelligent woman, Marcia, and can outwit Max, just give him a certain amount of information, enough to keep him happy, and I promise you I will come up with something to help your son escape his clutches." Marcia felt no relief from Suzette's promises. She may have Suzette and Greg on her side and her own intuitive ability to guide her, but these were ruthless people, not the type who would allow an act of betrayal to go unpunished.

By the time Max rang, Marcia had mostly regained her control and gave Max the answers she felt best suited his questions. She had given him the description of the fair-haired female, who she had warned Jimmy would likely betray him. She added a bit more about his future and gave him a warning about dealings with a man in an official uniform who would eventually double-cross him. Max had asked her if she could describe the uniformed man. Marcia told him that was all the information she was receiving, but advised him not to give out too many details about his future to this man.

"However, I do see you are going to have a powerful ally in the guise of a foreigner who will aid you in the near future," Marcia explained.

That seemed to appease Max slightly. He told her to tell Suzette that he wished to speak to her. Marcia placed the phone on the table with a huge sigh of relief and left the room, leaving a hovering Suzette to take the phone.

. . . .

Suzette used as much charm as she could muster with Max, sweet talking him incessantly. He appeared to be listening, she thought, but clearly, he was just waiting for an opportunity to announce his bombshell news. When eventually Suzette came up for air, he informed her that she would be leaving for Thailand the following Sunday and taking Marcia with her. Rooted to the spot in shock by this turn of events, she tried every way to get out of it, as she told him she wasn't up to such an arduous, long trip, but he brooked no argument, stating she was the only one he trusted.

"I've got a deal going down, Suzie, and only you can oversee it for me." Suzette knew there was no point in protesting. "Stay a week," he stated. Once everything is sorted, you girls can please yourselves. Enjoy some of the sights of Pattaya. I'm sure the change of scenery will do you both good. I will ask Mikey to book you both business class seats to Bangkok. When you arrive, there will be someone waiting for you at the airport."

Suzette felt as if her life were spinning out of control; there was no way out of the situation because if she refused Max would take it as a personal affront. Both she and Marcia had little option but to follow his orders. Max told Suzette she would have to vouch for the quality of the drugs on offer and he wanted Marcia's expert opinion on the trustworthiness of his contact in Thailand. Suzette was no expert in narcotics but, Graham, the Australian guy that Max informed her she'd be meeting, was. She'd had a brief encounter with Graham previously when she and Max had met up with him in London once for business. She felt a little more comfortable that she had at least met the man before.

. . . .

Marcia was aghast as Suzette relayed Max's orders. Thailand was the country that had lured her son Reuben into the biggest mistake of his life, leading to their forced estrangement and his now clandestine life. Marcia was horrified that she was being ordered to go there to ensure that the man who was overseeing the drug shipment was reliable. She couldn't understand why Max required her verification that the man in Asia could be trusted.

"I'm not happy with this, Suzette. It's one thing having to read these men's cards, but now I'm expected to give the go-ahead on a drug deal that's taking place halfway across the world?"

"What you fail to understand, Marcia," Suzette said, "is that everything is riding on this deal for Max. He can't afford to take any financial risks without your sanction. You've proved yourself to him that you are totally reliable with your tarot readings, and for him, there is no way this is going to happen without you."

Marcia knew there was nothing she could say or do that would prevent her life's downward spiral. She was almost resigned to the fact that she was no longer in charge of her own destiny.

Suzette decided that the days leading up to their flight to Thailand would be filled with the two women getting everything in order, in preparation for their relocation to Spain. It was a whirlwind of shopping and packing. Suzette told Marcia that once they had appeased Max going to Thailand, upon their return, if they required a quick exit from the UK, they would be ready.

Marcia shook her head in wonderment as Suzette gave her instructions. She made it seem as if it were all quite normal to pull the shutters down on your whole way of life and move to another country under cloak and dagger. There were times when Marcia wondered what planet her friend was on.

This is total madness! Marcia thought as the graceful Thai hostess welcomed them on board the Double Decker A380. Glancing at the ticket, she said, smiling, "Royal Silk," indicating towards the stairs that led to the upper-class section of the airbus. Both women were quiet, deep in their own thoughts as they settled in while the passengers boarded. Marcia looked out at the greyness that hung over Heathrow airport. As the engines roared into life and the plane moved along the tarmac gaining speed and lifting into the air, she felt numb. She wondered if the pilot ever had the same feeling as she did, holding people's lives in the palm of his hands. Her clientele were like the passengers on this plane. People came to her for advice and direction and all it would take would be for her to abuse her power, or to make a mistake, and they would all come crashing to the ground.

The flight attendant's voice broke her reverie as the plane reached 36,000 feet and they were offered champagne and strawberries, which Marcia declined, asking for just mineral water. They were given a menu and a form to fill in with their details and the address where they would be staying. Marcia felt in no mood to eat. Her fears of travelling to a country such as Thailand, with its zero-tolerance policy on drugs, were mounting. She'd read enough terrifying stories of the consequences faced by those foolish enough to break the country's narcotic laws. She felt the quicker this trip was over with and they were back in the UK the better she would feel. Even Suzette's plans to live in Spain paled in comparison to this.

Marcia's nervousness had been noted by Suzette, who asked her if she wanted a sleeping tablet. Suzette knew that if Marcia slept through the twelve-hour flight she would be in a more positive frame of mind. Against her better judgement, Marcia took it. She never took any form of prescription medication as a rule but felt the circumstances warranted it. She needed the oblivion of sleep.

Thailand

Suzette had not mentioned to Marcia that when she'd spoken to Greg before they left, she'd informed him of the details of their trip to Thailand and that Greg was furious over what Suzette had told him.

He railed about Max. "How could that selfish bastard put you in such a dangerous position?" He had begged her to be careful and not to take any unnecessary risks. Greg informed Suzette that he would put plans in motion to enable her to join him in Spain as soon as she got back. She felt comforted as he spoke of the changes he would make to ensure that they could spend their lives together.

Suzette smiled wistfully at her sleeping friend. The tablet had worked. She knew she had Marcia's arm forced behind her back regarding her plans to leave England, but once Marcia settled in Spain, she knew the country would open up a whole new way of life for her. She wasn't going to allow Marcia and her powerful gift to be wasted. Suzette had become very fond of Marcia, and she wanted to make it up to her, as she planned a new business venture for them both, and Greg had agreed to help her. Suzette was now in a more positive frame of mind about this trip to Thailand since she had spoken to Greg, who restored her confidence about her future with him. She eventually slept for the last few hours.

. . . .

The women were awoken by the flight attendant who asked them to put the seat in the upright position and fasten their seatbelts, as the plane would be landing shortly.

After they'd cleared customs and collected their cases, Suzette spotted a young Thai man who was holding up a sign with her name on it. He bowed his head, smiling from ear to ear as he welcomed them, asking the women to follow him. As they exited the air-conditioned terminal going through the revolving doors at Suvarnabhumi airport, the fumes from the traffic hit the back of their throats. The driver opened the awaiting car doors, and then he put their cases into the boot. Marcia reeled from the sensory overload. Not only was the heat stifling, the Bangkok air was acrid, and she had never heard such a cacophony of noise. Loud whistles competed with the shouting of traffic police. The air conditioning in the car was like a breath of fresh air compared to the heavy, humid air outside. She slumped in her seat gratefully. The driver hopped in front, introduced himself as Nai, and without indicating, pulled into the traffic mayhem and sped away from the airport. The death-defying manoeuvres of the cars narrowly missing hitting one another and car horns blaring was something that Marcia had only seen in movies.

"Don't worry," Nai said. "Me good driver. It Bangkok," he laughed, indicating the chaos. In broken English, he told the women his family history at rapid speed, which they only caught snippets of – although they both understood when he smiled, "Me, half Thai. Father, he go home to Australia."

Nai drove expertly at top speed, weaving in and out of the traffic. Marcia thought he would have done well in a James Bond movie. She had never been driven at such a fast pace in all her life. Nai continually shouted, "Crazy Thai driver!" as car after car seemed to come within inches of wiping them out.

Despite the speed, Marcia took in the sights as they travelled further out of the city towards their destination. She had never seen poverty like it, but amongst it, all were huge golden statues of Buddha and ornate temples, which Marcia was in awe of. Three hours later, with Nai's chatter now falling on deaf ears, the car entered Pattaya, which lay along the east coast off the Gulf of Thailand. Nai manoeuvred skilfully along the beach road, amongst the throngs of people that seemed to have a death wish, before turning off to the right.

"Soon we be there," he stated, pointing to a road sign, "only three," he said, which Marcia took to mean three kilometres to Jomtien. She heaved a sigh of relief and nudged Suzette lightly. He eventually pulled up at the top of a long drive that led to a house that was surrounded by high walls with large ornate gates. Nai spoke into the intercom and as they drove through.

A tall, blond, muscular man, flanked by two menacing-looking dogs eyed Marcia and Suzette suspiciously. The man appeared to be in his early fifties. On recognising them, a warm smile lit up his face. Startling blue eyes edged with black lashes were his main attraction, contrasting with his somewhat worn, craggy face.

Marcia felt uneasy as the man greeted Suzette and proffered his hand to her. He introduced himself to Marcia as Graham. When he clasped Marcia's hand, she sensed a darkness that surrounded him. She was taken aback as it seemed at odds with his friendly energy. Before she could fully understand this strange mix of energies, a dark premonition connecting a violent situation flashed through her mind.

Feeling greatly perturbed, she followed Suzette and Graham up to the magnificent house where his stunning daughter and lovely Thai wife were standing at the top of the steps waiting to greet them. Marcia's foreboding didn't dissipate however and she was glad when Graham excused himself, saying he had an urgent appointment and would return in an hour. As he exited, the ominous cloud that followed him dissipated. Marcia sensed that he was in grave danger.

She had no time to ponder it though as the two women, Graham's wife Aye, and daughter Stephanie, gave them the customary Thai greeting. Bowing their heads with raised hands palm to palm, they welcomed them. Marcia was enchanted. Stephanie, being mixed race, was the most beautiful girl Marcia had ever seen. Her long, chestnut brown hair with copper highlights, coupled with her father's sapphire blue eyes certainly gave her a striking look. Marcia was taken aback to then hear her speak in a cultured English accent. She wouldn't have expected this teenage girl, who conversed with her mother in Thai, to immediately revert to an upper-crust accent that wouldn't have been out of place at Oxford University.

Marcia noticed it was the daughter who did all the talking, slipping naturally between Thai and English. Stephanie showed them to their bedrooms and then said that they were preparing food for them and to make themselves at home.

As Marcia unpacked, she thought of how Suzette had been unduly quiet during the trip. She knew that Greg was on her mind, as the night before they left, Suzette had been on the phone with him for nearly two hours. Although she had told Marcia that Greg would help them, she sensed Suzette was withholding something from her. She hoped that Suzette would use caution with Max, as Marcia had so much to lose and, when it came down to it, Greg was Suzette's ally. Marcia had no one. The air conditioning offered some relief from the heat, which was oppressive even though there was a breeze from the ocean.

After a cool shower, Marcia wrapped a towel around herself and lay on the bed. She cleared her mind, shutting the door on all negative thoughts as she began to meditate. This, along with Hatha yoga, which she had routinely practised for many years, was the only way she could wind down, control her mind and aid her well-being. It was as necessary to her as breathing and she was going to take this opportunity to indulge in the discipline now that she had a quiet hour to herself. Marcia drifted, calm taking over her mind, and the familiar feeling of relaxation spreading through her.

The tension had all but left her when she felt pressure at the back of her head and blackness filled her mind. As if being struck by a bolt of lightning, she jolted upright, her senses hyper-alert. Overwhelmed with a feeling of dread she felt that some misfortune was going to occur in this house. It was utterly pointless for her to try to relax and rest now. The bad sign had left her feeling very disturbed. Slipping into a light blue cotton dress, she left the bedroom and headed towards the large shaded wraparound veranda.

She was acutely aware that fate had thrown her from a relatively unobtrusive life into the vortex of the underworld, steeped in narcotics and criminal activity. Since studying astrology, Marcia had always been drawn to the eighth house of Scorpio, more so than any of the others. It ruled death and the afterlife, the underworld, crime, psychology, hidden secrets, one's soul mate and sex. *How ironic,* she thought, as she sat quietly listening to the whirr of the ceiling fan. Apart from the sex, I'm practically living the eighth house. My new life is certainly at odds with this beautiful view. She gazed out at the Gulf of Thailand Andaman Sea in the distance, which was filled with the activity of jet skis and para sailing.

Despite the worrying thoughts, she was beginning to feel an affinity with this country, and under different circumstances, she would have enjoyed the culture, the people and the sights. The sound of Graham's vehicle returning as he drove in broke her reverie. He smiled at Marcia, jumping out of the jeep with the agility of a much younger man. She watched his jaunty walk as he moved towards her. Marcia was puzzled by her earlier dark feelings surrounding Graham, as his overall impression gave her nothing untoward – no duplicity, no underhandedness – he seemed a real genuine sort of guy. He asked for Suzette, who was still in her room, then said to his wife that they would eat lunch on the veranda.

Marcia pushed aside the ominous feeling that had begun to creep back, as he informed her that he and Stephanie would show them the local sights in Pattaya later that evening. Graham seemed like a typical Australian, disarming and with a dry sense of humour. Marcia very much enjoyed his company over lunch and wished she could shake off the sense of foreboding surrounding him.

He explained that he had met his wife in the country when he'd been a young man, then went on to set up a successful fishing business. His daughter, he said, came along much later. When he spoke of her, it was clear that Stephanie was his pride and joy. He went on to say that he'd sent her to the most prestigious private school in the area and that she spoke four languages. Her English would enable her to mix with the top society in the world, he said proudly. Suzette, late for lunch, as she had been napping, suddenly appeared, in high spirits.

"I'm starving! I hope you've left some for me?" She waltzed over to Graham and kissed him on the cheek. The only thing Suzette knew about Graham was when she first met him in London with Max. The men had a "business" connection. Suzette hadn't delved into her husband's work when they were in the early stages of their relationship but became aware over time that Max dealt in illegal operations, and by then it was too late for her to back out. She was head over heels in love with him. Suzette was back to being her normal talkative self, taking over the conversation, unaware of what was going on in Marcia's head. Her non-stop chattering about the beauty of the house and the amazing views over the Gulf of Thailand and what she was intending to wear that night gave Marcia the perfect excuse to leave the table, saying she was going to rest. She knew that it was imperative Suzette and Graham have some private time to talk, and she certainly didn't want to be a party to that conversation.

Graham had been given the nod via Max to allow Suzette to join him when he tested the cocaine sample. It was Suzette's job to verify the consignment was the correct weight before the deal was given the go-ahead. Feeling slightly uncomfortable by her husband's obvious mistrust of Graham, Suzette stated that it was highly irregular for her to accompany him, but the laid-back Australian waved her concern away. He told her that whatever it took to allay Max's fears as to the quality and quantity was fine by him. Suzette knew that Max had dealt with Graham in the past and he had never let him down, but because of the way Max had been double-crossed of late, Suzette totally understood his paranoia.

. . . .

That evening, Graham and Stephanie introduced Marcia and Suzette to the delights of Walking Street. The women were astonished at the sight of beautiful women parading around. Graham informed them that they were actually men, "lady boys" or "katoys," as they are known in Thailand. He laughed at the surprised look on their faces. As Stephanie was only a teenager, it came as a surprise to them that she said it was her favourite place of enjoyment. She relished the opportunity to show them the highlights of Walking Street, which was a tourist hotspot that always went down well with visitors to Pattaya.

Graham told them that the clubs put on shows that left little to the imagination. He said if they wanted to see a performance, he would return another evening with them while his daughter stayed at home. The lady boys were usually the main attraction and drew people from all walks of life into the dazzling array of clubs. Marcia could totally understand the draw for Western men, as she marvelled at the lady boys' glamour, long legs and waist-length hair that shone like jet-black stone, all of them strutting like peacocks. From one end of Walking Street to the other, the women felt as if they were in another world – the colours, gaiety and party atmosphere enthralled them. Stopping at bars for a drink and talking and laughing with the lady boys, Marcia soon forgot her previous worries. They totally lost track of time and Marcia found that she didn't want it to end, as she was kept entertained all evening.

At the end of the evening, Marcia thanked Graham and Stephanie for a lovely time and retired to her bedroom. She had a shower because although it was past midnight, the humidity still lingered. As she relaxed and got into bed, she tried to organise her thoughts. She decided she would tell Suzette tomorrow about the dark feelings of foreboding that she sensed surrounding Graham. She couldn't shake off the warnings her senses were giving her, though Marcia felt nothing untoward around Stephanie or her mother Aye. She knew she was obligated by Max to do her part in the deal, however. She couldn't allow anything to jeopardise Reuben. Her thoughts were of her son, and after being in Thailand for 24 hours, she now understood why he'd fallen in love with the country.

It was around midday when Marcia woke up the next day. She apologised to Aye, explaining that it was so unlike her to sleep in. Aye asked her to take a seat on the veranda and said she would bring her something to drink and eat. Marcia thanked her, returning her beaming smile. Suzette had gone out early with Graham, Aye informed her, but they would be returning soon. Marcia asked Aye to join her at the table, as she was hoping Aye would educate her on the Thai way of life as Marcia was already quite fascinated by it.

Over a jug of mint and ginger-infused water and a delicious variety of sliced fruit, Aye began her story. She had been brought up in the north of Thailand helping her mother in the rice fields at the tender age of three. She laughed as she told of her grandmother who used to make rice whisky, which was illegal, and was once locked up in the "monkey house." Marcia gasped and asked her to explain what she meant by that. Aye, grinning, explained that it was the local prison. Marcia was horrified but intrigued to know more. She continued by telling Marcia how she had to go to work for an army couple at the age of fourteen who had treated her as little more than a slave. Marcia was immediately overwhelmed by an element of sadness she felt for Aye but, confusingly, she knew it wasn't related to the story of Aye's young life, more so, she felt it was something still to come. Aye was clearly happy in her life now. With a broad grin on her face, she told Marcia how her luck had changed the day she met Graham and how the birth of their adored daughter had made her life complete. She went on to say that Graham had provided her family with the means to have a better life and she sent them an allowance each month.

Marcia felt Aye's demeanour change to one of sadness when she asked if she visited her family.

"Not too many times," she replied, her eyes downcast, but didn't elaborate.

Marcia wanted to delve deeper, but Aye excused herself saying that she must prepare lunch as Stephanie was out visiting her friends and she too would be returning very hungry. Marcia sat looking out to sea, the gentle breeze was a welcome relief, as the midday sun was stifling and she could see the haze across the water. Without warning, a chill ran up her spine and a horrendous feeling of sadness engulfed her. She knew, without doubt, it concerned Aye, her wonderful Thai hostess.

A short while later, Graham and Suzette pulled up at the front of the house. The smile on Suzette's face indicated that all was well. Graham called out to his wife to bring drinks and they both joined Marcia at the table. There was no mention of what went on. All they talked about were the island trips that Graham was going to take them on over the next few days. Although nothing could take away from how beautiful Thailand was, or how friendly the people were, the circumstances of their trip made Marcia feel very uneasy. She so wished she were here under different circumstances.

The following morning, the women joined Graham and his daughter at the boat that was to take them on the twelve-kilometer trip to Koh Larn coral island. They were going to spend their time snorkelling, swimming and looking up a friend of Graham's who owned a restaurant on the beach. The speedboat, on full throttle, whisked them to the island in just under an hour, although the ride was bumpy. Aye had given the women dried ginger to chew – these boat rides could make you feel sick, she'd advised. Suzette and Marcia clung on for dear life as the pounding waves hit the speeding boat. The ginger did its magic; there was no sickness or nausea, only a feeling of disorientation.

Eventually, they began moving through calmer waters and, as the island came into sight, Suzette told Marcia that it had been worth the roller coaster ride. It was a truly stunning place. Graham and the women were met by the local diving expert who gave them brief instruction, then swam alongside them pointing out the different species of exotic fish. Neither woman had snorkelled before, but as they went down amongst the sea-life and saw the amazing colours of the coral, they felt as if they had entered another world. Marcia likened it to an underwater Walking Street, so bright and busy was the marine life. Graham and Stephanie were expertly swimming a few feet away from them. Marcia marvelled at the vision of Stephanie, who she thought looked like a mermaid with her gorgeous copper hair fanning out behind her. It was with reluctance they got out of the water, but Graham had made them a lunch reservation at his friend's beach restaurant. As the day came to an end, tired and happy, they returned to Pattaya.

Marcia hadn't said a word to Suzette about the feelings of foreboding that she had regarding Graham. She was biding her time, wanting to wait until they were out of earshot of anyone else. She didn't think there was anyone she could confide in about her dreadful feelings concerning Aye though. Graham had been such a gracious host. He had taken them to many places, the river restaurant, temples and the night markets, not to mention the snorkelling, fabulous meals and the never-to-be-forgotten Buddhist temples. It had been a whirlwind week, so exhilarating. Considering how she had felt before she arrived in Thailand, Marcia couldn't believe her reluctance to leave the country that she now felt she had an affinity with. She had become especially fond of Aye and would miss their friendly chats, particularly about the Buddhist religion that Aye practised. She sincerely hoped that she would see her again one day and that she had been mistaken about the sadness Marcia had perceived was awaiting Aye.

It had only seemed like yesterday that they had arrived in Thailand as the car sped back to Bangkok airport. She was relieved that this unnerving trip was nearly over; however, she knew she'd left a part of her heart in Asia.

. . . .

Marcia hadn't had a chance to speak to Suzette on her own until they were seated in the business class and waiting for take-off on the flight taking them back from Thailand to the UK. She expressed her fears for Graham and the feeling of pressure to the back of her head that had awoken her so violently that she felt as if her head would explode. Marcia tried to explain the ominous feeling of foreboding that she sensed, along with a deep sadness she felt when she was in his company, despite his cheery demeanour. However, Marcia didn't share her worrying thoughts about Aye. Suzette dismissed Marcia's agitation and told her that it was likely due to an anxious state of mind because of the reason they were in Thailand. She informed her that Graham had taken her to inspect the "goods," which he had verified were first class, so all was well.

"Your only job, Marcia, is to inform Max whether you trusted Graham or not. Stop being paranoid."

"I am positive that Graham's life is in jeopardy. Please believe me," Marcia implored.

Suzette brushed her off by telling her that they had done their part and to focus on making plans to move to Spain. Marcia couldn't be dissuaded against what she had sensed and felt. She switched off to Suzette's ramblings and mentally prepared herself for the future upheaval she was to face.

UK

Greg hadn't been a man who would let anyone get in his way in the past, but since he had become financially secure, his life had turned a corner. He had put all criminal activities behind him, or so he thought. He hadn't bargained on falling in love, however, and his overriding need to protect Suzette meant he would stop at nothing to ensure their future happiness. Greg believed in behaving like a gentleman, but on the same note, he wouldn't be anybody's fool. When Suzette returned from Thailand, she rang him immediately and Greg informed her that he had put everything in place for her relocation to Spain and that no matter what she heard, she was to keep her cool with Max.

Max had impatiently phoned Suzette the minute she was back home after her flight touched down in the UK. She had barely put down her suitcase and kicked off her shoes when the phone rang. Marcia accepted the invitation to stay over at Suzette's, as the long journey had been taxing. Tiredly, she told him that all went well with the deal, whereby he insisted upon speaking to Marcia.

Marcia tried to explain to Max the conflicted feelings that she'd experienced around Graham. Marcia was usually very articulate in describing her perceptions, however, she was struggling with extreme jet lag and finding it difficult to communicate to Max exactly what she meant.

"He is one hundred per cent trustworthy," she reassured him, "But I just feel that something terrible is going to happen to him…"

Max didn't let her finish. "How on earth can it all be … *fucking fine,*" he shouted, his temper flaring, "when YOU are predicting doom and gloom? I seem to be getting mixed messages here. You are saying one thing and I'm hearing another," he raged.

Marcia held the phone away from her ear. The aggression in Max's voice was unnerving her. Thankfully, he ended the call.

Suzette comfortingly put her arm around her shoulders, as she could see Marcia was visibly shaken. Marcia took a deep breath and regaining her control she turned on Suzette. "I'm warning you for the last time about Max," she said, raising her tone more out of fear than anger. "If you think, Suzette, that you can play games with Max, forget it, as he will turn on us. I heard the menace in his tone," she stated wearily.

Suzette looked at her. "Marcia, please, I promise you that once we are in Spain, Greg will protect us both. He told me as much."

"I am sick of Max's demands," Suzette declared. "I don't care about his bloody deals. The sooner we can get away from him, Marcia, the better." Suzette took Marcia's hand. "We will get through this together. Please don't fret," she stated in earnest.

Marcia was sick to death of being emotionally blackmailed by Suzette and Max. She wished she were a million miles away from the pair of them. As much as she was fond of Suzette, she knew that she was only out for herself, always glossing over the real dangers. There was no denying she was a very generous friend, and Marcia had enjoyed the trappings of their friendship, but there was too high a price to pay. Suzette's demands and hare-brained schemes were wearing thin. Suzette cocked her head to one side, smiling warmly as she got out two glasses and poured the wine. "Let us sit and chill out, the past weeks have taken its toll on both of us."

Marcia sank into the overstuffed leather chair, sipped the wine and spoke forcibly. She was determined to get her point of view across and try to drum it into Suzette's head the absurdity of her idea that Max would relinquish his hold on both of them. "This is the stark reality of the situation Suzette. I know you are desperate to get away from Max and go to Greg. I can understand that. It isn't the fact that you two are not going to be together. You will be. But the price you and I are going to pay is what concerns me."

"If we stand strong, Marcia, we can make it," Suzette counter argued. "I know life is difficult, but things will change for the better. You know that more than most that nothing stays the same, and I cannot do this without you," Suzette implored. "I know, Marcia, under different circumstances our paths wouldn't have crossed, but I feel this is our destiny."

"Destiny…" Marcia replied sarcastically.

Suzette ignored Marcia's retort. "You have spoken in the past of your belief that our lives are mapped out and how you believed in destiny. Are you being hypocritical?" Suzette queried.

Marcia sighed, "Not at all," she answered flatly. After a lifetime of studying astrology and tarot, she knew very well how destiny could throw you into the deep end when you least expected it.

Suzette smiled. "Then we are meant to go on this life journey together, Marcia. I will look after you in return for you helping me. There are two weeks before this shipment arrives and then Max will be a happy bunny. We have plenty of time to finish tying up loose ends while I wait for the word from Greg to make our move, and in the meantime, I will search the internet for available long-term villa rentals in Greg's area."

Marcia nodded in resignation, as she felt she was just kicking against inevitability.

Fate was to play its hand the very day that Max's narcotic deal was due to be finalised.

The two women, at Suzette's insistence, had spent the last three days on a shopping spree in Brighton and Knightsbridge. Marcia had felt fed up with traipsing in and out of so many designer shops. Money was no object for Suzette but Marcia's enthusiasm began to wane after what seemed like trying on a thousand dresses. She was visibly wilting on the third day, unlike Suzette, who Marcia thought had been born to shop. Marcia took Suzette's announcement that they were going to eat out that night with a sense of relief. *At least I'll be able to sit down,* she thought.

Marcia hadn't been overly enthusiastic about making an effort to dress up, but Suzette was insistent, encouraging Marcia to wear one of her numerous designer dresses. "There is no need to unpack any of your new ones; this particular dress of mine will look stunning on you. You are going to make a huge impression on Karl who owns the restaurant. Max and I have known him for years and I know he is going to be thrilled to meet you," Suzette enthused.

Marcia stayed at Suzette's at her insistence – she said it was easier for her to be at her home, in case Max wanted to speak to her. Marcia knew that Suzette didn't like to be on her own, as the large house was in an isolated area. Marcia looked at her reflection in the full-length mirror in the bedroom. She had to admit she was amazed by the transformation. Although she had baulked at the idea, she now realised Suzette had been right to suggest her change of hairstyle. It was now cut shorter on one side and longer on the other, the dark red and soft gold glint of highlights, just as the stylist had recommended, suited her skin tone to perfection.

"Wow," Suzette exclaimed at Marcia's reflection. "That Alexander McQueen had never looked like that on me!" It fitted Marcia like a second skin. The olive green dress with the cutaway neckline and capped sleeves accentuated her toned figure, her shapely legs emerging from the knee-length hem. "You look stunning – so hot! That dress was made for you. I never did it justice. I want you to have it," Suzette said in admiration.

Marcia said she couldn't accept it. "You've bought me enough things already, Suzette."

"Get used to wearing haute couture, Marcia, because that is why I purchased your dresses and accessories from the top houses. You and I are going up in the world. We will be masters of our entwined destinies," Suzette laughed.

Marcia had an unaccustomed feeling of pride, even as they departed for the restaurant; she was still taking sly glances at herself in the mirror. She couldn't remember the last time she had felt so glamorous and feminine.

The women got out of the taxi outside the restaurant. Marcia felt more uplifted, although somewhat conspicuous, as she was so unused to dressing up, unlike Suzette who looked glamorous from the moment she woke up in the morning. Marcia was surprised by the attention they received when Karl the maître d' and owner of the restaurant, walked towards them as they entered. He kissed them on both cheeks and fawned over the pair them as they were shown to a table at the back of the restaurant. He signalled to the waiter and ordered a bottle of champagne, which he said was on the house and to order anything on the menu as his complimentary gift. "For my two beautiful friends," he said.

Suzette tried to insist that she wouldn't expect him to foot the bill. He waved the suggestion with a gesture of finality by raising his palm towards her. "Suzette if you can excuse me for a moment I have to instruct my staff in the kitchen, but I will return shortly to chat with you."

Marcia suddenly realised how hungry she was. Suzette ordered for them both and they chatted animatedly over their champagne while waiting for the first course. Marcia felt more relaxed than she had for a long time. The ambience, the alcohol, the good food to come and even Suzette's idle chatter was having a positive effect on her.

Karl returned to their table just as they had received their desserts. Sitting down to join them, he asked Suzette how Max was coping. At the mention of Max's name, Marcia paled. Even here, that man had to somehow be involved.

"Not too bad under the circumstances," mumbled Suzette through a spoonful of sorbet, "you know Max, he's made sure that things are easy for himself in there."

"I've just been informed of a shooting," Karl said casually, draining the last of the champagne bottle into Suzette's glass and pushing it towards her, "by one of the old faces that pop in from time to time."

Marcia suddenly had no appetite for dessert. It hadn't occurred to her that to know Max so well Karl must also be caught up in the criminal world.

"Yes," Karl said warming to his subject. "Apparently some sort of gangland hit."

"Oh my God," Suzette exclaimed. "Where?"

"That's the weird thing," Karl mused, "Thailand of all places."

Under the starched linen tablecloth, Marcia's legs turned to jelly. Suzette had gone deathly white and she was barely audible when she asked Karl, "Did he mention a name?"

"No name was mentioned but he did say that the murdered guy was an Australian who owned a fishing business in Jomtien."

Nausea rose from the pit of Marcia's stomach. Her head reeling, she glanced across at Suzette who appeared stunned. Karl, oblivious to the shock that registered with both women, was taken aback when Suzette announced they had to leave immediately. He had hoped the ladies would have stayed for more drinks and a catch-up.

They barely took time to thank him and say goodbye before hurrying out. Neither spoke on the taxi ride home.

Inside the house, Suzette slumped into a chair, turning to Marcia who had sat opposite her. "Surely, it cannot be Graham that's been shot?" Suzette asked.

Marcia couldn't trust herself to answer. She was still feeling nauseous and her hands shook. She just stared straight ahead as Suzette continued rambling, "Oh God if it is, Max will hear of it in no time, you'd better prepare yourself for a phone call Marcia, this is not looking good."

Marcia was dumbstruck. Every nerve in her body was as taut as piano wire. She walked deliberately, on wobbly legs, over to the sideboard and poured them both a large brandy. She didn't need the phone call from Max to tell her that it was Graham who had been murdered. She knew it with every fibre of her being.

Max rang Suzette the following day, screaming abuse at her down the phone. His informants had wasted no time getting the news to the prison that it was Graham who had been murdered, and Max was out for blood. He said Graham was shot in the head while sleeping. Suzette sat down heavily, the receiver in hand, trying to make sense of what Max had just told her.

After a few moments, she composed herself enough to ask if Aye and her daughter were unharmed. "They're fine. The bitch didn't even wake up! More to the point, my fucking shipment, which I have heavily invested in, is nowhere to be seen," he barked at Suzette. "I am warning you, if this goes haywire I'm putting you two in the frame." Suzette, visibly shaken, tried to calm him with reassurances that all would be fine.

"There is a grass somewhere down the line," Max fumed, "and when I find out who it is, they are fucking *history*." Max ended the call abruptly.

Suzette, beginning to grasp the extreme seriousness of the situation, turned to Marcia. "Max will be financially wiped out, he won't even be able to pay the extortionate rent on this place anymore if this deal goes wrong for him," she said.

Marcia was more than relieved that he hadn't asked to speak to her. She had been dreading a confrontation with Max over the phone. She hated his volatile nature and was secretly pleased that maybe Suzette was beginning to grasp the danger they were both in.

"I am scared, Marcia. Why didn't I listen to you? I could have phoned Graham to warn him if I'd only paid attention to your feelings," she groaned.

"It's too late now, Suzette," Marcia replied. "We need to have a serious think about how we are going to manage all this."

Suzette put her head in her hands. "I've been so selfish, Marcia. I'm sorry." Marcia moved over to her friend and put her arm around her shoulder, trying to comfort her. Much as

Suzette exasperated her, she hated to see her so upset. Despite her fear, Marcia found herself intrigued. It could scarcely be a coincidence the amount of "bad luck" Max had been experiencing lately. She couldn't put her finger on it just yet, nor did she want to dwell on it any longer. Her overriding thoughts were for Aye and Stephanie, tragic victims in this whole sorry mess.

....

Suzette had called Greg immediately after she had spoken to Max, nervously filling him in about Graham's murder, and Max's fury over his consignment of drugs, which appeared to be missing. She had no doubt whatsoever, that even from behind bars, Max would stop at nothing to put paid to the bastards who messed with him.

Greg could hear that Suzette was petrified. He told her not to worry and offered financial help, reminding her that it wouldn't be too long until she would be joining him in Spain. He wanted nothing more than to sweep her up in his arms and protect her from that mad son of a bitch, Max Greenaway. "Listen to me Suzette, I want you to lay low until I'm able to finalise my plans," Greg reassured her. Greg knew that Suzette took comfort from his words and knew she wasn't looking forward to keeping up the pretence with Max. He knew if Max had the slightest inkling of what she was up to, he would ensure she would be going nowhere … ever!

....

While Suzette had been on the phone most of the day, Marcia had taken the opportunity to meditate and get her thoughts in order. She was beginning to get some distinctly unnerving thoughts about someone close to home. Someone who she had practically disregarded, but the more she mulled it over, the more she realised that he could be the spy in the camp. It made total sense and over dinner that evening, she warned Suzette that she felt that Mikey was not to be trusted.

Marcia cast her mind back to the times Mikey had watched them in the rear view mirror and how Suzette had never thought it necessary to guard her speech around him. She had been lax in thinking of Mikey as no more than an odd job man and their occasional chauffeur. She had now concluded that Mikey could well be the main player and she wanted Suzette to take on board how treacherous to them he might be.

This time, Suzette seemed to pay heed to Marcia's warning. She announced that there was no way she was going to be so blasé about Marcia's feelings ever again.

After they had cleared the table, Suzette asked Marcia for a tarot reading. "I need some guidance, Marcia. No matter what you see in the cards, I don't want you to withhold anything from me."

Marcia turned the first card over. The Tower stared back at her. She felt a heaviness overcome her. Tapping the card without looking at her friend, she said, "There is going to be news of a death which coincides with a major change in your life. You are going to be knocked off your feet by this unexpected news."

Suzette looked stricken. "Marcia, we have only just received the news of Graham's death. Do you think you are getting confused?"

Marcia stared into Suzette's eyes. "I never get confused when reading the tarot," she stated flatly. "This news is imminent and there is deceit surrounding it. It will bring an ending, but as your life transforms you must be wary of a man who will cause you harm."

Suzette placed her hand upon Marcia's to prevent her from continuing. "Please, Marcia," she said, close to tears, "Don't tell me this is all going to go wrong. I couldn't bear to be without Greg."

Marcia was filled with a powerful energy as she removed Suzette's hand, laid each card out, and continued speaking. "These two cards both signify the ending of a situation which will have a great impact upon your life." She smiled as she placed her finger on the card of the lovers and the card of the Sun. *Thank goodness for that* Marcia thought to herself. Her serious demeanour changed to one of lightness as the significance of the cards she had turned filled her with relief. "Don't worry, you are going to be extremely happy and your love life will bring you great joy, but please don't rush into anything. You must have the patience for this situation to unfold."

Marcia didn't reveal that there was actually much more that she had seen in the cards. She knew Suzette was going to be with Greg, but the emotional connection between them was linked somehow to the news she was to receive.

Suzette didn't want to hear anymore anyway. She was satisfied that she and Greg were going to be together. Hugging her friend, Suzette said, "I know that you think this is all about me, but once our lives change for the better and we settle in Spain you will look back and be thankful we left our past behind."

Marcia smiled thinly. She was under no illusions about Suzette. She knew full well that no sooner she was riding the waves of happiness with Greg than Marcia would be put on the back burner again.

....

Max was struggling with his feelings. This was the first time in his life that he'd been in such a dilemma. He felt at rock bottom. He'd been certain that he'd covered all eventualities. This latest investment should have gone without a hitch. Instead, he was facing financial ruin and without his wealth, he was a nobody. Being a nobody was not an option, but without the payment from the consignment, Max could not employ the contacts needed to track down those responsible. A longer stretch in prison didn't bear thinking about. His musings turned to his wife. What a fool he'd been, imagining he could still control her while he was locked up. He had let her dalliance with Gary slide, believing that she had just been naïve, and the ponce had worked his charms on her and used her. Max had forgiven her indiscretion but not forgotten it. He knew Suzette loved all the trappings of the lifestyle he had given her, and she would never leave him, but with that bitch Marcia on the scene, she was far less gullible.

Max realised he had grossly underestimated Suzette. When Marcia had given Suzette the first tarot reading, and she came home and told him how she predicted a police raid, he had gone along with Suzie more to humour her than anything else and had all the incriminating evidence removed from their home. When the police had raided his house on the date that Marcia had predicted, he couldn't believe his luck. Very swiftly, he'd checked out Marcia's background. He found out that she struggled for money and the news that she had a son in a safe house was all he needed to persuade her to work for him. What woman wouldn't be tempted by his offer of ready cash or the threat of blackmail?

However, his heart sank into his boots now it dawned on him that Suzette was most definitely employing Marcia too. Max realised too late that he was doomed, having chosen to believe Suzette's story of misery and depression over reports that she was looking radiant and was regularly out with Marcia on shopping sprees. Sick as a pig, it dawned on him that Suzette had played him at his own game.

....

Marcia was awoken by Suzette shaking her urgently. She sat bolt upright as Suzette sank down on the edge of the bed, sobbing and shaking.

"What on earth is the matter?" Marcia said, concerned.

"Max is dead!" Suzette said, incredulously.

Sidling out of bed, Marcia took Suzette by the hand to the lounge. She sat her down on a chair and perched herself on the arm next to a staggered Suzette. "Tell me what you have been told about it, Suzie," she said.

"I just can't take it on board," a tearful Suzette said, "A prison official told me that Max hanged himself with a bed-sheet last night. I know, Marcia, that he had lost everything on that missing consignment, but he was hell-bent on finding out who was responsible for it. There must be more to it than that. Something must have sent him over the edge," she sobbed.

Marcia was as dumbstruck as her friend was. She told Suzette she would make them both a strong black coffee. She thought back to Suzette's tarot card reading and her prediction of death only last night, which gave her a surreal sensation of the news of Max's demise. Marcia knew that Max's death would have an enormous impact on their lives. She was now free of Max's hold over her. But she still had Suzette to contend with. She knew Suzette's upset wouldn't last long, and a friend or no friend, she'd been pulling the strings. Marcia was aware that Suzette didn't have a guilty conscience. She hadn't batted an eyelid when she had stolen a vast amount of money from her husband, so Marcia wasn't expecting any preferential treatment for herself.

Suzette thanked her for the coffee. "I know you may think that I'm a hypocrite as I planned to leave him for another man, Marcia, but Max was my first love," she said, sadly.

. . . .

Later that morning, Suzette had phoned Mikey to inform him of Max's suicide. Stunned beyond comprehension, he told her that he'd be straight over to see her. Grief-stricken by the death of his closest friend, he could barely drive through his tears. Mikey pulled up outside the gates, pressed the buzzer and Suzette let him in. Despite Suzette's upset on the phone, upon his arrival, he immediately noticed that in his opinion, she was hardly playing the grieving widow. She couldn't look him in the eye, nor did she seem sympathetic to his overwhelming feelings of grief. Mikey found his feelings of sadness overcome by those of anger. He was seeing Suzette in a whole new light as she prattled on, thanking him for being such a loyal friend to Max and telling him that she felt that she needed to get away, take a break abroad in the sun and try to come to terms with the impact of her loss. Mikey wasn't buying any of it. Max may be dead, but he wasn't. If Suzette thought she could pull the wool over his eyes, she was very much mistaken.

Mikey could now understand why Max had revealed to him his closely guarded secret, it was Max's surety that if he was no longer able to use it as leverage, Mikey could. After comforting Suzette and promising to help her in any way he could, he left, planning to keep an eye on the two of them and make a few more enquiries about Marcia and her son. His gut feeling was that the two women couldn't be trusted. He hadn't forgotten that Suzette had gone behind Max's back with that low-life, Gary Wiley and he was certain that if she'd done it once she was more than capable of doing it again. One thing Mikey wasn't going to do was sit back and let his pal Max be taken for a fool, even in death.

Mikey chewed over the fact that Max had left a note, which was found in his cell, explaining that he wanted no one to attend his funeral. When Suzette rang him a fortnight later and told him the service had taken place that day, Mikey sat in his car and sent up a silent prayer to his dear friend, vowing that he wouldn't rest until he got revenge on those who had betrayed him.

Word had recently got back to Mikey from a pal in Spain that Suzette and Marcia were going to attend Jimmy Grant's daughter's wedding shortly. What intrigued Mikey was that Max knew that Jimmy had turned his back on him, so why would Suzette and her friend attend a family celebration of the man who had suspiciously let down his cousin on an important deal. Mikey saw him as no more than a Judas and he was disgusted that Suzette would want anything to do with him. He concluded that Suzette was so shallow that she put pleasure, enjoyment and showing off before loyalty to her dead husband. She was only out for a good time and she was taking her psychic mate along with her for the ride.

Mikey had rung his pal Johnny, whose top security company he knew handled all the high profile events and asked him a favour to keep a watchful eye on Suzette and Marcia in Spain. He wanted reports to be sent back to him on everything the pair got up to.

. . . .

Marcia couldn't shake off the strong feelings of mistrust she felt about Mikey, he had turned up unexpectedly, saying he wanted to see how Suzette was coping. Although he smiled at her, she knew full well he had an ulterior motive. Marcia had a hunch he was checking up on them. "I know he is up to something," she warned Suzette after Mikey had left.

"Okay," Suzette said, to appease Marcia, "I will. But Mikey won't be around much now Max has gone, so your worries are needless."

"Don't you ever listen to me, Suzette? Don't brush it off. I'm telling you the man isn't what you think he is." But almost as soon as Marcia formed those words, she blurted out, "He is ill."

Gobsmacked, Suzette frowned. "Whatever do you mean, ill?"

"I can see it in his eyes, he has cancer ... I have seen it this way many times before," Marcia said, emphatically. "It comes out of nowhere, and I can't stop myself. If I feel it, I have to say it."

. . . .

Suzette turned her face away from Marcia, smiling. That sounded like good news to her. Perhaps it would stop Marcia from going on about Mikey. In an instant, she had refocused her mind on much more important things. Phoning Colin, she arranged to pay him and Madge a visit, telling him that she planned to arrive at midday the next day. She wanted to retrieve the money that she had stashed there, as soon as possible. She decided that she would inform Colin of Max's death only after she had the cash safely back in her possession. It wasn't that she didn't trust him, but where the money was concerned, she was going to heed Marcia's advice to use caution.

....

They spent a happy hour with Colin and Madge. Suzette discreetly handed Colin a wad of cash, careful that Madge didn't notice what she was doing. Tears had welled up in his eyes when she had told him about Max's death but whether it was because of the sad news or Suzette's generous gift, Marcia couldn't tell. Suzette told him to purchase a new car and that there was enough money for them to pay a visit to their son as well.

The women took their leave and returned home. Suzette looked elated, now that she was financially independent. She told Marcia how she could set up a new business on the Costa Blanca and be with Greg. She asked Marcia to go into business with her. "You can do all your psychic work and earn a fortune and I will pay someone to work for me in the beauty business. We will be made for life," Suzette told her excitedly.

"I would like to think it over," Marcia said. She knew it would be a golden opportunity for her, but, equally, Suzette would be exerting an awful lot of influence over her. She had been freed of Max's influence but despite that, she was aware that she was still very much at Suzette's beck and call and she wasn't sure if she wanted that.

"What is there to think about?" Suzette asked, "What life do you have here? Come on! Soon we'll be living it up in sunny Spain!" Marcia didn't feel she had any other option but to go along with Suzette's wishes. Suzette knew about her son Reuben, and Marcia was uneasy about this.

....

Greg had received a phone call from Jimmy about Max taking his own life. Although Greg gave his condolences, he was secretly ecstatic because his plans to be with Suzette were now without any obstacles. When Suzette contacted him to give him the same information, he couldn't contain his joy. They agreed that they would have to play it cool and keep their relationship under wraps for a while, then, once the way was clear, they could appear as a couple.

They didn't want people to think that they only just had got together so quickly after Max's death, as it would raise suspicions. Otherwise, Greg knew that even with Max dead there could be dire consequences. He and Suzette were both anxious to forge ahead with their new lives in Spain but he was under no illusions of the need to tread very carefully.

Greg suggested that Suzette should get involved in the beauty business, opening a parlour, employing anyone she liked and he would administrate behind the scenes.

"I miss you so much, Greg," Suzette breathed huskily down the phone.

"It won't be long," Greg replied. "I'm aching for you too, my darling. It's driving me wild thinking of you next to me," he groaned.

"Wait till you see what I've bought on my latest shopping trip," Suzette teased, "Bedroom wear only, of course."

. . . .

Suzette could hear Greg's breath quicken and he answered in gasps. "Stop it, Suzette, please, or I'll have to put the phone down on you," Greg moaned.

Suzette was feeling more than a little horny herself but cooled down the conversation by promising Greg that they would finalise their plans when they saw each other at the wedding, and Greg assured her he would have found suitable accommodation for her and Marcia by then. He had already looked at several villas and had one in mind that he thought would be suitable for the discreet visits he would be making to it.

With a warm glow, Suzette put the phone down. She had her man, her new life in the sun and, thanks to Max, money. Indeed, she was very much looking forward to spending Greg's money too.

....

Mikey had been coughing up blood, and unexplained bruises had started appearing on his body. He had always been fit and well, so he knew these signs warranted investigation. He had a few quid tucked away, so decided to book an appointment with a private doctor.

A week later, the doctor had the results from the tests he had conducted. The diagnosis came back revealing that Mikey had an aggressive form of leukaemia. He was told he had six months to live, at the most. In his heart, he had known something was seriously wrong. He wasn't afraid to die. He was looking forward to it, as he would finally be back with the love of his life, his old childhood sweetheart who had passed away years ago. He had many happy memories and no regrets ... there was just one last thing he must sort out in Max's memory. *I need to get my suspicions out of the way about Suzette, and if I am wrong, the woman can live in peace,* he reflected, *but woe betide her if she has betrayed Max. I will bring her down and anyone connected to her.*

....

Time flew by and it was only a few days until the women would arrive in Spain for the wedding of the year. Suzette and Marcia had shopped until they dropped. Suzette footed the bill and brushed off Marcia's embarrassment at the extortionate price tags on the dresses, shoes and bags. "Don't worry about money," Suzette told her, "We are heading for the big time now."

Sitting in a restaurant enjoying lunch after one of their shopping sprees, Marcia spoke of the uneasy feeling that she couldn't shake off. "I can't explain it, but I feel as if something around us is not right, it's all going too smoothly for my liking."

Suzette told her not to worry since they'd be in Spain before long. She had phoned Mikey, she said, to arrange their transfer to the airport.

Marcia's tension increased at the thought of Mikey She didn't know why Suzette hadn't booked a taxi instead of phoning him. He gave her the creeps. He exuded deviousness, and the sooner Suzette broke contact with him the better Marcia would feel.

The car was outside waiting for them. Mikey was all smiles as he put the women's cases in the boot of his car. Complementing them on how great they both looked, Marcia picked up on his energy and the cadence of his voice. There was something dark going on with him, she thought. Whatever he was up to she didn't like what she was sensing, but equally, she knew he hadn't long for this world. She hoped with all her heart that his death would outrun his deviousness.

Spain

The two women strolled out of Alicante airport into radiant sunshine that was matched by Joyce's beaming smile. Joyce's happiness was infectious and dispelled the heaviness that Marcia hadn't been able to shake off regarding her feelings surrounding Mikey. Joyce's effervescent energy was infectious, making Marcia smile as she hugged them both.

Joyce looked wonderful. Her blonde hair was piled into a topknot and she was wearing a red and white striped summer dress. Marcia thought that Joyce had more of a spring in her step since she last saw her. She put it down to her daughter Sara's forthcoming marriage and her excitement about becoming a grandmother.

Joyce gave her condolences to Suzette on Max's passing. In typical fashion, Suzette waved it away. "Thank you, Joyce, but let us try to think of the forthcoming happy event. Life is too short to let us become bogged down by tears and sad reflections."

Marcia noticed Joyce's momentary surprise by Suzette's seemingly blasé attitude to Max's death, but, equally as quickly, Joyce laughed it off too. Marcia was not surprised that the women weren't dwelling on Max's death. In her limited experience of both Jimmy and Max, both were controlling men.

The buzz of excited talk filled the car as the three women chatted excitedly about nothing but the upcoming wedding. Joyce told them that Sara had arrived a couple of days earlier and that Matt would be flying in that night. In those few minutes, Marcia felt a change in her mood. She couldn't deny that good company, sunshine and the chance to dress up was just the uplift she needed.

. . . .

As soon as the women pulled up at the villa, Jimmy appeared on the top step. Walking towards them, he offered to help with their cases. Marcia sensed his agitation as he took her luggage. She was not in the least surprised when he said he would like to speak to her in his office. Marcia smiled thinly at him. She didn't unpack; she instinctively took her tarot cards from her hand luggage and went to Jimmy's office. She knocked once and he told her to come in. He stood up and greeted her warmly, asking her to take a seat.

"I will get straight to the point, Marcia. I have worked hard to stay at the top of my game and I now realise I need your insight. I can't afford to let anyone get the better of me." His piercing blue eyes bored into hers. Marcia remained impassive, listening to Jimmy as he leant back into his chair with a smile on his face "Do we understand one another Marcia? His tone wasn't threatening, but she knew she couldn't refuse him. She hid her feelings of disdain for him. He made her flesh crawl.

"I want a reading now, if you don't mind, as there are one or two things I need to focus on."

Marcia had anticipated this and took her cards from her bag. Once he had shuffled the cards, Marcia took them without glancing in his direction. She turned each card over slowly and with deliberation, keeping Jimmy in suspense until the twenty-two completed the layout. She let her eyes scan each card, knowing her silence was causing him discomfort.

It was Marcia's turn to be in control, and when she felt that Jimmy had reached the end of his patience, she looked directly at him and held his gaze. An uncustomary tingle of power rose in Marcia and, with growing confidence, she spoke slowly and deliberately. "I feel you are in danger and there is a connection from your past that will rear its head."

Involuntarily, she immediately picked up her train of thought and continued, "There is a connection to Scotland in this warning. I know that because I can hear the bagpipes playing," she advised. Marcia noted Jimmy's look of alarm.

"Can you throw any more light on this Scottish situation?" he asked, leaning forward, his eyes flitting from the cards to her.

Marcia held him transfixed as she said, "I feel you were involved in a dispute with someone in your past and that you are going to somehow be reconnected once more."

Marcia could see that Jimmy was struggling to keep his composure when he asked, "Does this connect up in any way to my family?"

"Yes it does…" she replied, "I must repeat that I feel you are in danger, so please tread carefully because if you do not heed the warning you will end up the victim, not the victor."

"Is there anyone in particular who I should be worried about?" he asked.

Marcia held him in suspense as she perused the cards. "Men plot against you. They want your downfall and are out for revenge."

A pale Jimmy regained his composure and thanked her.

"Was there some other query that you wished to ask for guidance on?" Marcia asked flatly.

A troubled looking Jimmy rose from behind the desk and mustered up a weak smile. "You've told me all I need to know at the moment. Now go and join the women and catch up on all the small talk." He dismissed her with a hollow laugh.

. . . .

Jimmy locked his office door and sat down at the desk with his feet up, contemplating what he had just heard, trying to piece it all together. His anger was building. The Scottish link could only mean one thing. It had to be something to do with Sara and her fucking bloke Matt's bastard of a father. He brooded. Jimmy would have pulled out all the stops to prevent his adored daughter from marrying Matt but not at the risk of losing face with all the big guns from his world in attendance at the wedding celebration. Now with a grandchild coming, he couldn't see any way out, but he was thankful for small mercies. At least Matt's mother had legally changed her married name from MacDonald to her maiden name of Bennett. It gave him some small comfort that Sara and her child would not be linked to that scum by name.

. . . .

As Marcia joined the women out on the terrace, she noticed that Cindy was with them too, dressed in a multi-coloured sleeveless jumpsuit with a matching band tied in a large bow on top of her dark hair. She was an attractive woman and the more Marcia saw her the more she liked her. Cindy's outgoing, sunny disposition always brought gaiety to any gathering.

Joyce and Sara were sitting at the table listening to her giving her opinion about the seating for all the wedding guests, laughing in all the right places. Suzette had changed into a bikini and was lounging on a sunbed by the pool, looking as glamorous as ever in her swimwear with a wide brim hat and over large sunglasses.

Marcia felt at ease and intended to enjoy herself wholeheartedly. "I will leave all the hard work to you," she grinned at the women as she left to change into her swimsuit. She had purchased bikinis but decided to wear a black racerback swimsuit that she used at the fitness club in the UK. Showing too much flesh when Jimmy was around made her feel distinctly uncomfortable. It hadn't escaped her notice how lecherous he was and she didn't want to encourage him in any way.

Stepping into the cool water, she leisurely moved with measured strokes, and, as she reached the far end, she began to feel the gradual release of endorphins. She swam from one end to the other of the large pool, and with each lap, her mind became clearer. The pent-up pressure caused by Jimmy's reading started to dissipate. Swimming and yoga were her mainstays. It enabled her to clear any residual energy that clouded her thoughts. The feel of the water on her skin always worked like a tonic. Swimming enabled Marcia to retreat into her private world where no one else could enter. Marcia completed forty lengths of the pool, climbed the steps and reached for a towel. Wrapping it around herself, she gazed out across the bay and the vast expanse that lay beyond. Without conscious thought, Reuben came into her mind. She felt suddenly felt guilty at the good time she was having, not knowing what he was doing or where he was. Distractedly, she slipped her feet into her flip flops, turned and her eyes met Eamon's. He was sitting on a chair with his long legs stretched out, watching her intently over Jimmy's shoulder. She felt the colour rise in her cheeks and her body responded of its own accord, sending a thrill from neck to feet. Eamon continued to hold her gaze, transfixed.

Feeling as embarrassed as a schoolgirl, she cursed herself for being taken so unawares. Realising the effect he had on her, a hint of a smile crossed his handsome features, and then he looked away and turned his attention back to Jimmy. Disconcerted, Marcia wondered how long he had been watching her and worryingly found herself not displeased at the thought.

. . . .

Eamon had seen her enter the pool as he walked with Jimmy to a more private area on the large terrace away from the women. Marcia had been brought to Eamon's attention when Jimmy nudged him, making a lewd remark about how he would like to try his luck with her, and the fact she was single. Jimmy smirked, "I bet she's gagging for it."

Eamon had chosen to ignore him but was grateful when Jimmy took a chair with his back turned towards the pool, so he had an uninterrupted view of the shapely figure cutting through the water. He let Jimmy rattle on, catching a word here and there, nodding where he thought appropriate but he couldn't take his eyes from the sight of the woman who had constantly been invading his thoughts, but whom he'd been unsure he would ever meet again. Now here she was before his eyes and he could not pull himself away from the sight of her. He admired her shapely body at length as she emerged from the pool and felt rather than saw her distractedness as she looked out over the bay. He knew that out of decency he should have averted his eyes when she turned, but instead, he quickly took note that she had changed her hairstyle. Eamon thought the sleek new cut really suited her and added to her already classy look. He noticed that she was not wearing makeup. Her fresh-faced beauty was a refreshing change from the heavily made-up women in his circle. How artificial they now seemed. In moments, he had taken in her small, straight nose, her dark eyes, eerily like his own and her sensuously shaped mouth.

He'd caught her eye and knew he had unnerved her. She looked distinctly uncomfortable when she caught him staring but he knew his attraction to her was reciprocated when he spotted her cheeks redden and her body posture tighten. In order not to embarrass her further and to distract himself from what were becoming very inappropriate thoughts, he gave her what he hoped she'd interpret as a friendly welcoming smile, and turned his attentions back to Jimmy. Trying to focus, he caught only two words "traitor" and "camp" and thought that perhaps he should have paid a bit more attention to Jimmy and a bit less to Marcia.

....

Suzette informed Marcia that she would be meeting Greg and she had booked her in for a three-hour spa treatment. Marcia was not entirely happy about having to cover for Suzette's tryst but she felt she had no other option but to go along with, it. *At least,* Marcia mused, *I can look forward to some beauty treatment at Suzette's expense. She could have quite easily just dumped me in a grotty old café for three hours.* While contemplating this situation, a large shadow fell across the two women.

146

Both looked up to see who had obscured the sunlight they had been dreamily enjoying. Suzette smiled immediately as the imposing figure of Eamon stood over them. Marcia, on the other hand, had never felt more vulnerable or exposed as she lay looking up at the ridiculously handsome face of the towering Irishman. Her cheeks coloured instantly and she felt the same tremors throughout her body that she felt when he was near. He had just returned from a spot check with Jimmy at his haulage depot to ensure that Jimmy's drivers only carried his goods and no contraband. He wanted to say goodbye to Suzette and Marcia before leaving, hence his appearance at the poolside.

He smiled disarmingly at Marcia and, without a pause, he asked if they were enjoying the sun.

Angry about the effect this man AND his voice were having on her, Marcia answered just a touch sharply, "we were until you blocked it out."

Eamon chuckled a silvery throaty sound that made Marcia instantly forget her annoyance with him. Eamon took one huge stride sideways and both Marcia and Suzette put their hands up to shield their eyes as the Spanish sun hit them again.

"Enjoy it while youse can," came the soft brogue, "I don't expect the weather in the UK will be the same."

Marcia finally found her voice and replied, "It is beautiful here. So tranquil, unlike the wind and rain of England."

Suzette interrupted, "It won't be very long before those heavy clouds of the UK are all behind us and we will be living out here in the sunshine permanently." Marcia could see that this caught him off guard.

He pressed his lips together, nodding slowly in Marcia's direction then smiled warmly at her. "Youse be attending Sara's wedding then? It's going to be a grand affair."

"Yes, I am looking forward to it," Marcia smiled her reply. In her mind's eye, she was already planning what she might wear that Eamon would approve of.

"To be sure ladies, I am taking up too much of your time and Jimmy's waiting on me. I'll say goodbye for now."

As he turned and left, Marcia did to him what he had done to her that morning and admired his body from the rear view, taking in the broad shoulders, long legs and the way his hair glinted blue-black in the sunlight.

Suzette waited until he entered the house through the terrace doors and was out of earshot. She turned to face Marcia, grinning. "My God! That man may have recently been bereaved but he can't take his eyes off of you, and please don't try to tell me you don't fancy him, because I could have cut the sexual tension between you with a knife. I felt like I had a ringside seat but the players had forgotten their audience."

Marcia tried to brush off her remarks but knew she was fooling no one, least of all herself. "Suzette, Joyce spoke of his devotion to his dead wife and I think his penetrating look is part of his personality."

"Ha," Suzette laughed. "Do you think you can fool me? You are an expert at receiving messages from others and yet you are telling me that you are not reading Eamon loud and clear?" She cocked her head to one side, smiling.

Marcia was aware that Eamon was creeping under her skin and the last thing she wanted was the complication of a relationship, especially one with a man whose wife had only recently died. It puzzled her though that since she was last in Spain, Eamon's grief seemed much diminished. She mustn't be taken in by his charms, she thought to herself. What sort of man can forget his wife that quickly and then openly flirt with another woman? It was one she must steer clear of, she concluded.

Suzette had dropped Marcia off at the spa to enable her to sneak off to spend time with Greg. Marcia, relaxing with the full facial and body treatments began to enjoy the luxury of being pampered. She knew Suzette had prepaid for the three-hour session, which must have cost a small fortune, as the wellness centre was upmarket. But knowing Suzette as she did, her friend wouldn't have flinched at the cost. Having completed the treatments, the young beautician asked her to relax for a while in the lounge. Marcia sat by the floor to wall windows that looked out onto manicured lawns enclosed by palm trees. The serenity of the setting helped her to reflect on her decision to give up her old life in the UK and move to Spain permanently. Suzette had painted a picture of the good times to come for them both out here, which she could now foresee. Word had spread like wildfire about Marcia's tarot card reading abilities and the clients were lining up in readiness for the opening of Suzette's salon. She would have no financial worries. She had learnt how to deal with Suzette, but still, Marcia couldn't shake off the feeling of disquietude that engulfed her.

She had never encountered the type of men whose circle she now moved in. Each one of them was intimidating in their own way, even Eamon. Despite his sexual allure and his easy-going way with her, she did not doubt that he had a core of steel. She thought of him now and how he made her feel when he had caught her unawares after her swim. She reflected on the intensity of his dark, smouldering eyes and what lay behind them. Yet later that day, when Suzette had informed Eamon that they were moving to Spain, Eamon's unspoken words, as his eyes held hers, told Marcia he was a safe port for her in a storm. The powerful attraction she felt for Eamon was frightening but intensely exciting at the same time, and she found the mixed feelings bewildering.

Suddenly aware of how long she had been at the spa, Marcia checked the time. She knew Suzette and Greg were snatching every spare moment to be together, but Marcia hoped that her friend would err on the side of caution because if anyone suspected that they were an item, Suzette and Greg would find everything blowing up in their faces.

Marcia hoped that with all the women wrapped up in Sara's wedding plans, no one would notice that Suzette was most definitely not a grieving widow. Marcia felt sure the other women would be distracted by more pressing matters, but the same couldn't be said for the men, who Marcia knew would be much harder to deceive. She smiled with relief as a text came through. Not only was Suzette right on time for a change and was coming to collect her but she also gave her some good news about a villa viewing.

. . . .

Joyce and Cindy had all the wedding arrangements now in place. They had left themselves three hours in which to get ready and opened themselves a celebratory bottle of wine. The huge marquee was up and overflowing with gigantic blooms, the caterers were ready for the reception and local hotels had been booked for the number of people that had come from far and wide. Cindy had ensured that the seating was arranged so that the guests would not only have the bride and groom in their sights but also the vista of the sparkling bay. Baby pink and white roses, to match Sara's bouquet, hung in abundance from the arbour under which she and Matt would take their vows.

Joyce sipped at her wine and allowed herself a few moments of self-pity. The wedding would be a bittersweet affair. What should have been the happiest day of her life, to see her only child married to the man she loved, had been ruined by Jimmy wielding his control over her as usual. He had devastated her when he had announced they would have no association with Sara and the baby once Matt established himself in America. Joyce would have to put on a brave face for Sara's sake, though she was dying of heartbreak inside. Even though Jimmy loathed the thought of his daughter tying the knot with Matt, Joyce knew he would carry off his role as the father of the bride with aplomb. The wedding would be an impressive affair and allow him to show off how it should be done. It was the sort of one-upmanship that his associates had come to expect from someone of his standing.

. . . .

Suzette and Marcia had offered to share a bedroom since Cindy was staying and the other room was taken over with wedding presents. The two women stood side by side looking in the large floor-to-ceiling mirror. Marcia hardly recognised herself in the Valentino black dress and the emerald green wide-brimmed hat.

Suzette stood back admiring her. "Look at how the smooth crepe moulds around your curves and the sweetheart neckline reveals just enough cleavage. You look so chic." Suzette had insisted Marcia tried on the dress when they were shopping in Oxford Street. Marcia had emerged from the changing room and Suzette had told her she looked amazing. When Suzette told the assistant they would take the dress, Marcia tried to resist, pulling Suzette to one side, stating that it was far too expensive.

"Marcia, please don't fuss. Just think of it as an investment," Suzette had told her at the time. Suzette hadn't baulked at the cost of the £3,950 dress. "You look so elegant. The reception will be crawling with eligible men and you are going to be a great catch for one of them."

Suzette was wearing a cherry red silk dress with a matching pillbox hat. She looked every part of the high society woman she always projected, positively oozing glamour. She put her arm through Marcia's, smiling. "Here's to us, Marcia. This wedding is the start of things to come. It's the high life for us from now on. Clients are queuing up who will pay top dollar for your predictions. We are both going to be very wealthy women."

Suzette's optimism did not instil Marcia with enthusiasm. She still couldn't shake off the unsettling feelings she had about Suzette and Greg's relationship. It wasn't Greg that was her concern. There was something linked to Suzette that she yet couldn't put her finger on. She needed to make a serious attempt to put all this to the back of her mind, as she fully intended to enjoy the day without letting any negativity take root.

The jolt she needed came in the form of Cindy, who popped her head around the door. She looked striking in a soft blue dress with a wide-brimmed hat. Her dark eyes sparkling and her full mouth split into a grin.

"Wow," Cindy said, beaming, "You two look a million dollars, but you better get a move on. There are only fifteen minutes before the wedding begins and we need to take our seats." Cindy's eagerness gave Marcia the boost she needed. Laughing, the three of them linked arms and proceeded outside.

After sitting down, Marcia began scanning the throng. She didn't know the majority of the guests, but there were two familiar faces she was thrilled to spot. She couldn't believe her eyes when she looked over to see Aye and her daughter Stephanie from Thailand. Marcia did a double take. Curiously, Eamon was sitting on Aye's left, speaking to her. Marcia's breathe caught in her throat. She thought he was the singularly most handsome man there. She couldn't help her sidelong glances at him, all the while trying to concentrate on the bride and groom's vows. She was baffled by his connection to Aye. Their smiles and animated conversation indicated that they knew each other well. Aye's invite could only mean one thing – that she was far more involved in the criminal world than just having been married to Graham. She noted that Aye did not seem unfamiliar with Mr O'Donally either. Her heart sank as she watched Eamon put his arm around Aye's shoulder and kiss the top of her head, while in the same instant looking directly at Marcia. God, the man had a nerve, Marcia thought.

She whipped her eyes to the front, determined not to let him get to her, but as the cheers erupted, signalling that Sara and Matt were now man and wife, she took the opportunity to glance Eamon's way again. She watched as Aye and Eamon rose, his arm around her shoulder, protectively. Stephanie seemed as happy as her mother in Eamon's presence. Marcia interpreted this scene in the few seconds it took for her heart to plummet. She felt so angry that she'd allowed herself to think she was more to the captivating Irishman with the beguiling smile than a mere flirtation.

Dispiritedly, Marcia forced a smile at Suzette and Cindy and resolved to forget the sight of Eamon and Aye together, as surely that's where his romantic interest lay. Marcia was about to do justice to all her friends' hard work and planning as the three of them headed towards the huge sweet-scented marquee.

Suzette, forever the organiser, took Marcia by the arm. They entered the cavernous interior of the marquee and were blown away by the myriad of fragrant blooms. Marcia had never seen so many beautiful flowers all in one place, and she found the scent quite intoxicating.

"Take your jaw off the floor, Marcia," Suzette laughed, "We are going to circulate. There are many influential men and women here who will be able to open doors for you and me. I have already spoken to one woman who Joyce introduced me to whose husband is a powerful man from Andalusia. His wife appeared interested when I informed her about my plan to open up a beauty salon, with you as the resident psychic." Suzette gave a conspiratorial smile. "Come, my friend, we are going to drum up the clientele." The marquee was starting to fill up with guests in designer suits and dresses getting ready for the toast.

Marcia advised Suzette to go easy on the champagne, "You mustn't drop your guard, Suzie. You have to keep your wits about you when you are in Greg's presence. All eyes will be on you," Marcia warned.

Suzette patted her arm reassuringly and gave her the withering look that Marcia knew only too well meant Suzette was only appeasing her. Suzette had spotted Aye and Stephanie looking lost amongst the crowd and, without hesitation, grabbed Marcia's arm and headed towards them. Slightly ashamed, Marcia felt a pang of guilt at the envious thoughts she had rising to the surface. She had no right to question Eamon's interest in Aye. He was a single man and could do as he pleased. Her previous thoughts disintegrated as Aye's friendly face lit up upon seeing the women. Marcia and Suzette offered their commiserations over the tragedy with Graham.

Stephanie spoke first. "My father will be reincarnated," she stated emphatically. Marcia was relieved to hear that their Buddhist belief was of great comfort to them, as she had often wondered how mother and daughter were coping.

"We are so happy to be here," Aye said. "Eamon is very kind to us. He was a good friend to Graham and he phoned me to tell us both to come to stay at his home. Eamon helps us now we no longer have Graham. He has lost someone too. We love Eamon." she added, "He is a very good man."

Marcia had no time to dwell on this revelation as cheers rang out and drinks were raised to toast the entrance of the bride and groom. Glasses drained, Stephanie made their excuses, "Please forgive us. I must eat as I am famished." She took her mother's arm and made their way to the tables that ran from one end of the marquee to the other, laden with food. Chefs and waiting staff stood by in readiness to serve the hungry masses.

Marcia watched them retreat and endeavoured to push back down the feeling of envy towards Aye that had begun to rise again. Marcia realised she had foolishly thought that her strong attraction to Eamon was recip-rocated. It didn't help matters that Sara and Matt were so clearly in love and embarking on a new life together. She felt almost tearful watching the radiant Sara and beaming Matt taking the stage for their first dance. Suddenly, a tap on her shoulder broke her thoughts. She whirled round to find Joyce and two glamorous women standing behind her.

"I have been looking all over for you, Marcia," Joyce said, smiling. "I want to introduce you to Vicky and Natalie from Moraira who, along with their friends, are anxious to make an appointment with you for tarot readings." It came

155

as a welcome distraction for Marcia, but before she could answer, Suzette piped up.

"Marcia will be conducting her tarot business from my new beauty salon, which will have the latest luxury spa and beauty treatments along with the top hair technicians – all under one roof," she announced with a flourish. Marcia had to hand it to Suzette – her sales pitch was second to none. "We already have a waiting list," she told the two women, but, as you're friends of Joyce I can give you a concession if you would like to combine an appointment." Suzette beamed a triumphant smile as they walked away verifying they would ring to be put on the waiting list as soon as possible. "Killing two birds with one stone, Marcia" Suzette smirked. "Didn't I tell you I would sort everything out? Let us waste no more time. We need to mingle and celebrate."

In one swift movement, she took two glasses of champagne from one of the waiters. Suzette sipped at her beverage as her eyes ran over the heads of the crowd. "Greg's here," she breathed, excitedly, draining her glass in one she began pushing through the throng, making her way to where he had just entered the marquee. Marcia dutifully followed at her heels.

The champagne had been flowing for hours and Suzette was more than a little tipsy. She was spending more time in Greg's company than it warranted, and Marcia was beginning to worry that their body language would give away that they were more than just acquaintances. Marcia grew tired of warning her to be careful. Women were constantly vying for her attention. Word had circulated regarding her psychic ability and Marcia was feeling distinctly claustrophobic. She made her way to the entrance to get some fresh air, unaware of the man who had been biding his time to get her on her own.

. . . .

A pair of unseen eyes had been trained on Suzette and Marcia from the moment they took their seats at the ceremony right through to the reception. Johnny Smart's security company had supplied the bodyguards for the wedding. He prided himself on his twenty-year reputation of protecting his high-profile clients. His code of confidentiality was pressed home to all in his employ. It went against the grain to pass on information regarding guests of his clients; however, these were special circumstances. Jimmy Grant was paying him well, but Johnny had no compunction about what he had embarked on. He knew there would be no comeback, as the favour he was returning was for a man who Johnny knew was one hundred per cent kosher and whatever Johnny revealed, his name wouldn't be brought into it. His old dad's boxing pal Mikey from Peckham had asked a favour of him. It was one Johnny felt obliged to return, as Mikey had seen to it that Johnny's mum didn't go without when Johnny's dad did seven years in Wandsworth prison.

Johnny had both women under close observation all day. He watched Max Greenaway's widow make a beeline for Greg Davidson as soon as he entered the marquee, the other woman following closely on her heels. From his vantage point behind the expansive foliage, Johnny took note that Greg didn't take his eyes off the widow, who was approaching him. The other woman, the psychic redhead, was secondary to Greg's attention. In fact, after a brief hello, the redhead became invisible to the couple. Johnny was more than a little interested by the way Greg placed his hand on Suzette's arm as he kissed her on the cheek. He smiled to himself as he saw Greg's forefinger brush back and forth over her skin as he spoke to her. Their body language and eye contact alerted Johnny to the knowledge that this couple had been intimate. He ascertained, as Suzette linked her arm through Greg's, and Greg, thinking himself unobserved, placed his hand on a well-rounded buttock, that these two were much more than mere friends. Watching the pair disappear giggling into the crowd he scanned over the heads of the milling guests searching for Marcia. When he first noticed her at the wedding, she stood out in the elegant black dress and emerald green hat. She was different from the other women in so much as she wore no diamonds or expensive jewellery, nor lashings of makeup, just a soft hint of pink lipstick and a natural tan. Nothing about her was artificial, he thought. She was classy and a head turner but she appeared to him to be a duck out of water.

Johnny had been given the rundown on both women. Mikey told him briefly of how Marcia had a gift for seeing into the future, and how she had worked for Max while at the same time being in Suzette's employ. Johnny was intrigued by this information. The psychic must have brains as well as beauty, he mused, as he caught sight of Marcia's red hair. She appeared to be surrounded by women and looking distinctly uncomfortable with the situation. From where he stood, he watched her disentangle herself from the group and head towards the entrance. From a discreet distance, he was intrigued to notice a man following closely behind her. Without ado, Johnny made his way outside and lit a cigarette, his back to Marcia but within earshot. Johnny recognised the voice instantly. Jimmy Grant had grabbed his opportunity as soon as it presented itself. Marcia stood on her own outside the marquee. Elbowing his way through the crowd, Jimmy caught up with her on the lawn. Johnny lit a fresh cigarette from the butt of his finished one and listened in.

. . . .

Marcia turned round as her name was called and was unnerved to see Jimmy Grant approaching her. She felt a distinct sense of unease as he announced, "I wanted to speak to you, Marcia. A little bird has told me that you are moving out here to Spain?"

Marcia was uncomfortable as Jimmy invaded her space and stood inches from her. Her flesh crawled as she realised his intentions. His proposition to her was heavily loaded with sexual innuendo. "I would like to set you up with a nice apartment, for when you felt like some male company," he breathed over her, leaning so close Marcia could smell the alcohol on his breath. You are a very desirable woman, Marcia, and I would see that you are well taken care of."

Jimmy had emphasised the "well taken care of" and Marcia almost gagged. Her cheeks flushed from the anger she felt at his arrogant manner and the fact he thought he could buy any woman that took his interest. She was speechless. She wanted to turn him down flat but was wary of his wrath. He smiled, smugly placing his hand on her shoulder. She recoiled under it but did not move away as he whispered to her, "I will expect your answer in a week."

He walked off leaving her aghast. Her head reeled as she walked towards the terrace. She couldn't believe the man's audacity. She found Jimmy Grant abhorrent. He was everything in a man she despised. She barely glanced at the man stubbing out his cigarette end and taking a glass of champagne from one of the waiters as she moved to the quiet end of the terrace, sitting down at a table by the pool.

She sipped her champagne and turned her gaze upwards at the starlit sky. In a few months, her life had changed beyond recognition, but some things would never change she reflected sadly. The men she had encountered since her involvement with Suzette all seemed to be cut from the same cloth. It disillusioned her that these men appeared not to find just one woman satisfactory. From Jimmy Grant's outrageous proposal to Eamon's interest in her AND Aye, she had concluded that she was far better off on her own. No man would have her at his mercy. She felt a glow of satisfaction as she formulated these thoughts, thinking smugly what a great lifestyle the new business was going to bring her. In her mind's eye, she was already planning the décor and fitments she'd have in her villa. How sweet life was going to be as an independent woman, Marcia pondered. Unusually, for she rarely drank, Marcia finished off her third glass of champagne. Her hand froze halfway between lips and table. Even over the heady scent from the marquee – she smelt him. Four or five seconds before he spoke she inhaled his male scent and the heat of his masculinity. She became aware of the delicate under-notes of his aftershave mingled with the clean freshness of a newly laundered shirt. He had come up behind her with a silent tread, his powerful presence only centimetres away. Her body responded accordingly – her nipples hardening and, unbidden, a warm receptiveness spreading from her stomach to her thighs. Traitor! Marcia thought of her own body even as she ached for him, wanting him so badly she almost moaned. Her pupils already dilated from the darkened evening thankfully couldn't give her away, but she was certain he would hear her heart pounding he was standing so close.

From directly behind her she heard, "A penny for them, Marcia." Startled out of her thoughts by Eamon's Irish brogue, she turned her head to be greeted by his handsome features and seductive smile. He stood with his legs slightly apart, a bottle of champagne in one hand and two glasses, the stems between his fingers, in the other. He took a seat opposite her and held her gaze. His eyes were as black as night. Hers, equal in darkness, gazed straight back. "Have I offended ye in some way?" he asked.

Marcia felt her throat constrict. Her hands interlocked around her glass, she couldn't trust herself to let go, such was the effect he had on her. Regaining as much composure as possible, she answered him frostily, "Why would you offend me?" He leaned forward across the table studying her intently. Much as he mesmerised her, she felt empowered to give a good account of herself. She had noticed him throughout the day but had chosen to stay as far away from him as possible. It hadn't escaped her notice that if he wasn't with Aye he wasn't lacking other female admirers. His lips pressed together. He gave a measured nod, pouring out two glasses of champagne as he did so. Taking her hand away from the empty glass, he put the full one in it instead, leaving his hand encircling hers.

"Because, Marcia, you have been deliberately ignoring me all day haven't you?" With a strength of will that she didn't think she possessed in his presence, she slid her hand and glass out from under his.

"Well you weren't exactly short of the company, Mr O'Donally," Marcia retorted. "For someone who just lost his wife you have wasted no time in replacing her."

Eamon rocked back in his seat, his expression grim. "What the hell do you mean by that?" he replied menacingly.

Too late Marcia realised she had touched on a raw nerve. She drained the full glass and letting Dutch courage speak, she answered, "I know it's not my concern, but I couldn't help noticing how close you have been with Aye all day. I didn't realise you knew her well enough to ask her to move in with you?"

"Ye don't know what ye are talking about woman," Eamon replied, angrily.

Marcia had gone past the point of no return, fuelled by her fourth glass of alcohol, and standing up to leave, she gave him her parting shot. "But I do have eyes, Eamon … you're all as bad as one another."

Eamon's look changed to one of barely contained anger. He rose to his full height, towering over Marcia as she turned to walk away "Aye is my former sister-in-law," he fairly spat at her. "If ye feel ye need to throw accusations at anyone I'd advise ye to get your facts straight … and there was I thinking ye were a cut above the rest. I got it wrong," he ended, before striding away from her across the terrace.

Marcia was devastated. She couldn't believe her stupidity. She desperately wanted to apologise but wondered if she would ever get the chance. Dear God, to go in blindly with an accusation of which she had no proof and to see the hurt in his eyes as he stood over her, had stirred emotions in her that had laid dormant for so long. Eamon O'Donally had aroused such intense feelings of anger, jealousy and pure passion in her that she hardly knew what to do with herself. *Damn the man,* she thought.

. . . .

Johnny watched Marcia and Eamon O'Donally on the terrace from the marquee entrance. Their body language was intriguing. This Marcia was evidently in popular demand, but unlike Jimmy's overtures towards her, which she had rebuffed, He could see Eamon O'Donally had the opposite effect. The two were attracted to each other. Eamon was being full-on flirtatious and she was trying to keep herself under control. From where Johnny stood, he could see Marcia gripping her glass tightly and he wondered what Eamon had done to upset her. Within moments, voices were raised and the two parted company. *Interesting,* Johnny thought, withdrawing a cigarette from its packet, *if I didn't know any better I'd say that was a lovers tiff.*

. . . .

Marcia composed herself after returning to her room to freshen up. She was mortified that she had insulted Eamon with her accusations about Aye. Feeling dispirited that she had let her emotions get the better of her; she returned to the marquee and looked over the heads of the packed area for Suzette. There was no sign of her or Greg. Marcia heard an American accent and was aware of someone close behind her.

"May I introduce myself, I'm Brandon, a friend of Jimmy's," the American said, moving alongside her. "I was speaking to the men outside and I noticed as you walked across the lawn that you appeared somewhat distracted. Are you here on your own?" As Brandon introduced himself to Marcia, he lent forward and kissed her on the cheek. Marcia flashed a look of annoyance at him. Apologising, he stood back and smiled at her. "Forgive me for being so forward, but you are an attractive woman whom I'd like to get to know." Marcia, still in turmoil from her encounter with Eamon was in no mood to entertain another member of the male species, but she felt his warm congenial energy and decided it would not harm to speak with him. Despite the bad feelings and hurtful words when she and Eamon had parted, Marcia was aching for male attention.

"My name is Marcia," she returned his smile.

"The music is loud," Brandon said, raising his voice over the noise, "and it's so hot in here, perhaps it would be better if we spoke outside on the terrace where the air will be cooler."

Marcia hesitated. This Brandon didn't seem lecherous like Jimmy and she needed a friendly face right now.

"Why not," Marcia said, as he stood back for her to lead the way, and with his hand on the small of her back, Brandon guided her out of the marquee. Marcia guessed that all of Jimmy's associates were from the criminal world and she wasn't foolish enough to think that Brandon was an exception, but she didn't feel intimidated by him.

Marcia studied Brandon as he spoke in a slow, Texan drawl. She found the way he prolonged his vowels very engaging and easy on the ear. She judged him to be in his early fifties. His salt and pepper hair and tall, muscular frame gave him a certain attraction. His twinkling hazel eyes spoke of a genuine kindliness – a man, Marcia sensed, who would take care of a woman. But she didn't feel the magnetic allure with him that she felt with Eamon O'Donally, although she felt she should make a determined effort to concentrate on Brandon while he was speaking to her and diligently tried to look interested. Brandon told her about his life and the fifty-nine-acre horse ranch he owned in Jeff Davis County in Texas. Marcia smiled and thought she could picture him in a pair of Levi jeans, cowboy boots and a Stetson hat, sitting easily in the saddle.

"Do you ride?" he asked.

Marcia shook her head. "It's something that one day I would like to learn and perhaps there will come a time when I will get round to it."

"Problem solved, Marcia," he laughed showing even, white teeth against his weathered tan. "You are most welcome to visit my ranch and I will teach you. There is nothing quite like riding out on the range on the back of a Morgan horse. I do own American Quarter horses but I think they'd be a bit too high-spirited for an inexperienced rider."

"You make it sound so tempting. Perhaps one day I will take you up on your proposal, Brandon."

Despite herself, Marcia was finding Brandon to be entertaining company.

"The sight of the beautiful West Texas sunset is something to behold, Marcia, and one, I might add, you shouldn't miss."

Marcia fleetingly thought how easy it would be to take him up on his offer, but she knew she couldn't feel physically attracted to him, whereas just visualising Eamon made her feel physically weak. Her heartbeat had already started to rise just thinking about him. Redoubling her efforts, she focused once more on Brandon, encouraging him with a friendly smile to continue. Brandon went on to tell her that his two grown-up sons helped him run the ranch and that he had a daughter whom he hadn't seen since she'd left home at the age of eighteen. Marcia sensed a deep sadness as he spoke of his daughter. He continued, "My wife died after a riding accident."

Marcia told him snippets about her life, though nothing about her son. He asked her if she had a career, with a soft smile.

Marcia kept it short. "I advise clients who require direction in their life with business or relationships."

He raised his brow, smiling. "I am impressed. I admire an independent woman." He held her eyes. "You haven't said if there is a man in your life, as I'd find it hard to believe that you are not attached," he said.

Marcia laughed softly. "My life is too busy and at the moment I am planning to move to Spain with my friend and start afresh with a business venture." Marcia wasn't intending to go into anything more about herself.

Brandon took the lead as he asked her if she would like to dance. Marcia smiled, rising, as he took her by the arm. "Let us enjoy the rest of the evening, as my stay in Spain is unfortunately too short."

But Marcia found she enjoyed his company and his easy manner. She felt she had found a friend in Brandon, and hoped that they would stay in contact, although she didn't want to lead him on to make him think there would be anything more. She had found that conversation flowed easily between them and hoped Brandon wouldn't take advantage of her relaxed attitude towards him. They moved onto the dance floor and Marcia confidently moved to the rhythm of the music. Brandon was a natural and enthusiastic dance partner and, Marcia, for the first time that day felt light-hearted as she thoroughly enjoyed herself. When a line dance started, Brandon tried to show her the moves with his expertise. Giggling, Marcia attempted to follow the moves, foot-stomping and twirling in time to the beat.

Eventually, he excused himself and told her he needed the restroom. "Wait right here. Don't move and I will be back," he insisted.

Marcia felt she had known Brandon for more than just a few hours. He was growing on her and she was having great fun with him. The music changed to a slower beat. Adele's words of lost love resounded across the marquee as couples took to the dance floor. There were so many people that she couldn't see the familiar black bobbed hairstyle of Suzette. Marcia sincerely hoped she hadn't snuck off with Greg, as it wouldn't take much for someone to notice their absence. She felt the heat travel through her as a hand touched her shoulder. Marcia didn't need to turn to realise who it was, his mere presence and mesmerising dark eyes held her transfixed

"If ye are free would ye like this dance?" Eamon didn't wait for her to answer. Firmly, his large hand took her arm and, guiding her back to the dance floor, he pulled her close. The length of their bodies joined and, encircled by his strong arms, Marcia melted into him. She could feel him hardening and her own body responding to it. Eamon's dark chocolate eyes drew her in, reaching into her soul. Unashamedly and oblivious of anyone else, they drew each other closer still. The music had been replaced by their pounding hearts and Marcia was aware of her pulse beating in her ears. She felt an overwhelming desire to fall into him and let him carry her away and do as he wished with her. Her hands, on arms that, up until now, encircled his neck, found themselves travelling up the nape of his neck and into his thick hair. This first real touch of him coupled with his male musk and his bear-like embrace electrified Marcia.

Eamon's voice was husky with desire. He knew their sexual attraction was overpowering but strove to keep himself under control as he spoke. "I see ye are entertaining the Texan," he held her slightly away from him and his dark eyes challenged, "and there was I thinking that the emerald green hat ye wore at the wedding was a nod to me," he said, with a touch of sarcasm.

Breathlessly, Marcia stepped back into his embrace and tilted her head back. Eamon brought his down and his mouth moved slowly over hers. His kiss was warm, soft and lingering, and Marcia wanted it to go on forever. She surrendered herself to him, intoxicated and drunk on desire.

As the music finished, Eamon broke away from her, thanked her for the dance, turned on his heels and strode off without looking back. Marcia was left excruciatingly embarrassed. She felt disoriented and flummoxed by the way he had dropped her like a hot coal. Feeling all eyes on her, and still flushed, lips tingling, she made her way back towards where Brandon had left her. She felt outraged with herself. How could she have allowed him to pick her up like a puppet on a string, leaving her like a love-struck teenager? She was thankful that Brandon hadn't returned yet. She wouldn't have been able to explain her behaviour to him. Marcia, in truth, couldn't begin to explain it to herself.

. . . .

Jimmy's curiosity got the better of him when he saw Eamon enter the marquee. He followed, observing from the sidelines, as his right-hand man made a beeline for Marcia. He was quietly seething that Eamon had made a play for her, but Jimmy knew that with a bit of manipulation he could have the psychic for himself, just like Eamon's former wife Eve, and many others. Jimmy smugly recalled the times he had enjoyed Eve's body. She had been an easy lay, eager to jump into bed with him. He loved the thrill of the chase and took pride in knowing how to please a woman between the sheets. He intently watched Eamon and Marcia together on the dance floor. The dynamic attraction between them was there for all to see, but his interest was piqued even further when Eamon extracted Marcia and left her floundering alone on the dance floor. Now would be as good a time as any to make his move, he mused. Whatever was going on between the two of them it was obviously not all plain sailing. Eamon O'Donally may be a good-looking guy and, under normal circumstances, Jimmy wasn't egotistical enough to think that he'd be able to compete in the looks department, but there was more to getting a woman into bed than good looks, and he had the power and prestige, not to mention the money to achieve his aims. As the main man, Jimmy never dealt in refusal. He knew there was more than one way to "skin a cat" and it would be easy to remove his rival to ensure that he'd have a clear path. Jimmy wasn't at all worried about the

Texan Brandon Daniels either. He'd watched him with Marcia and was astute enough to know that he wasn't her type. Besides which, he was flying home soon. After Marcia and Eamon's shenanigans on the dance floor, any fool could see where that was going to eventually lead, Jimmy thought. *I need to intercept sooner rather than later* he said to himself. A caustic smile played on his lips. He wasn't going to let anyone get in his way.

. . . .

Johnny Smart had seen for himself that the Irishman Eamon O'Donally had had his fair share of female attention throughout the day and he thought that the man's powerful position as Jimmy Grant's right-hand man, coupled with his swarthy good looks warranted it. But Johnny soon came to realise that Eamon O'Donally was only interested in one woman – the attractive redheaded psychic. In Johnny's observation, she was more than just of fleeting interest to the Irishman. He sensed something was going on with the pair of them, their upsetting exchange earlier on the terrace denoted a depth of feeling more akin to lovers. The eye-opener came when he saw the couple dancing, wrapped in one another's arms, then, to Johnny's amazement, they kissed long and hard. It was doubtful you'd get a sheet of paper between them, Johnny concluded, and despite Eamon abruptly dumping Marcia when the music stopped, he wasn't fooled. These two will be an item before long. He would lay money on it. Johnny had so much information to report to Mikey about the two women. He sensed Suzette and Greg Davidson had sneaked off to a rendezvous in some discreet place, but he knew it would be only a matter of time before the pair resurfaced. Johnny paused, cigarette in hand, just as he had thought, he detected Greg Davidson appearing from the side of the villa. Johnny watched as he strolled across the lawn making his way towards Jimmy Grant and the men gathered around him. If his assumption was correct, it wouldn't be too long before Max's widow appeared. Smiling to himself, he spotted her a few minutes later coming through the terrace doors. The age-old trick, Johnny chuckled to himself. He'd seen it all before.

....

Joyce and Cindy had kept the wedding running smoothly and were enjoying a glass of wine on Joyce's private balcony, sipping the second glass that they'd allowed themselves. They'd needed a clear head to keep on top of the guests and arrangements. Speaking aloud, but to no one in particular, Joyce said, wistfully, "Well a new day dawns and tomorrow my baby girl will be off on her honeymoon and when the baby is born she will begin a new life in the US."

Cindy picked up the sadness in her friend's voice and put her arm around her shoulders. She knew that Joyce had put up with so much from Jimmy, carrying on with whoever took his fancy over the years. She was aware that Joyce's lifestyle was on a par with the best of them, but for all of that, Cindy thought Joyce was only Jimmy's dogsbody and that he didn't care for her. All she was to him was someone in the background to fall back on when he tired of his latest conquest. Cindy had even experienced his wandering hands herself, though she'd never mentioned it to Joyce. She wouldn't upset Joyce for the world. On one occasion when Joyce had confided in her after discovering makeup on Jimmy's shirt, Cindy told Joyce that she wouldn't want a man like Jimmy even if he draped her in diamonds. Joyce sighed as she looked out at the vast grounds, "Once Sara is gone I won't be able to visit her and the baby," she said sadly.

Aghast, Cindy spun around to face her and told her not to be silly. "Of course you can. There will be nothing stopping you. It's not like you can't afford it!" Cindy declared.

Joyce looked serious, shaking her head. "You have no idea what he is capable of, Cindy." Joyce turned to her, looking into her trusted friend's face. "Jimmy has told me as much. He loves his daughter but he said that Sara has made her bed and she can lie in it. You know, Cindy, that Jimmy's word is the law and I won't be able to go against him." Joyce couldn't control the heartache she was feeling as she revealed the story of Jimmy and Matt's father and the hatred that Jimmy felt for anyone connected to him. He told me there will be no contact once she leaves for the States, as he feels betrayed beyond words, even though I begged him … saying Sara is innocent in all of this, but he's having none of it."

Cindy's anger burst forth. "He is an absolute bastard! Why can't the man fuck off with one of his fancy women and at least you would be able to enjoy your life with Sara and the baby." Joyce let the tears flow as Cindy reached out to comfort her. "Please listen to me, Joyce. You don't know what is around the corner. Destiny is a funny thing. We'll ask Marcia for a tarot reading when everyone is out of the way and then you will know what's on the horizon."

Cindy, smiling reassuringly got some tissues and wiped Joyce's tears. Sounding more confident than she was feeling after Joyce's revelations about Jimmy's plans to keep her away from Sara and the baby, Cindy hurried Joyce along. "Now go and freshen up and we will go down and join the others." Cindy knew what Joyce would be up against if she disobeyed Jimmy Grant's orders to visit her daughter behind his back, but she realised that if they had Marcia on their side, Joyce would be able to foresee any eventualities before they arose. He had wiped the floor with Joyce emotionally, Cindy thought. He'd flaunted all the dalliances he'd had over the years and Joyce had put up with it, all for Sara's sake. But his latest demands would be the straw that broke the camel's back. If there was any way Cindy could help her dear friend she was going to, and if they had Marcia guiding them then it would give the women the upper hand. It was the only solution she could come up with. She was aware of the risk she was taking by trying to help Joyce because if Jimmy discovered they went against him, all hell would let loose and he would put a stop to her and Joyce's close friendship. But this aside, she was willing to take that chance if it enabled Joyce to break free of him.

. . . .

Marcia's mind had been churning ever since her encounter earlier with Eamon on the dance floor. When Brandon had returned to her in the marquee, he apologised for being so long but explained that an old acquaintance had waylaid him, wanting to catch up. Marcia, unable to think straight, made her exit by telling Brandon that she must seek out her friend and thanked him for the pleasurable time she'd had with him.

Brandon, appearing bemused, thanked her back. Marcia could see he looked crestfallen as she walked purpose-lessly away from him.

Marcia was determined to avoid Eamon O'Donally like the plague. Humiliation swept over her when she thought of the way he had treated her on the dance floor. *Who does he think he is?* she thought, angrily. Eamon O'Donally may think he is in a powerful enough position that entitles him to use any woman when he feels like it, but I won't be one of his playthings. Marcia was becoming tired of feeling used, first by Max, then Suzette and now by Eamon O'Donally leading her on and then dropping her. Although Marcia had grown fond of Suzette, and she couldn't dispute the fact that she had been extremely generous, it didn't alter the fact that Marcia had been forced into a world of crime by Max and Suzette's emotional blackmail. With fierce determination, she left the marquee seeking some fresh air and a moment to herself. Almost immediately, Marcia saw Suzette walking across the terrace, the radiant flush on her face told her that she had spent the last few hours in Greg's company, no doubt at his villa. Suzette walked hurriedly towards Marcia. Taking her to one side, she lost no time in relaying to her about how they'd left the wedding reception and spent a couple of hours in bed. Marcia felt it was fruitless to keep warning Suzette about bringing her affair with Greg to anyone's notice. She knew that Suzette's brazen attitude wouldn't have been missed by anyone, especially the men.

"What have you been up to tonight? Has there been any nice man that's taken your interest?" Suzette said, looking around in the hope that Marcia had found herself a male friend. Before Marcia could reply, she saw Brandon heading towards them. "WHO is this?" Suzette asked, out of the side of her mouth, then beaming at him as he approached. Marcia introduced Brandon to an enraptured Suzette.

"Brandon, this is my friend, Suzette. I'm moving to Spain to begin a new venture with her."

Brandon, projecting a radiant smile answered, "Very pleased to meet you, Suzette. I don't mean to interrupt y'all, but before I lose sight of you, Marcia, I was wondering if you would like to have lunch with me tomorrow, as I leave for

Texas the following day, he quickly added. "Y'all are welcome too," he said, looking directly at Suzette.

"Thank-you, Brandon. I would like that," Marcia replied without hesitation. Suzette, surprised at Marcia's quick response, declined the invitation, saying she had other arrangements. Brandon asked Marcia if one o'clock was fine and she nodded in agreement. As he sauntered back across the lawn, Suzette faced Marcia, cocking her head and grinning.

"You are acquainted with that Texan hunk? OH, his drawl!" she swooned, laughing. "You are a dark horse, Marcia, so that is what you've been up to, and very nice too," she added.

Marcia told her about his ranch in Jeff Davis County in Texas.

"A horse ranch"? Suzette queried.

"Yes, he has many horses and Brandon said he would teach me to ride."

Suzette laughed. "I imagine it's not only horse riding that he would teach you. An experienced horseman such as him must be amazing in the saddle." She turned, watching as Brandon joined the men.

"He is a nice guy, Suzette, and very entertaining. But don't bother trying any match-making, Suzette," Marcia said, "I am going out for lunch with him tomorrow and then he will be will be gone from my life."

"Watch this space," Suzette laughed. Changing the subject in typical Suzette style, she informed Marcia that she was going to look over some business premises tomorrow and if it was anything like the way it looked on the plans, then within a short while they would be ready to "rock and roll" with their business. Greg was going to get his workers in on the job to complete it in double-quick time.

Marcia wasn't really listening to Suzette. Her mind was working overtime. She knew she had to find a way to remove herself from Spain and perhaps Brandon could be part of that plan. He was clearly smitten with her and she enjoyed his warm, friendly personality. It wasn't a heaven-sent match, but it would mean Marcia would have peace and security – something that was sadly lacking in her life now.

Much as she tried to fool herself that she could cut Eamon O'Donally out of her life, she was fully aware that if he frequented the same place as she did, it was like a spark to a tinderbox. He was creeping into her heart. His kiss had brought feelings to the surface that she knew would be all too easy to succumb to. He was far too dangerous a temptation. She felt she shouldn't stick around.

Brandon had picked her up at one o'clock the next day. As she walked towards him, Marcia could see by his expression that he liked what he saw. She had chosen a sky blue, thin-strapped dress that enhanced her golden suntan, coupled with a darker shade of blue stilettos and clutch bag.

"Wow," was all Brandon said, beaming from ear to ear, as she approached. He opened the car door for Marcia and she slid into the seat without revealing too much thigh. She knew that the dress, which was above the knee, had risen enough for him to avert his eyes as she clicked the seatbelt in.

Brandon was cheerful, chatty and animated – it was what made him such pleasant company. He had the knack for being able to distract her, and she was genuinely looking forward to having lunch with him. He certainly wasn't boring, Marcia thought, as she settled back to enjoy the drive and listen to Brandon's running commentary about where he was taking her. He said he'd booked a restaurant that he'd used on previous visits to Spain but didn't elaborate, which made Marcia wonder what had previously brought him to Spain.

The maître d' welcomed them, recognising Brandon, which increased Marcia's curiosity. The waiter showed them to the private booth that Brandon had requested. Then Brandon ordered the best house wine and leaned back into his seat, appraising Marcia.

Marcia had never been so forward with a man before, but she knew that time was of the essence seeing as Brandon was leaving Spain the following day. She leaned towards him to speak, watching as his eyes fleetingly swept across her cleavage. "I want to know more about you and your life Brandon," Marcia probed, gazing into his eyes. It's such a pity that we only have a short while together and then we will have to part company."

Brandon told her again that he would like it if she could spend time with him at his ranch very soon. "I will make all the flight arrangements and you can visit for as long as you wish. You never know, you might like it so much that you'd want to stay," he proposed eagerly.

Slowly drinking her wine, she listened to him telling her of his everyday working life on the ranch, which seemed to her like nothing but hard work, but she'd never been scared of that. Even if she couldn't make a go of it with him, Brandon was her ticket out of Spain, and, drastic as it seemed, Marcia knew she had to get away as soon as possible.

Placing her hand over his and leaving it there for a few seconds longer than necessary, Marcia excused herself to use the ladies' room. Brandon could see that he took in her shapely form as she deliberately moved slowly away from him. Marcia knew her toned body in the dress, which left nothing to the imagination, would have the desired effect. This, in combination with the five-inch stilettos nearly drove him to distraction.

Upon Marcia's return, he asked her questions about her life, which she was more than happy to answer. She needed Brandon to feel she was being open with him, though she would never normally be so forthcoming. She leant forward and held his eyes as their animated conversation went back and forth. She made it clear with her gentle laughter and occasional hair flicking that the attraction was mutual. He listened, transfixed, as she described her life as a mystic, lightly touching on varying circumstances she had had to deal with, but omitting her involvement with Max Greenaway. All of which only added to Brandon's fascination with her.

. . . .

Eamon watched the couple intently from the far corner of the restaurant. He had only just placed his order when Marcia walked into the eatery ahead of the Texan. She sat with her back to him, but he could see that she was leaning towards the man, who was doing most of the talking. He knew a great deal about the wealthy rancher's life and the fact that his original riches came from his talent as a gifted artist, but, nowadays, Brandon Daniels was in great demand as a forger. Brandon was raised in Texas, but he had lived in New York as a young man, returning to his family home when he inherited his father's ranch, ploughing his ill-gotten gains into breeding horses.

Jimmy valued Brandon Daniels' expertise and, although his services didn't come cheap, Jimmy didn't baulk at the man's fees, as his penmanship was second to none. Eamon watched as Marcia rose from her seat. He ran his eyes hungrily over her, remembering the feel of her body next to his, and a fire lit in the pit of his stomach. She stood up and headed towards the ladies' room. His groin ached as he watched her firm buttocks sashay rhythmically with each step in the high heels. He was filled with intense fury, his hands unconsciously clenched into fists. He was sickened that Marcia, who aroused such desire in him, was dining with the Texan and had dressed so provocatively for it. Suddenly he had no appetite. He was ablaze with a mixture of passion and anger and he hardly knew what to do with it.

Upon her return, Eamon concluded that she was blatantly flirting with Daniels. He felt like he was about to explode. Remembering the last time he'd felt this angry was when he'd discovered his wife had been playing him. This woman was in his head, driving him to distraction. He needed to leave the restaurant before he did something he would later regret. Torn between throttling the Texan and sweeping Marcia up in his arms, he stood up to leave. Hell-bent on removing all trace of her from his mind, he knew of a sure way to exorcise his demons. The waiter arrived, just at that moment, placing his meal on the table. Without hesitation, Eamon took out 50 euros and told him to keep the change. "Business beckons," was all he said, leaving a stupefied waiter shaking his head, then smiling when he looked down at the large tip he had in his hand.

. . . .

Johnny Smart's security company was synonymous with not only its protection but also its discretion where its clients were concerned. For the first time, Johnny Smart broke his own rule and would pass on information regarding two guests of his high profile client, and it didn't sit easily with him. Johnny rang the number and within two rings, Mikey picked up his phone. Johnny had a great deal of respect for Mikey and he knew that for him to call in a favour, that there was no other way.

Johnny laid it on the line. "I know you don't need reminding, Mikey, but this is a one-off, regarding the information you wanted on the two women. It repays the debt my old mum owed you for seeing us okay while my old man was in prison."

Mikey said he appreciated the job that he'd asked him to do. Johnny recalled what he had observed. "Max Greenaway's widow Suzette, and Marcia the psychic, appear to be popular with the men out here, but both women appear to have their particular favourites". He went on to tell him how Suzette Greenaway went on the missing list for a few hours with Greg Davidson, the big building contractor who is close to Jimmy Grant.

"What about the other one, anything on her?" Mikey asked.

"The pair of them are as thick as thieves and whatever Max's widow is up to, the psychic is in cahoots with her," Johnny laughed. "The redheaded psychic seemed to have a few of the men vying for her attention," Johnny went on to tell him. "Jimmy Grant has the hots for her and a Yank with a Texan drawl was on her tail all night. But the one that grabbed my attention was the Irishman Eamon O'Donally, Jimmy Grant's right-hand man, who, I was informed by one of my men, has recently been faced with the tragedy of his young wife's death in a car accident. Though by what I saw of him, he didn't appear overly heartbroken."

Johnny went on to tell him about the scene on the terrace with the Irishman and Marcia, and how it had looked to him. He then enlightened Mikey as to what occurred between the couple as they later came together on the dance floor. "It had been pretty entertaining to watch them during a slow dance. They couldn't have got any closer if they'd tried, and then they snogged the faces off each other, if you catch my drift," Johnny said, remembering how he thought that the couple should have got a room somewhere. "But then, without so much as a bye your leave, the Irishman dumps her and walks off. From where I was standing, she definitely hadn't expected that." Johnny continued. "To be fair, I was embarrassed for the girl."

Johnny finished by saying, "Mind you, as soon as she left the dance floor, the big Texan's on her, but it's the Irishman I'd put my money on."

Mikey thanked him and clicked off. He sat on the arm of his old armchair in his small flat trying to take in all the info Johnny had given him. Mikey wasn't overly interested in the psychic's private life. It was more her collusion with Suzette that was concerning him. He'd been somewhat surprised by that revelation. What a dark horse that Marcia had turned out to be. He wouldn't have put her down as a woman that put herself about, but as the old saying goes, Mikey thought, *You can't judge a book by its cover*. He wasn't in the least bit surprised by Suzette's behaviour. She was clearly up to her old capers with some bloke out in Spain, just as she had been with Gary Wiley. He'd hoped for her sake that she would have played it straight. If there was one thing Mikey knew about Suzette it was that she loved the high life. Max had always spoilt her, she'd always worn top drawer clothing and driven the latest model of Mercedes. He'd like to lay money on it that Suzette had a plan and one that would take her to the top rung. He made a vow to his dead friend Max. *She may have disrespected you, mate, but if it's the last thing I do, I will bring her down to reality.*

....

Eamon had watched Marcia come into the restaurant with the Texan. The sight of her in the blue dress and high heels in the company of another man had affected him to the point where he'd felt nauseous. He'd observed her playing up to the man, and from his vantage point, he could see that Brandon Daniels was enamoured with her. Eamon couldn't unwind. His gut felt like it was tied up in knots. He was agitated and angry with himself for allowing her to invade his every waking thought. To watch her game playing made his blood boil. He was plagued by his wanting of her and here she was pretending to offer herself to the Texan on a plate. *What the hell was she playing at, and why? What the fuck is going on with me, why should I be bothered about who she sees?* he asked himself. She had practically thrown herself at the guy in the restaurant. Anybody could see what she was up to. Disgusted with the whole situation he removed himself. He returned to his villa in a foul mood with only one aim – to rid this woman from his mind once and for all. The battle of voices competing in his brain continued, even as he was taking a cool shower, deciding what to wear that night and arguing with himself against the stupidity of his decision. But there was only one sure-fire way to render himself sufficiently brain dead to wipe Marcia from his mind. He hit the bars that night. In the first one, he downed a large brandy that quickly took effect, and he began to calm down, succumbing to the voice in his head that told him that he knew he was only fooling himself. *Bejesus, I'm fucking besotted with the woman, it seems like she's put some sort of spell on me,* he thought, leaving the bar and walking to the next one. The Irish bar was an old haunt of his before one of his previous futile attempts to give up drinking. Michael, his old pal who owned the place for years, called out to Eamon as he came through the door, "Ye'r a sight for sore eyes my friend, I'd never thought ye would have fallen off the wagon after all this time, what's up wit ye?" he continued concerned. "Is it the loss of yer wife that's caused this?"

Eamon sniggered, "Ye can be sure it's nothing to do with HER!" Before he could say another word, Michael raised his hand and informed him, shaking his head, "There'll be no drink fer ye here. I won't see a good man go down the drain, in the same way ye were heading in the past. Now I don't know what's eating at ye, but whatever it is, to be sure, I'll find the remedy." He smiled, "Let me make ye some good Irish coffee and we'll sit in my private quarters and have a man-to-man chat."

Eamon smiled thinly and followed him to the back room, as Michael told the bartender to take over. Michael had known this man from way back when they were youngsters growing up in Dublin. Michael asked him if he wanted to tell him his problems, knowing full well that he was barking up the wrong tree. Eamon had always been a closed book. He hated to see his good friend out of sorts and reckoned he knew the solution, guaranteed to put a smile on any man's face. "I'll tell ye what I will do for ye. I know a young lady who will give ye some distraction away from whatever's bothering ye. She's not your run-of-the-mill kind of girl that does that sort of thing. She's a bit classy like."

Eamon pursed his lips and then nodded. Michael grinned and made the call, telling her this was someone special that needed to be treated right. "Just a word before he arrives…" Michael told the woman, "I have to inform ye that discretion is of the utmost importance with this man, but he's a gent and he'll look after ye." He hung up then phoned a taxi. "Okay my friend, go and blow your socks off. I can promise ye that this girl has a few specialities up her sleeve."

182

Michael saw Eamon to the outside of the bar and opened the taxi door for him. Both men slapped one another on the back and went their separate ways.

. . . .

Anna, upon receiving the phone call from Michael cancelled her plans for that night. She was going to have a girly night in as her young daughter Chloe was staying over with her close friend, Dee. Michael owned the Irish bar on the beach road where Anna decided one night to have a glass of wine. She had sat in the booth at the back of the bar, nursing her drink, trying to sort out in her mind how she could survive, as her child's father had left them penniless. Anna had been at her wits end as to how she could find the money to pay the rent, feed her daughter, not to mention Chloe's private school fees. Michael had been collecting glasses and made his way to her table. He noticed the young woman appeared to have the world upon her shoulders and being one to lend an ear Michael had bought her a drink and sat down to listen. Anna had bared her soul to him about her dire situation. Her long-term boyfriend had left her for someone much younger. At the time, Anna had thought Michael wasn't overly attractive to look at, but his wit, added to his charm, made her warm to him. Over the course of the next few weeks, with Michael insisting that her drinks were all on the house, they became remarkably close. On one of these evenings, Michael told her that he was happily married and didn't want anything to change but that his wife wasn't interested in sex. It wasn't long before they came to a mutual agreement. It worked well. He looked after Anna, made her laugh and, whenever they were together, Anna saw to it that they had a good time. They didn't love each other but enjoyed their time together. She was happy to take up Michael's suggestion that she get a couple of regulars, giving her and her child a bit of financial security and allowing her to keep up Chloe's school fees.

Tonight Anna was getting ready to entertain Michael's friend, a man who needed his identity kept secret. She was intrigued, to say the least, hoping that it wasn't some short, fat, balding guy. Still, it was a favour for Michael and he told her the man would look after her. She knew Michael meant she would be paid well. Anna put her lustrous dark brown hair up, slid out of her dress and ran the shower. She was twenty-six and she knew that her body was good. She was 5' 8" and a shapely size twelve. Taking care of herself was something that had been a priority since her teens. She hadn't been the best looker on the block, but her body and ability to make the most of what she had made her a head-turner. Anna now used her looks to keep her head above water since her ex Leon had left her and her child high and dry. As she stepped from the shower, drying herself, she put on a black thong, toying with the idea of wearing a bra, but after slipping on a black dress with thin shoulder straps, she decided to go without. Anna admired herself in the mirror as she applied a hint of pink lipstick to her naturally plump lips. She was pleased with the effect. The buzzer sounded, filling her with a sense of unease as to what she could expect once she opened the door. Moving across the room, she flicked the intercom switch, "Hello," she said.

"Is that Anna?" the voice answered.

She detected an accent. She hoped Michael's friend was eager. That way it would be over in minutes and she'd be able to get rid of him and enjoy her previously planned night. Anna braced herself. Smiling, she opened the door and became rooted to the spot at the sight of the tall, dark-haired man standing before her. He was incredibly handsome with an air of authority about him. His dark chocolate colour eyes gave no indication as to what he was thinking. Anna stood to one side as he stepped into the room. She caught the subtle fragrance of his aftershave. His bespoke attire pointed to a man who knew how to dress well. Anna wondered who he was, as he didn't look the type to frequent Michael's bar.

She offered him a drink, hoping it would break the silence. "I only have whisky," Anna said, as she was in the habit of keeping a bottle of single malt, which Michael would have enjoyed after she had pleasured him.

"I'm grand, thank ye," he replied, walking towards the window without looking at her. Although Anna only had a couple of regulars apart from Michael, she had quickly learnt to take the initiative and get the job done as soon as possible. However, Anna thought she wouldn't mind prolonging it with this handsome stranger. Rarely had she seen a man with such a striking presence and, as she walked towards him, she was already planning what she intended to do to him. When he didn't turn, she moved to stand beside him. But as she went to place her hand on his thigh, he caught it in mid-air. Then turning to face her he stepped back and released her hand. Anna realised she was out of her depth with him. This was a man who couldn't be manipulated. He turned and ran his eyes over the small flat, catching sight of a child's shoe peeking out from under the sofa, and asked her in a measured tone, "Why do ye take risks, doing this sort of thing?"

She was silent, not knowing what to say.

"I'm not chastising ye," he added.

Anna was taken aback. She felt like a child being caught with her hand in the cookie jar. When she didn't reply, he moved to the small table and, taking a chair, he turned it around and straddled it, facing her. "To be sure, you're an attractive young

185

woman, so don't be thinking I'm spurning ye, but I can't do this and I shouldn't be here."

His directive was straight from the hip. "Take a seat," he said, proffering his hand to the chair opposite him. Anna obediently sat down. "Do ye want to tell me about your life, Anna, as it strikes me that some misfortune has brought ye to this?"

Anna had been prepared to give this handsome man a good time, but, instead, she felt tears well up. She tried to keep them in check as she looked away from his intense glare. She told him how she had run away from an abusive mother who was always drunk, and had met an older guy and ended up pregnant. She said he'd promised to take care of her and the baby, so she followed him to Spain.

"The details are quite boring," she said, with a pained smile. "He left me but I do have my beautiful daughter, Chloe, and I do what it takes to ensure she doesn't go without."

Eamon studied her. Rising to his full height, he sucked air through his teeth as he gave a measured nod.

"Understandable," he said walking to the window. A solution to a family problem had just presented itself to Eamon. He wondered if this Anna would be interested in turning her life around with a proposition he was about to present her with. He knew from Michael that she was trustworthy and reliable and if she accepted his offer, it would kill two birds with one stone.

"I may be able to help ye and your child, but it would mean that youse would have to leave Spain."

Anna gave a soft laugh. "Leave Spain! I have no money to go anywhere I …"

Eamon interjected, "I will see to all yer finances such as flights but before ye answer, think it over, as I must warn ye if ye take this job on, there can be no half measures." He told her about his brother Patrick's daughter, who was severely disabled, and they required help with her and their small boy. He explained that life in County Armagh in Northern Ireland on the smallholding was worlds apart from the Costa Blanca. "To be sure, youse will have security, a wage and a roof over ye head."

Anna let the tears that had been threatening to spill over, spring forth, as she accepted his offer.

"Dry ye tears," he said, moving towards her, placing his hand on her shoulder. "Write down yer phone number, bank account details and name. I will transfer enough money to tide ye over and to pay for taxis, flights and to buy ye some warm clothing, as County Armagh isn't the Costa Blanca," he smiled.

As he walked out of the door, he turned to face her. Anna threw her arms around his neck and hugged him. "I can't thank you enough, I won't let you down."

Eamon nodded. "I will phone ye tomorrow and give ye the details. So get things moving as ye will be out of here by the end of the week."

Stepping into the cool night air, Eamon decided to walk towards the beach road. He was in no hurry to return to his empty villa. He understood the girl's plight. He had been down that road himself, with a younger sibling to look out for, and as soon as he had been in a strong enough financial position, he'd purchased the smallholding in County Armagh to keep his brother Patrick from continuing to tread the wrong path. His brother, true to his word and, much to Eamon's relief, had turned his life around, which was something he was proud of. He felt his effort and money had been well spent. That was ten years ago and Eamon felt he could rest easy as Patrick settled down to country life. His gut feeling told him that Anna and her child would be all right with Patrick and his wife Rosie. He knew the pair needed a hand on the smallholding as they struggled with Catherine, their ten-year-old daughter whose mental age was of a three year old due to severe autism. They also had a two-year-old boy, Conner, and a menagerie that Patrick had accumulated along the way, as he loved animals. His earlier anger at himself over Marcia had now dissipated. The chill air from the Mediterranean Sea helped clear his mind as he leisurely strolled along the promenade. Eamon realised his error of thinking that he could have released the tension tonight through sex, but when Anna opened the door to him, he knew he'd had to make a judgement call. He hadn't ever paid for sexual favours, but when Michael had suggested Anna, he'd thought it would have resolved his frustration. It wasn't the fact he wouldn't have enjoyed an hour or so in her bed, she had everything in the right places, but he knew sex with another woman wouldn't give him what he yearned for. He reminisced over his dance with Marcia – the heady feeling of losing control, as a compelling force brought them together. He had never experienced anything like it before, feeling the touch of her body and their kiss. It was as if two lost souls had found one another and, as they joined, went tumbling together into the. *How the fuck do I ever explain that if I hadn't walked away from her at that moment, I wouldn't have been responsible for my actions?* Eamon's overwhelming desire for Marcia ran in tandem with his hatred of Eve and Jimmy's supreme betrayal of him. *I'm fucked if I know how to move on from that,* he thought, stumped.

. . . .

As Marcia sat on the plane going back to the UK, she tucked Brandon's phone number back into her purse as she recalled their meeting. She had felt no physical attraction to him, although he was a good-looking man with many good attributes. She had enjoyed his company, his easy-going manner and the picture he painted of the life he lived on his ranch in Texas. By the time Brandon had said goodbye, Marcia realised he had strong feelings for her. He asked if he could ring her. Marcia had given him her phone number and returned his hug, kissing him on the cheek as she thanked him for an enjoyable time. However, in the cold light of day, Marcia was aware that using Brandon as she had planned was not an option. She felt slightly ashamed about how she had led him on so badly and, hopefully, he would get her out of his system now they would be thousands of miles apart.

After the initial panic about having to remove herself from Spain, her intuition was telling her that there were calmer waters ahead. Marcia's main concern was Jimmy's proposition, which had unnerved her. She was fearful that if she disclosed what Jimmy had proposed to her, Suzette would let it slip. It wasn't the case that she thought Suzette wouldn't sympathise, but Marcia was aware of pillow talk and Suzette's loose tongue, and with Greg and Jimmy being close friends she couldn't afford to take that chance. She didn't know how Greg would respond to it.

Deep in thought about the matter, Marcia was only half listening to Suzette, as all she could talk about was the beauty salon and the plans that had been made for their big move to Spain. Marcia was happy that Suzette had met Greg, a very influential man who would give her the moral support she needed to ensure her transition to Spain went unhindered. *How ironic,* Marcia mused, turning her head to look out of the plane window as the sound of the powerful engines lifted them from the tarmac, *I now have offers from two powerful men,*

Jimmy and Brandon who would both support me if that's what I desired. But only one man permeated her thoughts – the dark-haired Irishman, Eamon O'Donally. She tried to rationalise why she'd felt mesmerised by him when her sensibilities were screaming at her to stay away. She knew he operated in a world of criminal activity. Being Jimmy Grant's right-hand man, narcotics and violence were normal for them but completely alien to the way Marcia lived her life. Marcia didn't need to be told; she had seen in Jimmy's tarot reading the scary situations that surrounded him.

Eamon had aroused feelings in her that she had thought she'd put to rest after her husband had passed away. She was in a quandary. Should she remain in the UK where she would have no contact with Jimmy Grant OR Eamon O'Donally, and hope that Suzette, now she was involved with Greg, would release her? Or should she settle in Spain to appease Suzette and remain at the mercy of Jimmy? She never considered for one moment putting Eamon in the same category as Jimmy. He was certainly dangerous, but Marcia felt an inexplicable thrill from the danger that Eamon presented.

Marcia was jolted out of her thoughts by Suzette. "What's bothering you, Marcia? You haven't been yourself since we left. Is it that hunky Texan that's distracting you?" she said, raising an eyebrow quizzically, and smiling.

Suzette ordered a bottle of wine for them both as the flight attendant with a trolley pulled level with their seats. As they sipped their drinks, Suzette turned to Marcia. "Well, are you going to tell me, or am I going to have to keep probing?" she laughed, topping up their glasses.

Marcia sighed. Before she told her about what Jimmy had proposed to her, she asked her to give her word that she wouldn't say anything to Greg. A curious Suzette promised to keep it to herself. Marcia relayed how Jimmy propositioned her and that she felt she couldn't live in Spain under that sort of duress.

Suzette's jaw dropped. "I don't know why I'm shocked, as Jimmy is notorious for having affairs. I can understand your concern because I know what he's like. Jimmy is a law unto himself and he won't let up until he gets what he wants. Poor Joyce, putting up with him," Suzette said, sympathetically.

Placing a comforting hand on Marcia's, she asked her to let her speak to Greg. Seeing the look of consternation on Marcia's face, Suzette reassured her, "Honestly, Marcia, you don't know Greg. He will help. He won't go against me. Even he knows what Jimmy is like."

Reluctantly, Marcia agreed.

"I am not going to let Jimmy Grant put a stop to our business plans or the wonderful new life that awaits us. Leave it to me," she declared, raising her hand to the flight attendant for more wine. Marcia felt a certain sense of relief now that she'd confided in Suzette who seemed confident that Greg would come up with something to prevent Jimmy from coming on to her. She had to put all her trust in Suzette's plan that Greg would let them know when the problem with Jimmy was sorted. Marcia knew that the minute they landed Suzette would be on the phone to Greg putting her plan into action. Everything rested on Greg pulling it off for Marcia; otherwise, it would mean her staying behind in England. There was no way she would ever become Jimmy's mistress. She hoped with all her heart that Greg was successful because even if she could only gaze on Eamon from afar, it had become unthinkable to her that he in some way or another would not be present in her life. Settling this matter in her head made her realise that her heart belonged to this man no matter where he was. She felt

strangely reassured now she had come to this obvious conclusion and wondered why she had fought against it for so long.

UK

Although Marcia felt that things would run smoothly for Suzette and Greg, she couldn't shake off the feeling that they weren't out of the woods yet – she could sense danger lurking. There was something she couldn't quite put her finger on, but now with Jimmy Grant putting Marcia under pressure, she knew Suzette was right in speaking to Greg about the matter. She prayed that he would be on her side. Sitting in Suzette's lounge on their first day back in the UK, Marcia felt she had nothing to lose now and, throwing caution to the wind, she spoke to Suzette about her feelings for Eamon. She revealed to her what had gone on between them on the dance floor, and how he had suddenly dropped her like a hot coal and just walked away.

Suzette laughed at her friend. "You may be a powerful woman, who can see into the future, but it's a pity you can't see what's right in front of your nose. I have seen the way Eamon looks at you. It was so obvious that day at the pool that he has the hots for you."

Marcia sighed. "He assumes I will be available for him, playing with my emotions by turning his attention on me when it suits him. I wouldn't put up with that from any man, no matter how attracted he was to me. I have too much respect for myself," she added.

"That man has you under his skin. All Eamon is doing is battling with himself and you're telling me you can't see or sense that?" Suzette asked. "Look," she continued, "I don't know everything, but one thing I do know is that you should pack up your things and move out to Spain with me." Suzette looked serious. "If you turn your back on him, you will be sorry for the rest of your days … and don't worry, Greg and I will put a stop to Jimmy's little game one way or another."

. . . .

Suzette hadn't been able to get hold of Greg until later that night, and when she spoke to him, she begged him to help Marcia. She had come up with a plan and, hopefully, Greg loved her enough to go along with it. Greg listened to everything Suzette had to say. She declared that she'd be unable to live in Spain without Marcia by her side and that she desperately needed his help. Greg remained silent while she informed him about Jimmy's proposition to Marcia and, unless it was resolved, Marcia would not come back.

When Greg agreed, Suzette knew that he couldn't live without her. "Ok," he said, "What is it that you propose I do? Please bear in mind Jimmy's no fool, Suzette."

"All you need to do, Greg, is whenever you're in his company, mention that you've heard from a source that Suzette's friend Marcia has an STD. By saying that, he should lose interest immediately."

Greg laughed heartily, then became serious. "Suzette, I'm not ridiculing you, but think about what you're asking of me. How on earth would I know anything as personal as that about a woman? Do you honestly think Jimmy is stupid? You will have to come up with something more concrete than that."

But Suzette remained sombre, "Greg, please I am at my wits end. Can't you think of anything that will stop him sniffing around her?"

He pondered before replying, "Why doesn't she tell him indirectly that she has an ongoing medical condition that requires treatment and when he asks the nature of it, Marcia informs him it's personal. That is a sure-fire way to get Jimmy to back off."

Suzette squealed with delight "Darling, you are amazing!" she said, thanking Greg and telling him she loved him and promised to speak to him a bit later.

. . . .

Marcia had been nervously waiting for Jimmy Grant's phone call, which she knew would come. When he finally called, asking how she was, Marcia steered the conversation towards the topic of medical treatment. She tentatively told Jimmy she was feeling unwell and was being treated by the doctor.

"What's your problem?" he asked, sounding sympathetic.

She hesitated.

"What's the matter, Marcia?" he asked again. Reeling him in, she suggested that it was a personal issue – a recurring problem. To add to the drama, she quietly told him that there was no cure and she would have to put up with it forever.

Marcia thought he had put the phone down. "Jimmy are you still there?" she asked. She now had a different Jimmy on the other end of the phone. The tone of his voice changed from sexy-husky to one of detachment. Indifferent now, he told her to take care of herself and, hopefully, he would see her when she returned to Spain.

The women were ecstatic. They laughed at their triumph. Jimmy had dropped her like he'd been burned. She had performed the best act of her life.

"You should have taken up acting. Even I believed you," Suzette giggled.

"Suzie, I can't thank you enough for getting that letch off my back, he makes my skin crawl," Marcia told her.

"Right," Suzette declared, "Now that we have removed that obstacle we can begin to pack up and say goodbye to our lives here for good."

Greg had sealed the deal for Suzette and Marcia's business premises. Marcia was beginning to see her path was looking clearer. She was still perplexed about Max, though she knew he was dead, and she was still mistrustful of Mikey. He would often turn up unexpectedly, and each time she noticed how his physical appearance was rapidly declining. His breathing was laboured and he had a persistent cough. *I feel he is not long for this world,* she thought, but her senses told her he still posed a danger to them. It continued to frustrate her that Suzette was not taking her seriously about being on guard with Mikey. Suzette protested his innocence, insisting that his desire to help her was genuine. Marcia was more than annoyed that Suzette's loose tongue had run away with itself again. She'd told Mikey about how she planned to make a clean break and move out to Spain. She didn't stop there. "Marcia is coming with me and with her 'gift' she will be in great demand," she told him excitedly.

When Marcia reprimanded her about the disclosure of their plans, Suzette brushed her off. "Max is dead and Mikey understands that I am making a clean break to try to get over my heartache," Suzette exclaimed. Marcia resigned herself to the fact that Suzette's naïve outlook was dangerous. She hoped that Suzette would be more careful around Jimmy Grant because if he discovered that Suzette had been seeing Greg while Max was alive he would be less than amused.

Marcia had been living at Suzette's house since being back in the UK only returning to her flat to deal with the removal of her unwanted furniture. She had given back the keys on her rented property and the things she was taking with her were packed into two large cases. As Suzette seemed to spend most of her day speaking to Greg on the phone, Marcia found herself with plenty of free time to meditate, which suited her fine. In the run-up to them leaving for the UK, she had been in a whirlwind of emotions and not had the time to relax and recuperate as she normally would. With regular meditation now and nothing more difficult than packing to worry about, Marcia finally felt emotionally balanced again.

One afternoon, Suzette tapped on Marcia's bedroom door, telling her excitedly that Greg had paid for six months' rent on a villa for them not too far from his place and near the new business site.

"Once the way is clear for Greg and me, and a respectable time has elapsed, there will be no more living this cloak and dagger life and we will show the world that we are together," Suzette clarified.

She's like a bloody teenager ... bless her, thought Marcia. Greg's name came into every conversation. No one else seemed to exist for Suzette. Marcia had to admit that Greg was dynamic and organised, having settled everything for their relocation – also he was incredibly generous, just like Suzette.

Marcia joined Suzette in the lounge where she was opening a bottle of wine to celebrate. Marcia declined but Suzette ignored her, passing her a glass.

"This is a great day, Marcia, and I want you to join me in a drink," she said, smiling. Marcia raised an eyebrow, leaving the wine untouched. She was taken aback as Suzette pressed a monetary gift of £10,000 upon her, adamant that she accept it, as she told her it was from her stash of Max's money. "Don't you worry, there's plenty more where that came from," she reassured Marcia, "and when Greg has everything finalised and we open the doors on our new venture, the money will start pouring in and you and I will never want for anything again."

Marcia was reluctant to accept such a large sum of money but, at Suzette's insistence, she did so, hugging and thanking her for her generosity. The move to Spain was such a giant step for Marcia and although money wasn't that important to her, she knew Suzette's gift would enable her to live independently until the business was up and running.

Spain

"Well, we have done it," Suzette beamed, triumphantly.

Suzette was buzzing with excitement as she and Marcia clipped their seat belts in on the plane. They'd both given up their rented accommodation and were taking only necessities. All the furniture had been sold to a dealer. Suzette informed Marcia that she would purchase anything they required for the rented villa. Marcia had packed only her cherished photographs along with her laptop and her newly purchased clothes. She couldn't shake off the feeling that she was abandoning her son by relocating to Spain, even though he hadn't been in contact with her for years. She worried that he would never find her without a forwarding address. These thoughts were intermingled with those of excitement and the exhilaration of running into Eamon again. All she had to show from her previous life was stashed in the hold of the plane and she was silently thankful that she had got herself into a better place emotionally, in readiness.

Marcia knew no matter where she went she had her "gift" that enabled her to survive. When the plane landed and they cleared customs, going through departures with their cases, they were approached by a man that Greg had sent to pick them up, deeming it unwise to do so himself. The driver, who introduced himself as Mario, the son of the owner of the rented villa, constantly chatted in excellent English, though they were too preoccupied to listen. The women gave one another a con-spiratorial look. The women had been on high alert walking through customs, as they had brought Max's money with them in Suzette's case. Marcia had been racked with nerves when Suzette first mentioned it. She had asked Marcia to look at the tarot cards to see if there were going to be any problems. Reluc-tantly, she had laid out the cards and was relieved to see that there would be no hiccups.

"Now can you understand why I couldn't move to Spain without you, Marcia, you're indispensable to me?" Suzette had laughed.

Now they were home and dry. Marcia was light-headed with relief and infected by Suzette's jubilant attitude that all was going to plan. She couldn't wait to see their new home. Greg was waiting inside the gates as the driver turned into the prop-erty. Suzette hugged and kissed him as he passed her the key.

"You carry on and I'll see to the cases, Greg said, smiling. Marcia returned his smile as Suzette led the way up the steps. Bright sunshine filled the lounge, which was not overly large but big enough to hold three large armchairs, a table and four chairs and a breakfast bar. There was also a bedroom for each of them. Marcia's interest was drawn to the outside. She walked towards the glass doors and asked Suzette to open them to allow her to take in the sight of the luxurious swimming pool, its azure water sparkling.

"You see how easily pleased Marcia is?" Suzette said, turning to Greg as he brought the last of the cases in. "It was my stipulation," she said to a beaming Marcia, who was stand-ing by the poolside. Marcia couldn't fault how Suzette and Greg had come together to make the transition flow. She knew they were a perfect match and they looked so much in love as she observed them standing together in the doorway.

Her thoughts turned to Eamon. She felt nervous yet excited by being on his home turf, knowing he was but a short distance away. She realised that now he was single, there would be plenty of women who could snatch him up.

Greg said he would give them time to freshen up then he would take them to look at cars. This was a priority, he told them, and his pal owned the best car business on the Costa Blanca, so he would be the man to sort them out with a reliable vehicle.

"You don't want anything too flashy for now. It's advisable not to attract too much attention." Greg said, adding, "I'll be back in an hour."

Marcia and Suzette were ready and waiting upon his return and Greg informed them he was purchasing cars for both women. Marcia insisted that she would pay for her own car. Greg tried to dissuade her, telling her that once she became established, if she wanted to she could repay him then. But Marcia didn't want to be beholden to anyone. She wanted to be independent and she had the money that Suzette had given her, so she stood her ground, thanking Greg nonetheless for the offer.

It was a short ride to the car salesroom and it took no more than half an hour for them to settle on two clean, dependable run-arounds. Greg struck a deal with Joey B, telling him to sort the paperwork and bring the bill to him that night once he shut up shop. Greg explained to them that Joey B was from Hackney, Greg and Jimmy's neck of the woods. Greg's construction company had designed and built Joey B's villa on the opposite side of the hill to where most of the ex-pats lived. Marcia had warmed to him as soon as they'd met. His natural-born wit added to Joey B's charm and Marcia and Suzette found him very entertaining. He invited Greg to his daughter's twenty-first birthday party at the weekend and told him to bring Suzette and Marcia with him.

The women got into their cars to follow Greg back to their villa. Marcia was slightly hesitant, as she hadn't ever driven on the right-hand side of the road before, but positioned in the middle with Greg in the car in front and Suzette driving behind her, she soon gained confidence. She was sorry to have to pull up at the villa; she had enjoyed the short drive so much. Greg took his leave, kissing Suzette. He invited them out for a meal that night. Suzette retreated to her room and Marcia took the opportunity to swim and to get in half an hour's yoga to wind down. She showered and changed into a microscopic black bikini that exposed more flesh than it covered. Marcia's preference was to swim naked whenever she could but that hadn't been possible while staying at Joyce's, but now they had their private pool, she opted for the next best thing. The bikini was one she'd purchased on her first visit to Spain but had never dared to wear it as she'd always felt uncomfortable in Jimmy's presence. But with the seclusion of their private villa, she was at ease as she stepped into the pool, feeling instant relief from the heat. Marcia found being able to swim near-naked delectable as the cool trickle of water on her flesh gave the sensation of seductive fingers, reminiscent of Eamon's when he had encased her in his arms on the dance floor. She wondered dreamily what it would be like to make love to him. She found it amazingly easy to fantasise about Eamon as the delicious sensation of the flowing water, created by her powerful strokes, caressed the most intimate parts of her. Marcia had been surprised at how gentle yet urgent his kiss had been. Although their embrace had been short-lived, she had felt his vulnerability underneath his steel-like torso. Lost in her body's sensations and the exquisite pictures she was conjuring in her brain, she powered through forty lengths of the pool. With a satisfied smile on her face, Marcia rose from the water. Picking up the towel, she dried herself and walked to the far end of the terrace where she had previously placed the yoga mat. A peaceful calm overcame her as she put the towel aside and sat down in the lotus position to begin her Hatha yoga routine. Oblivious to the world around her she drifted deep within herself, at one with life. The physical exercises required discipline and deep breathing techniques, which she had mastered to a high degree. The combination of a healthy vegetarian diet, her spiritual belief and regular exercise had kept Marcia in superb shape, a factor that hadn't gone unnoticed by her watcher. As Marcia held the position of the shoulder stand, with her body weight resting on her shoulders, her immense core strength held her spine and legs in a vertical line. Slowly relaxing into the completion of her routine, she opened her eyes, lazily reaching for the towel, Marcia turned around and a bolt of fear struck her in the chest. Jimmy Grant was lounging on a chair at the garden table leering at her, one hand over the crotch of his trousers, covering his swollen cock. Initially, Marcia felt frightened but she swiftly felt her anger rise. She was furious at his voyeurism, the position of his hand and his smug smile told her he'd been observing her throughout. Composing herself as well as she could, her fury bubbling below the surface, she tried to act as if he hadn't unnerved her, praying that Suzette would emerge. She wondered how he'd discovered so soon where they were living, but common sense told her that nothing went on that he didn't know about.

"I am pleased to see you looking so well Marcia," he said sarcastically, rearranging the front of his trousers.

Marcia averted her eyes and didn't reply, knowing he was referring to their last telephone conversation. She wasn't concerned whether he believed her made-up story about a medical condition. Marcia knew he couldn't prove that it wasn't true. She glanced at the bottle of Krug champagne on the table.

"I have brought you both a moving in gift," he said, without dropping his intense stare. His blue eyes bored into her. "I noticed you both have wheels, you girls don't let the grass grow under your feet."

Marcia's anger had cooled and she was beginning to feel distinctly unsettled by Jimmy's nearness, standing as she was with just a towel wrapped around her near-naked body. Jimmy rose to his full height and Marcia instinctively stepped backwards. Looking casually around him, he nodded. "Nice little place you've got here, and a pool too … but heed my warning…" Jimmy's tone held a definite hint of menace. "I would be careful of intruders up here, especially if you're swimming alone, with your mind on other things." He emphasised the word *things,* and Marcia flushed.

Oh God, had it been that obvious what she was thinking about? Marcia thought, mortified that this pig of a man had studied her that intently. As he left, her legs refused to hold her up any longer and she sank onto the garden chair with relief. She couldn't stop the nervous fluttering in the pit of her stomach caused by his unexpected visit. Where the hell was Suzette?

....

Greg had picked the women up that evening, wined and dined them and afterwards had taken them to show them around the new complex where the beauty salon was taking shape.

Marcia looked around the large building. All the plumbing and electrical wiring was complete and all Suzette had to do was to be there the following day, ready to take delivery of the expensive furnishings that Greg had bought for her. No expense had been spared. This was going to be "the place" to go to for every form of beauty treatment that money could buy. Suzette had previously placed adverts in the UK and Spanish papers, looking for the top beauty therapists and hair stylists who wanted to work for a new, notable beauty therapy salon on the Costa Blanca. Suzette had been inundated by applications and would be interviewing for two days next week.

"This unique venture is going to be on every woman's lips; we will not only be providing high-end beauty treatment but also an in-house spiritual medium." Suzette stated confidently, adding, "We'll blow all competition out of the water." Marcia didn't doubt the salon's future success as she had been kept busy conducting tarot readings from the villa and had taken plenty of appointments for when the business opened. She was grateful her days had been so full that she'd had no time to dwell on Jimmy's appearance at the pool earlier that day.

Marcia arrived home, locking the gates and double-checking them. This would be the first night that she would be staying in the villa without Suzette and she knew she had to conquer her fears. Marcia wasn't used to someone holding her hand and she didn't intend to start now. Suzette, though, itching to stay at Greg's overnight, had been reluctant to leave Marcia on her own. After she learnt from Marcia how Jimmy had entered the grounds and had observed her without her knowing, she had Greg change all the locks throughout the villa. Marcia reassured her that she'd be fine and she entered the villa determined to enjoy the evening on her own. Locking the front door, she opened her laptop that she'd brought with her from the UK and found the music she'd saved. The melodic and tuneful voice of Barbra Streisand filtered through the room, the words of the song "Why Did I Choose You," resonated with her, conjuring Eamon O'Donally. Although Marcia loved most of the songstress's recordings, that song and "Woman in Love" were among her favourites. She showered, wrapping a towel around her. She placed the computer by the open patio doors so she could hear the music by the pool. Letting out a breath, she hadn't realised she'd been holding, she glanced around half expecting to see him sitting there. Instead, all that greeted her was the soft lights playing over the water, the balmy air and the visible starlit bay in the distance. Relief flooded through her and with a sense of contentment, Marcia started to look forward to the way her life was beginning to turn out. No Jimmy Grant was going to stop her indulging in what she loved doing most. She let the towel fall, revelling in the feel of the night air on her bare skin. Walking down the steps devoid of clothing into the aqua freshness, her nipples erect as she submerged, the seductiveness of swimming in her natural state felt like a liberation. As Marcia leisurely swam, she thought about her earlier life and her husband Andrew came to mind. She'd been a naïve sixteen-year-old and by the time she approached her next birthday, Marcia had a baby boy in her arms. That child, Reuben, was now eighteen and she was thirty-five. She wondered where Reuben was and how he was getting on. A pang of guilt hit her. She couldn't spend the rest of her life punishing herself, she thought. She knew she wasn't in any position to aid Reuben yet, no matter where he was in the world. Being estranged from him was like a double-edged sword – she missed him so much but strangely did not worry about him. Her acute perception told her that wherever he was he was okay. All these thoughts receded to the back of her mind as the ballad changed to "Evergreen," a harmonious duet with Kris Kristofferson. Eamon returned to the forefront of her mind as she immersed herself in the lyrics about a deep love.

Marcia still couldn't understand how someone she hardly knew could invade her thoughts as Eamon O'Donally did. She'd never before longed for a man as she did for him. Marcia realised, looking back on her marriage at a young age, that it hadn't been real love. They'd only been teenagers and had only married because of her unexpected pregnancy, although Andrew had proved to be a good and kind man. For the first time in her life, she wondered if an all-consuming love might be hers to experience. She was still a young woman and one that had looked after herself, treating her body and mind as a temple. Perhaps now was *her* time. Finishing her swim, she felt exhilarated, her mind cleared yet replaced with her inner reserve, determined to enjoy her new life out in Spain.

That night Marcia slept like a baby. Suzette arrived early the next morning to change her clothes. Marcia had completed her yoga routine; upon hearing Suzette calling her, she came out of the bedroom to find her looking stressed-out and flustered.

"I am running late, Greg delayed me," she laughed, and Marcia smiled, knowing that Greg had kept her longer in his bed. Suzette continued with the conversation as she entered her bedroom stripping her clothes off. "I need to be at the beauty salon as all the fixtures and fittings are being delivered and put into place today by Greg's men. As you know, Marcia, the grand opening is scheduled in two weeks' time."

Marcia popped her head round the door as Suzette zipped her dress up and slipped into high heels. Marcia never failed to marvel at how Suzette always looked effortlessly glamorous.

"Joyce phoned to say that she and Cindy wouldn't be too long. They're coming over for a coffee," Marcia said. She didn't mention they'd had to wait until Jimmy and Eamon went out before they could make their escape so that Joyce could have a tarot reading. Marcia promised to keep Joyce's secret that she wanted to flee from Jimmy's control.

Suzette told her she would ring later as she rushed out the door. Marcia felt apprehensive, wondering what Jimmy's next move would be. She didn't trust him. Even though he seemed to have accepted her mistruth, she wasn't foolish enough to think that she was on safe ground with him. She was aware of the consequences for all three of them if he discovered their disloyalty, but it was a price Marcia was prepared to pay by helping Joyce.

Joyce arrived with Cindy and all three women went into the lounge and sat around the table. There was a lull in the room as Marcia removed her tarot cards from their silk wrapping, passing them to Joyce whose eyes reminded Marcia of a scared deer caught in the headlights. Joyce shuffled the cards and once completed handed them back. Joyce and Cindy, with their eyes glued to the table, watched as Marcia turned the first three cards over.

"I see a trap and danger around Jimmy." She made a circle of 360 degrees with her middle finger. "He is surrounded by deception. People are plotting and scheming to put an end to him."

Joyce gasped holding her hand across her chest looking stricken as Marcia continued. "I feel that shortly there will be a sudden ending."

Cindy leant over the table, scanning the cards. "What are you saying?" she asked, trying to see what Marcia was seeing.

"There are men who are in collusion against him. They come from across the water, but there are others closer by," she added. Marcia experienced a feeling of sadness as she placed the rest of the cards on the table. Trying to break it to her gently, so as not to alarm Joyce, Marcia eyed the Grim Reaper.

"There are going to be big changes in your life that will bring a transformation, and once the dust has settled I can see a remarkable twist in your destiny that will bring your wishes to fruition."

Cindy shook her head while Joyce sat stunned in silence.

"Marcia, please be more specific. You're confusing Joyce," Cindy said eagerly. Marcia wasn't going to be coerced by Cindy into divulging more.

Turning to speak to Joyce, Marcia smiled thinly. "You are to sit back and wait for situations to unfold. I can assure you that Sara and your grandchild will be in your life and you will pull up your roots and cross the seas."

Cindy sat back in her chair and asked, "How would she get away from him? Because I know Jimmy. He's a nasty bastard and ..."

Marcia intercepted, "All I know Cindy is that Joyce will be happy and have a better life."

"Well," Cindy chirruped, "that piece of good news should put a smile on your face, Joyce. If you are not going to lose Sara it doesn't matter how the situation comes about. But what about Jimmy? He should be warned," Joyce stated, her voice trembling with emotion.

Cindy's eyes flashed, temper rising as she pushed back her chair, "What about Jimmy!" she stated loudly. "WHAT ABOUT YOU JOYCE?" she yelled, exasperated.

"Are you always going to put him before your daughter? Let's not forget your future grandchild!"

Cindy's outburst visibly upset Joyce. She put her head down on the table and tears began to flow. Cindy put a comforting arm around her and lowered her tone. "You've got to think about yourself for once, Joyce. Let us put the tarot reading to one side and remember that Marcia has given you hope. So we'll wait to see what happens."

To lighten the mood, Marcia asked the women out onto the terrace. Picking up two glasses, she brought out the champagne, placing the bottle before them.

On catching sight of the label, Joyce remarked, "You must have the same expensive taste as Jimmy," she held the bottle aloft. "Krug champagne is his absolute favourite."

Marcia flushed, feeling guilty.

Cindy caught her eye. "Aren't you joining us?"

Marcia lifted her bottle of mineral water in answer.

"I've drunk more since I have known you ladies than I have ever done in my life. I don't want it to become a habit." She laughed and rapidly changed the subject, telling them about the friendly car dealer Joey B who they'd purchased their cars from and how being new to the area he'd invited them to his daughter's twenty-first birthday party. "He was very welcoming. He made us both feel as if we had known him for ages," Marcia said. "Will you two be going too?"

Joyce and Cindy both replied that they wouldn't miss it for the world.

"Everyone loves Joey B and his lovely wife Mel. We all know that if you enjoy a great party, you shouldn't miss one of his." Joyce said that Jimmy was fond of him too since they went way back, being members of the same gang in London once. Jimmy had gone into big-time crime, while Joey B had gone straight,

Joyce and Cindy knew of Suzette's new business venture, which she had been keeping under wraps. She was going to tell them that she had gotten a bank loan for fear of Jimmy delving into how she could financially invest in such a big enterprise. But Max's death had changed everything and Suzette had lied by saying that her dead husband had provided for her. Suzette told Marcia that no one would know how much money Max had had. What with her ill-gotten gains stashed away and Greg's generosity, Suzette was in the clear. The women were itching to see the completed salon. Joyce, seeming more cheerful, asked Marcia if Suzette might let her manage the salon for her. "It will keep me occupied," she said.

Marcia didn't think that Joyce would be in the position to work, but kept her own counsel. Cindy piped up that she used to be a qualified hairdresser and would be willing to retrain under whomever Suzette took on.

"I will speak to her, don't worry. I can think of nothing better than having you both onboard. I'll choose the right moment to broach the subject. Suzette is under a lot of pressure at the moment and she has so much to deal with." But she promised to put in a good word for them.

Joyce and Cindy hugged Marcia, thanking her for the tarot reading, saying that they would see her and Suzette at Joey B's party on Saturday. The ever-loyal Cindy had spent the previous day shopping and had the bags in her car so Jimmy would think they had been out all day buying new clothes. Cindy made no bones about her dislike of Jimmy and his treatment of Joyce. But Marcia knew they were all playing with fire. She hoped that Cindy realised the man was ruthless, and that he wouldn't think twice about retaliating if he thought anyone was being duplicitous.

. . . .

Eamon and Jimmy had been discussing a big business trip to Miami. Jimmy wanted Eamon to oversee a shipment of cocaine that was coming from a new source into the Florida Straights. The vessel, which was en route in the Gulf of Mexico, would be received by Carlo Gabrette. Eamon had had dealings with his father Alphonso Gabrette in the past. He classed the old Italian as a friend, and his trustworthy family name went before him. But due to Alphonso's ailing health, his son Carlo would be stepping in. Although they hadn't ever dealt with Al's son before, the old man's word was enough of a guarantee. This new contact, Jimmy informed Eamon, would funnel untold millions their way if all went well. Eamon knew there was no need for him to stay in Miami more than a couple of days to sort everything out, but Jimmy had insisted that Eamon have a break after what he'd been through with Eve's untimely death. He had told him to take a holiday and see as much of the region as he could.

"Take a flight from the Florida Keys to the Bahamas. It's only a matter of a six-hour trip. My mate Ricky has a place there. I'll give you his contact number," Jimmy encouraged.

Eamon knew Jimmy wasn't the least bit concerned about his welfare. He knew he only ever thought of himself. Eamon wanted out and the thought of being far away from Jimmy Grant for a couple of weeks suited him down to the ground. He loathed Jimmy from the core of his being ever since he'd found Eve's diary and read every sickening detail of their affair. He had zero loyalty to Jimmy now. Eamon knew that once you entered this world there was no easy way out. He'd have to play the game, bide his time and wait for the right opportunity to make his move. He planned to eventually return to Ireland and have a quiet life like his younger brother Patrick had in the Irish countryside. He was tired of the circle he'd been mixing with and the type of women who frequented it. He wanted someone decent. Eve, like the rest of them, had been so superficial. All of them were out for themselves. It made his blood boil thinking of her and the way she had cheated on him. He'd been steeped in crime for a long time, but this turn of events had pushed him towards wanting to make long-overdue changes. He'd had a hard job keeping his emotions in check when Jimmy had told him in detail, how he'd turned up at Marcia's villa while she was swimming and doing yoga in a tiny bikini that left nothing to the imagination.

"She'd been totally unaware of the show I was enjoying," Jimmy had leered and continued to boast about the huge boner he he had had, and what he had wanted to do to her.

Eamon was sickened. Marcia was by far the most respectable woman to have crossed his path in years. He felt a sudden rush of protectiveness towards her, thinking about how frightened she must have been when she discovered the pervy bastard watching her.

Eamon's admiration for her had gone up a notch when Jimmy had added, "Shame she's untouchable, though. The silly bitch should have been more careful when she'd put it about before."

Momentarily mystified by this outburst, it had taken Eamon all but a few seconds to realise just how clever Marcia was. Jimmy had fallen for the oldest trick in the book, and the only thing that would have kept him away from her. Eamon smiled to himself. He was already attracted to her physical beauty and now it seemed she had the brain to match. He hoped that she'd forgive him for his behaviour on the dance floor at Sara's wedding.

....

Marcia and Suzette lay by the pool, taking a well-earned break after a busy day decorating the villa and making it homely and sorting things out with the business. Suzette had overseen the delivery at the salon, and Greg's men were working hard to have all the fittings in place.

Marcia confided in Suzette about how under the starlit sky she'd swum naked. "I felt like a water nymph. It was so sensual and now that the locks have been changed and it's secluded here, I feel safer about making it routine," she smiled.

Concerned, Suzette warned her, "I wouldn't advise it, Marcia. I know we've made the place more secure now but I'd still worry that we could get an unexpected visitor."

Brushing off her fears, Marcia told her she would be fine. "I can't live my life worrying about what might happen, Suzie. It's only you and I that know, so please don't worry."

Marcia brought up the subject of Joyce helping to manage the salon. She didn't mention anything about Joyce's tarot reading, though. "Even if it's part-time, at least it will give her some distraction away from the villa for a few hours."

Suzette shook her head. "Do you think that Jimmy would tolerate her not being at his beck and call? I would love to but dare not invite trouble from his direction."

It was disappointing, but Marcia could understand the reasons why. She asked about the possibility of Cindy working at the salon as she'd had previous experience and Cindy had said she would be willing to retrain under the expertise of any hairstylist that Suzette employed.

"The more trustworthy employees you have on your side the better, and then you will be able to spend more time with Greg," she advised.

"Hmmm," Suzette said, "Although I find her outspoken manner refreshing, Cindy would have to learn to curb her fiery directives. There is such a thing as the right time and place."

Marcia reassured her that Cindy's personality could be an asset, as she would stand no nonsense from difficult clients.

Turning her attention to Marcia, Suzette smiled. "Now let's forget about the others and talk about you. We must find you a man. What about Eamon? He has his eye on you." Suzette said.

"Eamon has recently lost his wife in a tragic accident. He isn't interested in me, I'm sure," Marcia said. "I know he kissed me when we danced but maybe he just got carried away by the moment."

Suzette threw her head back laughing. "Please," she said with a touch of drama splaying her long red painted nails for effect. "Eamon O'Donally is a handsome man who's now available and plenty of the women would be interested in him. However, I have never heard any gossip about him. The man is straight. He's no Jimmy Grant. Trust me, I would have heard about it if he were."

Marcia was heartened by these remarks. Her attraction to Eamon was compelling, but she just knew her personality wouldn't be compatible with a man who was a player.

"I've seen the way he watches you," Suzette continued, "and mark my words, it will happen at some point with you and him."

Marcia shook her head in denial.

Suzette grinned mischievously. "Are you telling me that you wouldn't want that dark-haired handsome hunk in your bed? Imagine being encased in those powerful thighs of his?" Suzette elevated her brow.

Marcia smiled embarrassedly, remembering how often she fantasised about him. She couldn't deny that just the mention of his name brought back the feeling he had given her on that night, how protected she'd felt in his powerful arms and what he'd awakened in her.

"Don't try to tell me that Eamon isn't under your skin. It's written all over your face. I have my man, now you get yours."

"But Greg has a regular type of job," Marcia said, "Unlike Eamon, he is…"

Suzette interjected. "Greg told me about his past and how he was deeply involved in crime but through a lucky break via Jimmy, he got the big contracts and his small building business turned into a multi-million euro empire."

Marcia nodded.

"The time has come to live your life more dangerously, Marcia. You've been wrapped in cotton wool for too long," Suzette laughed, "At least your life wouldn't be tedious with a man such as him, and I should imagine with the quiet sexual magnetism he projects, that he'd be extremely fulfilling in the sack."

Marcia blushed, but couldn't hide a grin.

The buzzer on the gates echoed through the villa. It was Mario. Marcia told him to park up and join them at the front by the pool.

"We have a guest," she told Suzette.

The landlord's son joined them on the terrace. He asked if there had been any problems with the villa and passed on an invitation from his father, who wanted to offer them dinner at his home the following week. Mario's mother was a superb cook and the family wanted to welcome them to Spain. His eyes were everywhere. Marcia could see him scrutinising them as he spoke. He tried to work his magic on them, flashing his beautiful white teeth and making full use of his stunning, dusky looks. Marcia wasn't impressed though. She recognised the overconfidence of a man who saw himself as the local stud. She made a note to herself to avoid him at all costs. Suzette also saw through him and thanked him for the invitation, saying that they would get back to him about going to dinner with his family some other time, as they had a busy schedule with the business. Marcia walked with him to the front of the villa.

Before she could stop him, Mario kissed her on the cheek. "If you need any company, I am always available to show you the beauty of my country."

Thanking him for the offer, she cut him dead. "I am an extremely busy woman and my boyfriend will show me all I need to see."

Apologising, Mario looked her up and down and said, "This man is a very lucky person."

He got into his car and drove off. *Idiot!* Marcia thought. Mario had been annoyed by her blunt refusal, and she knew that they wouldn't get rid of him easily. She had lied about the boyfriend to stop him in his tracks. They had to be careful though. He was the landlord's son, after all, and they needed the villa for at least twelve months. Once things had taken off financially, she could see about getting a place of her own. She knew that Suzette would be moving in with Greg after a respectable time.

Suzette had laughed when Marcia told her about Mario's offer and the lie she'd told him.

"I feel like he's bad news," she told her, "and he should be discouraged from coming here. I know we can't prevent him turning up like the proverbial bad penny, but I don't trust his motives. He gives me the creeps."

An ideal solution sprang to her mind. "How about we get a dog, Suzie?" Marcia enquired, "The contract says animals are allowed and we could ask Joyce or Cindy about how to go about getting one."

Suzette agreed, as she knew that Marcia would be on her own in the villa most nights. She decided to get one as soon as possible and the bigger the dog the better. With that thought in mind, Suzette phoned Cindy. After a brief conversation, Suzette came away armed with the name and number of a local dog breeder and trainer who she said would be able to help. Suzette had thanked Cindy for the information and said they would see her at the party the next night.

"Right, that's underway," Suzette told her friend, "Once we have a guard dog, I'll feel better about leaving you at night, especially with you swimming in the nude. I'll be able to rest knowing that you have some protection."

Marcia, though having little knowledge of dogs, was comforted by the thought that she would be protected and have some company when Suzette was not around.

"After we've shopped for a new dress and shoes I'm buying you for the party," Suzette said, "we'll give this dog breeder a ring."

She handed Marcia the piece of paper with the breeder's details and trotted off to the villa to get herself a bottle of wine. Marcia stretched out luxuriously on the sunbed. She was looking forward to their shopping trip in Malaga tomorrow morning and Joey B's party in the evening.

Her friendship with Suzette had gone from strength to strength, even though the start had been somewhat forced. Marcia had grown close to her, against all the odds, and if she could prevent anything from happening to her she would.

They shopped until they dropped the next day. Marcia had tried to resist Suzette's offer to pay for the clothes, exclaiming that she had already given her so much.

"Not only am I financially independent, but Greg will not allow me to pay for anything. He's footing the bill for the salon as well," she grinned. Marcia knew it was pointless arguing with her and that Suzette wouldn't take no for an answer. They came out of the shop laden with designer dresses, lingerie, shoes and bags. An assistant carried the purchases to the car and Suzette gave her a 50 euro tip. Marcia was astounded by her friend's overwhelming generosity. She'd never in her wildest dreams thought she would ever see so much money change hands in one transaction, let alone have thousands spent on her. Back at their villa, Suzette hurriedly put her purchases away as Greg had an interlude and she was meeting him at his place. Marcia thought how happy Suzette was with her new love and she was pleased for her. They had gone to the salon on their way home to check out how the builders were faring. They were astounded by the progress they were making, as the building was a hub of activity.

As they left, Suzette winked. "Did you notice how many handsome men there were? Bent over showing the firmness of their buttocks. Not that I'm interested, as I have more than enough with Greg, but one can be allowed to admire," she laughed.

The villa was quiet as Marcia hung up the dresses. She was unsure which one she would wear to the party, as she was spoilt for choice. She shook her head in amazement as she looked at a price tag. Holding a dress at arm's length, she thought it was a good choice for the party. Placing it back in the wardrobe, Marcia changed into a pale lemon, shoestring strap dress, deciding to lay in the garden in the shade and relax. She wanted to be rested before Joey B's party. She wasn't going to think about anything, apart from enjoying herself.

. . . .

Eamon clicked off the call from his brother Patrick in Ireland. He sat at the table running his forefinger across his chin in contemplation. Patrick had informed him that since Anna and Chloe had arrived, they had been a blessing for his family. Anna had taken a huge burden off Rosie's shoulders by helping with the 24/7 care that Catherine required. He said Anna and her daughter had taken to country life and they were all getting along grand. Patrick added that Anna was helping with the care of the animals too and that he was now teaching her how to ride a horse. Eamon sucked air through his teeth as he thought of how his younger brother Patrick's dark good looks were very popular with the local girls when he was younger. But it was the plain-looking Rosie who he succumbed to after a few drinks one night at the local dance, and that one slip had cost Patrick his freedom. With no choice but to do the right thing, Patrick had married her.

Patrick had been earning his income from gun-running, but with a child on the way and a family to look after, it was a recipe for disaster. Eamon stepped in to bankroll his sibling to try to prevent him from fucking his life up.

Eamon smiled wryly to himself. He was no fool. Patrick's constant referral to Anna and the amount of time he was obviously spending with her had him wondering if it had been such a good idea to send her there to help out, putting temptation in his brother's path. *For fuck's sake,* he thought, *there's not much I can do about it now.*

He needed all his wits about him for the impending trip to Miami the next day. His last night in Spain was going to be spent at Joey B's party and he had already collected his suits from Eugene, his tailor, who had convinced him he needed shirts and silk ties to complete the picture. He had to hand it to the Frenchman – he certainly knew his job.

Eamon was going to decline the invitation to the party at first until Joey B put the pressure on. He told him that he'd be offended if Eamon didn't show up. He had laughed jovially, "After all, it is my girl's twenty-first birthday and you know how fond my wife Mel is of you, so stop being a stranger to us."

That clinched it. Eamon confirmed that he would attend. He was fond of Joey B and his family. The man would always go to lengths to find Eamon whatever car he wanted, and always at a fair price. Over the years, Eamon had often attended Joey and Mel's lavish parties, which were legendary – adding to which, Eamon found Joey B incredibly entertaining. All the men in Eamon's circle considered Joey B to be Spain's Danny DeVito. Eamon's mind wandered. Joey had said to bring someone, so Eamon mulled over who that might be. He thought about Vonja, the estate agent who valued his villa. He'd had her on ice since she passed him her calling card. He was considering putting his villa on the market to rid himself of any reminders of Eve.

He didn't want to look like a spare prick at a wedding arriving on his own but, in many ways, Vonja was just another Eve. Eamon didn't know if he could cope with yet another blonde airhead on his arm all night. He picked up the phone, she answered in an irritating pseudo-sexy voice, which she clearly considered a big turn-on. It had the opposite effect on him. Jesus, he was sick of false women. Still … he reflected, that goes with the territory and I won't have to hang out with her all night. Vonja was elated with the invitation and asked Eamon, giggling, if she should bring an overnight bag with her. Eamon hesitated, "Why not," he replied curtly, before abruptly clicking off the call.

He ran his fingers through his hair, wondering why he was going through with it when Vonja was already annoying the fuck out of him. Upon reflection, he knew in his heart that he wanted more out of life than what he had had over the past couple of decades. He was forty-five and lived many of those years dealing with the criminal world with nothing but money to show for it. He would have liked to have had children, but Eve had informed him that because she suffered from endometriosis she couldn't give him children. He had come to terms with the fact that they wouldn't be having a family together, but when he'd read Eve's diary he discovered that she'd lied to him, as written down in black and white Eve had expressed a wish to have Jimmy Grant's baby. Sickened by her double betrayal, he'd searched her cupboards and drawers, eventually finding what he suspected she had hidden. Tucked away were packets of contraceptive pills, which she had obviously been taking for a long time. He vowed that no woman would ever deceive him again. "Once everything is done in Miami, I am going to sort my life out," he promised himself.

....

Vonja was thrilled, she had been hoping Eamon O'Donally would call her and now she'd be on his arm at one of the year's most prestigious events. She clapped her hands with glee at her triumph. Vonja was thick-skinned and determined to work herself into Eamon O'Donally's life. She knew he was next in line to Jimmy Grant and she'd set her sights on him the moment that the news spread about his wife's death in the car accident. "Shit happens," she said aloud as she went through her vast wardrobe to see which dress she'd wear to impress him. Being one to grab an opportunity when it came her way she was ecstatic to get an opening.

Vonja had worked her way through Jimmy Grant's men and knew she wasn't immensely popular with the women, but Vonja wasn't out to make friends. She wanted a luxury life-style and all the trappings that went with it. Admiring her reflection in the long bedroom mirror, she flicked her long blonde hair back, adjusting the mini dress that showed her toned thighs. She smiled as she thought of the sexual delights she would give Eamon O'Donally later that night. She wasn't fazed by these men from the criminal world – on the contrary, she enjoyed the aggressive passion that they acted out behind closed doors.

Vonja valued herself highly. She knew she was a head-turner. It hadn't come easy – it took discipline and every spare hour in the gym for her to stay on top. Appraising what she saw in the mirror … the boob job, Botox, the regular facials … all gave her a body that she found no man could resist. Vonja worked at the high-end estate agents for Rupert Hatchet; she'd become an invaluable asset to his company as she sold more properties and earned the highest commission that her boss had ever paid anyone. When Rupert informed her that Eamon O'Donally wanted a valuation on his property, he had set Vonja to the task. She couldn't believe her good fortune, as this had been the first opportunity to get near to her target. Rupert told Vonja that Eamon O'Donally would be a hard nut to crack, as he was known as a no-nonsense, private man who couldn't have the wool pulled over his eyes. Rupert informed her that although he only wanted a valuation of his villa and wasn't interested in purchasing another yet, he put Vonja on a promise of a large commission if she got a sale from him.

UK

Back in the UK, Mikey Paige had tears of joy running down his face. He was the happiest man on the planet, even though he knew he was on borrowed time. At first, hearing the caller's voice on the other end of the phone, he thought it was someone trying to get one over on him. He was elated when he realised it was bona fide and not a hoax. Mikey didn't ask for or need any explanations. Hard on the heels of that call, Mikey received another, this time from Johnny Smart, whose security services had been used at Jimmy Grant's girl's wedding in Spain.

Smart's security company had also been hired for Joey B's girl's twenty-first birthday bash – where the who's who of the criminal underworld would be all gathered under one roof. Mikey's suspicions about Suzette and her sidekick psychic mate Marcia had been confirmed. The two of them had men in their sights, and not just any men. The pair had aimed high. Suzette was with Greg Davidson, the wealthy construction boss, and Marcia the psychic had been seen with Jimmy Grant's right-hand man, Eamon O'Donally. Mikey continued to listen politely, although he didn't need to hear any more. Debts would be honoured. Mikey would die a happy man.

Spain

Marcia had arrived at Joey B's with Suzette and the party was already well underway. They could hear a rock band blaring – the headbanging noise was deafening.

"Good God!" Marcia said, laughing.

"Well, it is the girl's twenty-first," Suzette shouted back.

They couldn't hear themselves think and decided to move further away from the live music. Just as they managed to get through the throng of youngsters, Joey B appeared with his wife on his arm. He called out to them.

"Come on ladies, don't worry about all the commotion. The tempo changes at seven. That lot has been banging away for the last three hours," he said pointing to the temporary stage.

He introduced his wife Mel who explained, "The rock band has been flown in from the States as a surprise for our daughter Sophia. The silly old sod paid an arm and a leg for that racket." Mel said, laughing. "Still, his baby girl can have the proverbial top brick. Security is tight though. You know what they say about sex, drugs and rock and roll." Mel told them that Joey B had warned the lads in the band that if there were any drugs on the go, they wouldn't get paid. Anyway, there's me rabbiting on and I haven't even asked your names!" Mel reproached herself.

Suzette introduced them and took the opportunity to inform Mel about the opening of the beauty salon. She explained how Marcia would play a role in the business with her gift as a psychic. Suzette had been prepared and planned to reveal her new enterprise at the party, as Greg had told her that the place would be packed with many influential men with their women. Mel couldn't contain herself when she realised who Marcia was.

"I have wanted to get hold of you, but then I was told you were back in the UK, and here you are at my baby girl's party! Well," she stepped back in admiration, "I must say, the picture I had in my mind's eye of a mystic was much more gypsy Rose Lee. You're enough to warm any man's cockles, isn't she, Joey?" Mel laughed. Her husband nodded in agreement. It hadn't escaped his notice how elegant Marcia looked.

Marcia was enjoying Mel's cockney directness. She thought Mel was a woman that she could become friends with. Her warm energy reminded her of Joyce. Suzette made her excuses and disappeared into the crowd that was gathered at the opposite side of the villa, Marcia knew she'd be on the hunt for her man. Mel took Marcia's arm, moving her towards a large gathering of glamorous women on the terrace.

"Ladies listen up," she announced loudly over the chatter, "This is the lady I was telling you all about … Marcia is the psychic medium. Can you believe it, girls? She is now living only half an hour away on the other side of the hill!"

Marcia was hemmed in by all the women asking for tarot readings and her contact details. Suzette had given her business cards for the new salon, which had Marcia's details on them. She reached for them in her clutch bag and placed about thirty on the table. Within minutes they were all gone. She hadn't realised just how much in demand she would be. It was a little overwhelming, as they clamoured for her attention, vying with each other to get their questions answered. It wasn't the type of evening Marcia had planned and, without Suzette there to rescue her, she didn't quite know how to make her escape without appearing rude. They were all friendly – their camaraderie was infectious, but Marcia still felt like a fish out of water. The women reminded her of shop mannequins, dripping in haute couture and expensive jewellery. Most it would seem spent their husbands' generous allowances on cosmetic surgery.

In contrast, Marcia was wearing a classical but under-stated Alexander McQueen dress. The style suited her shape perfectly. She had chosen the black sleeveless double-breasted dress with the figure-hugging belt specifically so as not to stand out. It was elegant and comfortable and coupled with the plain black stilettos made her feel confident but not showy. Marcia, still hemmed in by the excited women, was oblivious to the eyes watching her.

. . . .

Eamon had been talking to Joey B just behind the group of women when he'd heard all the commotion. He'd looked up and was momentarily taken aback to see that Marcia was the centre of the women's focus. He knew she was now living in Spain, but he hadn't expected to see her at Joey B's party. He wondered if she was on her own. He thought she looked even more desirable than when he'd seen her last. She stood out like a sore thumb – unadorned and so natural in comparison to all the heaving bosoms spilling out of dresses and the acres of thighs and buttocks barely covered by designer fabrics. She had no idea just how different and mesmerising she was amongst the others. He couldn't take his eyes off her – her soft curves accentuated by the black dress, and the high heels that showed off her shapely lower legs. Sucking air through his teeth he wished now he'd come to the celebration alone. He was getting a distinct ache in his groin and he was fighting to regulate his breathing. Out of necessity, he turned his attention back to the conversation with Joey B.

. . . .

Vonja was no stranger to men's moods and desires and observing Eamon, she knew full well his attention was elsewhere. The object of his desire appeared to be a redheaded woman who was surrounded by Spain's most influential wives and girlfriends. Suddenly, Vonja felt threatened. His look had been one of longing, not mere male hot-bloodedness.

No one is going to have him but me, she vowed to herself, directing daggers at the woman. She was going to make it her business to find out who she was. Slipping her arm into Eamon's, she turned her attention back to him, busying herself smiling in all the right places as they talked shop. Out of the corner of her eye, she recognised a familiar figure. It was Cindy, who she previously had property dealings with. Excusing herself, she walked over to where Cindy was talking to Joyce.

Vonja complimented both women on their gorgeous dresses and then slyly turned her attention to Marcia who was still surrounded by a circle of interested females. "The redheaded woman in the black dress seems to be popular, who is she, Cindy?"

Joyce answered before Cindy could reply, "Her name is Marcia. She has moved here to start a business."

Interesting, Vonja mused, hoping that she had a man in tow. "What type of business?"

Cindy was now the one to speak. "She is a psychic medium with an amazing gift and, I would add, a truly lovely person." Cindy had emphasised the word "lovely," as she could sense that somehow Vonja had been unsettled by Marcia and saw her as a threat.

"Her new business ... is that with her husband?" Vonja asked Cindy presumptively.

Taking great pleasure in twisting the knife, Cindy replied smugly, "Not only is she single but I'm sure it won't be long before she was the centre of some lucky man's attention. She has so much going for her."

. . . .

Ignoring the open hostility emanating from the other women surrounding Marcia, Vonja held out her hand, introduced herself and told Marcia how much she would love to book a reading with her as soon as possible. Marcia was immediately taken aback by the woman's energy. There was a sense of cold ruthlessness about her and she wanted to move away from her as quickly as possible. Marcia had one last business card remaining and passed it to her. Vonja beamed her thanks before telling her, "I can't wait to tell my man Eamon that I'm going to have a tarot reading with you."

Marcia's heart contracted at the mention of his name. The woman had completely taken her by surprise. She hoped that the surprise hadn't shown on her face. A lead weight settled in her stomach at the thought of him with this brash and arrogant creature.

Marcia fought to overcome how dispirited she felt, knowing Eamon was with the leggy blonde. She would never have put the two of them together. Thoroughly disillusioned and feeling irrationally emotional, she decided to get drunk for the first time in her life. She plucked a couple of glasses of champagne from one of the waiters who was circulating in the crowd and swiftly knocked back both drinks. She moved onto the packed dance floor and began to sway. Suddenly there was a hand on her shoulder and she whirled round to see that Mario had joined her. Marcia could smell the alcohol on his breath as he pulled her in close. She leaned her upper body backwards trying to escape his tight grip. Her struggle to get away only seemed to encourage him – he seemed even more turned on. Marcia was raging. She couldn't believe the little idiot thought she'd be interested in him.

"You're the last person I expected to be here," she fumed.

"Why wouldn't I be?" he purred in her ear. "Joey B has been a family friend for years." He lowered his hand and gripped her right buttock, grinding himself into her.

"You haven't really got a boyfriend, have you?" he breathed, "because if you had he would be here." Marcia gagged as the alcoholic fumes hit her. She wanted nothing more than to knee him in the crotch but instead, she dug her nails from her freed hand into his wrist, and putting her mouth close to his ear warned him in no uncertain terms to let her go. In a heartbeat, everything changed. Mario squealed in pain before a huge hand gripped his shoulder from behind. In the same moment, the tempo of the music changed and the sensual, soulful voice of Lionel Ritchie reverberated across the marquee. "You are my destiny." Mario looked up at the big Irishman and conceded defeat. He skulked off, holding his wrist.

"It seems like I'm just in time, my little mystic," Eamon put his arm gently around Marcia's waist, "May I have this dance?" he whispered.

Marcia wanted nothing more than to dissolve into Eamon's toned frame but instead, she stiffened and replied, "I don't think so Eamon, I've had very bad experiences on the dance floor."

Eamon chuckled softly as she tried weakly to move away from him, but his hold tightened.

"To be sure, I thought that ye would be thankful that I acted as your knight in shining armour," he smiled, nuzzling into her neck.

She could offer up no resistance, her physical self had taken over completely. The two moved rhythmically to the music, Eamon's powerful arms were up her back, his fingers playing the skin on the back of her neck. He raised his head and looked down directly into her eyes. "How is the Texan?" He smiled sarcastically.

Marcia was pulled up short – her eyes flashed.

"You dare to question me about my friend when YOU are here with that unpleasant blonde," she said, indignantly.

Eamon laughed, "Oh indeed, and to be fair, it was pure stupidity on my part to have brought her." Looking into her eyes, he reassured Marcia, "She is nothing to me but there are times when a man needs company."

Marcia looked up into his handsome face and knew he was being sincere. His words had softened her.

"The Texan," Marcia said, "Is just a friend, nothing else."

She blushed, knowing at that moment she wanted nothing more than to make it clear to him that she had no romantic attachment to Brandon.

He pressed his lips together and nodded. Eamon's fingers moved down her jawline and cupped her chin. Smiling, he said, "That's grand, now we've got that out of the way." He brought her mouth to his.

Marcia responded urgently. She felt electrified – her hands were inside his jacket exploring the warm maleness of him. The combination of the champagne, music and her longing for him made for a heady mix.

From out of nowhere and without warning, a sharp pain shot through Marcia as her head was knocked back. She was thrown like a rag doll, and losing her balance, she struck the side of her temple on the hard floor. The world swam away, her hearing faded as the commotion around her became more distant. Marcia fell into unconsciousness.

Smart's security company had a reputation for stopping any trouble if anything kicked off, which was the reason Johnny's protection business was in high demand. Johnny Smart gave his security men the nod as he stood on the sidelines, avidly watching the play unfold between the big Irishman and the redheaded psychic on the dance floor. Johnny and his men went into action, removing the screeching blonde assailant.

. . . .

It had all happened in an instant. Eamon scooped Marcia up from the floor in one powerful movement. He held her limp body protectively against his and made his exit. Drawing level with Johnny Smart on his way out Eamon growled, "Keep that bitch well away from me." With a supportive arm around a dazed Marcia, he helped her into the passenger seat of his car.

Eamon drove straight to the local hospital. He insisted upon Marcia being checked over even though she was now lucid and insisting she wanted to go home. He felt guilty, knowing that he'd been the reason why Vonja attacked her, and he waited on tenterhooks while the nurse took her through for triage. After Marcia had been checked over and been given the all-clear, Eamon drove her home. Not only was he concerned for her welfare but he also offered to replace her dress, which had been torn when she was attacked. Marcia insisted that he wasn't to blame and that she hadn't helped matters herself. She continued to reassure Eamon that she would be fine and not to worry about her torn dress.

"The course of events was entirely my fault," he said, broaching no argument. Eamon insisted on escorting her into the villa. He had noticed that the place had all the lights on and wondered why.

"Is Suzette at home?" he asked.

"I don't think so, Eamon," she replied softly.

At that moment he glimpsed her vulnerability and realised that whatever she was not telling him had to do with her loyalty towards Suzette. His heart lurched. Strong though she was, there was no way he was going to leave her alone until he was certain she was quite safe.

"In that case, I'll see ye inside," Eamon insisted, guiding her with his hand on the small of her back. Marcia would never have admitted it but the comfort that hand gave her was overwhelming. After the evening's earlier escapade, Eamon's reassuring presence filled her with gratitude.

"Do you mind waiting while I quickly shower and change? There is wine if you wish to pour yourself a drink," Marcia invited.

Eamon told her to go ahead. Pouring himself a small glass, he watched Marcia disappear off to the right. She was feeling frail and he guessed she was in some physical pain, yet she'd shown him what a tough cookie she was, shaking off the encounter and insisting she was fine. Eamon could hear the shower running and without hesitation knocked back the glass of wine, and with silent footsteps, he crossed the few feet to the door Marcia had gone through earlier. Entering her bedroom he knew that what he was about to do would be either the best decision of his life or the worst. The door to the en suite was open and through the misted glass Marcia was enjoying the healing power of the water. Time stood still as Eamon slowly undressed. It was almost a ritual, removing his jacket, trousers and shirt, he laid them across a nearby chair. Removing his underwear, he clasped his turgid member to ease the discomfort. He took two steps forward and from that angle, he could make out Marcia's silhouette more clearly. A sweet clean fragrance was suspended in the steam. She had her back to him, face uplifted to the spray. A few more silent steps and he slid the shower door open slightly. His heart was thumping uncontrollably in his chest – it was a sight he would never forget for the rest of his life.

Eyes closed, Marcia had no idea he was standing there. Eamon stood transfixed. Marcia's hair fell in wet tendrils with water cascading over her shoulders, running in rivulets over her pert buttocks and trickling down through that dark space between her thighs. Eamon was as hard as he had ever been and there was no going back now. He reached out and touched her tenderly. He knew that the worst-case scenario would be if he alarmed her, but he was certain he'd read all her signals correctly. As if expecting it, Marcia turned at his touch, her eyes sweeping over him. His magnificence took her breath away. She just managed to breathe his name before he crushed her to him. They embraced, the water crashing down on them.

He lifted her easily and she wrapped her legs around him, his hardness against her hip bone.

Light as a feather, she rained kisses on his ear, neck and throat as he carried her ceremoniously onto the bed, the clean, sweet smell of her driving him crazy. Crumpling in a wet heap, Eamon paid service to her, starting at the hollow at the base of her throat. He suckled her nipple, teasing her with teeth and tongue. She groaned and squirmed beneath him and he could hold back no longer. Marcia threw her head back in ecstasy as she took the length of him inside of her.

Eamon gazed down at the woman who had plagued his thoughts every night for months and his desire heightened with each thrust as Marcia's rapture reflected his own. He put his hand down between them and felt their combined wetness. Marcia moaned with pleasure. He wanted to make it last if he could. He knew her urgency was in part due to her abstention and had promised himself he would make their first time together most memorable. He hadn't bargained on the way their lovemaking was making him feel though. It was taking all his control not to succumb to the intense emotions aroused in him.

Marcia inhaled the male scent of him, every nerve ending wired and responsive to the man on top of her. She raised her head, hungry for his mouth and kissed him deeply, her tongue pushing to the back of his throat. It tipped Eamon over the edge. As one, the powerful energy of their simultaneous climax brought them both to sexual heights that they had never experienced before. Afterwards, Eamon rolled languidly off Marcia, their steaming bodies parting reluctantly.

"Jesus, woman," Eamon gasped, propping himself up on one elbow and looking down into Marcia's contented face.

Marcia shyly pulled the coverlet up over her bare breasts. Eamon smiled seductively and put his hand tenderly against her face.

"I am going to see a lot more of ye, my little mystic, before this night is out," Eamon breathed huskily.

Her legs parted voluntarily as his hand moved downwards under the flimsy sheet. They took each other in their mouths until both were satiated. Fulfilled and entwined in each other's arms, Eamon felt in a deep state of contentment. He gathered her small, perfect form to him and knew at that moment he would never let her go. With a deep pang of sorrow, he announced softly that he would have to leave first thing in the morning on a business trip, and he would be away for two weeks, but he reassured Marcia he'd keep in regular contact.

. . . .

Marcia could not hide the disappointment in her eyes. She couldn't believe she had only just found refuge in Eamon's arms and he would be gone from her so suddenly. She was missing him already.

Tenderly he lay his cheek next to hers and whispered, "Upon my return, I will make plans for our future. I don't intend losing ye, my little mystic."

It was little consolation, but Marcia knew that the promise was what she needed to hear. He was dehydrated and rose to get a glass of water, which was on the chest of drawers. Marcia felt his annoyance at having to leave their warm bed. She feigned sleep as he crept from the bed and came round to her side. She opened one eye just a slit, enough to observe his physique in silhouette. He was an incredibly impressive man – a lean, toned torso, broad muscular back tapering to hardened buttocks. His

236

lower legs were in shadow but his thighs and resting sex were clearly outlined. Her breath caught in her throat, responding to the sight. As if he had read her thoughts, he replaced the glass and turned to face her. In the semi-darkness, she very slowly closed her half-open eye.

"I know ye are not asleep, Marcia," he murmured.

He moved swiftly and slid into bed behind her. Marcia's arousal was at fever pitch. One powerful arm encircled her and she could feel his heat and desire down the full length of her. She moved ever so slightly backwards and tilted her lower half just enough to bring herself correctly angled to him. Marcia thought she might die of the wanting. He was supremely hard and she was very wet. He nuzzled her below her ear, his free hand gripping her hair and pulling her head gently but firmly backwards.

"Is this what ye want, Marcia?" His breath came in great catches as he fought to pace himself. Eamon's other hand moved down over her thigh and slipped from behind between her legs. With his fingers, he gently opened her and inserted himself. His hardness filled her, her pulse was drumming in her ears, her breath came in short gasps and quiet moans. She felt the silkiness of their conjoined moistness between her thighs and gave her whole being up to him. Eamon moved deliberately slowly, the whole length of him driving her to the edge of desire. Their bodies were mercurial, flowing away from and then rejoining each other in an exquisite rhythm.

Soft as velvet, his hand spread over her lower stomach, he stretched his middle finger forward and gently worked away in unison with their every movement. An electric current surged through Marcia, nerve endings responding accordingly. The ebb and flow of pulsations rippled through her body, her legs deadened and Eamon, hand entwined in her hair still, shuddered violently as he climaxed with her.

....

Two men passed through the Spanish border control at the airport. They had arrived on the afternoon flight and walked towards the car hire booth in the airport. The vehicle was booked for two days, but if all went according to plan, they would be returning to Scotland in twenty-four hours. They were an ominous presence, reminiscent of the notorious, east London Kray twins. The brothers' background was similar, being sired and raised by the powerful gang leader Alastair MacCallum, who was known throughout as Mac. His formative years and his old stomping ground had been Glasgow's Gorbals on the south bank of the River Clyde. Now the boys' fathers' realm was situated in Edinburgh although it extended far beyond. Mac had given his two sons an assignment, and upon completion, it would be retribution for the unsightly scar that ran from his cheekbone to the top of his upper lip, inflicted many years ago by Jimmy Grant. This was a golden opportunity brought about by a phone call to an old contact who Mac discovered to his delight also had an axe to grind with Jimmy Grant. When Denny Wakely told Mac that Jimmy Grant had been sniffing around his twenty-two-year-old daughter, wining and dining her, it was music to his ears. Denny learnt through his wife, as the girl had confided in her mother, that Jimmy Grant had got her into bed and then ditched her. Denny had spat venom and he vowed he would have Grant's blood. Now Mac had an ally in Denny Wakely, who resided a short distance from Jimmy Grant. Mac discovered that his estranged firstborn son had married Jimmy Grant's daughter, who was pregnant, but Mac wasn't going to swallow the pill of sharing his grandchild with that piece of shit.

Everything was in place. Denny and Alby Wakely had been associates of Jimmy Grant for years, and one thing the brothers knew was that Jimmy loved a good deal and beautiful boats. The plan was to take Jimmy out to Denny's yacht, which they knew he would be eager to buy. Mac's boys would be on the boat on the pretext they were deckhands, on the understanding that the lads couldn't open their mouths, as their Scots accent would be a giveaway. Speed was of the essence if they were to carry out the plan successfully. Denny knew Jimmy well enough to know he would jump at the chance of buying the yacht at a ridiculously low price. To make it believable, Denny had put it to Jimmy that he wanted a quick sale due to a big gambling debt that was being called in. Denny's brother Alby, who knew the score with Jimmy Grant and his niece Caroline, was eager to jump on the bandwagon and assist in the removal of the man. Alby had no difficulty in recognising Mac's sons by his description, and his role was to take them in the speedboat from Murcia and meet the yacht at anchor somewhere quiet between Malaga and Almeria, after which he would pick up Jimmy and take him to the rendezvous. Denny and Alby Wakely were expert seamen and had the yacht positioned to their best advantage, in deep waters.

Overcome by greed, Jimmy's smug smile reflected the fact he thought this deal would be like taking candy from a baby. Barely glancing at the two "deckhands" working on the rigging as he boarded, he was oblivious to the danger he was in, even when Denny had introduced him to the two men. They nodded in his direction, without speaking. Jimmy was anxious to get on with the deal before Denny changed his mind over the stupidly low price. Glancing over the yacht's sleek lines and elegant woodwork, Jimmy didn't even offer a lower bid. "Let's shake on it," he announced, gloating over his bargain, and then gleefully stated, "Let's christen my yacht boys."

Jimmy jauntily walked the length of the boat, heading towards the well-stocked bar. Mac's son, who had been given the weapon by Denny, raised the firearm and put a bullet through the back of Jimmy Grant's head. Moving quickly, the four helped tie him up, attached weights to the body and heaved him into the murky Mediterranean depths. Mac's son told Denny that their father would soon be in touch as they left with Alby in the speedboat. The plan had been executed without a glitch.

....

Eamon and Marcia could barely disentangle themselves from each other. Marcia was on the threshold of tears but steadfastly held them back. She didn't want to make Eamon feel guiltier than he already did about leaving her. She held on to the feeling of his final embrace. He had told her to ensure the gates were locked and warned her not to swim naked at night by herself, until his return.

Marcia let the tears fall as the engine on his powerful Maserati started up and roared away. She was thankful that Suzette had returned to the villa in such a rush to change and prepare herself to get to the beauty salon that she didn't question Marcia about last night's events. She couldn't have faced the barrage of questions that would have ensued.

Marcia hadn't booked any clients in for that day, and she was grateful for the free time she had, as her mind was filled with the events of the hours she had spent in the arms of Eamon O'Donally. She could barely concentrate, her head was sore from Vonja's hair pulling and a lot else was tender from Eamon's administrations. She smiled seductively to herself, cocooned in the bliss of their lovemaking.

It took a supreme effort for Marcia to throw herself into her routine, but she swam and then completed her yoga. She needed to clear her thoughts if she possibly could, to make sense of the whirlwind her life had just become, at the centre of which was Mr Eamon O'Donally. She didn't quite know how she would survive without him for a whole two weeks.

Moving into the shade out of the rising heat, Marcia pondered on their pillow talk in the early hours. She had been hesitant at first to reveal details of her son, knowing instinctively that Reuben's betrayal wouldn't be tolerated in Eamon's world. Marcia quickly learnt that Eamon wasn't the type of man who would leave any stone unturned, as he cajoled and probed until it left her no option but to tell him the full story. She hadn't mentioned anything about Suzette's role in forcing Marcia to leave the UK, only mentioning the emotional blackmail by Max Greenaway. Marcia didn't want to lie or withhold anything but she felt that she couldn't betray Suzette. She went on to tell him how Jimmy had propositioned her and how she had needed to lie to him about an ongoing personal medical condition to try to keep him at bay. At this news, she had felt Eamon physically tense and she thought she may have said too much, but after a moment, he had relaxed again and gently kissed her. Eamon didn't reveal much in return. She understood he was a man of few words but he gave her a few insights into his brother Patrick in County Armagh. He promised her he would take her there one day.

Going over their conversation in her head, she realised Eamon hadn't divulged anything about himself, but when he spoke of his concern for his younger brother Patrick, it confirmed to Marcia that beneath his tough exterior, Eamon was a solicitous man.

Marcia smiled to herself as she remembered Eamon calling her an undine – a water spirit – with her preference for swimming naked, and he said that upon his return he would take great pleasure in watching her. Marcia knew she was head over heels in love with him. She had tried to deny it right up until he came to her in the shower, her subconscious paving the way. She had no idea what his business deal entailed and preferred not to dwell on it. She hadn't sensed any undue concern for his safety, but she felt that he was walking into a form of entrapment and felt compelled to tell him not to take people who he didn't know personally on face value. His fleeting look of concern vanished as he'd nodded.

His parting words to her had been, "I'm coming back to ye. We've got a lot of living to get through together my little mystic."

. . . .

Joyce had returned home alone from the party. As always, Joey B and Mel had excelled themselves. Their daughter's birthday party had been a fabulous affair. Even with Jimmy hitting on one of the women, Joyce hadn't allowed it to dampen her spirits. She and Cindy had danced the night away and although she'd noticed earlier that night Jimmy was preoccupied, it hadn't bothered her. Joyce was now past caring what he was up to, there had been so many nights in the past, crying herself to sleep over the smell of perfume or lipstick imprints on his shirt when he had returned in the early hours. When she had discovered Eve's missing diamond stud in the back of Jimmy's car, she didn't have to guess what the pair had been up to on the backseat. That incident, along with Jimmy dictating that she was not to visit their daughter Sara and her future grandchild, had been the final straw. Jimmy had betrayed her and Eamon, his trusted right-hand man, by having an affair with Eve along with numerous other women. Joyce now saw him for what he truly was – a tosser, a loser – she knew Jimmy only looked out for himself and he was nobody's friend.

Jimmy had acquired a vast fortune through crime and she had stood by him, putting up with his controlling ways. She remembered Marcia's reading of her tarot cards. She prayed silently as she lay down to sleep. All she wanted was to be left in peace so that she could enjoy the rest of her life.

Joyce woke up late, which was unlike her, and glancing at the clock, she noticed it was 10:25. She walked out onto the terrace and peered over the side noticing that Jimmy's car wasn't there. The thought crossed her mind that he was in another woman's bed. Around midday, she phoned Cindy and arranged to meet her for lunch at 3 pm at the marina. At the restaurant, Joyce told Cindy that Jimmy was on the missing list.

Joyce laughed at what her friend said. "Good, perhaps the bastard's had an accident. But thinking about it, the police surely would have got in touch if that were the case. Judging by his behaviour at the party last night he is probably tucked up with some bird somewhere," said Joyce, dismissively.

"Don't worry, he will turn up like the proverbial," Cindy advised, but deep inside, she hoped that someone had paid the prick back.

Joyce, unconcerned about Jimmy's whereabouts had left phoning his number until 8 pm that evening, but it seemed to be switched off. She had the home phone number for Eamon, which rang and then went to voicemail. She opened a bottle of wine and an hour later rang Greg, dutifully playing the worried wife. With Greg not answering either she put her feet up and poured herself another glass of wine.

. . . .

Greg and Suzette had been at the salon all day and, that evening, after they'd both taken a shower, Suzette crept up on her man, put her arms around his neck, and whispered to him, "Come to bed and I will show you my appreciation for all your hard work." They had been in bed for over an hour when Greg's phone rang. Suzette nuzzled into him telling him to leave it. Engaged in their lovemaking, Greg was reluctant to answer the phone himself but he thought he recognised a familiar voice on the voicemail. Half an hour later, dragging himself away from Suzette's embrace, he played back the message. He could count on one hand the number of times that Joyce had ever rung him, and knowing that something must be wrong he returned her call. Joyce told him that Jimmy hadn't been home all night and his mobile phone was switched off. She asked Greg if he had any idea of his whereabouts. Greg knew that Jimmy was a prolific womaniser but reassured Joyce that he was bound to turn up soon.

"Jimmy's not come home and Joyce seems concerned. She told me his phone is turned off, which is unlike him," Greg told Suzette.

. . . .

Knowing how close Greg and Jimmy were, Suzette kept her own counsel. She was aware of how badly Jimmy treated Joyce and presumed, like everyone else, that he was off getting his leg over elsewhere, as per usual. Thinking about women on their own, Suzette realised with a jolt that she had been neglecting Marcia and had left her on her own at the villa. When she had last spoken to her, Marcia had assured her that she had a book to read and was fine. Suzette decided that Marcia would probably be glad of some company and asked Greg if he'd mind her joining them as they were going out for a meal the following evening.

"Ring her in the morning and don't take no for an answer. Tell her I will pick her up on the way," Greg replied.

. . . .

Suzette called early the next morning, telling Marcia she would be going straight to the salon, but she invited her out with them that evening. Marcia had tried to refuse, but Suzette wouldn't hear of it. She said they would pick her up at 7 pm. They spoke briefly about Joyce's late phone call to Greg. Marcia felt an ominous sensation flow through her at this news but said nothing to Suzette. She said she would contact Joyce to see what was going on. Joyce answered after two rings. She told Marcia that Jimmy still hadn't returned home. Marcia was surprised by Joyce's unconcerned voice, even though Marcia knew Joyce had had more than enough of him. Marcia told Joyce if she heard any news to contact her. Her thoughts turned to the last time she had warned Jimmy about the circle of deception around him and the danger she felt he was in. Having no time to think about it further, she put it to one side and prepared herself for the three tarot readings that were booked in later.

As the last client left, Marcia locked the gates, waving goodbye as the woman drove off. Even though it was daytime, she wasn't going to take any chances after Jimmy's unexpected visit. Marcia had been on a euphoric high since her night with Eamon, now with time to herself, she was going to endeavour to relax in the shade. After changing into a bikini, she picked up the book she had tried to read last night, but after going over and over the same page, with nothing sinking in, she had given up and let her thoughts wander to where they wanted to go.

Her thoughts of Eamon were all-encompassing. She had barely eaten since he'd been gone, and every minute had seemed like an hour. She knew her appetite had diminished but she forced herself to make a small salad, knowing that in her constant state of elation she would be burning the calories at twice the rate she could eat them. The sky seemed brighter, the flowers more vibrant, even the very air she breathed seemed sweeter. It was akin to walking on air. She couldn't remember ever feeling as she did now. If she closed her eyes, she could feel his soft kisses, his fingertips making her skin quiver, the all-embracing feeling of safety in his powerful arms. He had been such an amazingly considerate lover. She knew he was undoubtedly very experienced, whereas she had lived a sheltered life and the only man she'd ever slept with had been her husband. But Eamon had awoken in her a latent, voracious sexual appetite that she didn't know existed. Time and again, throughout that night with him he had continued to pleasure her. He'd taken her to unparalleled sexual heights and she had reciprocated in kind. It wasn't just the sex that had gratified her – it was everything about him, the soft way he spoke her name with his lilting Irish brogue and his dark chocolate colour eyes that mirrored her own and seemed to see into her very soul. Marcia was brought back to the moment by the sound of her phone ringing. It was Cindy to say she would take her tomorrow at 11 am to see the woman who bred the dogs. Marcia asked her if there was any news from Joyce about Jimmy.

"No," perhaps he has pissed off with a bird and at least Joyce will be free to live her life." Cindy retorted.

Marcia could understand Cindy's dislike of Jimmy as she and Joyce were such close friends, and Cindy knew how he had always disrespected her. Marcia thanked her for contacting the dog breeder and said she would see her in the morning. Marcia didn't feel Jimmy was with a woman. She pondered on Joyce and Jimmy's previous tarot readings. She had an overwhelming feeling that Jimmy wouldn't be returning to Joyce. Marcia switched off any dark thoughts in her mind about Jimmy Grant. She wasn't going to allow him to infiltrate. She finally relaxed, taking in the warm sun rays and drifted off to sleep.

Marcia awoke and checked the time on her mobile phone. She had drifted off for an hour. It was unusual for her to feel tired during the day but with the lack of sleep when Eamon stayed over coupled with her inability to sleep the night before thinking of him she now felt at least a little rested.

. . . .

Suzette rang the intercom informing Marcia of their arrival. Unlocking the gates with her key, Greg drove through as Marcia came down the steps. Suzette hadn't seen her friend since Joey B's party and was taken aback by the changes in Marcia, who was wearing a sky blue linen dress with colour coordinated shoes – she looked radiant. Suzette knew it wasn't the golden tan that gave Marcia her glow. She smiled knowingly, catching Marcia's eye as Greg opened the door. The conversation between the two of them centred on the salon and Suzette told Marcia how she had chosen, out of all the applicants, two hair technicians who were also beauty therapists, both were gay, good-looking men whose expertise and personality had won her over. She added she was prepared to let Cindy retrain as both men said they were more than happy to comply. Greg took them to a quiet out of the way restaurant that he knew no one in their circle used. He wined and dined the two women and Suzette made plans for lunch and a girlie catch-up with Marcia the next day as soon as Marcia returned from her visit to the dog breeder. Dropping her off, Suzette could barely contain her excitement over what might be revealed the next day. She watched Marcia lightly ascend the steps, illuminated by the security lights that Suzette had insisted Greg install. Suzette was no stranger to the feeling of being in love and if she wasn't very much mistaken, Marcia had fallen for someone hook line and sinker.

Miami

Eamon's flight had arrived at Miami International airport right on schedule. Taking his case from the baggage carousel, he moved with purposeful strides towards the exit doors. The cacophony of noise from the traffic-filled street jarred his senses. He flagged down a yellow cab, which swerved in beside him. The cabbie took care of his case and Eamon settled in the back seat. Eamon had used the Oriental Hotel on the waterfront many times in the past. It wasn't only accessible for his assignment, but he favoured the skyline suite, which gave stunning views that traced the outline of Biscayne Bay. He'd done a great deal of thinking on the flight over and decided that this was going to be the last time he was going to work with Jimmy. Eamon knew that it wouldn't be easy; no one left Jimmy Grant without a death threat hanging over their head. He wasn't afraid for himself, but now he had Marcia to consider. His soul searching had led him to the conclusion that the time had come to get his house in order. Marcia had given him many a sleepless night over the past months, the culmination of which had ended in their momentous night together. Eamon was a driven man, hungry for success and he'd always put business before pleasure, but now he had a higher goal. His voracity for Marcia surpassed any monetary value. He replayed Marcia's unquenched desire for him. "Jesus!" he muttered to himself. If it weren't for the fact that he would arouse Jimmy's suspicions, there would be no way he would be spending a fortnight in Miami, away from Marcia. And if Jimmy knew he had slept with Marcia, he would find out that she had deliberately lied to him about having a medical condition. Eamon wasn't intimidated by Jimmy Grant, but he needed to protect Marcia at all costs. His mind turned to the task at hand. Jimmy had set the wheels in motion with the Italians in Miami. The vast quantity of this shipment would see Eamon financially set up. Jimmy had told him that the street value was £150 million. He had to finalise the deal with Carlo Gabrette after he looked at a sample to ensure it was pure cocaine.

The container ship had brought in the narcotics via Mexico to the Florida Keys, and it was now safely stored in a warehouse awaiting Eamon's go-ahead before being shipped to the UK. Jimmy and Eamon had dealt with the Miami organisation many times over the years and each time the pay-out had grown bigger. Eamon had the greatest respect for the old Italian, Alphonso Gabrette who had become a father figure to him over time. Jimmy's original introduction to Alphonso had come via a guy named Randy, who Jimmy trusted. Contact with Alphonso had expanded their network.

Eamon undid his shirt buttons, got a bottle of water from the minibar and picked up his phone to call his contact and let him know that he would be with him in two hours. It gave him time to shower and change into something lighter. His hire car was ready and waiting, having been booked in advance.

Eamon stepped under the refreshing, cool jets of water, unconsciously raising his face. His psyche responded to the trigger. Deep inside a primaeval tension gripped him. The fine hairs on his limbs raised themselves and his testicles tightened. He was primed for sex and in response, his maleness rose huge and ready. Thoughts of Marcia flooded his being. The scent of her body, her breasts, cherry ripe nipples erect, the soft, secret place between her legs, her limbs toned and pliant. His heartbeat was frantically hammering in his chest, his breath got heavier … quicker. The water rippled down his muscular torso, every drop catching for a nanosecond in the dark hairs that adorned the various parts of his body. It continued its way, stirring where it touched, like waves lapping the sand. Eamon ran his hand down the smooth plane of his stomach and reverently enclosed his erectness in his palm. The film running inside his head played out his night with Marcia, freeze-framing the scenes over and over. He pleasured himself as slowly and as deliberately as his desire would allow. Legs planted slightly apart, buttocks taught, one arm outstretched … hand flat against the tiles, the other stroking as she had stroked. Eamon convulsed himself to orgasm.

It had exhausted him. He was spent from his ardency, weak limbed now that his pent-up urgency for her had been released. He longed to hear her voice. He checked the time, knowing that Spain was six hours ahead of Miami. Eamon sank into the armchair and stretching his long legs out, he rested them on the coffee table. Toying with the thought of ringing Marcia, he didn't know if he could handle hearing her voice and not be able to hold her in his arms. Sinking back in the chair, he sighed wistfully. Replacing the mobile phone on the table, he decided for the moment not to contact her. He couldn't afford any distractions until he got this meeting out of the way.

As the sky darkened into evening, Eamon set off. He cruised at a steady pace as he drove in his rental car along the coast road heading towards the marina. The rendezvous point was in the heart of downtown Miami. The guy he was meeting was Alphonso Gabrette's son Carlo. Although he'd never dealt with Al's son before, Eamon had been introduced to him in the past when he had been invited to Alphonso's and his wife Marcella's family home. Due to the old Italian's health issues, he had put his only son in charge of the negotiations. Eamon looked up to Al. The man commanded and received respect. Eamon thought about Carlo Gabrette and he hoped that his son was of the same mettle as his father. Under any other circumstances, he wouldn't have dealt with someone he didn't know, but Carlo Gabrette didn't have any history.

Fleetingly, Marcia's warning about not trusting someone at face value came to mind. He hadn't previously given it too much thought when Jimmy informed him he had put Marcia on the payroll, but now his mind was working overtime. It suddenly occurred to Eamon that Jimmy must have used her insight ahead of this deal. Eamon's loathing for the man went up a notch. She had to be worth her salt because Jimmy Grant was no fool. With the hood down on the rented Corvette, the tendrils of the warm breeze from the Atlantic played through his hair. He took in the serene ambience that this waterline always gave him.

As the skyline of downtown Miami came into view, Eamon's business head switched on. Parking up at the front of the hotel, the valet opened the car door and Eamon passed him his key. He strode up the steep flight of steps, through the revolving hotel doors. Stepping into the lobby, he headed towards the lift and pressed the button for the penthouse suite.

Spain

When Cindy pulled up at Marcia's she asked her if she would be alone when they came back from the dog breeder's.

"Yes, although I am meeting Suzette a bit later for lunch. Why?" Marcia asked.

"Could you give Joyce a reading? She's frantic about Jimmy, as he still hasn't returned home. I'd be pleased he's still on the missing list but Joyce is worried, and I told her I would ask you as I was seeing you this morning."

Marcia answered, "Let's get this visit to the dog breeder done as quickly as possible then."

Meeting Jane was an eye-opener. She seemed to have quite a few dogs, all in various stages of training and she explained to Marcia that it wasn't just a question of choosing a dog, but that dog would need to fit into the new owner's lifestyle.

Jane herself preferred to meet with prospective new families in their own homes. Jane had arranged with her to come to the villa at 11 am the following morning with one of the dogs she thought might be suitable. Marcia instantly liked Jane, who seemed genuinely concerned for her dogs' welfare and was no fool. On the drive home, Marcia told

Cindy to bring Joyce straight over as soon as she dropped her off.

Joyce and Cindy pulled into the drive of Suzette's and Marcia's villa. There was still no sign of Jimmy, and Joyce had a terrible feeling that something serious must have happened to him. Although Jimmy had been the cause of her heartache over the years, he had never been gone for this long before and it was worrying her. Somehow, her instincts were telling her that there was no woman involved this time. Cindy had persuaded her to wait until 36 hours had elapsed before ringing Marcia because she didn't share Joyce's concern over him and was convinced he was just out with another woman.

Marcia could see the change in Joyce as the women got out of the car. Gone, the familiar smiling face, she looked drawn and it appeared she had hardly slept. She took the women onto the terrace and went to fetch a bottle of wine. Joyce slumped on a chair at the garden table as Cindy took the wine, passing Joyce a glass. Marcia knew Joyce no longer cared for Jimmy but with him making no contact for so long Joyce was unnerved about his disappearance. Cindy was unusually quiet as Joyce spoke.

Joyce took a large gulp of her wine and said, "I cannot get my head around it, Marcia, I know what I've said about him and I won't back down but this sinking feeling in my gut tells me that something bad has happened to Jimmy. I have tried to ring him but the mobile is dead," she said dejectedly. "I need to know if you can tell me, one way or another what's happened to him."

Marcia rose. "I will get my tarot cards," she said, asking Cindy and Joyce to go into the lounge.

They convened around the wooden table, as Marcia passed Joyce the twenty-two cards that would reveal the mystery of Jimmy's absence. The pregnant silence hung over them as Joyce returned the pack. This was the side to Marcia's work that she had always been uncomfortable with. Joyce wasn't just a client, she was a friend and she'd be expecting answers and Marcia would have to be brutally honest with what was about to be exposed in the reading. She turned the first card over and looked at the Tower worriedly, bracing herself as a feeling of gloom descended upon her. She looked at the second card – the Grim Reaper. It confirmed to her only one outcome. Marcia broke it to Joyce as gently as she could – that Jimmy wouldn't be returning.

Joyce's face drained of colour, tears spilt over as Marcia and Cindy attempted to console her. Cindy retained her silence as Marcia made to pack the cards away, but Joyce composed herself and smiled thinly, "You may as well continue, Marcia, because you have confirmed what I already felt. My gut feeling told me he was dead."

Looking into Joyce's stricken face, Marcia continued, casting her eyes over the full layout. After a few moments, she took Joyce's hand and announced, "There is a bright light at the end of the tunnel though and you are going to have a happy and contented future, Joyce."

"Can you see what happened to Jimmy or am I asking too much?" Joyce queried.

Marcia had seen that Jimmy had been surrounded by deception and was engulfed by deep waters. Leaning back into the chair, Marcia said quietly, "Don't you think that it is better to let sleeping dogs lie, Joyce?"

Joyce sighed then slowly nodded, thanking Marcia. She said she wanted to return home as she felt drained. Cindy said on their way out that she would stay with Joyce to watch over her. Marcia bade them farewell and locked the gates as they drove off.

The impact of Joyce's emotional pain weighed heavily on Marcia. She went through the lounge into the garden to get some air. She suddenly felt very alone and longed to hear Eamon's voice. She prayed he would ring her so she could unburden herself over what she had seen in the cards.

Suzette came through the terrace doors smiling "Well," are you going to tell me WHO has made this impact upon you because that radiance you exude must mean you have met a MAN." She raised an eyebrow, grinning as she walked towards the garden table, and then sat opposite Marcia.

"Suzette so much has occurred since the party."

Marcia briefly told Suzette how Eamon had been at the party with a leggy blonde that had upset her so much that she took to the dance floor on her own only for a drunken Mario to try to take advantage of her. Eamon had intervened and had asked her to dance.

"It was a slow dance and we were both oblivious to anything going on around us. Out of nowhere, my head was ripped back with such force that I was thrown to the floor." Because of what happened at the party.

Suzette's jaw dropped, aghast by the attack Marcia had experienced.

"But Eamon insisted on taking me to the hospital. Thankfully, it wasn't a concussion," Marcia said.

"Good God!" I feel so guilty for sneaking off to Greg's villa and not being there. You shouldn't have had to spend the night on your own after that ordeal."

"I wasn't alone, Suzie. Eamon stayed to ensure I was alright."

As the penny dropped, a smile spread across Suzette's face. "Do you mean ALL night?"

Marcia nodded as Suzette squealed with delight jumping up and hugging her. "You had Eamon O'Donally in your bed for hours?" Suzette exclaimed, laughing.

"Yes, but he left in the morning as he had business to attend to and won't be returning for two weeks."

Suzette clapped her hands, genuinely happy that Eamon managed to break through Marcia's barrier.

"For the man to leave you looking so radiant, he certainly must have given you much pleasure. I told you Eamon had the hots for you," she giggled delightedly. Then she added on a more serious note, "Marcia did you use contraception because…"

Marcia interjected, "I tried for another baby when Reuben was two years old but nothing ever happened. I don't think I'm particularly fertile anyway."

Suzette nodded, and then smiling, said, "I am going inside to get us some wine to celebrate." She put her hand up to stop Marcia's refusal. "You and I both have gorgeous men now what more could a woman need … apart from money?" she added winking.

Marcia smiled at her retreating back as she sashayed in her high heels across the terrace, her glossy black bobbed hair completing the picture of the glamorous woman she was. When she returned with two glasses, Marcia asked her to sit alongside her on the other sun lounger.

"Suzette, I did a card reading for Joyce because she was concerned that Jimmy hasn't been home since the party."

Suzette was not unduly surprised, as Joyce had previously phoned Greg looking for Jimmy. But she was gobsmacked by what Marcia told her next. She revealed to Suzette what she hadn't divulged to Joyce.

"I saw Jimmy engulfed in deep water and he was surrounded by deception," Marcia related. "I could see it as plain as

I can see your face, *and* I sensed that someone from Jimmy's past is connected to the killing."

Suzette poured them each a large glass of wine as Marcia, lowering her voice and leaning in towards Suzette warned, "This has got to stay between us. There is no way we can let on how Jimmy ended up. It's too dangerous Suzette."

"Have you told Eamon?" Suzette asked.

Marcia shook her head. "No, he told me once he has sorted out what he has to do, then he will ring me."

"I will tell Greg," Suzette said, "that there is still no word from Jimmy." Suzette and Marcia suddenly lost their appetite as the seriousness of the situation hit them.

Miami

Eamon walked into the sheer opulence of the penthouse suite and took in the amazing views of the ocean through the floor-to-ceiling windows. Carlo Gabrette's right-hand man frisked Eamon as he stepped into the room. Standing in his socks at 193 centimetres tall and weighing over 200 pounds, he wouldn't be someone who Eamon would want to argue with. He'd met the bodyguard before when he was by Alphonso's side. After spreading his arms and letting him pat him down, he walked over to Carlo, who was standing by the window admiring the view. The men shook hands and Carlo asked him if he'd had a good flight. Carlo was a good-looking lad, Eamon thought, and a dead ringer for his father as a younger man. But from what Eamon sensed from the handshake, the comparison stopped there. Eamon felt, through that fleeting gesture, the lack of his father's strength of character. Alphonso Gabrette was one of the big players in Miami. He was a man who commanded respect and anyone who crossed him would end up as fish food. But to Eamon, the old boy had always been an old-school gentleman. Al and his lovely wife had found themselves spending more time at their palatial condo on the Golden Beach waterfront, allowing Carlo to take up the reins of his father's empire. Al and

Marcella were Sicilian-born. They'd both come to the States with their respective families. After an introduction provided by a friend of Alphonso, they'd formed a successful alliance, opening their first restaurant and working all hours with Al running the show and Marcella working in the kitchen. After a successful third restaurant, Al had started a drug business on the side and had quickly moved upwards in the criminal food chain.

Carlo nodded to Joey who went to a case, brought a package and placed it on the table. Joey slit a small hole for Eamon's inspection. After the test, Eamon nodded. The men shook hands. Eamon knew that Carlo's father was a man of his word and the rest of the consignment would be of equal quality, so he was happy to give the go-ahead, and now the wheels could be set in motion for it to be transported from Miami to Malaga, then onto Southampton docks in the UK. Business complete, Carlo extended an invitation to Eamon. His mother was cooking that evening and she wanted Eamon to join them for dinner at their family home. Eamon thanked him. He had enjoyed his evenings with the Gabrette family before. Alphonso's home was beautiful and Marcella cooked some of the best Italian food Eamon had ever eaten.

They entered the gated estate and stopped outside Alphonso's magnificent multi-million dollar condo. The property had eight sumptuous bedrooms and six grand bathrooms. Owning a property in this vicinity was the mark of a man who had made it big. And Alphonso owned two like it. It never failed to impress Eamon each time he saw it.

Marcella had been cooking in the kitchen when Carlo and Eamon came in. She threw her arms around him, kissing him on both cheeks, and she welcomed him warmly into their home. Alphonso was seated in a large leather recliner chair. He rose as Eamon walked towards him. Grasping Eamon by the shoulders, he insisted that he sit in the chair opposite. Carlo took his leave as he said he had made previous arrangements.

"I hope that your appointment is with a nice Italian girl, Carlo," she beamed, hugging him.

Carlo smiled into his mother's eyes, nodding towards Eamon as he left and Marcella disappeared back into her kitchen. The old man sat back in his chair smiling.

"My Marcella has been cooking all afternoon for you," Alphonso smiled.

"To be sure, I do appreciate it," Eamon said. "There is nothing that competes with her cuisine." Eamon was saddened to see how much the couple had aged since he'd been there two years ago. Al's health had taken an unfortunate turn for the worse since he'd suffered a stroke nine months earlier. Al told him that Marcella was now undergoing treatment for breast cancer.

"We are both taking life easier now," he said, "and the boy has taken over running of the show."

Al asked Eamon about how things were going in Spain – and how Jimmy was and how the business was going. Eamon passed on the news about Eve's death. Alphonso gave him his condolences.

Al's three daughters were to arrive later, and his daughter Estelle was bringing her new husband, Rocco, who was now the family lawyer. Alphonso guarded his three beautiful daughters like a Rottweiler. Each one of them had flirted outrageously with Eamon the last time he'd been there, and he was looking forward to seeing them again that evening. Eamon spent a pleasant hour listening to the old Italian's tales and the rundown on what was going on in Miami with various drug lords. The sound of the girls' laughter as they arrived signalled them to the large open plan kitchen where a feast awaited. The next few hours passed in a haze of laughter and good food. Eamon took his leave around midnight, full to bursting and smiling inwardly at the girls' antics. On Eamon's drive back to the Oriental Hotel, he mused over the evening's events. The old Italian's declining health worried him, but surrounded by his daughters and Marcella, it was apparent that whatever time he had left would certainly be full of warmth and laughter. Eamon hadn't taken to the son-in-law. He might be a high-flying lawyer, but Eamon thought he was a ponce. Though for his host's sake, he'd behaved politely to him over dinner. Marcella had invited him to come back soon to stay, promising to find him a nice Italian wife.

"No man should be on his own, especially someone as handsome as you," she'd smiled playfully at him.

Eamon kicked off his shoes, undressing down to his underwear after hanging his suit and shirt in the wardrobe. He propped himself up on the bed and reached for his phone on the bedside table. He checked the time. He knew it would be nearly 8 am in Spain.

Marcia answered the call after the fourth ring; her soft, sleepy voice melted him as she said, "Hello?"

He wanted nothing more at that moment than to be in her bed, holding her in his arms.

"Did I wake ye, my little mystic?"

Marcia was instantly awake. "I am so pleased you did," she purred back. "I had a disturbed night and didn't get to sleep until late."

"I hope I'm the reason for your disturbance?" he asked, feeling the familiar ache in his groin.

"Yes you are," she answered. "I have missed you so much Eamon." She admitted feeling tearful when he left. "Eamon," she continued, "I need to speak to you about something very important. Joyce is concerned because Jimmy is missing. He hasn't been home or in touch since the night of the party."

That caught Eamon's attention. He had known Jimmy to stay out all night with whatever woman took his fancy but never for that length of time. He had Jimmy's private telephone number, which only he knew and which was only ever used in times of emergency.

"To be sure, Jimmy will turn up, Marcia. I think Joyce is overly worried about him without reason," Eamon reassured her.

Marcia's voice rose an octave. "Please, Eamon, I know Jimmy is dead."

"Dead!" he exclaimed, "How could ye know that?"

Tentatively she told him about the outcome of Joyce's tarot reading. "I have seen his death … he is surrounded by water. Eamon, please, believe me, Jimmy isn't coming back," she implored.

Eamon went quiet then said gently, "I will call ye back shortly, Marcia."

Going to his briefcase, he switched on his other phone and punched in Jimmy's private number. He stood by the window, his mind in turmoil as the burr of the connection broke the silence in the room with its monotonous tone. With the sound still ringing in his ear, he called the hotel reception and asked them to book him the earliest business flight from Miami International to Alicante in Spain.

Eamon told Marcia that with the two-hour stopover and without any delays, he would be back with her around 10.30 pm the following evening.

On the long flight back to Spain, Eamon tried to make sense of the fact that his unanswered phone call to Jimmy could only mean that Marcia was right and that Jimmy was indeed dead. There was no other explanation. The realisation that he was the only one besides Jimmy that knew of the deal he'd just made with Carlo hit him in the solar plexus. This would change his life immeasurably. The natural progression would be for him to step into Jimmy's shoes. He hadn't disbelieved Marcia about what she had foreseen, but with the confirmation of Jimmy's private phone being dead, it was the first time the magnitude of Marcia's psychic abilities had involved him personally. He now knew without the shadow of a doubt that someone had wiped out Jimmy Grant. Eamon smiled sardonically and stretched out in his seat. One thing was certain, Eamon mused, as poetic justice came to mind. The man certainly wouldn't be missed, especially by him. It couldn't have happened to anyone nicer. Eamon smirked to himself as he settled back. Closing his eyes, he fantasised about the warm reception he would receive from Marcia.

Spain

Cindy had stayed over with Joyce throughout all the drama. Jimmy's disappearance had been reported to the police who hadn't seemed particularly interested. They'd made all the right noises about making enquiries, but Cindy felt that they were not that bothered.

The Spanish police knew all about Jimmy, however, they had never managed to pin anything on him to warrant putting him behind bars. There was relief amongst the local establishment that Jimmy had gone off the radar and it was agreed by the comisario that after a short period, they'd close the case and it would be filed away as no more than a missing person investigation.

Later that day, Joyce received a call from Matt to say Sara had given birth to a beautiful girl. She'd had a quick labour, Matt had said, and mother and baby were doing fine. Joyce didn't mention Jimmy being missing and told Matt to make sure Sara gave her a call once she'd had some rest. Joyce was over the moon at the news of her new granddaughter. Jessica Joyce, they'd named her. *How ironic,* Joyce thought, *a death and a new life.* Her world was certainly changing in a big way. It was being turned upside down. Joyce felt that she needed to speak to Eamon. He was someone that she trusted. Her thoughts turned to Marcia's first tarot reading and how since then events had unfolded exactly as she had predicted. She knew that once she'd sorted out Jimmy's legit business she would be free to do whatever she wanted. Jimmy had never divulged to her exactly how many fingers he had in which pies but she wasn't a fool. She'd suspected that most of his deals were dodgy. Everything was discussed behind closed doors, Jimmy and Eamon would spend many hours locked in his office. She hadn't been interested then and she wasn't interested now. It was most probably some double-dealings that had brought about his end, she thought. Cindy broke her reverie, telling her that she was going to get her out of the villa and was taking her to Marcia's for a coffee, as Jane the dog trainer was coming over.

When they got to Marcia and Suzette's villa, the women rendezvoused in the beautiful garden. Jane arrived with a magnificent red-coated Belgian shepherd dog alongside her. She introduced herself and asked the women to ignore the dog, which she commanded to lay at her feet. Marcia was impressed at how quickly the big dog settled. She asked Jane if she would like a cool drink. Jane declined, explaining that she couldn't stay too long. She passed an introductory file outlining everything they would need to know about the nutrition and care of the dog, which she asked them to read through thoroughly after she'd gone. Getting out her mobile phone, she asked them to gather around and watch a video of the dog working. The women watched in awe as the dog was put through his paces, instantly obeying Jane's every command. They were slightly unnerved however to observe the dog lying so quietly a few feet away from them, move with lightning speed to bring down a man wearing a protective sleeve. Jane's authoritative voice rang out.

"Leave!" and the Belgian shepherd released the man. "So this is Roman," Jane grinned. "Come and say hello," she commanded the dog. "Sit and be gentle." The big dog pushed himself up to a sitting position, extended his noble head to greet the women, and as they took it in turns to stroke his head and scratch behind his ears, his tail swept back and forth.

Marcia was amazed at his gentleness.

"I have chosen Roman for you ladies as he would very much enjoy being part of a household. He's a particularly gentle and intuitive dog who can turn it on when necessary. He's not only trained to a high standard in obedience and protection work but he is also one of the few of my dogs that is trained in scent work. Unfortunately, I cannot stay too long today but I would just like to look quickly around the villa and grounds before I go." It fell to Marcia to show Jane and Roman around. She admired the way Jane and the dog seemed to be in complete harmony. She hoped Roman would transfer those affections onto her when he came to live with them.

"Well do you think you could cope with Roman?" Jane asked as the dog jumped up in the back of the Land Rover. "I will make daily visits while he is transitioning but in the meantime please read the manual and realise what a big commitment you'll be taking on."

Marcia thought that she would be fine with a dog like Roman, with Jane's help and advice. Jane seemed solid and dependable and not one to suffer fools gladly. She thanked her for bringing Roman over and waved goodbye, as Jane, blonde ponytail swinging, jumped into the front seat and drove off. Marcia returned to the women and asked them what they thought.

Cindy answered first, "He's adorable Marcia, you'd be mad not to have him."

"I think so too. I'd feel much safer with him around. I hope she thinks we're suitable for him."

Suzette looked up. "Jane has an amazing figure, pity she didn't make more of herself. Is she married, Cindy?"

"Only to her animals, Suzette. She lives and breathes those dogs."

"I would love to get her in my salon and let my new beauty technicians loose on her. The boys would have a field day." Suzette beamed and said, "And speaking of the salon, when we have finished here ladies, I'd like you all to come and see what you think of it, as it's almost completed. And afterwards, I'm treating you all to a meal."

Joyce interrupted, "Can we have less beauty talk and more baby talk now ladies, please?" Marcia observed the change in Joyce. She'd seemed more like her old self. She passed on the good news about her new granddaughter and then touched upon the situation with Jimmy. She told them that Greg had been supportive but that he was at his wit's end wondering where Jimmy was. The women's excitement was infectious and Marcia was glad of the diversions keeping her occupied.

That evening, Marcia had returned to the villa feeling exhausted, although the thrill of knowing Eamon was coming home kept her adrenaline-filled. She locked the gates, thankful that the property was illuminated as she went into the villa. She made her way to her bedroom. Removing her clothes, she wrapped herself in a bathrobe and walked out onto the terrace towards the pool. Like a delicious secret, Marcia knew Eamon's arrival later that evening would mean they would spend the rest of the night in bed. She smiled to herself, getting ready to ease herself into the water. The chill of the evening breeze raised goosebumps on her flesh as she walked down the steps into the water. The sensuous liquid enveloped her as she submerged her nakedness, stimulating her nipples. Swimming slowly, her thoughts turned to Eamon. She couldn't wait to feel his strong, protective arms around her and his lips on hers. Feeling exhilarated, she finished the laps and moved up the steps, shivering in the rising wind. She reached for her bathrobe, quickly tying it around her. Suddenly she was in a vice-like grip and screamed out as strong arms from behind forced her towards the doors. A hand, palm damp with sweat, clamped over her mouth. Terror flooded through her. Struggling manically, she fought against her attacker, but his overpowering physical strength dragged her into the lounge and through the open bedroom door. Heels dug in, Marcia tried to slow down the inevitable. Her fight or flight response was going into overdrive … but it was futile. Deranged with fear, she struggled to lash out with her feet. Tightening his grip still further to keep her under control, her aggressor back kicked the bedroom door shut and forced her onto the bed, her head snapped backwards and a strong hand gripped her throat. Her heartbeat was banging in her ears as the assailant's face loomed above her and the reek of alcohol hit her nostrils.

"You've been asking for this," Mario sneered in her face. "I expect you willingly gave it to the Irishman the other night, didn't you? You whore!"

He bent to kiss her and Marcia, free arms flailing, ripped at his hair, in a desperate attempt to keep him at bay. The backhanded slap that followed rocked Marcia's head sideways. Momentarily stunned, she felt him shift his weight as he straddled her, holding her down with one arm while unzipping his trousers with his free hand. Stars floated before her eyes as he forced his mouth down upon hers again, his acrid breath making her stomach heave. Adrenaline pumping, Marcia's inner savagery rose to the surface and she sank her teeth into his face. Mario fleetingly loosened his hold. Seizing the moment, Marcia, with renewed might brought her knee up and aimed it at his crotch. Face contorted in agony, Mario's eyes widened with shock. Pitching forward, he automatically loosened his grip. With her last remaining reserves of strength, Marcia shoved Mario's fetid, heaving body off her and twisted away. Throwing herself from the bed and quickly scrambling to her feet, she ran into the bathroom locking the door. Abject terror filled her as she thought of what he might do next. She had no defence if he broke the door in. Remembering the small nail scissors in the bathroom cabinet, she shakily opened it. Clenching them in her hand, heart thumping, she put her ear to the door. She listened tensely for any sound of movement from the other side. As the minutes ticked by, she had no idea how long she had stood there for, scissors poised. She didn't know if he was waiting for her in silence or if he had left the villa. She summoned her last vestige of courage, praying to herself as she tentatively opened the door. Taught as a bowstring she crept out, her eyes sweeping the bedroom from left to right. Tiptoeing into the lounge, long shadows greeted her but only of familiar things. It appeared that Mario had fled the villa. On wobbly legs, she hurried across the room and slammed the terrace doors, locking them. She willed herself not to look out through the glass for fear of seeing him lurking there. Locking herself in the bedroom, she pushed the chest of drawers up against the door, returned weakly into the bathroom and vomited into the toilet. Tears streaming down her face, she sat collapsed on the floor, violated, the pain of his physical assault crawling up into her temples, her head throbbing with the impact of the blow. Hauling herself up, she took Suzette's strong painkillers from the cabinet and took several before running the shower. She needed to rid herself of him and to wash away the feeling of his hands on her. She needed to rid herself of the thought of how close she had come to being raped.

Marcia, overcome with exhaustion, removed her robe and crawled into bed. The attack played over and over in her mind and she longed for the oblivion of sleep. Fortunately, within minutes the tablets took effect.

. . . .

Eamon's flight had landed at 10 pm. He came through the airport doors and rang Marcia. He knew that she wouldn't be asleep and that she'd be waiting for his call. He was puzzled when she didn't answer. He didn't leave a message on her voicemail. Eamon got into the taxi. He intended to tell her that he would drop his case off at his place and drive straight to hers. He tried her number once more with no response. He gave the driver Marcia's address. By the time he reached his destination, his agitated mind was battling with the alarming thought that something was wrong. Throwing his baggage over the locked gates, he shimmied over after it. He walked around to the side of the property and a feeling of uneasiness overcame him. There was an eerie silence about the place. He was instantly on high alert. Moving to the terrace doors, he tried them but they were locked. Peering inside and seeing nothing untoward, he strode to her bedroom window. Panic choked him, seeing her sleeping form in the bed and the chest of drawers up against the door. Frantically banging the window until Marcia stirred, Eamon was horrified by her immediate response. He instantly recognised her wide-eyed look of fear and alarm. Marcia's face turned to one of recognition as she scrambled out of bed and Eamon, mind in turmoil, tried to figure out what the hell had happened.

Marcia unlocked the terrace doors. Eamon pushed them open and scooped her up in his arms as she collapsed against him. He held her to him as between broken sobs she relived the event of Mario's assault and attempted rape. Holding her tenderly, Eamon listened in stunned silence, torn between white-hot fury and the overwhelming love he felt for this woman. Her strength of character astonished him as she relayed how she had fought Mario off.

Marcia had stopped crying now but her eyes were swollen and sore and she wouldn't release her hold on him. Very carefully, he unwrapped her and encouraged her to get back into bed. He insisted she had a small glass of brandy for the shock and gratefully she felt the warm glow of it spreading through her. As she lay her head down, Eamon lightly brushed her hair away from her anguished face. The livid red weal on her cheek drove the breath from him. Removing his clothes he climbed in behind her and lay as close to her as he could.

Gathering her to him, he whispered to her, "I'm here Marcia, I'm here. I swear no one will ever hurt ye again."

For the longest time, he waited, until he was certain she was asleep. He then extricated himself gently and got out of bed.

Pulling on his trousers, he walked outside. Moving out of earshot, he fought to control the molten heat of his destructive inner rage that threatened to spew over. He was going to obliterate the low-life who attacked Marcia, whatever it took, and Eamon knew the best man for the job. The man he planned to use came with top credentials.

"Torture," he said out loud to himself, "will take on a brand new meaning, by the time I've finished wit ye. Ye'll be wishing that you'd never been born." Eamon punched in a number and told the voice at the end of the line to meet him at his place at 10.30 the next morning. Seething with anger and out of control, Eamon took himself back inside for a shower. Directing the powerful jets of water on his body, he could see the outline of Marcia's sleeping face through the glass of the shower door and his heart broke for her. Turning off the shower, he took a towel, wrapped it around his lower body and went to get himself a drink. After pouring a small brandy, he walked back out onto the terrace. The nectar took almost instantaneous effect, quietening his rage. Taking in the damp night air and the brightness of the celestial bodies, he looked out to beyond the bay, where dark clouds were forming, threatening an incoming storm. His anger abated and he returned to the bedroom where he slipped into bed next to Marcia. Taking her gently in his arms, he watched the quiet, steady rise and fall of her breathing. This was the woman he loved with such a passion that he was willing to kill for her.

....

Suzette was flabbergasted to find Eamon at the villa when she returned the next morning. Marcia was sitting up in bed with a bruised face and Eamon was administering to her needs. He had made her breakfast as she was draining what looked to be a cup of black coffee. Without any attempt to explain anything, he ordered Suzette to stay with Marcia, as he had business to attend to, but he would be back as soon as possible. Suzette watched, mouth agape as he kissed Marcia gently on the lips and left.

....

Dan Fisher entered Eamon's living room and Eamon proffered him a seat. "This is a matter of the utmost urgency. There's a piece of garbage that I want obliterated. After..." he added, smiling caustically, "he has been treated to some of your specialities."

Dan pursed his lips, nodding.

Eamon continued, "I want to watch this piece of filth being taught his final lesson on this earth and, of course, there will be a five grand bonus on top of your usual fee." He gave Dan Mario's name, description and the father's details and address from the villa rental contract. The two men shook hands and Dan told him he would keep him informed.

Dan was built like a pit-bull terrier, Eamon mused, not only in stature. Tenacious could be his middle name because once Dan got his target in sight, there was no chance of getting away. Eamon was aware that Dan Fisher could be mentally unstable at times, but then again, he concluded, weren't we all. Eamon had no worries that there would be any comebacks. Dan had been used extensively in the past by Jimmy to wipe out adversaries, and he knew him to be trustworthy. Dan was an ex-paratrooper and a former member of the Special Forces and consequently was fearless in any situation. He could dish out the type of "medicine" that would make the bravest of men wish they'd never crossed his path. He was no stranger to maltreatment, having been captured behind enemy lines in Afghanistan and subjected to torture without giving anything away. Back then, his army buddies had surrounded the enemy's place, killed everyone in their sights and succeeded in releasing Dan from his cell. It had taken six months for him to recover from the physical toll but then his commanding officer had broken the news to him: he'd been assessed as suffering from post-traumatic stress disorder and was unfit to continue in the armed forces. Dan had relocated to Spain and went into private work. His reputation as a man who kept his word preceded him and Dan hadn't looked back since.

. . . .

On the night of Joey B's daughter's party, Mario had been rebuffed by Marcia and the big Irishman Eamon O'Donally had given him his marching orders. He'd nursed his pent-up desire for Marcia ever since and when a golden opportunity came his way, via an associate at the Bistro club making enquiries about Suzette Greenaway and her psychic friend Marcia, he jumped at the chance. Passing on the information about them, Mario was asked if he would like to earn a lot of money. The man had a contact in the UK that required the psychic to be taught a lesson. She only needed to be slapped around a bit. Suzette Greenaway was to be left untouched, the man would deal with her himself. He would receive 5,000 euros on completion and he would be able to satisfy his lust and have the opportunity to relocate away from the scene of the crime.

Mario Lopez settled into his window seat ready for the early morning flight to take off for Gatwick. He was smug in the knowledge that he had stolen 20,000 euros from the box under his parents' bed, which along with the payoff, was going to finance his new life in London. He had crept out of the family home without a thought of anything but the bright lights of England's capital city. His father had bailed him out many times before, even paying the Spanish police a bribe to keep him out of jail, and clearing debts with drug dealers for him. But the way Mario looked at it, it was down to his old man's stupidity. He felt safe in the knowledge that his father wouldn't report the theft to the police, as it wasn't the first time he had helped himself. His only regret was that he had failed in his attempt to rape Marcia. He hadn't bargained on the little bitch fighting back so ferociously. He winced inwardly at the memory of the excruciating pain he'd suffered by her powerful knee to his testicles, which had put paid to his erection. He'd fled the villa seething, wishing he had slapped her far more than just the once. He put his hand protectively on his crotch massaging his manhood where Marcia had kneed him.

....

Dan had arrived at the house on the pretext of being Mario's friend, and he was warmly received by his distressed parents. Dan stood listening as Mario's parents poured out their grief over their errant son – the son they'd spent their lives bending over backwards for, to try to keep him out of trouble. Tears streamed down the old boy's face as he related to Dan in broken English that Mario had stolen their life savings and had disappeared. Mario's passport and bags were gone. They didn't know if he had left the country or if they'd ever see him again. They'd seemed relieved to have a sympathetic ear to talk to. Mario's father broke down, telling him of the pain and suffering they'd experienced over the years, and his devoted mother's heart problems, which had been largely brought on by the stress caused by their only child. Dan revealed nothing of what Mario had done. The old couple had already been through enough. Instead, he quietly asked them if they knew of anyone that Mario might have contacted.

"He could be anywhere," his father mumbled dejectedly as the old man walked to the door alongside Dan to show him out. Mario's father took a moment to reflect, "Wait! I remember now. His favourite place to hang out was the Bistro club on the waterfront. I had to pick him up from there a few times after Mario had been taking drugs." From out of his cardigan pocket he pulled a well-fingered photograph and handed it to Dan. "Here," he said, "this might help."

Thanking him, Dan promised to keep in touch if he heard anything about Mario's whereabouts. He decided to head down to the club later to make some enquiries.

. . . .

Concluding his business with Dan, Eamon drove straight over to Joyce's. As he drove, he thought about the impact that this big deal would have on his life if Jimmy didn't return. One hundred and fifty million street value was a stupendous amount. Eamon knew if the deal went wrong he could kiss his life goodbye, as smuggling that vast amount of narcotics carried at least a 30-year tag behind bars. He had many things to deal with and business was the last thing on his mind, but he knew it was imperative that he to speak to Joyce. He recognised the fact that, apart from him and Jimmy, no one else from their camp knew about the big Miami deal, as Jimmy wanted it to be kept secret in case of any leaks. The shipment was coming into the quay in three days and if everything went according to plan, Eamon would be in the driving seat and he would be a great deal richer. Eamon was not one to jump the gun. He knew he would have to bide his time for a while, even though Jimmy had never been gone this long before and he believed Marcia's prediction that he was dead.

Dan Fisher had had a bite to eat and then he took himself off to the Bistro club. He tried the doors and found that they were unlocked. Stepping inside, the dank smell of sweat and beer filled his nostrils. He glanced around to see that the tables were still full of the previous night's dirty glasses and overflowing ashtrays. The door at the back of the dance-floor was slightly ajar and there was a light showing through. Dan moved silently across the floor, stopping outside to listen for movement. As Dan quietly pushed it open, a man who was hunched over a computer, suddenly became alert and jumped up.

"What the fuck! Can't you see we're shut!" he shouted. Suddenly his face changed from anger to worry as his eyes swept over Dan's bulky frame.

Dan smirked. "I need some information about a Spanish guy who frequents your club," Dan said, holding the terrified man in his gaze, Dan gave his name and description. The manager recognised the name.

"He's a bit of a regular here but I can't tell you any-thing else. Perhaps you'd find out more from the guy he's been hanging around with lately."

Dan sucked air through his teeth, "I want a name," he stated coldly. The manager dutifully sang like a canary, telling him how Mario had been spending time with a guy called Giuseppe. Over the past few days, the pair have had their heads together.

"The last name," Dan said exasperated.

"Layou, Giuseppe Layou." Beads of sweat started forming on the manager's forehead and his voice had gone hoarse. He suddenly seemed eager to tell Dan what he wanted to know. "He stays nearby at the lodging house, which a lot of my regulars use," he stammered.

As the manager showed him out, Dan smiled to himself as he heard the bolts sliding into place behind the door.

Dan arrived at the lodging house within fifteen minutes. The old Spanish woman told him that Giuseppe was having his regular siesta and didn't like to be disturbed. Dan passed a 20 euro note and said that he wanted to surprise his friend. Smiling, and taking the proffered money she told Dan the room number on the first floor. Dan walked up the stairs, stopped outside of number 13 and put his ear to the door. One powerful kick and the door had swung open to reveal a slob of a guy, spread-eagled on the bed and still out of it. Dan wedged a chair underneath the door handle and then slowly walked around the bed, glancing down at the mess of the man. He picked up the full jug of water on the bedside cabinet and poured the contents onto his head.

The man, rudely awakened, struggled to work out what was happening. "Who the fuck are you?" Giuseppe gasped, trying to sit up.

Dan grabbed him by the throat, squeezing as he pushed him up against the headboard. Dan, not being one to mess around, took out a taser gun and a reel of tape from his jacket pocket, watching with Arctic cold eyes that held the terrified man transfixed. Sweat was now running into Giuseppe's eyes as Dan started to pump him for information on Mario's whereabouts. Giuseppe knew that he couldn't tell him and it wasn't because he gave a fuck about Mario. It was the guy back in the UK that worried him. Dan yanked him to his feet and told him to strip, not happy with the man's declarations of ignorance.

"OK, so I..." he croaked, throat constricting. "I was with him for a few nights, but listen, mate, I'm not his fucking keeper."

Dan slowly raised the taser gun. "Listen to what I'm going to say and be warned. I'm an impatient man who doesn't like to repeat himself. If you don't tell me what I want to know about Mario Lopez and where he's gone to, I can guarantee that I will be the last person you'll ever be seeing because I'll fry your fucking eyeballs," he growled. The 50,000 volt taser hovered less than an inch in front of Giuseppe's eyes.

"OK," he whimpered, wetness spreading across the front of his trousers. "Take that thing away and I'll tell you everything."

Satisfied, Dan left the lodging house and returned home. Booking his flight and a hotel for that evening, he then called Eamon with the new information. He said, "the bird has flown," and that he was going to London, as he had names and addresses.

. . . .

Eamon parked up in the sumptuous grounds of Jimmy Grant's villa. He had been thrilled by Dan's news and with how quickly things were moving. Joyce was beaming as she welcomed Eamon at the door, kissing him warmly on the cheek and inviting him to join her outside on the terrace. Eamon thought she didn't appear like a woman who was missing her husband. He'd never seen her look so radiant. As if reading his thoughts, Joyce spoke of her joy about her new granddaughter and of her plans to visit them in America. She mentioned the strong possibility that she would move out there to live with them.

Eamon nodded, smiling. Then he broached the subject of Jimmy.

"At first," she said. "I was upset when he hadn't come home, but I don't feel like that now, Eamon," she confided in him. She told him how she'd known about all the women he'd slept with over the years. "But that is all in the past. Please let us talk about the future, Eamon, because I need to discuss Jimmy's legitimate business with you."

"To be sure, Joyce, with the haulage depot and Diego continuing to manage it, I can oversee the company for ye."

Joyce shook her head. "I don't want anything to do with his business. I want you to take it off my hands."

Eamon looked perplexed. Joyce told him about a large amount of money she'd discovered in the safe, and revealed how Jimmy had given her the combination a while back. He said at the time that it was in case anything should ever happen to him. Marcia had warned him about a ring of deception surrounding him and it must have put the wind up him. "Two and a half million euros were sitting in there. I couldn't believe there was so much money in the house!" She chuckled gleefully, placing her hand on his across the garden table. "I am offering the haulage company to you at a low price."

Eamon frowned as she continued. "I have seen the paperwork on the monthly returns, so I know how much it brings in, but if you'd like to take it off of my hands for 20,000 lock stock and barrel, it's yours."

"I can't do that. I would be robbing ye, Joyce," Eamon declared.

She put her hand up to stop him. "Eamon when I sell this place for a couple of million, I will have far more money than I ever will need. You and I haven't had an easy time of it with Jimmy and I know you're loyalty has gone without question, as has mine," she added wistfully. "I trust you Eamon," she told him, "more than any man I know. Shall we shake on it?" she laughed as he shook her proffered hand.

. . . .

Eamon left the villa and got into his car. He looked back at the stunning building, his thoughts drifting back to the time when

Greg had been constructing the place, to Jimmy's specification. So many things had happened since Eamon had met Jimmy all those years ago. Eamon had been the muscle and Jimmy had the money to set the big deals up. Eamon had always conducted Jimmy's deals, but, although he had done well for himself, it had been Jimmy who had raked in the big money. *Now,* Eamon thought, getting into his car, *the wheel has begun to turn full circle.*

Suzette and Marcia were lounging in the shade, deep in conversation about the assault. Suzette was wracked with guilt because she had left Marcia alone that night.

"Please don't blame yourself; it was my fault for swimming alone at night. If I had listened to you and Eamon, I would have been behind locked doors."

"You do realise, Suzette said, "that Eamon will not let him get away with it. Anyone who harms one of their own will be hunted down and punished accordingly and don't think that Eamon would be any different."

A shiver ran the full length of Marcia's back. Eamon hadn't said a great deal since he found her after the attack, but she knew he was only keeping a lid on the fury simmering inside of him.

"He has been so gentle and caring, Suzie, I'd rather not think about what he is capable of. Eamon has promised me I won't be left on my own until Roman arrives and I cannot allow something like this to spoil my life by living in fear of it happening again."

The buzzer from the gates sounded in the lounge. "That will be Eamon," Marcia said.

"I will let him in, then make myself scarce," Suzette announced, "I want to make sure Greg and Eamon will be sleeping here tonight. Suzette rose, then turning to Marcia, she

282

said, "Eamon must know I have a man in my life as he has slept here and I wasn't at home all night."

"Jimmy was the one you were worried about finding out about you and Greg," Marcia replied, "but Eamon has more than enough to contend with to be worried about you two, so hurry and let him in." And, Suzie," Marcia called, "Please ensure you lock the car doors."

. . . .

Eamon lay on Suzette's vacant sun lounger, propped up on one arm facing her, tracing his fingers on her arm with the other. "I have big plans for us, Marcia, and as soon as I get everything sorted…"

Marcia interrupted him, "I'm frightened, Eamon. Not only for me but for you."

He took her hand in his. "There is nothing for ye to be worried about, Marcia. I will protect ye." Leaning across, he kissed her.

"Eamon, I know, you will be in a powerful position, but I can sense there is so much out there that can cause you harm and if you are taken from me…"

"Hush," he said, his fingertips brushing her lips.

She continued, "Eamon, I don't need you to tell me what is going on in your life. She reached across to him. "I can't explain how I know – I just do," she whispered. "My life has been on hold ever since my son … and now I've found you, but I'm so scared that things will go wrong."

"We will become powerful allies, my sweet little mystic." He smiled reassuringly at her. He desperately wanted to make love to her but he knew it was too soon. She was too delicate. To defuse the situation and move it away from danger and sex,

Eamon laughingly said, "Go and get that dog manual ye been telling me about and we'll read it together. Let's see what we need to do to welcome the boy home."

They had been lounging in the shade all afternoon. Their time together had been enlightening. Eamon couldn't remember when he'd ever felt so at one with a woman as he did with Marcia. Her head was bent while she pored over the dog breeder's instruction manual. He had studied every part of her. Her firm, tanned limbs, shapely figure with rounded behind, perfectly formed feet and hands, nails painted in soft pink. He physically ached to kiss the base of her slender throat and take her heart-shaped mouth to his own. She was intelligent, feisty and so natural. And those eyes, as dark and as fathomless as his own. When she glanced up coyly and held his gaze, he felt his insides dissolve. Never had he felt such a yearning to be with someone, breathing the same air and sharing the same space forever. Jesus, he never wanted their time together to end. They talked about everything and nothing as lovers do, revelling in each other's company, until Eamon was interrupted abruptly by his rumbling stomach, making Marcia giggle.

"Now, ye have two options, either I phone to order us some food, or…" he smiled, "ye take a chance on me to rustle up something. I'm not too bad at throwing a few things together," he laughed.

"I know, you made me a mean omelette this morning," Marcia responded. "But let's order in."

Eamon opened the fridge to take them out a bottle of water each, and laughed, shaking his head when he saw what was inside. Eamon quizzically held up an avocado. Marcia laughed, explaining that she was a vegetarian.

"I need meat and ye need a substantial meal inside ye, Marcia. I'll ring Marco who will send me a steak and one of his chef's special fish dishes." Eamon placed an order at his favourite restaurant.

Eamon busied himself while Marcia showered. The sound of the spray, the thought of the water touching every part of her transported him instantly back to their first night together. The phone ringing pierced his thoughts – a welcome distraction. Eamon picked his mobile up and upon hearing Dan's voice, walked into the lounge. Dan told him that he'd arrived in London and was meeting up with a pal. He advised that he would video the event as it happened. Although Eamon was gutted that he wouldn't be there to oversee it personally, he had to accept the situation as it was. Dan told him he'd keep him updated. Eamon pondered Dan's abilities and trustworthiness and decided what an asset he would be to him. Upon completion of the mission, he was going to offer him the position of his right-hand man.

Marcia stepped from the shower glistening, soft unwiped drops on her velvet skin, her hair piled up in a towel. The bruised cheek somehow just added to her strength and beauty. It was all he could do not to step forward and crush her to him, feeling her heat, drowning in her scent. He wanted her so badly he almost wept. Still, he knew he had to go slowly and carefully. She'd had a bad experience and he was unsure how she would react to him. She'd not shied away from him though, seeming to welcome his gentle kisses and the reassurance of his hugs. He held her robe open for her as she moved towards him. "I don't need that Eamon," she smiled up at him. It took a moment for him to register her words.

"Marcia, we don't have to." His response was low and gentle. Her hand slipped into his and she led him to the bed. Sitting down on it, she unzipped his fly. A bolt of pleasure surged through Eamon, charging him like electricity.

He yanked down his trousers and in one fluid motion laid Marcia on her back and kicked them to one side. He covered her petite body with his, taking care to keep his weight on his elbows. Marcia moaned in delight as their bodies made contact. The towel released her damp tresses and Eamon buried his face into their freshness, inhaling deeply. Marcia could feel him, huge between her thighs, and she wriggled in anticipation, slippery with desire for him. They kissed deeply, tongues exploring. Marcia's hands caressed his strong arms, her breathing synchronised with his own. Their pulses began to race, hearts pumping furiously, blood surging to the most delicate of body parts, readying themselves for the act. Finally, he entered her. Marcia was so ready for him she felt she would explode with want. She held his massive solidness to her, wrapping her legs around the back of his thighs. Eamon took her with long deliberate strokes, slowly, even hesitantly at first, but she squirmed beneath him, bringing her legs up and clasping him firmly to her. They swept along on a tide of euphoric pleasure, moulding themselves together, drowning in each other's fulfilment.

Eamon was deliberately making love to her and Marcia was reciprocating in full. Every embrace, movement and touch in complete harmony. Conjoined bodies responding as one, bringing themselves to a fever pit of ecstasy. It was long and sensuous, and heart-stoppingly gratifying. Eamon had never felt such fulfilment. He had delayed his gratification several times throughout their lovemaking through it had taken every fibre of his being to control himself. He had just wanted it to be perfect for Marcia, wanting her to know he could be gentle and considerate as a lover. They didn't need to speak. Their bodies had spoken for them. Locked in each other's arms, suspended in satisfaction, Eamon watched over Marcia as she drifted off.

Marcia was asleep when the call came through from Carlo in Miami. Eamon moved into the lounge, closing the door.

"All has gone according to plan," Carlo Gabrette said cheerily, "It will arrive on Wednesday evening if everything goes to schedule."

It was at that moment that Eamon knew, beyond a shadow of a doubt, that Jimmy was dead. Because with Jimmy laying out such a large amount of money and knowing the massive investment he would have reaped from it, he would have reared his ugly head before now.

Eamon lay next to Marcia as she slumbered, mulling over his next move. He would arrange for the men on the quay to split the cargo between three vessels, which would give them better odds. Once everything was sorted, Eamon decided to book a couple of days away so that Marcia could recuperate.

UK

After Dan had left Mario's place, he'd studied the photograph intently. The image of Mario Lopez was now imprinted on his brain.

Dan had contacted Billy Mackenzie to ask if he was up for a nice little earner. Billy had been at a loose end and was eager to help as they'd worked on a fair few missions together in the past. Afghanistan had nearly seen the end of Dan when he'd been captured but when he'd been set free by his comrades, it had been Billy Mackenzie who had been his solace throughout, and they'd stayed in contact ever since. The two men were like chalk and cheese personality-wise. Dan was sombre, tight-lipped and brooding, whereas Billy was animated, always using a barrage of tongue-in-cheek quips that at times were close to the mark, but his cheeky boyish grin always got him out of trouble. What the two men had in common was the recognition that they were both from the same "tribe."

Billy was living in a rundown house in Dagenham, left to him by an elderly great uncle. Billy had picked Dan up at the airport after Billy told him to stay at his place and cancel the hotel. Billy pulled up in an old Ford Transit van to take Dan back to his place, which was only ten miles away from where

Mario Lopez was lodging. Dan filled Billy in on the way, offering him a large payout once the mission was completed.

"Phew," Billy said, grinning. "You've certainly saved my fucking bacon, Dan. I'm on the bones of my arse, even the mice have moved out," he laughed.

Pulling up at the back of the house Dan suddenly wished he had stayed at the hotel. If the overgrown garden was anything to go by, he didn't have much hope of the gaff being any better on the inside.

Billy pushed the weather-beaten door with his shoulder. "My great uncle was ninety-four when he died and didn't do a thing to the place for the years he lived here, as you can see," he laughed, ramming the door shut. After a few hours catching up, Dan spent the night in a single "put-you-up" bed whose bedding had seen better days.

The following morning, they set off in the pouring rain to an address in Ilford, which was only just over five miles from Billy's house. By the time they turned onto Clements Rd and took a slight right, they had reached their destination. Billy wiped a spot on the misted windscreen and peered through it. They parked up to stake out the house.

"The weather's on our side – slashing it down. Not many people about. Let's hope the ponce ventures out later," Billy stated.

Nearly five hours later, Dan nudged Billy's arm. Mario Lopez came through the door and stood on the top step, pulling the collar up on his leather jacket as he came down the steps. Billy turned the key in the ignition, then jumped out and opened the back door of the car. Like a bolt of lightning, Dan struck, as Mario started to walk in the opposite direction. He grabbed him from behind and with a vice-like grip held him by his neck. With his other hand across Mario's mouth, he lifted him into the back of the van. Mario's eyes flew open in terror before Dan's fist made contact with his face, sending him into oblivion. Slamming the doors shut, Dan jumped into the passenger seat and they sped off. Billy weaved expertly in and out of the traffic.

Pulling around the back of the house, they parked up. Billy and Dan supported Mario on either side, hurrying up the garden path to get out of the torrential rain. Billy kicked the back door open shoving Mario inside.

As Mario's head started to clear, he tried desperately to get to his feet, only for Billy to kick him with such force that he sailed across the kitchen and smashed his head into a cupboard. Billy grabbed the one chair in the room, picked Mario up by his hair and forced him into it. Dan tore a length of carpet tape in readiness. Twisting Mario's arms behind his back, he wrapped it around his wrists and secured his ankles to the legs of the chair. Dan smirked as he took the pliers and taser gun from Billy and placed them on the cupboard.

He passed Billy his phone. "When I say... start recording."

Mario began to plead with the men, asking why they were doing this to him. Dan folded his arms sucking air through his teeth, glaring directly into Mario's petrified eyes.

"There is someone in Spain who is extremely pissed off with you. Not to mention, you scummy bastard, the money you've stolen from your parents."

Mario was squealing. "Please, it's the man in Ilford who wanted the redhead psychic slapped around. I'll give the money back. It's in my room..."

"Give me this man's name," Dan commanded.

"Sure, anything you want to know," he stuttered. "Max Greenaway paid me via a contact in Spain. The psychic, along with his wife double-crossed him, and you know how it is," he forced a grin, "I thought I would have a bit of fun with her…"

"Listen, sleazeball," Dan growled, smiling at Billy and giving him an inconspicuous nod. "You are going to put on a show for a friend of mine, and my colleague here will record it," he spat as Billy came up behind him and put the carpet tape over his mouth.

Mario Lopez's bowels exploded when the first fingernail was ripped out. By the time they employed the taser to cook his testicles, Mario had lost consciousness for the last time. The sickening odour of faeces and burnt flesh filled the room and Billy had captured every second of it on film.

Billy leant forwards and felt for a pulse, "Dead as a fucking dodo," he confirmed.

Dan lit a cigarette and booked the earliest flight back to Spain.

The men patted each other on the back, and Dan gave Billy his fee plus a bit more on top. Billy would sort out the body.

Dan placed a call. "All complete, home tomorrow." Dan made a mental note to see if there were any openers for Billy in Spain.

Spain

Eamon sat in his office, a heavy silence filled the room, as he watched with loathing the piece of scum Mario Lopez being tortured. Once he'd seen it, Eamon passed the phone back to Dan who removed the sim card. Taking it outside, he put it in a small metal bucket then proceeded to pour acid over it. Upon Dan's return, Eamon passed him the Manila envelope, smiling as he leaned back in the leather chair.

"I'm more than satisfied with your work, Dan, even though that piece of shite came out with a load of bollocks about doing a dead man's dirty work. I know for a fact that Max Greenaway topped himself in prison. Anyways, it was an extremely well-executed job, which brings me to what I wanted to talk to you about. I would like ye to work alongside me as my right-hand man."

He sat up then, leaning forward and placing his fore-arms on the desk. "I can promise ye I will be fair. There will never be any double-crossing on my part, plus on top of any earners, ye will have a big bonus."

Dan smiled. "There is only one condition if I am to accept. I want the guy who assisted me in London to come on board too. Billy Mackenzie and I go way back. The man would be an asset to you and it would be doing me a big favour," Dan added.

Eamon put his hand up. "Say no more. If ye say the man is grand, then it's done." And they shook on it.

Eamon had received news that all three vessels had cleared Southampton docks in the UK and he was home and dry. The payment was en route via a fishing boat. The pay-out would be tucked away, safe with a proven, trusted professional investor.

He had booked a two-night break in Marbella. He wanted time to be with Marcia, and two days out of his hectic schedule was all he could spare.

Eamon had discovered that Suzette was seeing Greg Davidson, a man he held in high esteem. He admired the way Greg had turned his life around, owning a large construction business and was as straight as they come. Greg had told him about his relationship with Suzette when he paid Eamon a visit to try to get to the bottom of Jimmy Grant's disappearance.

Eamon knew that Greg and Jimmy had had a strong bond since childhood. Greg Davidson had been brought up by Jimmy's mum in the east end of London. Eamon was guarded, but to his surprise, Greg thanked him for taking over and helping Joyce with Jimmy's business.

"We both know Jimmy isn't going to return, Eamon," he said as the two men sat at the table in Eamon's garden under the shade of a large umbrella.

"I have spoken to Joyce to see if she wanted any assistance with the haulage company and she informed me that Jimmy had put the company in her name for legal reasons and she has sold it to you."

Eamon gave a measured nod. He didn't like discussing his business with anyone, even if he respected the man.

"Eamon, you and I have known one another for a long time and I hope we can be honest with each other. I intend to have Suzette permanently in my life and I know you and her friend Marcia are now an item." He smiled warmly. "Max Greenaway hasn't been in the ground long and we both know that in our world it's frowned upon, to put it lightly, to step into another man's shoes so quickly."

Eamon interjected, "Let's make this clear, Greg. Max Greenaway and Jimmy Grant were cousins, which says it all about bad blood." He waited for Greg's reaction. When he smiled and offered Eamon his hand, he clasped it. Greg rose to his full height.

"I knew what Jimmy was like and we both know there would have been a long list of people wanting to top him, so I offer you my congratulations, Eamon, on stepping up to the position which I always thought should be rightfully yours."

When Jane arrived at Marcia and Suzette's villa with the dog, Eamon and Greg were there to be introduced to the magnificent animal. Eamon had previously told the women that he would be happy to purchase the dog, as it would be protection for Marcia.

Jane put the dog through his paces. Eamon observed in awe as the Belgian shepherd went from being a killing machine to a pussycat each time she changed a command. Jane had Roman sit at Marcia's side while she fired questions at her regarding his health, training, feeding and general husbandry. Jane was more than a little surprised that both Marcia and Eamon had obviously read the instruction manual from cover to cover and answered all her questions unhesitatingly.

"I can see you've done your homework and my boy is going to be in good hands. I know you are planning to take a few days' break, so I'll bring Roman back on your return. I've been impressed with the way you have handled the dog this afternoon and I'm happy he is going to the right home."

As Jane got up to leave, taking hold of the dog's lead, Eamon stepped forward and spoke. "Let me show you out, Jane. I have a matter I'd like to discuss with ye."

Eamon walked her to her Land Rover and watched as the powerful dog jumped inside. "Tell me, Jane," he said, "would ye be having another dog for sale as well trained as Roman?"

Jane laughed, knowingly. "I have two dogs trained to Roman's standard and three not quite at that level yet, plus a couple of six-month-olds who have just started working. Why do you ask?"

"I'm in need of another dog. I own a haulage company and without going into details, I require a dog with a good nose on him."

Jane laughed, "You mean you need a sniffer dog for narcotics? One of my boys excels in that line of work."

He had no idea why, but he trusted this woman. She was straightforward and didn't indulge in small talk. "That's exactly what I want," Eamon replied. "Would he be ready in a couple of weeks?"

"He'll be available whenever you want him, Eamon, but he won't be cheap."

"Money's no object, Jane; we'll discuss the finer details when I come back."

Eamon thanked her and went to open the gates for her to drive out.

Eamon decided to pay a visit to his old friend Dominic O'Reilly, an old-school cockney with Irish parents, who was living the good life in Marbella with his wife Maureen.

Dom was now out of the drug game and living his life to the max, tootling about the Mediterranean on his luxury cruiser. Dom and Eamon became pals when Jimmy Grant had introduced them. The two men had clicked immediately.

Originally, Dom had no problem with Jimmy Grant, who had taken an interest in a yacht that Dom was selling a few years back. The deal had gone smoothly. What disturbed Dom was when he was told by his wife that Jimmy Grant had tried it on with their sixteen-year-old daughter, Sheila. Dom had been in the dark about the situation until a few years later when Sheila revealed to her mother that Jimmy Grant had chatted her up and patted her rear. It had only been Maureen's intervention that had prevented Dom from putting a hit out on Jimmy Grant.

Eamon knew that no one could have been more pleased about the rumours of someone bumping off Jimmy Grant than Dominic O'Reilly.

Eamon and Marcia, with Dan at the wheel, pulled into the marina. Dan had taken the scenic route at break-neck speed, reaching their destination in record time. Eamon had wanted to fly but Marcia had asked to go by road so she could take in the stunning views on the way. The speed at which Dan drove had terrified Marcia though, and now she wished that she'd gone with Eamon's original suggestion to fly. Eamon heard the voice that couldn't be mistaken for anyone else's, even before his old pal came into sight. Dom waddled along the boardwalk, beaming like a Cheshire Cat with arms akimbo in welcome.

He kissed Marcia on the cheek. "Excuse the belly," he grinned as his wide girth pressed into her. "It's the wife's Irish cooking," he chuckled.

Marcia instantly took a liking to him. He reminded her of Joey B and seemed just as jovial. Dom, cocking an eyebrow towards Dan, prompted Eamon to introduce him. Dom pressed Dan to stay at his place too but Dan told him he had booked into a hotel along Golden Mile beach to enable him to do a bit of sightseeing.

Dom grinned and winked, "I understand, lad."

Dan followed Dom in his car as they drove to the villa that Marcia and Eamon would be staying at for the next two days. Dom left them with the reminder that he'd take them out on his cruiser the following day around noon.

. . . .

Marcia and Eamon were staying in the villa of a friend of Dom's, who was away in Mexico. The housekeeper had opened the vacant villa for them and had it all ready for their arrival. Marcia took in the luxury of the furnishings and the breathtaking views from the balcony. She sensed that there was something on Eamon's mind, but she knew him well enough by now to let him come round in his own time. She told him that she was going to shower and change into something cooler. The temperature was rising into the thirties.

Upon Marcia's return, she was pleasantly surprised to find that Eamon had prepared lunch. He said he would bring them out a bottle of wine. Marcia admired the scenery, her thoughts dwelling on Eamon. As much as he wanted to get away, he seemed subdued. She was aware of his dual personality. She had fleetingly seen the other side of him in the steel glint of his eyes on the night of Mario's assault. An icy coldness sometimes lurked behind his dark chocolate eyes, which at times she found unnerving, although as a lover and protector she couldn't fault him. He was so gentle and caring in every way with her. She had been so deep in thought that she hadn't heard him approach.

"Penny for them," he said, bending down and kissing the top of her head.

She saw the flicker of ice in his eyes as she looked up, sending a shiver down her spine. He took her hand and walked towards the table holding her eyes. He sat opposite, pushing the salad dish towards her. Although he was smiling, Marcia tried to make sense of what she was receiving from him that was making her feel so on edge. She couldn't think of anything she had done which may have upset him.

"Eat," he smiled thinly, leaning back in his seat, studying her intensely.

He waited for her to finish most of her lunch before he spoke. Marcia was aware that Eamon was waiting for the appropriate moment to reveal what was on his mind. She took a large swallow of her wine, apprehensive of what was to come.

"I want ye to tell me everything about ye and Suzette," Eamon began. "Leave nothing out. I want the truth between us. I know ye have told me some of it but take it back to when ye gave advice to Max Greenaway while he was imprisoned."

Whatever Marcia had thought was coming, it wasn't this.

"Did youse two double-cross the man?" He held her gaze, as Marcia blushed. "Please listen to me, I need ye to tell me it all. I'm hearing strange things that I can't get my head around. So for me to fathom it out ye have to tell me the truth. In return, I will tell ye all I feel is safe for ye to know."

Marcia took another mouthful of wine and then placed the glass on the table. She realised she couldn't leave anything out and told him of how she'd given a tarot reading to Suzette, about Max's imprisonment for drug dealing and Max's emotional blackmail regarding her son. Marcia told Eamon that Suzette wanted her to withhold anything she saw about her in Max's tarot readings.

"Which ye did," he said, without wanting a reply. "Go on." He sipped his wine, watching her.

Marcia continued – she didn't leave out a single detail. She informed him about Suzette and Gary's affair and how Gary had deceived Suzette over Max's drug money and how she'd felt that his right-hand man Mikey Paige was watching them. "And then the telephone call came from the prison to say Max had taken his life," Marcia said.

Eamon concluded, "Suzette stepped in where Max Greenaway left off. Then why did ye come to Spain with her?"

"Because I had no choice, Eamon."

He raised an eyebrow. Marcia averted her eyes. Eamon reached across the table, cupping her chin. "Don't think for a millisecond that I'm not grateful to her for bringing ye to me."

She saw the hint of a smile play on his lips.

"But I need to know her motives because it's come to my attention that the low-life who attacked ye was paid via Max Greenaway."

Eamon had her full attention now. "We both know that Max is dead but for him to have wanted ye to be taught a lesson from beyond the grave, confirmed to me that he knew you were working for both camps."

Marcia was horrified to learn that Max had been behind the attack on her. For her own sanity, she knew she had to divulge to Eamon the role that Suzette played in her relocation to Spain. Over the next hour, Marcia filled Eamon in on her initial reluctance to come to Spain and how Suzette had insisted. She had felt like her back was up against the wall with Max's veiled threat concerning her son.

He waggled his head, weighing up the situation. "What we're talking about here then is blackmail."

Marcia kept silent, which was enough for Eamon to draw a conclusion.

"His right-hand man would have definitely kept tabs on youse two. "I heard Max Greenaway's man is dead, but I'd guess, that before he died he would have passed the info onto someone else to sort youse out."

"I warned Suzette time and again, Eamon, but she would never believe me that Mikey was untrustworthy," Marcia replied, putting two and two together.

Marcia defended Suzette, telling Eamon that she had proven to be a good friend, although she was still frightened regarding her son's safety. "As long as I draw breath, I would do what I can to protect him. He has no one but me," she added. With that, she pushed her chair back and walked to the edge of the balcony, staring out to sea. A wave of sadness came over her as she thought about Reuben.

"Please, Marcia, come and sit back down and hear me out."

Marcia walked slowly to the table, sitting quietly as he spoke.

Eamon talked about his life and the hardship he and his young brother experienced growing up. He omitted the details about his drunken and violent father. He told Marcia about his Thai wife, and about Eve. He recalled the day after she had been killed, how he'd found Eve's dairy and discovered his marriage was a sham. Eamon said how he had read all the explicit details of the affair she'd been having, and how he'd been led to believe that Eve's medical condition prevented her from having children, yet she wrote that she wanted a child with Jimmy Grant. He said that he had found the contraceptive pills hidden in the chest of drawers. He told her nothing about his business life. Eamon went into detail about how he had sent Anna and her young daughter Chloe to live with Patrick and his wife to help out with their autistic daughter Catherine and young son Conner.

"We all carry burdens in one way or another," he stated, smiling wistfully.

Marcia moved around the table and stood before him. He reached out, embracing her as she sat on his lap putting her arms around his neck. She felt him physically relax as she kneaded the taut muscles in his shoulders.

"Ye know what makes me feel good, my little mystic?" Eamon grinned, and she could feel him melting under her fingertips. "Let me shower and shave before we go any further," he laughed, his hardness becoming obvious beneath Marcia's lap.

Brushing her lips with his, Marcia responded, "I don't want you to shave, Eamon, I love your stubble. It turns me on." She kissed him softly along his jawline, his six o'clock shadow was already showing, even though he had shaved that morning. "Why don't you grow a beard, it would suit you, my handsome man?"

"How long do ye think ye could last out if I did. Ye'd lose control," Eamon chuckled.

"I would not, Eamon," Marcia answered with mock affront, "I don't know what you mean."

. . . .

"Let's put it to the test then, shall we?" Eamon replied, scooping Marcia into his arms and carrying her into the bedroom. She moulded perfectly into his body. He could smell the wine on her breath and the faintest hint of perfume on her neck. Her eyes never left his. This woman had so many dimensions and she had just added another by opening up about her involvement with Max and Suzette and the impact it had had on her life. It made

Eamon even more fiercely protective of her. Standing her down, he made short work of removing her dress and laid her sun-warmed body on the bed. She smiled up at him, dark eyes asking for his maleness, imploring him to take her. He knew she was ready for him, her limbs relaxed, her breathing heavy with desire.

"Lay still," he quietly commanded her. Legs astride hers, Eamon leant over her small frame, kissing her with a firmness that bruised her lips. She reached into the thickness of his hair, hands pulling him to her. He parted from her mouth reluctantly but continued, his lips pressing on her neck and throat, letting his tongue glide along her skin. Eamon rolled her erect nipple between his thumb and forefinger, his mouth and tongue paying homage to its twin.

. . . .

Marcia's grip tightened as she felt herself being swept along by a river of gradually intensifying ripples. Eamon's lips and tongue had reached her stomach and she writhed in anticipation, hollowing out a nest of crumpled quilt underneath her. Without conscious thought, she parted her legs. She clenched his hair as he journeyed down below. She made small gasps of delight as he pleasured her, teasing her with his tongue, the roughness of his bristles sending small frissons of what was to come. The slight pain of his stubble in contact with her delicate skin contrasted with the intense pleasure of his practiced mouth. Eamon held her legs open. His large, gentle hands explored every intimate part of her. His own suspense held at bay until she surrendered to him, shuddering with fulfilment.

Marcia took his mouth greedily, her tongue probing as she felt his length inside of her. She was lubricious and eager for him and he was no longer gentle.

"I need to be on top, Eamon," she gasped at the very moment he turned her with him into that position and clasped her waist either side. She squealed a little as she felt the full force of him, her weight driving down on his erection. Marcia watched his chiselled features contort in ecstasy as she rode him, her fingers spread across the iron hardness of his chest. She rose and lowered herself on him, over and over, skilfully using her suppleness to bring him to the point of no return. She felt the explosion of wet heat and his protracted moan as he released himself. Marcia remained in the same position, Eamon's hands still held her firmly by the waist. Beads of sweat glistened on both their foreheads. Slowly bending forward, Marcia laid her full breasts over the vast expanse of Eamon's chest, rubbing her silken skin over his salt and pepper hair. She nipped him playfully on the chin with her straight white teeth, and in response, he held the tip of her nose between his own, exerting just enough pressure to hold her still. His hands slid from her waist onto her buttocks each hand taking a cheek and feeling with fingertips in between." We're very wet, Marcia," he laughed, releasing her nose from between his teeth.

"I know," she replied delightedly, collapsing down onto him. The heady smell of him made her dizzy. His sweat and seed mingled with subtle notes of citrus, amber and herself on his mouth were intoxicating. Her heart physically ached for him and his touch. Marcia rolled off him and laid at his side, stretching her hand down as far as it would go and then ran it up his well-proportioned body. His hairs sprang up at her caress. Marcia nuzzled his ear and rubbed her palm gently over his muscular stomach, circling downwards and stopping at the triangular mat above his semi-swollen cock. She cupped his balls, still slick and warm and delicately fondled them. Above her hand, Eamon felt himself stiffen and his stomach contract.

With her other hand on his nipple, Marcia pinched it firmly, marvelling as he became fully erect again.

"Jesus, Marcia," a low groan escaped Eamon's lips "What are ye doing to me, woman?"

"I think you know," Marcia murmured, as she took the head of his swollen member into her mouth.

. . . .

Dom arrived the next day to pick them both up and was quick to notice the spring in Eamon's step. Marcia walked ahead of the two men towards the car. Dom nodded his head towards Marcia, grinning. "You must have had a good rest, or maybe it's your young lady that's put the twinkle in your eye," he laughed. "Mind you, perhaps I could do with some of that, as you look ten years younger!" Both men laughed.

Maureen had thrown her arms around Eamon and hugged Marcia in welcome. "Come and have a natter and let the men take over." Maureen linked her arm through Marcia's guiding her towards the stern of the boat. Dom was at the wheel in the helm with Eamon standing alongside, as the cruiser glided from its mooring towards deeper waters.

Eamon was usually a private man in personal matters but felt he owed Dom an explanation regarding his relationship with Marcia, so soon after Eve's tragic death.

He had been giving Dom the details on Jimmy – how Eve had been conducting an affair with him, and any love he thought he had for her had died upon reading her diary.

Dom said he understood and then revealed to Eamon that Jimmy Grant had tried it on with his young daughter and that she'd kept the burden to herself for years before eventually telling her mother.

Dom said he hoped someone had given it to Grant good and proper. "The fucking womanising bastard," he spat. "I know we all like a bit of skirt, but we also know which lines not to cross. But with him, he didn't give a toss who it was." His face reddened in anger. He turned to look out across the sea to the mountains in the distance. A smile broke out on his face as he turned towards Eamon, "Let's not let that toe rag spoil our time together. After what you've been through and then coming up smelling of roses with your lovely lady, I can understand why you look like the cat that got the cream." Dom grinned, slapping Eamon on the back.

"Have a quick look," Dom said, turning round to look at the women. "My Maureen hasn't stopped chewing your gal's ears off. Your woman won't get a word in edgeways!"

. . . .

Maureen had instantly taken a liking to Marcia. Maureen telling Marcia that she and her daughters loved anything to do with the stars, the spirit world and palm reading. Maureen said she couldn't believe her luck when Marcia had mentioned that she was a psychic medium. Maureen bombarded her with questions, telling Marcia that she was a Pisces and that Dom was a Scorpio. She went into detail about all her kids, barely coming up for breath.

Maureen was interested in auras and the energy surrounding people, telling Marcia that she thought she had a lovely aura, "I've got a thing about auras, I have, and you radiate kindness." She went on, "I feel that you two are made for each other even though he's a bit of a bugger, but that's what we women like, isn't it, Marcia?" she winked. "I blame it on the company they keep."

Marcia smiled as Maureen continued, "I know I shouldn't speak ill of the dead but that Eve who Eamon got himself tucked up with, I knew when I met her she wasn't for him. I told my Dom, you mark my words, she is nothing but a user, too flighty and up her own bum for my liking. Sorry, luv, there's me rabbiting on, but I'm one of those people that must get things off my chest. Now you and Eamon have to come and stay with me and Dom. I know the man's busy but I should well imagine you know how to get around him." She was laughing now. "Use your charms," she chuckled, "and get him to return soon."

....

Marcia had been relieved to have a man to lean on. Eamon was certainly that. He had taken charge over everything in her life up to this point, but she knew he had a weak spot – and that was her. She knew he felt it necessary to protect her at all costs and that he'd been let down badly by people in the past. She knew that there was a powerful union between them, which neither of them had ever experienced before. She hoped they could grow together as equals. However, Marcia's intuition told her that since Jimmy Grant's death, Eamon was now in an elevated position and she wondered what impact it would have on their relationship. She observed him up at the helm speaking to Dom, running her eyes over his muscular frame beneath a white shirt. He emitted a powerful energy that left no mistake of his position. Marcia smiled to herself as she looked at his strong, angular jawline, which sported the beginning of a goatee beard. Eamon had agreed to meet her halfway in the matter of his facial hair. Marcia smiled secretly to herself. Even Eamon O'Donally had an Achilles heel. She may not have his physical strength but with her powerful gift of insight, she could guard the man she loved with every fibre of her being.

Dom cut the engine and dropped anchor. Maureen had packed a picnic along with a couple of bottles of Dom Perignon and was busying herself in the galley as she prepared lunch.

Dom was divulging his problems to Eamon, telling him of his concern for his youngest girl Sheila. "I've just discovered that she is running around with an older guy called Robbie Marks who has a fucking big heroin habit and, from what I hear, an even bigger ego." Dom said, "I need to get the 'tosser' out of the picture. My Maureen had tried every trick in the book to get her away from the low-life scum, even getting her sister Andrea to talk to her to persuade her to move to Los Angeles for a few months. Nothing fucking works. My gal is besotted with him. I desperately need your help lad."

It was only because Eamon knew that Dom was a trusted friend that Eamon agreed to assist. Dom gave Eamon the rundown of what was needed to locate Robbie Marks and Eamon told Dom to leave it in his hands.

Thanking him, Dom declared, "No matter the price, I would have even sold this boat if it meant I could get her away from that fucking shyster."

"It will be a set fee, nothing extortionate," Eamon replied ending the discussion.

Maureen went to call Marcia, gently tapping at the cabin door. The door was a bit ajar and the movement caused it to swing open. Maureen caught sight of Marcia's face. The yellow and purple bruises, though faded, were still there for Maureen to see. Instantly forgetting about lunch, Maureen stood shocked beyond belief, as Marcia covered herself with a towel and took a seat on the bed. "Please don't tell me Eamon did this to you!" Maureen exclaimed.

"Oh my God no, Maureen," Marcia answered.

Maureen's heart went out to Marcia as she described the attack by Mario. Sitting alongside her, she smoothed Marcia's hair and offered comforting words. "I'm not saying you'll forget, but time's the best healer." Then she brightened trying to lighten the heavy mood, "Now get yourself ready. We have so much to look forward to. Come up on deck and get some food inside those skinny bones of yours."

Maureen had been trying to get Marcia to eat. She'd made Irish potato pie, and every type of salad – enough to feed ten people. There was wild salmon, homemade soda bread and apple cake to follow. Eamon looked like he had died and gone to heaven. Marcia sat alongside Maureen, who was not taking no for an answer, as she kept piling her plate with a bit of everything, insisting that she ate it all.

Marcia had never tasted anything so delicious in all her life. Maureen sat back with pride as Marcia finished every scrap. Marcia and Eamon agreed to visit them the next day, as Maureen had asked Marcia for a reading. Marcia assured her it would be no problem. Maureen was praying that Marcia would be able to give her some peace of mind about their daughter Sheila.

Dom and Maureen retired to their cabin for a siesta while Eamon and Marcia went up top to try to catch some sun and to relax for a while before they returned to shore. Marcia went back to their cabin and changed into a beautiful white bikini and matching dress. If Marcia and Eamon had been by themselves on the boat, the dress would have stayed in her small case, but, for decency's sake, she slipped the dress on over the bikini in case Maureen or Dom resurfaced.

Marcia moved seductively across the deck towards Eamon. She couldn't help but feel deliciously feminine and sensuous in his company. Eamon held out his arms to her as she approached. "Ye look beautiful," he murmured as he took her in a bear hug.

"Oh Eamon, this is paradise," she breathed back.

They held each other for a while, enjoying the closeness of their bodies, celebrating being alone under the cloudless azure sky. Marcia could hear the quiet laps of the waves against the hull and the lightest of breezes ruffled her hair. Just then, Eamon held her away from him and studied her cherished face, trying to suppress the urges arising in him. Marcia glanced down bashfully at the large formation in Eamon's trunks.

"Eamon, we can't," she said hoarsely, though her body did indeed want to – very much. He pulled her next to him once more. "Relax, Marcia," he directed, and she felt his powerful fingers lifting her dress and sliding sideways into her bikini bottoms, probing softly. She felt him cup one buttock, moving his hand under her dress. Deliriously, it ran through her mind why she had even bothered to put the bikini on as it barely covered her anyway. She could feel his solidity against her, and selfishly frenzied by Eamon's administrations between her thighs, she had lost all power of reason. She leaned into him and rocked with her surging impulses. Eamon expertly used his middle digits to enter her slippery depth while his other hand held her buttock in a vice-like grip, keeping her so tightly against his engorged cock she felt as if it was a part of her own flesh. The sensation of being held so securely that she could barely breathe, along with her mounting climax made Marcia whimper breathlessly.

As she reached her crescendo, the whimpering grew louder and Eamon, who up until that moment had been concentrating solely on her pleasure, clamped his mouth firmly over hers to prevent her from crying out. Marcia's legs turned to jelly and she slumped against him, entirely spent. Despite his own obvious discomfort, Eamon looked at her joyously.

"Oh Eamon, I'm sorry," Marcia gasped.

"Don't be," he laughed, "Ye need to lie down…" He indicated a pair of sun loungers. Eamon looked down slightly self-consciously at his burgeoning trunks "…while I go and sort myself out and then we'll catch some rays together."

Marcia's glow was not due to the sun nor the fresh salt air. She watched the stallion of a man that was Eamon O'Donally stride effortlessly across the deck. She couldn't wait for his return.

. . . .

Maureen listened to Dom snoring his head off beside her. "Bless him," she thought, bending to kiss his balding pate. She had just begun to drift off to sleep when from above, she heard the familiar sound of a couple discreetly trying to muffle their lovemaking. She sighed, remembering her own passion from the stolen moments that she had shared once with the man who lay beside her. She still had a deep love for the man who'd given her their five children. Oh, he had slipped off the path on a couple of occasions that Maureen had been able to suss out, but she wouldn't have ever given him up for some silly tart who thought that she could step into her shoes. Cuddling into Dom's back, she drifted off to sleep.

. . . .

Marcia tossed and turned as she slept and Eamon felt uneasy as he watched her. He gently smoothed her hair back, concerned that she wasn't sleeping easily.

He was going to make a lot of changes, he thought. There were so many things playing on his mind. Joyce had made arrangements with her solicitor to make him the CEO of the haulage company and he would pay her the £20,000 under the table. He also had plans to have a private word with Suzette. He knew all there was to know about the haulage business. He had helped oversee the thriving company for Jimmy for so many years. He was now in a financial position to put a stop to his life of crime. With Marcia in his life, he wasn't prepared to take any more risks that could result in him losing his liberty and becoming parted from her. He had spent so many years living his life on the edge, but now with this unexpected run of fortune, if he became legitimate he could stop looking over his shoulder all the time. To Eamon's advantage, he knew that his and Jimmy's financial adviser had a secret life, which meant Eamon was able to safely secure his newly acquired fortune.

. . . .

Marcia awoke with a start. She'd had a distressing dream which had imprinted itself upon her mind. She had the distinct sensation that a young girl needed help, but Marcia was unable to give it. There had been an evil male presence that disturbed Marcia. She wondered if the nightmarish dream was brought about by the recent trauma she'd experienced at the hands of Mario Lopez.

Eamon stood over her, smiling. He helped Marcia to her feet and put his arms around her. Marcia said nothing of the dream and pushed the feeling of despondency to the back of her mind.

Dom called out, telling them that they were heading back to the marina. Maureen's smiling face appeared from the galley and as Marcia looked at her, she had the overwhelming feeling that her dream was connected to her. Marcia kept her smile. She didn't want anything to spoil what had been an idyllic time.

Dom dropped Eamon and Marcia off at the villa. They'd set a date for dinner at his home the next day.

. . . .

While Marcia showered, Eamon gave Dan a call, telling him to come straight over. Dan and Eamon sat behind closed doors. Eamon gave him as much information as he could regarding the situation with Dom's daughter, Sheila, and Robbie Marks, including the bars they hung out in. Dan advised that he would phone Billy to catch the next flight to Malaga. He'd spoken to Billy only an hour before and he'd be up and running because he was itching to get out of the UK.

Eamon sensed something was disturbing Marcia. She had seemed preoccupied since she'd woken up on the boat, but he hadn't had the time up until now to talk to her about it. He walked out to where Marcia stood on the balcony, admiring the panoramic view.

He came up beside her, and turning her to face him, he asked, "What's bothering ye Marcia? Tell me," he said, cocking an eyebrow, "I can feel something is wrong?"

She told him about the dream, how she'd felt a darkness around Maureen. "I'm sure it's something ominous. There was a man in my dream who was looming over a young woman. I could feel his malevolent presence. It was so disturbing because I knew he was going to harm her."

Eamon felt his blood run cold. Dom had confided his fears that his daughter Sheila was already taking cocaine or perhaps something even worse. Eamon had been making other arrangements besides dealing with Dom's problem and these had been of a much more gratifying nature. To lighten the mood he said, "Let's not worry about anything like that, Marcia. I've got a surprise in store for ye."

Eamon brushed her neck delicately with his lips. "Go and make yourself glamorous. I have a car picking us up, as I need to call on an associate before I take ye out to dinner. Turning her around he patted her on the behind and sent her inside."

. . . .

Dan notified Billy that there had been a change of plan and that he was needed as soon as possible. He advised him to get on the earliest flight available and he would pick him up at Malaga airport.

Until then, Dan planned to frequent some of the haunts that Eamon had told him about. He knew through experience that this guy Robbie Marks wouldn't be too hard to find. Those sorts of people were creatures of habit. As he turned the key in the ignition he reflected that Robbie Marks shouldn't be a problem, but those connected to him could be. He wasn't one to take chances and knew if there were any problems Billy would be his backup.

. . . .

Amos Saggers' driver picked them up at the appointed time and drove them to a villa on the outskirts of Marbella. As Eamon and Marcia walked in, the old gay smiled. Moving around his desk, he proffered his hand and Eamon shook it, introducing Marcia.

Amos, kissing her on both cheeks, stood back. "Eamon, WHERE, have you been hiding her?" He feigned mock offence.

"Now! Can I have a look at what I asked ye for and stop your flirting with my woman." Eamon said with a serious tone, although the edge of his lips had a hint of a smile.

Amos flapped his hands. "I have a few stunning watches for you to browse over," he said, rising to go to the safe.

Eamon ran his eyes over the three beautiful timepieces that Amos had placed in front of him and picked up one that caught his attention.

"Ah," Amos said, "This is a masterpiece in the making, a Portugieser Perpetual Calendar made in Schaffhausen Switzerland in an eighteen-carat gold case, with one of the four dials on the face that shows the phases of the moon in the northern and southern hemisphere. The see-through sapphire glass…"

Eamon raised his hand to stop him. "I'll have it," he said brusquely. "Now let us get down to what I spoke to ye about earlier."

Amos smiled in a conspiratorial manner, returning to the safe. Putting on a pair of white cotton gloves, he removed a small pull string bag. Laying a protective cloth on the desk, he gently tipped the contents onto it.

Marcia's eyes opened wide in amazement as Eamon sat forward to get a closer look at the diamond.

As Amos looked at the couple from across his large Georgian-era desk, he knew for certain that this woman was a different class. Eamon had rung him that morning to tell him he wanted something special and he wasn't concerned about the cost. Amos had an exquisite four-carat diamond in mind for Eamon O'Donally, and looking at the woman, Amos knew it was as good as sold. He was an expert in reading body language, and judging from theirs, he thought that these two would be in for the long haul. "I shall leave you both to discuss it. I'll return in ten minutes."

Eamon cocked his head to one side, looking at her, "Do ye like it, Marcia?"

Marcia turned to gaze at the diamond. "Eamon, I have never seen anything, so beautiful."

"Well, if ye want me to buy it for ye, it comes at a price."

Marcia was overawed at the sight of the exquisite stone. Her voice trembled as she answered, "Eamon, I wouldn't expect you to pay what must be a small fortune on that diamond for me."

Eamon's dark eyes shone. Taking Marcia by the hand, he replied quietly, "That's not the sort of price I'm talking about Marcia."

He saw unbidden tears in her eyes as she realised what he meant.

"Marcia will ye marry me?" he asked, earnestly.

Marcia sprang from the chair, throwing her arms around his neck. "Yes," she answered, without hesitation, smothering his face with kisses.

"Okay," Eamon answered with a sigh of relief. "Let's get this sorted with the old queen." Eamon smiled, as, on cue, Amos stepped into the room brandishing a tray upon which sat a bottle of champagne and glasses.

Amos interrupted the joyous couple. "Am I jumping the gun or are congratulations in order?"

Marcia and Eamon smiled back at Amos. "To be sure, she said yes!" Eamon laughed.

"If I may say so, you are both very well suited to each other and I shouldn't imagine it would be too long before there will be wedding bells."

Eamon replied that the wedding would take place as soon as he had a few things sorted.

Amos, beaming, opened the champagne. Passing them each a crystal flute, he raised his and made a toast. Marcia and Eamon chinked theirs in unison as Amos wished them a happy and long union.

Amos offered up a suggestion that the four-carat diamond could be cushioned in a white band of nineteen-carat gold, encrusted with small emeralds, to signify Eamon's connection to the Emerald Isle.

Eamon looked askance at Marcia.

"I think that would be beautiful," Marcia smiled back at Eamon.

Amos advised Eamon that he would call him in the morning to discuss the particulars and that the ring would be on Marcia's finger in nine days' time. Amos wished them goodbye and told Eamon he would be expecting a wedding invitation for himself and his partner Levi.

"As if I'd leave youse two out," Eamon said, smiling as he and Marcia got into the car to go for their prearranged meal at the restaurant.

. . . .

Dan had been keeping himself busy, making enquiries at each haunt that he'd been informed Robbie Marks frequented, but up to that point, it had led him nowhere, despite having a name and a description.

Poking his head around the door of the last bar on the list, Dan was alerted to a guy sitting at a table towards the end of the bar with a mobile phone glued to his ear that fitted Robbie Marks description. He was one of those guys that judging by the "hip" way he dressed couldn't let go of his youth. He sauntered into the place and then took a seat at the bar a few feet away from him. The guy was oblivious to his presence. Dan ordered a drink and tried to overhear the guy's conversation but he could only catch the odd word as he was practically whispering into his phone. Dan's gut feeling informed him that this was his target.

After the guy finished his call, Dan projected a friendly smile at him, innocently asking if he knew the area, explaining that he was having a break for a few days and didn't know the locality. Dan smiled to himself as the "fish" took the bait.

He eagerly asked Dan where he was staying and what type of interests he had.

Joining the man at the table, Dan introduced himself as Brian Cole and told him that he was looking for some entertainment and something to get him high. "I'm a bit shaky," he lied, holding up his hand. Dan could do a good impression of a drug user needing his next fix.

The guy leaned forward, proffering his hand, "Hi, my name is Robbie Marks and this must be your lucky day," he said.

Dan's intuition had been spot on. He took out a wad of notes and offered Robbie a drink. He saw his eyes light up. Greed registered in Robbie's snake-like eyes. Dan peeled a 50 euro note from the roll and noticed they followed as he stuffed the money into his back pocket. He told Robbie that his mate was joining him later that night and that they would both appreciate a guide to show them around. Girls were needed, Dan told him, plus something to keep them going.

"My mate's a party animal," Dan said, "and he doesn't mind splashing his cash, but it will have to be around 10 pm tonight as we are night owls." Dan laughed. He had received a call from Billy to say he was on his way. Dan needed to have enough time to pick Billy up from Malaga airport, his flight with EasyJet was just under three hours.

Dan slipped Robbie a 50 euro note and told him to have another drink on him.

Dan drove like the wind from Marbella. He didn't want Billy taking any chances on public transport. Dan would drive and make the return journey in record time, as they had to move as quickly as possible.

Billy was waiting by the airport doors as Dan pulled up. On the return journey, Dan put Billy in the picture explaining the urgency of the job to remove this piece of scum from the young girl's life.

Dan had previously booked Billy a hotel room, which was two doors down from his own. The men agreed to play it by ear that night. The intention was to get Robbie Marks on his own. If Dan's intuition was correct, Robbie wasn't only a "coke head" but also a heroin user. He had noticed the familiar marks on his arm when Dan had shaken his hand.

"Maybe," he said to Billy, "we can give him exactly what he wants." Both men smiled and got into the hotel lift.

They'd deliberately arrived a bit late to put the guy on edge. Sure enough, Robbie Marks sprang up from his seat as the two men walked into the packed bar. Ushering Dan and Billy to his table, Dan introduced Billy as "Ryan".

Robbie said, "Meet Sheila," indicting a young, dark-haired girl.

As the two men greeted her, she appeared incoherent, and barely able to focus.

Noticing that the men looked concerned, Robbie explained that he was going to drop her off at his place on their way out. "Sheila always comes to the bar looking for me," Robbie stated exasperatedly.

Dan could see that the young girl was way over her head in the company of this low-life user and he could understand why her parents were desperate to get rid of him. Dan knew that there was only one way to deal with the likes of Robbie Marks – to permanently erase him.

Robbie said he'd seen his supplier and told him that he was planning a big session with a couple of buddies who he'd lined up for a night of fun. He told the men he had walked away with a stash of coke plus a bit of "white".

Billy took over, telling Robbie that he would grab a couple of bottles of whisky and bring them over to Robbie's place so they could have a few drinks and chill out for a while before hitting the town.

As the two men entered the flat with Robbie and Sheila, they had taken note of the address. The rancid odour of the filthy place filled their nostrils. Kicking out of the way full ashtrays and empty takeaway cartons, they made space to sit on the floor.

Robbie guided the girl to the bedroom and shut the door behind her, rubbing his hands together, grinning. "Hopefully, that's got her off my back for a while. To be honest with you boys, she's becoming a bleeding liability, forever on my tail." He sat on a pile of dirty clothing. "Are you lads single, or just letting your hair down?" he said, looking from one man to the other.

"Ryan," Dan said, speaking of Billy, "he's single. But I'm married with three kids, so I'm looking for a bit of respite." He laughed.

"Well if you wanted a quick jump before we head out, we can find you someone to give you a few hours of entertainment, Brian. She's not too responsive, but she's got great form, which works wonders when you want to relieve a bit of tension."

He smirked, showing what were once perfect, straight teeth, but which now had signs of decay through neglect and heroin use.

Dan took a swig from one of the bottles, offering the other one to Robbie, asking him to show him what he'd got for them.

Robbie, grinning, produced the cocaine and heroin. Dan knew that Robbie had doubled the price of the amount he would have to pay the supplier. But he didn't flinch, paying Robbie the money and gave him an extra 300 euros for good measure.

On the pretext that he wanted a drink first, Dan offered the drugs to Robbie, explaining that they'd had a bit earlier, which "Ryan" had managed to smuggle through customs. He pointed to Billy's rear. They all laughed as Robbie snorted a line of coke. Dan and Billy observed him as the drug took effect.

Billy started by asking questions about Robbie's life and family, trying to get him to talk about himself. He opened up eagerly and then told them what a good thing he was on to with Shelia, as she came from a wealthy family who owned a big golf course in Marbella.

Dan relaxed, knowing without question that this was the right man. He encouraged Robbie to help himself, and he greedily prepared the heroin, heating the spoon over the cigarette lighter.

The bedroom door opened, and the young girl pushed herself away from the door frame and staggered into the room.

Robbie swiftly jumped up, grabbed the girl by the arm and disappeared into the bedroom. Returning to the room with a syringe, he asked Dan if he could give his girl a bit of heroin to keep her quiet.

"Load it. Then we can get on with our night," Dan told him.

"Cheers mate," Robbie said, "won't be long. I'll put her out for the night."

Dan followed Robbie into the bedroom where he spotted the girl looking like death, lying on a stained mattress. In one swift movement, he grabbed Robbie's hair and wrenched his head back as Billy moved speedily, snatching the syringe and plunging the contents into Robbie's neck, killing him almost immediately. Checking his pulse, Billy was satisfied his work was done. Robbie Marks slumped to the floor. Dan called the emergency services and told Billy to bring the girl into the main room.

Dan retrieved the money he'd given to Robbie Marks. They waited until they could hear the siren approaching before leaving the flat. Dan prayed that the girl would survive as he watched from a safe distance across the road. She was being carried out on a stretcher and put into the back of the ambulance. The blaring sirens indicated that Sheila was still alive as the ambulance sped off to the nearest hospital. But the ambulance workers didn't emerge for a while with Robbie until Dan and Billy saw them leave the building with a shape inside a body bag.

Making their way back to the hotel, Dan phoned Eamon.

. . . .

Eamon and Marcia had finished a beautiful meal and Eamon had just ordered his favourite champagne when the call came through. He summoned the waiter for the bill and told Marcia that they needed to return to the villa as he had an important call to make.

An hour later, Dom returned Eamon's call to say that the doctors had put Sheila into an induced coma as her heart was beating too fast and they feared that she was at risk of a stroke. Dom said he wanted her transferred to a private hospital, but her doctor advised against it until her condition became stable. Dom said that he and Maureen wouldn't leave her side, and he told Eamon that they'd let him know of any changes. Eamon was pleased that his debt of honour to Dom had been repaid.

"Oh, I nearly forgot to tell you that piece of garbage Robbie Marks had been found dead in the flat," Dom said. The doctor had informed him that he'd overdosed on heroin. "What a pleasing bit of news," he said, scathingly.

. . . .

Marcia, although elated about their engagement and the stunning diamond and emerald ring Eamon was having made for her, sensed that something was occurring with Eamon, even though he was acting like there was nothing amiss.

Marcia was lounging on the bed in an ivory silk negligee, observing Eamon undressing. She was still on cloud nine from the excitement of the day and wanted to divert Eamon's attention back to her and away from whatever was bothering him. She had something special in mind. Admiring his flaccid penis, she unwrapped the tie belt of the negligee to reveal the ouverte panties and cup-less bra, smiling as she slightly parted her legs.

"Hmm ... I have to go to the bathroom and then I can have some of what ye had earlier on the boat," he said, smiling, walking to the bed naked and leaning across to kiss her. Marcia's hand enclosed his growing erection; her measured motion won the battle as she pulled him towards her. She wrapped her arms around him and he kissed her deeply.

....

Marcia lay in his arms as he told her the news about Dom's daughter Sheila. He had left telling her until now, as he didn't want to worry her unduly. Although he didn't tell Marcia the full circumstances of how Sheila O'Reilly came to be in hospital, he knew that the dream Marcia had previously on Dom's boat was precognitive. Marcia was extremely upset and Eamon reassured her that they would visit Dom and Maureen at the hospital the following day.

Amos had phoned Eamon to discuss the payment for the engagement ring. Eamon didn't quibble with him regarding the cost. When Amos began to run through the expense of the precious stones and the craftsmanship the design would require, Eamon shut him down. "Cut the spiel, Amos. All I want to know is the price." Eamon agreed to make the transfer and the ring would be delivered personally by Amos and his security staff.

Eamon smiled to himself as he put the phone down. He knew the ring would be elegant – he couldn't wait to place it on Marcia's finger.

....

Marcia and Eamon arrived at the hospital, making their way to the ICU. Marcia hugged Maureen, trying to comfort her as Maureen sobbed into her shoulder. Looking down at the young girl, Marcia felt a sense of déjà vu. She experienced a shiver up her spine. Sheila was the girl she'd seen in the dream. She took Maureen to the cafeteria for a much-needed break and left the men deep in conversation.

After a couple of hours, it was time for them to go, and they bid each other goodbye, promising to keep in touch. After the traumatic time at the hospital, Eamon suggested that they relax for the afternoon before leaving that evening. Marcia eagerly agreed, as she felt drained by Maureen's upset and desperately needed to recharge her batteries.

They lay side by side on the sun loungers, relaxing in the solitude. Marcia turned to face Eamon. "I didn't say anything to Maureen, but I feel that her daughter will pull through this. Sheila may have a difficult road ahead of her but eventually, I feel that there is a light at the end of the tunnel."

"Marcia, this is all new to me and, to be honest, I find it a bit spooky," he admitted. "But I think ye have proved your worth. I had heard things, such as reading tea leaves and the likes and talk about Banshees from the womenfolk while growing up, but it's something I used to shy away from, as my granny that would put the fear of Christ into me an' my brother," he laughed. "In fact, my red-haired granny warned us boys of women that could tempt us down the wrong road by their beauty. Maybe she had ye in mind."

Marcia smiled, looking into his eyes as her hand slowly moved down his stomach and onto his resting penis. "Do you think I could influence a man such as you to do as I bid?" she queried knowingly, her hand slowly caressing his growing erection.

He gently grabbed her arms and lifted her high, carrying her into the villa. "Ye, woman, can have yer way with me, and ye know it," he grinned, laying her on the bed and removing his shorts.

Marcia lay contentedly in his arms after their lovemaking. His sexual prowess had brought her to fulfilment, and a while later they co-joined, releasing their inflamed passion for each other. Marcia had never attained such heights of ecstasy. She understood that Eamon's expertise as a lover was because he had had far more experience than she had. He knew every erogenous zone of her anatomy, giving her multiple orgasms.

Marcia had learnt not to question Eamon about business matters, but she sensed there was a lot of activity going on behind the scenes that she would never be a party to. It was as if Eamon O'Donally lived in two separate worlds. She had observed how Eamon had become a major player, and, with that, she could recognise that the growing sense of responsibility was weighing heavily on him. Marcia was aware that Eamon possessed a harnessed potent intensity. She was mindful that Eamon wouldn't tolerate her keeping anything from him. When she had disclosed to him about the circumstances of her early relationship with Suzette, Marcia had pleaded Suzette's case, asking him to let it go because her bond with Suzette was now more one of sisters than of friends. Although Eamon hadn't responded, Marcia wasn't naïve enough to think that he would brush it under the carpet. She knew Eamon would confront Suzette but hoped he wouldn't be too harsh on her.

In their private time together, Marcia was able to quieten Eamon's innermost passionate storm and he became the most gentle, solicitous lover that any woman could dream of. Marcia knew all about energy – people's energy was something she had used in combination with her intuition and ability to read the tarot cards. She had studied astrology and the influence that the planets exerted on someone from their first intake of breath.

Marcia realised that trying to tame the destructive power within Eamon O'Donally would be a roller coaster ride. When she accepted Eamon's marriage proposal, Marcia didn't shy away from strapping herself in alongside him on that ride.

Suzette had phoned Marcia to ask if she'd had a nice break in Marbella. She said she was popping into the villa to collect a few of her things as she was going to Greg's after she had been to the salon.

As Suzette came through the door, she stopped in her tracks at the sight of Marcia. "You look radiant Marcia! Those couple of days have certainly put a bloom in your cheeks … or Eamon has," she laughed.

Marcia felt on edge. Eamon was walking in the garden as he said he had to make a phone call, and just at that instant, he stepped in through the terrace doors. Now that the three of them were in the room together, an overwhelming feeling of guilt came over Marcia. She felt as if she had betrayed Suzette.

"Hi Eamon," Suzette said, cheerily.

Eamon didn't return her greeting.

"May I have a private word wit ye outside in the garden?" He turned, not waiting for a reply.

Marcia put her head down and went into her bedroom not meeting Suzette's eyes.

. . . .

Suzette felt flustered by his tone of voice, and the lack of warmth unnerved her. She followed him out onto the terrace where Eamon took a seat.

"Please," he said, his dark eyes holding her's, as he indicated for her to be seated at the garden table. He sucked air through his teeth as he leaned back in the chair. "The reason I wanted to speak to ye is I need to clear up a few things. Before Marcia and I got together, whatever went on in her life was none of my concern. But now that's all changed, as everything that's Marcia's business is my business."

Suzette shifted in her seat.

"I don't need to explain to ye about the unwritten code of moral ethics, but if they have slipped yer mind, I will remind ye of a few of mine.

Suzette sat rooted to the spot.

"Let's start with blackmail. We can put adultery and theft from your husband to one side for the moment. I am the type of man that demands loyalty, and I have zero tolerance for lies and deception. Ye emotionally blackmailing her to suit yer own ends is something that I find despicable, to put it mildly, and it beggars belief that Marcia is still your friend. I most certainly wouldn't be," he said, scathingly. "The problem I have is that Marcia has told me that she values your friendship and has asked that I put it all behind me but wit ye being in a relationship with a close associate of mine, it puts me in a somewhat awkward position. Greg phoned me earlier and he insisted that we all go out to dinner this evening," Eamon continued. "I will be civil to ye in company, but that's as far as it goes."

He stood to his full height while Suzette crumpled under his glare, her mouth agape looking up at him, knowing she had no defence against his accusations.

Eamon had left Marcia to attend to some business and told her that he would return in time to get ready for their meal with Greg and Suzette.

Marcia walked out into the garden. Suzette looked up as she sat at the table opposite her and broke the silence. "I don't blame you for telling him, Marcia. I am guilty of all that Eamon accused me of," she admitted. "I know that you're in a relationship with him and knew that he would question you, if you remember?" She gave a weak laugh. "I was previously married to Max Greenaway, who controlled my world." Suzette looked at her pleadingly, "I am not asking for forgiveness, Marcia, but I couldn't bear to lose your friendship now," she said, sadly.

Marcia reached for her hands. "I know this all began with us being on shaky ground, Suzie, but I know that our friendship is solid and you have been very generous to me." She continued, "If you hadn't coerced me into coming to Spain, I wouldn't have met Eamon and I wouldn't be about to marry him!"

Suzette's jaw dropped. "Marcia, I am genuinely so thrilled for you, no wonder you look so happy!" Suzette jumped up to hug her, forgetting the earlier upset. "Please tell me all," Suzette said, back to her gregarious self.

"Before I begin to tell you about our engagement, Suzie, I need to explain why Eamon needed to know what occurred between Max and myself. I wouldn't jeopardise my relationship with Eamon by withholding anything, as all Eamon wants to do is protect me, which sadly has proved necessary." Marcia continued by telling her how, from beyond the grave, Max had sought revenge through someone connected to him who had paid Mario Lopez to assault her. Suzette was in genuine shock

"I am frightened for you, Suzie, I feel you are in danger," Marcia's voice took on a serious tone.

Suzette brushed her concern aside. "If I could ever make amends for placing you in such a dangerous position I…"

Marcia smiled warmly and interjected, "Forget the past, Suzie. I am not afraid of being on my own now, as I have got Roman to guard me." At the mention of his name, the dog, who was lying in the shade with his head resting on his forelegs, intently watching, raised his head, "and I also have Eamon," she added.

Marcia told Suzette about Eamon's marriage proposal and the beautiful ring that he was having made for her. "I understand that it will be rather uncomfortable when you are in Eamon's presence, Suzie, as he isn't the type of man to forgive and forget. But he is a beautiful man, who I deeply love, so for the sake of our friendship, please try and understand his point of view."

Suzette smiled wistfully. "I totally understand, and I would tolerate any situation rather than our bond be broken, Marcia."

"Now tell me what's happening with the beauty salon," Marcia enquired.

"Well, the two gay hair and beauty technicians have rented a place together and, by the looks of it, they have become a couple. The pair are so enamoured with each other, and the handsome beggars are so well suited," Suzette laughed, back to her usual self. She went into detail, telling Marcia how entertaining Lloyd and Kieron were. She said they bounced off one another with their banter. "The boys seem to have the full package, talent, good looks and stylish dress. Although Lloyd is rather outlandish, it does add to his attraction. I know that they will be an asset to the business, Marcia."

Her tone then took on a serious note. "This business with Eamon is not going to prevent you from working at the salon, Marcia, is it?" she queried, looking concerned.

"Of course not, I need my independence," Marcia reassured her.

. . . .

Eamon rang Joyce, telling her he wanted to see her. She invited him to come over straightaway since she'd just left Cindy and was returning to the villa. Joyce had changed, Eamon thought, as he watched the woman sitting opposite him. She had regained some of the spirit that she'd had years ago before Jimmy had caused her so much pain and torment. She said she had told her daughter Sara about Jimmy's disappearance and confirmed that it was highly probable that her father was dead. Joyce said she had been amazed by Sara's neutral reaction. "She said she loved him but, at the same time, she'd seen how he'd treated me. Sara also asked me to live with them to the States," Joyce said, gaily.

Eamon said he was pleased that her life was taking on a new meaning. "I need to have things sorted with the haulage business, Joyce, as for legal reasons, I require the majority shares to be in my name, which I will pay the going rate for."

"I will ring my solicitor to see what is the easiest and cheapest way it can be done, Eamon, so don't you worry, it will only take a couple of days. Then in a short while, I'll put this villa on the market and I will finally be free."

Business now out of the way, Eamon broke the news to Joyce about his engagement to Marcia. He'd felt apprehensive about her response given that Eve's death was still fresh in everyone's minds, but she surprised him by immediately leaping up to embrace him. Joyce wanted to know all the details about the ring, when the engagement party would be and when the wedding would take place. Eamon laughed and wondered what it was with women and weddings. He didn't go into detail about the engagement ring, only the fact that Marcia was overjoyed and that it would be ready in nine days' time.

Joyce sat back and looked at Eamon. "I am thrilled for you both," she confessed. "I know that you're made for each other, and I'm sure that you will treat her well. I've watched you in each other's company and, honestly, if a couple should be together it's you two." With tears glistening in her eyes, she said, "You both deserve happiness and, by the way, I love this goatee. It suits you!" She smiled, tugging the hair on his chin.

He smiled back, thanking her and told her he would await her call to sign the paperwork.

. . . .

As she stood on the top step watching Eamon walk to his car, Joyce thought about how many years she had known him and that she hadn't ever heard any talk of him being a ladies' man, unlike Jimmy. But now, with Eamon's rise to the top, Joyce knew from experience that there would be many women vying for his attention. She sincerely hoped, for Marcia's sake, that he wouldn't succumb to temptation.

He waved at her as he drove away. Joyce thought Eamon was by far the most handsome man she knew, and coupled with the Irish accent, the newly grown goatee beard, which Joyce was certain was Marcia's influence, only added to his attraction. Joyce knew from what Marcia had told her about her life that she wasn't from their side of the tracks and she wondered how she would cope with the testing times ahead. She had grown very fond of Marcia in the short time she'd known her. She judged Marcia to be a much stronger woman than she had been when she'd fallen hook line and sinker for the smooth-talking Jimmy Grant. Joyce went inside to call Cindy to tell her the good news about Eamon and Marcia's engagement.

. . . .

Eamon sat in his leather office chair talking to Dan and Billy. He passed them each an envelope. "I've given youse boys an additional bonus for a job well done." Both men gave a sharp nod of thanks. Dan had been right in recommending Billy, Eamon thought. He was satisfied with the part he'd played on both missions. He had gotten rid of three men who he thought weren't 100% kosher. His reshuffle, employing Dan and Billy had made him feel more at ease. He wouldn't have been comfortable retaining Jimmy's men. Every move the pair made was strategically carried out and completed with military precision. Dan had informed Eamon that both tasks were cut and dried, leaving nothing for the law to delve into.

"There is a situation that I'd like youse two to begin looking into for me, but what I need to know is if any of youse have an aversion to dogs. Bear in mind I'm talking of a Belgian shepherd and not a poodle," he grinned.

"Count me in," Billy said, enthusiastically. "I love dogs. They're more reliable than most people."

Dan smiled sheepishly. "I'm a bit wary, to be honest, boss. I've seen the dog handlers in the military working with Belgians and they can turn on a sixpence. One minute a pussycat, then a ferocious snarling nightmare."

"These dogs are trained by a woman who I trust. She is an expert and knows her stuff. In fact, I've already purchased one which stays with my woman. That is how much faith I have in this trainer, and in a short while, I will have a trained sniffer dog. Then let's see who thinks they can pull strokes with me by smuggling narcotics hidden in my lorries." Turning to Billy, Eamon asked him how he felt about being the dog's handler."

"In a flash, boss," then he hesitated, "but wouldn't the dog have to live with me, as I am staying at Dan's place and he seems a bit windy?"

Dan reacted sharply. "Fuck off Billy, I'm not scared of any dog, but I'm not used to being up close and personal with a living stick of dynamite."

"There you go, boss. Put my name down as the dog's new handler." Billy winked at Dan. "I thought you'd bite," he chuckled.

Dan playfully punched his arm.

"Right, that's settled then, I'll speak to Jane about the dog to see when she'd be able to fit ye in. But I do want youse two to go to the haulage company and put the frighteners on the drivers. We don't want them getting too comfortable now do we?" My manager Diego will be expecting youse. Just speak to him and he'll run youse through the list of employees."

Eamon had been having a good think about the depot and how he could reorganise it. Alejandro had worked the lorry run to the UK for three years. Eamon never liked the man, as he would never make eye contact with him. His hands had been tied though because Jimmy had hired him. His cousin, who worked for Jimmy already, had recommended Alejandro, but, recently, Eamon had been given some information that had raised suspicions. Eamon could rest easy knowing that Dan and Billy would set the cat amongst the pigeons. It was one job less for him to do, and after they'd gone, his thoughts turned to Marcia. He felt himself becoming aroused, checking his watch, he adjusted himself, there were three hours before the planned meal. Taking all he required to wear for that night he phoned Marcia to say he was on his way, he knew she would be anticipating his arrival too. As the car sped towards its destination Eamon's blood tingled. The powerful car ate up the miles between him and Marcia and by the time he arrived, he was hot with desire and couldn't wait to be welcomed into her arms.

. . . .

Their lovemaking had gone from hot and steamy to slow and sensuous. They had been so wrapped up in their enjoyment of one another, they'd lost track of time. "Jesus, Marcia," Eamon exclaimed, diving out of bed, "look at the time. We need to get ready."

Marcia took great delight and was amused by her man, naked and flustered. To save time, they showered together but were conscious of keeping themselves under control for fear they'd never get to the restaurant on time. To take his mind off Marcia's wet nakedness, Eamon thought about one of his best-kept secrets.

Eamon had always been careful about looking legit to show the taxman that he contributed his bit. He was aware that illegal money wasn't worth the paper it was written on, but he was thankful that he hadn't gone down the road that many in their circle had. He knew that ill-gotten monies needed to be filtered through legitimate businesses to make it work. Eamon was a man who kept his eye on the button, knowing that somewhere down the line you would get your collar felt.

He had purchased a fish restaurant many years ago and made himself the company director with the aid of his accountant and his solicitor, both worth their weight in gold. Eamon had learnt a big lesson in life early on and that was not to let the left hand know what the right hand was doing. Marcos, the efficient maître d' who ran Eamon's successful eatery like clockwork, was in the dark as to who the owner was. Eamon, whenever he'd booked a table at the restaurant always paid the tab and he'd never encountered a problem with how Marcos ran the place for him.

Eamon had told Greg that he would book them into his favourite restaurant and insisted that the meal was on him. He had taken Marcia there a couple of times before and knew she enjoyed the cuisine. Marcos the maître d' bowed his head as he stood back holding the door for them as they entered the busy restaurant.

"Welcome, Mr O'Donally," he said, turning his attention to the women and Greg and bidding them good evening. He ushered Eamon and his entourage towards their table at the rear of the restaurant. He told the hovering waiter to leave and Marcos poured the champagne himself. He continued to dance attendance on them and when Greg proposed a toast and offered his congratulations to Eamon and Marcia on their engagement, Marcos leaned in quietly congratulated Eamon. Marcos turned towards Marcia, bowed, and left them to it.

Eamon knew Marcos's game and smiled to himself as to what an old fox he was. But the man was harmless. He would give him the contract to supply the engagement and wedding catering. His service had been second to none over the years, but he would let him sweat for a while.

Over dessert, Eamon asked Greg if he would drop by his place early in the morning, as he wanted a word with him. He watched Suzette as she shifted uneasily in her seat, and knew she was wondering what Eamon would reveal to Greg. Then he reached across the table, took Marcia's hand, and told her that they would be married within six months. His public declaration was for effect. He wanted Suzette to read him loud and clear, making the point that he was the one that Marcia would rely on now. He went on to reveal that as soon as the ring arrived there would be a party to celebrate and they were both invited.

Eamon's phone rang and he excused himself. It was Dom, and he knew that something must be wrong for him to be calling so late. Sheila had taken a turn for the worse and

Maureen was beside herself with grief. After gathering all the details, and expressing his sympathy, Eamon clicked off.

. . . .

Marcia noticed Eamon's shift of mood but said nothing. She sensed that the phone call he'd just taken had troubled him.

Eamon and Marcia parted company with Greg and Suzette, dropping them off at Greg's villa. Roman's excited barking from inside the villa greeted them as they pulled up. He'd recognised the sound of the Maserati's engine just as Jane had said he would. The dog had cost Eamon a small fortune, but the peace of mind he'd brought them made him worth every penny and Eamon made a big fuss of him as they went in.

As they strolled with Roman around the garden Eamon revealed to Marcia that Dom had called to say that Sheila's condition had deteriorated.

"Eamon, I know she will survive. The girl won't have it easy at first, but she will adjust and have a healthy future."

Sensing that something was wrong, Roman's sharp eyes watched intently as Eamon took Marcia's hand.

Speaking softly, Eamon said, "Although I don't doubt what ye are saying, Marcia, because ye been 'spot on the money' with previous predictions, but I do find it difficult to comprehend that anyone without any medical expertise can predict an outcome like that. And yet, if I was a gambling man, I'd put my money on ye being accurate." He put his arm around her.

"Eamon, long ago I stopped questioning myself regarding how 'I know'. I accept the fact that I have an ability to tune into people's futures, which isn't always a good thing," she smiled, wistfully. "That is why I swim, meditate and practise yoga, as I find it helps me control my mind and enables me to switch off. The only analogy I can think of is that it's similar to a radio that tunes into varying stations."

A south-westerly wind rustled the fronds of the surrounding palm trees.

"I once read a book where an African man said that his tribe believed that the wind has ears and listens to what is being said, that we must be careful as words travel. I think words are a powerful thing Eamon." Marcia put her head on his shoulder as Eamon drew her towards him.

"Marcia, my life and the way I chose to live it before ye was different to how I would want it to be now. I am going to make changes so that I don't always have to be looking over my shoulder. I don't want to risk losing what we have." He kissed her softly. "I will sort my life out for ye, Marcia, but it will take a bit of time," he said, taking her by the hand and leading her into the villa.

. . . .

It was the middle of the night when Eamon's phone rang. His heart sank as he saw Dom's number.

Dom apologised for the late phone call. "I just had to tell someone, Eamon." He then went into details regarding Sheila's turning point. "Eamon, the blood clot has cleared on Sheila's brain. Maureen and I have been crying tears of joy. It's a miracle," Dom declared, happily. He told Eamon how Sheila had begun to respond when the nurses took over on the night shift and, shortly after midnight, Maureen had felt movement in her daughter's fingers. She summoned the nurses to the bedside and a further brain scan had been arranged. The signs were looking more hopeful. Dom said he would keep him updated.

Turning to gaze at Marcia who was in the foetal position, peacefully asleep, he pondered over her prediction. Against the odds, she had been proven right. Before Marcia, Eamon might well have believed it was sheer coincidence that Sheila had taken a turn for the better when it had all looked so hopeless. But Marcia had been adamant when Jimmy first went missing that the man was dead and nothing would dissuade her otherwise. He was convinced beyond a shadow of a doubt that Max Greenaway and Jimmy Grant knew the power of Marcia's gift and that was why they'd employed her. His blood boiled when he thought of how they would have taken advantage of her.

He thought about their future together. He would find a way out of the criminal world in which he'd lived for so long. He had stepped into Jimmy's shoes, which came at a price. Eamon knew that although he was now the man that calls the tune, he still had people to answer to. You simply couldn't ring these people up and tell them you'd changed your mind. He thought back to the many adversaries he'd encountered in his life, being of the opinion that the bigger they are the harder they fall. He had come across some big tough bastards in his time and had walked away the champion. Then destiny had the last laugh when it sent him this beautiful, petite redhead that lay in his arms, who could win him over every time. Eamon gently manoeuvred her sleeping form into his embrace. He smiled as even in sleep her body responded to him. He lovingly kissed the nape of her neck, and her eyes opened.

"Mm," she breathed, pressing into him, as he slowly guided himself into her. Dreamily, Marcia settled herself into him. The contours of their bodies fitted together as neatly as a jigsaw puzzle. Eamon's deft fingers caressed her nipple and his aroma drifted in a comforting haze around her, invading her sleepiness with warmth and comfort. She could feel his hot breath on her neck and the sensation of his coarse facial hair against her delicate skin caused goosebumps to rise. She readied herself for him even though she was still only half awake. His hardness filled her and rhythmically they took each other into a faraway place where only dreams exist.

....

Sheila had been moved to a private hospital. Dom informed Eamon that she seemed to be out of the woods now. The recent scan had detected no sign of the blood clot. The neurologist explained that Sheila had suffered a stroke while in a coma, which left her with damage to her eyesight. There was a probability that she wouldn't be able to drive again and only time would tell if she would be able to walk. Eamon had been given the full picture that morning and had been quick to fill Marcia in on the night's developments.

Marcia was so pleased for Maureen and Dom, she assured Eamon that Sheila may have to make some adjustments to her life in the future but she would be able to put the bad experience behind her.

Eamon smiled. "Okay, my little mystic, we can now get to the matter of the celebration. I need ye to write out a list of what ye want for this engagement party of ours."

"Eamon," she hesitated, "there is also the party that Suzette has planned to celebrate the opening of the beauty salon. I know how you feel about her but Greg has put so much into this new venture and we cannot…"

His smile didn't match the coldness she saw reflected in his unsmiling eyes as he interrupted, "To be sure, I'll attend.

339

I wouldn't upset the man. I've got too much respect for him. But make sure ours is a priority." He kissed her and then patted Roman who was observing them in their embrace.

Marcia said she was taking Roman out for a walk. She commanded him to sit and wait while she clipped his lead on. Eamon marvelled at how quickly Marcia and the dog had bonded. Roman never took his eyes off her and obeyed her without question. "It's not only me that woman has eating out of the palm of her hand." He winked at Marcia as he picked up his car keys, as he had to meet Greg at his place.

Eamon drove at speed. The much-needed cool breeze played over his face to clear his head. As much as he tried to put Suzette's misdemeanours against Marcia out of his mind, he knew he was fighting a losing battle. But for Marcia's sake, he realised he must tolerate her. He put all that to the back of his mind and concentrated on the surprise he had in mind for Marcia. He wanted a clean slate and no reminders of the old life he had lived with Eve. Greg was waiting in his car as Eamon pulled up at his villa. He opened the ornate gates and Greg followed him through. "Come on in," Eamon beckoned, "would you prefer to sit outside Greg, if it's not too hot fer ye?"

"Outside's, fine. Thanks, mate." Greg took a seat at the garden table. "Getting a bit overgrown," he said, smiling at the long grass and weeds.

"That will be sorted soon," Eamon replied, sitting down opposite him.

"How's the haulage company, now you've taken it over?"

"Grand," Eamon replied, curtly. Eamon didn't have any reason to doubt Greg's trustworthiness, but with Greg being in a relationship with Suzette Greenaway, it was pillow talk that concerned him. But with what he had in mind, he had to lay his cards on the table. He couldn't risk being investigated for money laundering.

"I don't need to tell you, Greg, that what I am going to say to you goes no further," he added. Eamon saw a flicker of annoyance pass across Greg's face.

"You and I are of the old school and whatever we discuss, never goes any further," Greg reassured him, "and, to be honest, Eamon I find it offensive that you feel the need to mention it."

"No offence meant, Greg," Eamon continued, "I want to purchase some land and have a home built for me and Marcia." Eamon told him exactly what he required. Greg pursed his lips, giving a sharp nod.

"You want my company to take on the task, which will be fine but why the need for secrecy?"

"It's more of a two-fold thing. I want the villa to be a surprise for Marcia as a wedding gift."

"I'm with you," Greg smiled, "so you don't want Suzette to hear of it and leak it to her friend."

"Something like that," Eamon smiled, "but obviously I'll put this place on the market which will offset some of the cost for what I have in mind."

"No sweat, I am about to complete a big project that my men have been working on. I have enough workforce to get your place done, at a push in six months, but it will cost you."

Eamon sucked air through his teeth as he stroked his goatee beard in contemplation. "I have a proposition that you may be interested in."

Greg smiled. "You have my full attention, Eamon; I'm always up for an earner."

"This is the other reason why I must insist on secrecy, and if you decide that you want to come in on it, you would need to be a silent partner."

Greg responded, "Sounds intriguing, I'm all ears."

Eamon disclosed that he was the owner of the restaurant that they visited last night.

"I'm impressed," Greg grinned, "tell me more."

Eamon told him how much money he wanted for 50% shares in the thriving restaurant. Greg nodded as Eamon told him that they would both be silent partners. "If ye want to think it over, Greg, that's fine."

Greg shook his head. "Look, Eamon, you know me. I've been legal now for the past fifteen years and I can afford to invest without the tax people making enquiries, but there would be a stipulation if you agree." Greg continued, "I intend to marry Suzette, and once everything is sorted I would want her to be the silent partner, as I have enough legal businesses on my plate. Is there any way we can work it without her knowledge? I know she will sign on the dotted line without asking me any questions." Greg took note that Eamon bristled at the suggestion. "Let me make it easier for you to understand my motives, Eamon. If anything should happen to me, I am making a will that will enable Suzette to inherit everything I own. There is no rush to sort out the restaurant partnership yet."

Eamon juggled the offer around in his head. Suzette was the last person he'd want to have as a partner, not that he could say that to Greg. Eamon knew he couldn't make any headway to legitimacy when his hands were tied. The two men shook on the deal. Eamon said he would arrange with his accountant for Greg to look at the books.

"I'm aware of what sort of money a popular restaurant like that, in such a prime position, is worth. And don't worry," Greg smiled, "both secrets stay with me." Greg told him that he knew a guy who had land for sale in the area Eamon had in mind for the new villa, not far from Altea Golf Club. "It's not on the market yet as the man only mentioned it to me two days ago. I know that his wife has left him and he's having a sell-up. I'll get the ball rolling, give him a call and then take a look at the land, and, if it suits you, Eamon, you can strike a deal with the bloke. In the meantime, I will get my architect to draw up the plans for the villa and then I'll give you a rough estimation on the completion date."

Eamon rang Dan, telling him to bring Billy with him to his home within the hour. Then he punched in Jane's number. He asked her about the new dog and told her that one of his men required training to be its handler. Jane told him that she had some free time and to come over.

Twenty minutes later, Eamon let his men in through his villa gates. Dan brought Eamon up to speed. They'd been to the depot and had a private talk in the depot office with the manager, Diego. He had revealed his suspicions about Alejandro, one of the lorry drivers who he suspected had smuggled a large package of drugs on his last trip. One of the younger yard lads had seen him acting suspiciously and putting a large package into a backpack when he'd been in the men's locker room. Dan said he asked Diego when Alejandro's next lorry would be leaving the depot, and Diego was quick to pass him the relevant paperwork, showing the delivery time and destination.

Dan said they checked over the lorry with a fine-tooth comb but hadn't found anything. Dan told Eamon that the lorry wasn't set to leave until 7 pm that evening. Alejandro had gone home, Diego told them, and wouldn't be returning until around 6.30 pm when he would start his journey to the UK. Dan felt sure that the drugs were going to be on Alejandro himself, and that their best plan was to waylay the lorry as it left the depot. They discussed the designated meeting point and Eamon said he would meet them there.

Eamon pulled up in front of Jane's house and called her so she could let him in. He could hear the barking of dogs as the gates slid open. He saw that she was surrounded by a pack of dogs of various breeds. She reassured him that he was safe as he gingerly opened the car door and approached her. With one command, Jane dismissed the dogs who instantly went to lounge in the shade of the veranda. She invited him around the back where there was a large wooden garden table with a sun umbrella. She asked him if he would like a drink. Eamon said he was fine. Eamon explained it was important that his haulage company didn't come under any suspicion with the law as he ran a clean business. Eamon enjoyed this new, relaxed side to Jane. He felt as if they were forming a useful relationship. He brought the conversation around to the narcotic-detection dog in which he was interested. Jane told him the cost of the Belgian shepherd and he didn't bat an eye at the price. He asked her if the dog could stay with her until his man completed the training, and would she work for him as and when required.

"If ye would be able to bring the dog along this evening to put it through its paces and let it go over the lorry, I would be very grateful," he said, quickly adding that he would give her 1,000 euros for the evening's work.

This she agreed to. "I am going to introduce you to Caesar," she said, walking towards the kennels. Eamon admired the powerful-looking dog who walked obediently alongside her. When Jane stopped, Caesar automatically sat by her side. His dark, intelligent eyes observed Eamon. He rose to his full height when Jane asked Eamon to give him a pat.

"What a magnificent animal, Jane," he declared, ruffling the dog's coat.

"May I ask you about this man who will eventually be Caesar's handler? Obviously, he must like dogs," she said, "but when he is experienced as a handler the dog will need to reside with him, of course."

"That's all sorted, Jane but ye can run tru all that with Billy."

"Billy?" Jane repeated.

"He's one of my men who used to be in the military. Tells me he likes dogs better than most people."

"He sounds like someone I'd be interested in meeting if his preference is dogs," she laughed.

Eamon respected her intelligence and straightforward manner and fleetingly wondered why such an attractive woman would tie her life to dogs. He arranged to collect her and the dog at 6 pm that evening and advised her that Billy and Dan would accompany them in a separate vehicle. Eamon was pleased with the afternoon's work. He called Marcia to tell her that he would pick her up around 8 pm. She said she had been busy arranging tarot readings, bookings and working with Suzette to prepare for the salon's opening night party. She told him she would be ready and couldn't wait to see him.

Eamon returned home and changed. He'd decided to go for a swim. He had only used the swimming pool a handful of times since moving there. It had been Eve who'd insisted that they needed one, although she told him she'd never had the time to use it, *sure she hadn't,* he thought, *Jimmy Grant had kept her occupied.* He dived into the deep end and glided beneath the surface, rising slowly at the other end of the pool. The cool water helping to clear his mind of Eve. His thoughts turned to Marcia as he swam. She was so different from the other women he'd met in his life. So many gold-diggers, hungry for flashy cars, huge villas, expensive diamonds. Marcia had told him that all she wanted was her independence and him. He smiled to himself at the memory of when he'd watched her do her yoga routine, then she had shown him just how flexible she was in bed. That memory alone made his groin ache He pushed himself on, swimming lap after lap, releasing his frustration. If she hadn't been so wrapped up in her work, he would have driven to her villa and enjoyed a couple of hours making love to her.

Eamon dried himself, wrapped a towel around his waist and walked to the bedroom. He hadn't used the room he'd shared with Eve since he discovered her diary. He picked up the phone to call Dom. The news was all good. Dom told him that they were overjoyed at the way Sheila was progressing and her chances of a positive recovery were gradually improving. Shutting the blinds, he lay on the bed. He couldn't think of the last time he'd enjoyed the luxury of a siesta. *I must be getting old,* he thought, as he drifted off to sleep.

Eamon had awoken with a start. He hurriedly dressed and drove to pick up Jane and the dog. When he arrived, Jane suggested they go in her Land Rover, as the Maserati wasn't suitable for Caesar to travel in.

He had previously gone over the plan with Dan and Billy. They were going to be waiting out of sight for Alejandro to leave the depot with his load. Once they'd stopped him, Eamon and Jane would appear ready to give the lorry the once-over with Caesar. If nothing were found, the driver could go on his way, but if it weren't the case then Eamon and Jane would leave Dan and Billy to do the necessary. Eamon wanted it to be known that he meant business.

Under cover of the trees in the lay-by, Jane and Dan's vehicles waited silently. Just after 7 pm, the HGV could be seen approaching. Dan waited until the lorry was at a reasonable distance before swinging his car round into its path. Alejandro, taken by surprise, slowly braked and ground to a halt in the road. Dan and Billy leapt out, yanked open the driver's door, and within a flash, Billy had him out of the cab with his arms forced behind his back. Alejandro was quivering with fear, which quickly turned to pure terror when his eyes fell upon Eamon and a woman with a large dog. Disregarding Alejandro for the moment, Eamon asked Jane to put Caesar to work on the lorry. Jane gave Caesar the command to seek and the dog rapidly and efficiently searched every inch of the lorry, often going backwards and forwards over the same area. When he got to the cab, he jumped in and systematically worked his way through. Moments later, they heard his persistent, sharp bark announcing he'd made a discovery. Jane jumped up into the cab and reached under the back seat where the dog was indicating. Pulling out a backpack, she praised Caesar, excitedly. She passed it over to a waiting Eamon before returning with Caesar to the Land Rover. Eamon opened the backpack and held up a suspicious-looking package. He opened it and nodded, telling Dan he'd leave it in their hands.

Jane was silent on the ride back. When Eamon got out of her Land Rover, he passed Jane an envelope, thanking her. He knew all he needed to know about Jane. He had made it his business to make a few enquiries about her as he did with anyone that piqued his interest, and he was anxious to have Jane working in his employ. He needed her invaluable talent, which would be an asset for his business. He'd discovered that Jane was a 38-year-old divorcee from England with no children who started up her dog business on the Costa Blanca eight years ago. Jane was a straightforward woman who didn't socialise in his circle, but he knew of people who used her ability to train protection dogs to a high standard. The woman had an affinity with animals, it appeared to Eamon. What female would be afraid to live on their own when they were surrounded by protectors such as the canine pack that guarded Jane, he mused, watching her as he got into his car.

Eamon felt drained and half-regretted the arrangement to take Marcia out that evening. His preference would be to order food in and spend a relaxing evening with her. However, he knew that she'd be ready, and didn't want to disappoint her. As he drove to her home, his mind strayed to thoughts of Billy, Dan and Alejandro. Eamon knew the man would have taken a beating – hopefully, one that would prevent him or anyone else trying to take the piss again.

Marcia buzzed Eamon through the gates. She came down the steps to meet him with Roman padding alongside her. What more could a man want, he thought, as he took in the vision of the woman who in a short while would be legally his. As she approached, he ran his eye over the classy sky-blue, figure-hugging dress she wore. He could see that there was no tell-tale panty line, smiling to himself that she'd heeded his suggestion that she could go without underwear only when he accompanied her. "Ye look stunning," he smiled.

Kissing him, she put her arm through his as they walked into the villa.

"You look so tired. Would you prefer if we stayed at home? We could order food in. I can make a nice salad but I know it's not your thing," she said.

"We'll go out, I'm fine," Eamon told her, as she stood in front of him.

"Eamon, I honestly don't mind. I will change and you can relax. We have both had a busy day." She helped him out of his jacket, seeing the relief in his eyes.

This was one of the many things that he loved about her – she could sense what he needed without words.

. . . .

Marcia disappeared to change into something more comfortable. She had been unsure earlier as to whether to tell him about a phone call she had received earlier, but after giving it some thought, she decided she would. She knew Eamon enough by now to know that if she withheld anything from him, it would cause ripples in their relationship, and she wasn't prepared to do that. Brandon had called her and had insisted on talking to her far longer than she thought was necessary. She realised the Texan still hankered after her even though she had told him that she was soon be married to Eamon O'Donally. It hadn't appeared to deter him. Brandon had asked her if they could keep in touch. Marcia explained that it would be better if they didn't, as she thought there was no reason to. She knew Eamon wouldn't be happy if she continued her friendship with him and tried to explain that to Brandon without hurting his feelings. Suzette was with her when she had gone outside the beauty salon to speak to Brandon privately and had been intrigued as to whom the caller was.

"You have been a long time on the phone, who was that?" Suzette pried. "Eamon?" Suzette pushed, wanting an answer.

Marcia sighed, "It was Brandon. I told him about my forthcoming marriage to Eamon, but it didn't seem to discourage him, as he asked if we could continue to keep in touch, but I had to tell him no."

"Well, you cannot blame the man for trying to hold onto you. I think if Brandon weren't thousands of miles away from you Eamon O'Donally would have had a fight on his hands."

"Suzie, I know Eamon has upset you and you don't like him, but please let me assure you, there would have been no contest between the two men. It's Eamon I love." Marcia had changed the subject, preferring to talk about the opening night party plans.

．．．．．．．．．．．．．．．．．．．．

Eamon sensed that there was something on Marcia's mind as he sat nursing a comforting glass of wine. He had placed a food order with Marco, who told him that he would make it a priority. He planned to share his own good news with her that evening. Amos Sagger had been in touch about the ring – it would be delivered in four days' time.

As they ate, Marcia spoke of the heavy volume of phone calls from women wishing to book an appointment with her for tarot readings.

"I understand ye be wanting independence, Marcia, but I'd prefer it if you worked at the salon only a couple of days a week. Ye need to make time for me as well," he joked.

Marcia promised him, "I won't let it interfere with our life, Eamon, but speaking of phone calls, I had one from Brandon today," she said making light of it.

Instantly his demeanour changed and he went pale. Refilling his wine glass he knocked it back, his dark eyes held her's as he sucked air through his teeth. He appeared as if he were struggling to contain his vexation. "How did he come to have yer number?" he asked, in a cold, threatening tone.

"Eamon, I gave it to him. But that was before you and I got together."

Marcia blushed, feeling uneasy, sensing that she shouldn't have mentioned it. "I told him about our engagement and our forthcoming marriage."

"What are ye telling me? That the prick said congratulations? Do ye honestly think I'd believe that? Yer forgetting that I watched ye playing up to him in the restaurant, leading the man on."

"Eamon, please don't let this spoil our evening. Brandon means nothing to me. I told you he phoned me because I wanted to be honest with you. He had no idea that you and I are together now."

"So how long were ye on the phone?"

Marcia hesitated. "Let me see the phone?" he said, holding his hand out.

Marcia went to the side cabinet to retrieve her mobile. "Eamon, I couldn't be rude and cut him off after I …"

He took the phone out of her hand. Scrolling the calls he stopped, then sneered, throwing it on the table pushing the chair back and rising, leaning across the table.

"Had a cosy chat with him for thirty-five fucking minutes, when all it takes is one, just to say, I am getting married!" he spat.

Marcia tried to pacify his rage. He grabbed his jacket and car keys and stormed out the door. She slumped onto the chair, stunned at Eamon's outburst. Roman was agitated by Eamon's raised voice and Marcia's tears. The dog sat there looking at her, head cocked to one side. Marcia's mind reeled as she heard the Maserati fire up and speed off.

. . . .

On the road and already five miles away, Eamon felt as if his head would explode. He drove at break-neck speed across the top of the hills. He hit a steep rise and then slowed to pull into a clearing at the side of the road. He looked across the bay at the

351

spectacular vista – it was just what he needed to help calm his inner rage. As his eyes took in the enormous sweep of the inky-blue sea and his skin felt the mountain air, the voices in his head began to dissipate. He needed to sort himself out, he thought. He couldn't withstand the pain of another betrayal. He tried to shake off how he'd seen Marcia behave with Brandon, and now she was in touch with him again. He would never hurt her, however, this evening he'd become so overcome by anger that he knew he had to leave before he did something rash. He knew where the anger stemmed from – it was a feeling of helpless-ness – there were events outside of his control. Images of being a small boy again taunted him. His mother had stood by as his drunken father had kicked and lashed him. He had taken the beating like a man even though he was a skinny kid of seven years old, curled into the foetal position trying to protect his face, stoically withstanding the searing pain, taking his child mind to another place.

Eamon turned the engine back on and became more sure of his intentions. He drove down the road towards a once-familiar strip of bars and restaurants. He couldn't show his face in his old pal's bar since the last time he was there. He knew Michael would read him the riot act, as Eamon had promised him he'd changed his ways.

No one was going to stop him tonight, though. He just needed to find somewhere where he could remain more anonymous. The lure of oblivion in the form of a large whisky was too tempting to ignore. He came to a stop alongside a bar. It was one of the more savoury joints on that stretch of the road. Eamon had frequented the place many years ago when he'd been getting rat-faced very night. As soon as Eamon approached the bar, Mateo, the owner, had recognised him. He had taken over the business when his father Tomas had passed away. His father had liked the young Irishman and had given him many a fatherly sermon over the years. Mateo gave him a warm welcome. The look on Eamon's face though was something else; he looked murderous, enough to make Mateo take a step back in surprise. Forcing a smile, Eamon asked after Mateo's family before ordering himself a bottle of whisky.

Eamon took a quiet booth at the back of the bar and glanced at his phone, which showed that he'd had three missed calls from Dan while driving. There were two from Marcia, he noticed. Eamon sipped the glass of whisky and the familiar warming glow came immediately. The peaceful numbing effect began to work its magic. He began to think about Marcia and Brandon without immediately becoming enraged. Why didn't she put the phone down after she'd told the Texan she was getting married? An inner voice popped up. *She must still be interested in him to be on the phone that long.* His stomach knotted again and he took another swallow of his whisky. A vision of Marcia appeared. Another voice chipped in. *Idiot, ye know Marcia isn't someone who would be out and out rude by cutting the man dead.* He knew she wasn't like that. He sighed as he thought of her and how he'd overreacted. He'd treated her as if he were dealing with some adversary, not as the woman he loved.

He sat there contemplating – running his fingers through his goatee. "What sort of man are ye to treat her like that?" he silently chastised himself. "When all she did was be honest wit ye."

....

Billy was on a high after the events of the evening at the depot. Dan had insisted that he go into town and enjoy himself. Getting Dan to join him had been impossible. Dan had been too wrapped up in trying to contact Eamon to update him on proceedings. Billy was on the prowl, looking forward to a skinful of drinks and a night with a woman. Most of the bars were heaving, so Billy headed out to the quieter end of town. He planned to make a few enquiries about where he could find a local good-time girl. He was surprised to see Eamon's car, which stood out like a sore thumb parked up outside one of the better bars in the area. Billy was in no doubt to whom the Maserati belonged. He didn't want to make waves with his boss, but something here wasn't adding up. This wasn't the sort of establishment that you brought a woman to. It was more a solo drinker's joint. As Billy walked through the door, he scanned its dozen occupants and spotted Eamon sitting in the back booth nursing a drink. His boss didn't look like he wanted company but Billy wasn't going to ignore him. He could see as he approached that his boss was troubled and wondered what the problem was. Eamon looked up as Billy sidled into the booth.

"Evening boss, you can tell me to fuck off if I'm intruding, but before I find what I need for tonight, I can join you if you want," he smiled, holding the bottle of malt whisky up and reading the label.

Eamon smiled thinly.

"To be sure, Billy, to be honest wit ye I could do with your company as I'm sick of talking to myself." Billy raised his hand for a glass. Thanking the bartender, he poured himself a small beverage.

"I don't intend to get rat-faced, boss, as I want to get laid tonight and this has an adverse effect on my performance," he grinned.

Eamon leaned back into the booth, smiling. "Woman problems boss?" he asked, not fully expecting an answer. He unhurriedly lifted the glass and tasted the golden nectar. "Nice," he said, placing the glass back on the table.

"My woman's not the problem, Billy. It's my fucked up brain."

"We all suffer from that shit, boss. It's called head fuck in the Services," he said, grinning, "but usually when I give myself a good bollocking I can then see sense. I don't know what's the problem but if I was in your position with a decent woman waiting on me, I sure as fuck wouldn't be sitting in this place."

Eamon nodded without replying.

"I am only on the hunt for a night's pleasure, but, out of choice, if I found myself a straight bird who'd clip my wings, I'd settle down." Billy contemplated the glass in front of him, then shook his head, putting his hand across his glass as Eamon went to top it up.

Eamon rose, and said, "Take the bottle wit ye, Billy. That's just what I needed to hear."

"See you in the morning, boss."

Eamon nodded. Billy turned to watch Eamon walk out. His eyes alighted on the sultry dark-haired woman sitting on her own at the bar. Billy read the invitation in her smiling brown eyes as they contacted his, she crossed her legs showing more thigh. Billy raised the bottle of liquor in her direction for her to join him. *I hope she has her own place,* Billy mused, as he knew he wouldn't be able to take her back to Dan's place.

The woman smiled as she walked towards him. Leila fitted the bill for what he had in mind that evening, but his heightened intuition informed him he wouldn't take it any further.

. . . .

Roman's ears pricked up at the familiar sound and he padded over to the door, whining impatiently. Marcia heard the Maserati's engine moments later. Her eyes were still swimming and she dried them hastily, not wanting him to see how visibly shaken she'd been by his verbal attack on her. She sat in misery since he'd been gone, her calls to him unanswered.

Eamon entered and Roman bounced with delight, rushing past him into the garden, expecting his evening stroll. Marcia, sitting in semi-darkness, watched Eamon's statuesque form fill the doorframe. His eyes were downcast and he had a dejected air about him, but even that couldn't distract from his handsome physicality

"Marcia, I…" he began.

She leapt up towards him. "I've been so worried, Eamon!" she cried. The whisky fumes hung heavily in the air as he spoke "I'm so sorry, please forgive me. I'm a jealous bastard. I can't help it."

Marcia could have cheerfully strangled him. He had caused the first major upset in their relationship and it had floored her. Initially, he had frightened her with his temper, but her fright had turned to anger. Her anger had produced hot tears, which in turn had become worried ones when Eamon didn't answer his phone. Sitting in the gloom, she had willed him back to her, and here he was. He reminded her of a small child and she held him to her. "It's okay, it's okay," she whispered over and over to him, laying her head against his chest, the familiar shape and feel of his warmth and his heart pounding in her ear.

"I'll never do to you what she did, Eamon," Marcia promised.

"I know," he answered, holding her in his customary bear hug, his hand tracing a pathway over her head, letting his fingers travel the length of her red hair. He breathed in her sweet-smelling fragrance and lifted her face up to his. Her eyes glistened as tears spilt over, but this time they were joyous ones.

"I love ye so much, Marcia," Eamon breathed.

"I love you too," Marcia answered, and taking his hand led him through to the bedroom. No more needed to be said.

Marcia felt as protective of Eamon as if he'd been a small boy. The plaintive look in his eyes had melted her heart. She loathed Eve for what she had put him through, and she understood his fear that it might happen again. She would never betray him. Words alone could not convey this. She cradled him into her, his thick dark hair across her shoulder, the weight of his head a heavy comfort to her. Her small hand ran down his massive back, soothing and calming him.

. . . .

His hand, strong and firm ran down her curves in response, following the contours of her body. She wanted him desperately and, knowingly, he took her mouth in his, hungering for her taste – her flesh. They kissed for the longest time as if they'd never kissed before. Eamon needed the closeness, the reassurance and feel of her. Her body was his and he wanted to worship it, to make her aware that every part of him was every part of her too. He was hyper conscious of her taste and smell, committing it all to memory. The feel of her plump breasts under his hands, the hardening of her nipples between his fingers, the moist eagerness between her legs. Her tanned limbs moving in impossible positions under him, willing him to drive into her, taking her soul with his into the sublime depth only they knew.

Marcia was alive with hungry intensity. Eamon was being sensitive to her wants, as always, but he also seemed to need extra; something deep within him wanted more from her. Her inner being responded, holding his huge frame tenderly, she kissed him with a passion that was soft and caring too. Her limbs entwined in his as she restlessly positioned herself in readiness for him. Her thighs were damp with desire – slick, hot and expectant.

Still, their mouths worked their magic, yearning, promising, committing to each other just as their bodies honoured one another, bonding, making a pact for eternity. When Eamon finally entered her, it was as if every nerve ending had exploded. Like a tidal wave, the pleasure of their joining took her to new and greater heights. They were moving along on something that was more than just physical. They breathed as one, as in tune as an orchestra. Their blood flowed, hot and tingling, pulses raced madly. Skin on skin, every sense was at screaming point, welcoming the honeyed saltiness of their taste, the mingled scent of man and woman and the sweet moans of ecstasy from them both. They were a lightning storm of tangled limbs and restless souls crashing and combining until they floated gently, peacefully back into the cradle of love that bound them to each other.

Without conscious effort, they took up position as before. Eamon resting his head on her, Marcia's arm cradling his broad shoulder, holding him against her as if to shield him from hurt. Soft shadows fell across his relaxed features and Marcia knew that without this man beside her there would be a ragged hole in her heart. As soft as angels' wings, she kissed his closed eyelids and wished him a deep and dream-free sleep.

....

Eamon listened as Dan brought him up to speed with what went on with Alejandro. He said that the man hadn't been immediately forthcoming when they'd demanded to know where the drugs had come from and who the supplier was. "However, after some physical 'persuasion'," Dan grinned, "he came up with both. I've got a name and the address for his supplier." Alejandro had revealed that he had previously done three trips, but pleading his case, he said that it was only under duress – otherwise he wouldn't have done it. Dan gave Eamon the details. He said Alejandro had implored, begging, telling them that he had a pregnant wife and young child to look after, that he couldn't afford to lose his job.

Eamon wasn't of the same mindset as Jimmy Grant, who'd turned a blind eye to anyone smuggling a bit of their personal contraband through, as long as the consignment reached its destination. Eamon was having a complete "shakedown." He was now at a place in his life where he was financially secure and determined to put his criminal activities behind him. Eamon knew he was a fortuitous man in every way. He had escaped a life behind bars and once he had fulfilled Jimmy's obligations, he did not intend to enter the narcotics arena again. Eamon knew that it made no difference to Jimmy Grant's contacts that he now ran the show. He had been Grant's right-hand man and had overseen the shipments for him. He had been in the firing line then as he was now. In this dog-eat-dog world he lived in, Eamon knew you couldn't easily bow out and leave the stage without taking the final curtain. But to make a start, he would ensure all his employees would read him loud and clear, as Eamon wasn't a man who liked to repeat himself.

Dan told Eamon, they would randomly subject all of the lorries and men to spot checks with the Belgian shepherd, which would guarantee to keep the drivers on their toes making them think twice about smuggling. Dan and Eamon talked about how the business was going to look, moving forward. Eamon asked Dan to give Billy a call – he wanted to get them all together to sort a few things out.

....

The launch party for Suzette's new salon, The Mystique, was a great success, far exceeding expectations. The place was absolutely heaving. Eamon was speaking to Greg. They had been privately discussing the restaurant and Greg had accepted Eamon's offer to repay the money for his newly acquired land to build a home for him and Marcia. Greg agreed to step back from the silent partnership, and Eamon would reimburse him at a low interest rate over twelve months. Playing it that way would enable Eamon to legally show the money from the income from the haulage company and his restaurant.

Eamon had reluctantly attended the opening. It was only to appease Marcia that he did. The last thing he wanted was to be in the company of Suzette Greenaway and all the other faux females that he now found distasteful. He looked around – each and every one of them appeared to come out of the same mould, each one battling to hold on to their youth. He observed Marcia who was encircled by women vying for her attention. Marcia didn't flaunt her sexuality as most of the other women in their circle did. The green Valentino dress that she wore didn't reveal flesh, yet spoke to him of the promise of what lay beneath – that small, curvaceous body that belonged to him only. It hadn't been Eve's betrayal that had changed him. It was falling in love with Marcia that had opened his heart, allowing his imprisoned emotions to begin their healing journey. He knew that there was still a secreted part of his damaged psyche that taunted him, but Marcia was slowly turning the key with her love and devotion.

....

Suzette looked thrilled. They had never seen so many designer labels under one roof. Marcia was now fully booked with clients for the next three months. The ladies who were in attendance appeared impressed with the range of beauty treatments and procedures that were available. The presence of a psychic medium on the premises was yet another asset and many of the clients doubled up their bookings. Suzette had stuck to her guns and hadn't given any concessions.

Marcia had to stop Suzette from overbooking her. She wanted some free time to spend with Eamon. She was fully aware that Eamon would have preferred her to stay at home, but he knew that her independence was important to her and he had agreed to her part-time work at the salon. Marcia had missed her friends, though, and was delighted when Joyce and Cindy arrived. Joyce was full of news about Sara and the baby and showed Marcia all the photos of her new granddaughter. She excitedly related her plans to move out to the US. She couldn't wait to leave Spain and kiss her old life and bad memories of Jimmy goodbye. Cindy, meanwhile, couldn't wait to retrain under the two top stylists that Suzette had employed at the salon. Marcia was pleased to hear their good news.

....

Eamon had taken delivery of the engagement ring from Amos and it was now locked away securely in his safe. It was absolutely the most beautiful piece of jewellery that he'd ever seen. Amos had told him to call as soon as the ring was on Marcia's finger, and Eamon had agreed, inviting him and his partner Levi to the engagement party.

Eamon had been busy on the phone to Jane that morning as well, arranging for Billy to get involved in handling Caesar. Eamon knew that Billy's charismatic nature belied a man who in a split second would snuff an adversary's light out and think nothing of it. Eamon thought he'd be the right man for the job, because not only was Billy an animal lover but he had also proved himself to be a man who wasn't afraid of any task that Eamon put his way.

Eamon had got rid of Jimmy Grant's men. He had no reason to keep them. He had a few men, loyal to him, who he knew he could rely on should the need arise. But now, the way things stood, Dan and Billy, along with Jane and the Belgian shepherd were sufficient.

....

Maureen had phoned Marcia. She said that Sheila was now speaking, but her words were slurred and it was difficult at times to understand what she was saying, although the doctors were happy with her progress. "No one had realistically expected my girl to pull through, except you, Marcia." Maureen was gushing with emotional joy and thrilled that her baby girl was fighting back. She told Marcia how the specialist had told them today that while Sheila was in an induced coma that she had suffered a stroke that had left Sheila's eyesight impaired, but Maureen said she would employ someone to drive her girl around. I couldn't have got through this without your conviction that she wasn't going to die," Maureen broke down sobbing. "Marcia, me and Dom want to buy you a gift, as you have been our rock and we don't know how we would have got through this without you and Eamon."

Marcia declined but thanked her. "When Eamon comes in I will tell him the good news," Marcia said, promising they would see them soon.

. . . .

Billy showered, splashed on some fresh cologne and got dressed in a smart shirt and jeans ready for his dog training with Jane and Caesar.

The time sped by so quickly, Billy found himself for the first time totally smitten, not only because Jane looked so good but also because he was fascinated by her intelligence and extensive knowledge of dog behaviour. He asked her out on a date and Jane accepted. From that moment on the pair became inseparable.

When Billy discussed this a couple of days later with his housemate, Dan revealed that he had gone for a haircut at the Mystique salon earlier that day and asked Cindy for a date.

. . . .

Eamon put the phone down, mulling over the offer that he had just received. Carlo Gabrette had given him three days to think it over, telling him that he'd need a definite answer within that time frame. He knew the pressure was on. Jimmy Grant had been dealing with the Italians for so long and Eamon would be expected to continue to do so. It didn't sit well with him, but he didn't know which way the wind would blow in Miami if he backed out of the deal.

The narcotic shipment from the Florida Keys could be a lucrative prospect, even though he didn't need the money. His thoughts were causing a maelstrom in his head. There had also been unrest at the depot over what had occurred with the Spaniard, Alejandro. The supplier who Alejandro dealt with was now demanding his money and had been threatening the man's family. Eamon knew he had to act fast. He could sense dangerous tensions arising with these small-time gangsters who weren't afraid to use violence. They thought they had carte blanche and could just take over Eamon's end of the business. He realised he had to be careful though. Things needed to run smoothly at the depot. He needed to avoid any trouble there. Half of the drivers were related to each other and family loyalties were bound to cause an issue. Suddenly a text alert from his phone jolted him out of his ruminations. Absent-mindedly he picked it up and noticed Marcia's number flashing at him. Opening the text, he smiled as he read about how much she was missing him. "Not as much as I miss ye, woman," he replied.

Marcia had sent some intimate photos to Eamon's phone. Eamon smiled at the first picture of her pert breasts, and he started to feel horny at the second one of her round bottom. The third photo of Marcia lying on the bed with her legs slightly parted sent his sexual desire through the roof. He responded immediately, telling Marcia that she was driving him absolutely demented. "I can only spare an hour," he texted back.

"I can't wait," she replied.

He shortly arrived at her place, keyed in the numbers on the gate and smiled as Roman accompanied him to the house. "Where is your mistress, boy?" he enquired as he strode round to the back of the villa and through the open terrace doors. He was greeted by the delectable sight of Marcia in the nude. Eamon smiled. Picking her up in his arms, he carried her into the bedroom, back kicking the door shut. "Sorry Roman," he said, as the dog tried to follow him, "but your mistress and I need some privacy." He stripped off as rapidly as he could. He had gained an uncomfortable erection on the drive over and he was more than happy to release it. Marcia was on all fours, doggy fashion, on the neatly made bed. He could see the dampness glistening where her legs were parted for him. Eamon stepped forward to claim what was his, kissing and licking Marcia's buttocks. She writhed and squirmed which only served to stimulate him further. But he did not intend to give her what she wanted straight away. He let his tongue torment her until she was gasping for more. She was nearly tipped over the edge before he guided himself into her moist warmth. She clenched her muscles around his taut penis, taking his full length as he hammered against her behind. His powerful hands almost meeting around her tiny waist, pinning her to the bed, head to one side, hair in a spray around her face. Panting and groaning in time to Eamon's thrusts, she climaxed a second before him. Feeling the familiar hot rush deep inside her, her legs gave way and they collapsed in a heap of wet satisfaction on the rumpled coverlet.

Eamon checked his watch as he hurriedly dressed. "Ye and I have unfinished business which we can deal with at our leisure this evening," he smiled. He leaned across her naked form on the bed, grabbing his car keys from the bedside table and kissing her.

"I have some appointments later at the salon. Thank you for the pleasurable interlude," she purred.

"The pleasure was all mine," Eamon winked as he instructed Roman to watch over her.

. . . .

The land that Greg had looked at boasted amazing panoramic views over the bay. He'd been quick to phone Eamon about it. Greg and the architect had arranged to meet him there. Eamon was sure that Marcia would absolutely love the stunning vistas the plot provided, and he felt certain that once this new home was built, it would be a true haven for them.

He spent several hours with the architect confirming the details on the style and layout. It all had to be perfect. He then shook hands on the deal with Greg. The plan was for Greg to go ahead with the land purchase, and once the architect had drawn up the plans, Greg would take over the entire project management as well. It seemed as if the future would be looking good for them.

Diego had informed Eamon that the men at the depot were afraid of the Eastern Europeans, as there were rumours that they were beginning to take over and they were well known for their violence. He also passed on his suspicions that Alejandro was not the only driver who the Bulgarians had got their hands on. He had heard rumours that there were now two more men in fear for their lives and worried about their families. Eamon advised Diego to go to Alejandro's home, to tell him to get his pregnant wife and child away from the area as soon as possible. He would ensure that there was enough money for them to get their lives sorted out. If Alejandro agreed, Diego was to come to Eamon's house to pick the money up. He wasn't to mention him by name; Diego could just inform him that the money was from

Diego's own funds. Diego assured Eamon that he would carry out his orders.

Eamon knew that he was many things – violence went hand in hand with his line of work. He was a fair man if he weren't crossed, but under no circumstances would he allow women and children to be threatened or put in danger.

Dan and Billy sat listening to their boss. He informed them to use their own strategy to stop the brothers. "Use any means youse see fit," he said, "I don't care, I just want them gone fer good," he ordered. Eamon had men on standby that he trusted and he would call upon them for backup if things got out of hand.

He also wanted as much information as possible about the Bulgarian brothers, he told Dan and Billy. "This job will require your full attention and has to be addressed as a priority, I'm sorry if youse boys had any other plans," Eamon told them, "but these scum are like a cancer. Once they get a hold there'll be no stopping them."

Eamon knew that the Bulgarians had put a price on his head, and he had no intention of losing it. As Eamon walked with Dan and Billy to their cars, Billy turned to his boss and told him with absolute certainty in his voice, "You can rest assured, these low-lives will disappear as fast as they arrived, and then the depot will be back running like clockwork."

Eamon thanked both men.

Dan and Billy returned to their home to make plans. It would be difficult for them to get any information from the workers at the depot, given their fear of the Bulgarian brothers. Alejandro could be the only person who would be able to provide them with any details.

They decided to go to the depot to speak to Diego to get Alejandro's address. After they'd beaten him that night, they hardly expected him to be happy to see them again. Speaking to him would be the only way for them to find out what they needed to know. They got into their car and sped off. On the way, Billy's thoughts turned to his boss, and he looked over at Dan as he drove, saying, "I know the boss is faced with a few problems now, which won't take us long to sort out. But I've noticed he looks chipper and he has a spring in his step, his woman must be keeping him satisfied in the sack. The old saying about women being the weaker sex is a load of bollocks," he laughed. "They're clever – they know how to give a man what he wants and..."

Dan cut in, "Are you speaking from experience? Someone must be 'training' you well too, I've noticed because all that applies to you too. The jaunty walk, the puppy dog look ... do you want me to continue?" Dan laughed.

Billy chuckled without replying. He hadn't realised it was that obvious.

....

Eamon was eagerly waiting and opened the gates for them. He invited them inside and listened carefully as Dan relayed the information from Alejandro. At first, Eamon appeared impassive. He was used to threats, but after Dan told him that there was a price on Jane's head, he responded. "I want this woman that's with them to disappear along with the brothers," he stated firmly. When Dan told him that another man, Axel Andreas was now working for the brothers through Eamon's haulage business Eamon knew instinctively that there must be more. These Bulgarian men were terrorising his men and he was going to put a swift stop to it. He knew it would only be a matter of time before the brothers knew about Marcia too, and then her life would also be in danger.

Eamon phoned Marcia at the salon straight away. He informed her to wait there. He was going to pick her up and she was going to move in with him. There was no room for discussion. He stated he would take her home to collect some of her things and that he'd be with her in twenty minutes.

. . . .

Marcia attempted to explain that she had appointments booked in, but Eamon wouldn't listen, telling her to do as he asked. Marcia couldn't take it in. "Eamon why the sudden change, what is happening?" she asked him, panic rising. She heard the urgency in his voice, and despite her protestations, knew that she had to do as he bid. Marcia quickly cancelled her afternoon appointments and had barely put the phone down before Eamon came into the salon.

. . . .

Suzette was fuming. Striding across to the reception, she challenged Eamon, "Who do you think you are, disrupting my business? Why don't you just get out of her life?" she exploded, holding nothing back. "I have worked hard to get my business up and running and you step in and try to ruin it, by taking…"

"Listen to me, yer skating on thin ice, Suzette," he growled. "Marcia is leaving right this minute with me, so I would think it wise if ye kept yer mouth shut." He turned around, taking Marcia gently by the arm, steering her towards the door.

Suzette was thankful that the two female clients were in the treatment room at the back of the building, relaxing in mud body wraps, and hadn't heard a thing.

Suzette acted as if nothing had happened. She busied herself with some paperwork telling the boys, who to her annoyance had been hanging around, to go check on their clients. She prayed that the scene went unnoticed as the last thing she needed was for it to become common knowledge that Eamon O'Donally had lowered the tone of her establishment.

Suzette thought about telling Greg about how he had spoken to her but then thought better of it. She knew that this would risk causing conflict between the two men, and Eamon knew too much about her past. Greg might view things a little differently about her if he knew how she had set Max up. No, she thought, wisely, I will apologise to Eamon and straighten things out.

. . . .

All that Eamon had told Marcia was that she and Roman needed to live at his place and that there wasn't any need for questions. Marcia followed his instructions without hesitation. She sensed that something was wrong, very wrong. Her bags were packed and she was sitting in the back of the car with Roman. She knew that when he was in a dark mood that he would not tell her what was on his mind, although she could see the burning intensity in his eyes when he glanced into the rearview mirror. She wouldn't want to be the person who had upset him to this extent, she thought to herself.

. . . .

Billy and Dan were observing the comings and goings at the Bulgarians' house. They watched as a car pulled up and a stunning dark-haired woman got out. She had raven black hair, skin-tight black jeans and she wore a very low-cut blouse which showed off her nice-sized breasts. She looked every part the femme fatale. Her appearance looked as dangerous as Alejandro had said. From the description they'd been given it was obvious that she was Catriona, Drogomir's mistress.

"I bet they share her, being brothers and all," Billy grinned. Dan just smiled and kept his eyes on the house, watching as Catriona put the key in the front door and entered. Five minutes later, Billy nudged Dan. One of the brothers had just left. "I'm going to take a look around as soon as his car is out of view," he told him. It was getting dark and he would have to move carefully in the dim light. He planned to sneak a look through a window, to try to see what was going on inside. "I'll go round the back to look for a possible entry point," he whispered to Dan.

Dan said he would keep watch in case the other brother returned.

Billy was used to creeping around in the dark. It was something that he'd done many times before in the mountainous regions of Afghanistan. This time was a little different – the place was like a junkyard, and the slightest sound would call attention. Any mistake would bring the Bulgarians running. At the back of the property, Billy could see a light on in a room. He watched as he saw the woman they'd identified as Catriona strip off. The man was naked and smiling, handcuffed, lying on a bed. Billy continued observing Catriona who was wearing a deep red basque, black fishnet stockings and stilettos. The bull whip in her hand completed the picture. Billy thought she looked menacing rather than sexy. On the bedside table was what appeared to be a thick cannabis joint or possibly even something more powerful smouldering in an ashtray. Billy's mind fleetingly went back to his past when he'd occasionally dabbled in drug-fuelled sex.

Billy smiled thinly as the woman straddled the man and his mind started to race at how much of a golden opportunity this created. Stealthily, he moved towards the back door and pressed the handle down. The door opened. He inched down the hallway until he was right outside the bedroom door. He listened – he could hear the movement of the bed and crept in unnoticed by the pair. In one swift movement, Billy grabbed Catriona's hair, twisting it so that she couldn't get away. The man's eyes bulged as he screamed at Billy in Bulgarian. Catriona was fighting like a tigress as he dragged her out of the bedroom towards the kitchen. She fought like a demon, her red painted talons trying to rip into his hands. He jerked her head away with his knee as she tried to sink her teeth in.

Once in the kitchen, he kicked her in the back of the legs and she fell to the floor like a ton of bricks. He held her hands clamped together and pulled out the tape and ties, securing her wrists behind her back. Quickly, opening the sink cupboard doors, he came across some plastic bags and, taking two, he yanked her to her feet. He put the plastic bag over her head and tied it as tightly as he could, while she spat and tried to wrestle away from him. He dragged her back to the bedroom, still kicking and struggling, and threw her to the floor. Taking the second plastic bag, he swiftly tied it around the Bulgarian's head. Billy then left as quickly as he had come, and by the time he had sat down next to Dan in the car, headlights came into view.

The second brother strode towards the house and put the key in the front door. Dan's fist smashed into his temple as it opened. Billy caught his limp body and they hauled his heavy, stunned body in. Once they had him in the kitchen, they trussed him up and repeated the plastic bag technique on him. Billy checked the bedroom, seeing no sign of life. Dan moved across the room, relighting the joint without putting it to his lips. He laid it on the cheap nylon bed covering, watching the embers start to smoulder. He then went into the kitchen, walked to the stove, and turned all the lighted gas taps on full, placing the oil-filled chip pan on the back burner. Signalling to Billy, the two men returned quickly to their car and drove quietly down the country lane.

. . . .

Marcia accepted that Eamon had his reasons for wanting her and Roman to move in with him. He didn't explain but said that although he hadn't wanted them to live together under the same roof that he had shared with Eve, circumstances had changed and it wouldn't be long before he had it sorted. He had put the ring on her finger that he was going to give her on the night of their engagement party. Marcia was overcome with emotion when she opened the box, gasping at the beauty of the diamond and emeralds on the gold band. Marcia forgot the trepidation she felt earlier – by all the upheaval. Throwing her arms around his neck, she kissed him, then, holding her at arms' length, Eamon said, "Ye go and sort yer things out, I have to speak to Dan and Billy and we'll have plenty of time tonight for ye to show me your appreciation," he grinned wickedly.

Looking through her suitcase, she found a swimsuit, changed into it and slid open the terrace doors that led out to the swimming pool. Roman's eyes were on her as she submerged herself in the pool. As always, he kept to his guard duties, lying near the poolside, watching her every move.

. . . .

In Eamon's office, behind locked doors, Dan and Billy sat opposite Eamon at his desk. Dan began by going through what had happened the previous night and explaining how there shouldn't be any more problems at the depot. Eamon was pleased that they had dealt directly with the issue. He advised them that he wanted the Belgian shepherd daily at the depot for a while. He was sure the drivers would soon get the picture. "Billy you and Jane can do the spot checks. By the way, how's your training with Jane coming on?"

"Swimmingly, boss."

"He's been a different man, boss, since Jane has been training him," Dan chipped in.

Billy shook his head, smiling.

Eamon elevated his brow and nodded, getting the picture, without commenting.

"We do have another small problem though, boss," Dan said. He filled him in on the situation with Axel Andreas, "If we let him go, then he'll think that he could start taking the piss again further down the line. Although the Bulgarian brothers are no more, you never know who might turn up in the future," counselled Dan.

Eamon nodded, he could see the sense in it and told the two to deal with him. They were to go to the depot the following day, locate him, and put the fear of Christ into him. "As soon as youse dealt with him get all the information from the man, ring me and we'll take it from there." Eamon thanked both men and wished them goodnight.

Alone in his office, Eamon thought about the criminal world he had been immersed in for most of his life. If it wasn't people across the Atlantic on his back, it was these poxy south-eastern Europeans that were trying to push their way in. He felt weary of the violence, narcotics and all the mayhem that went with it. All he wanted now was to settle down with Marcia and have a peaceful life. He thought again about the offer he'd received from Carlo and the decision he needed to make shortly. He was still uncertain and decided to sleep on it.

Eamon made a phone call to Dom and Maureen. Their daughter was slowly but surely on the mend. He told Dom he was pleased to hear it. The only lasting effect of her near-death experience seemed to be damage to her sight, which was very slowly coming back. The two parents were so thankful that their girl was still alive. Dom asked how things were with him and Marcia. Eamon revealed that she had moved in with him and that he would be sending Dom and Maureen a wedding invitation soon.

Dom said that Maureen would be itching to get involved with the arrangements. "She's like one of those bleeding wedding planners on the television," he laughed. "Still, if that's what makes her happy, it will help keep her mind occupied, what with all the worry she's had."

Eamon thought it was good to hear Dom laugh once more.

Eamon was relieved that the haulage business would now be running smoothly again. He ran his fingers through his hair, making a mental note to speak to his brother Patrick tomorrow. Eamon wanted to take Marcia back to his homeland and decided that he would make plans for it as soon as the business with Axel Andreas was sorted out. A few days with his younger brother, the only family he had, was what he needed. He switched the light off and locked his office door.

....

The terrace doors were open in their bedroom, and Eamon could see Marcia swimming in the pool. Momentarily, Roman lifted his head from the tiles, saw that it was Eamon, and rested his chin once again. Eamon smiled as he watched her, although she was unaware of his presence. Just seeing her lifted his mood and lightened his burdens. He observed her for several minutes before leaving to take a shower.

Marcia peeled her swimsuit off and wrapped a king-size towel around her petite frame. She then headed to the bathroom. A scented haze hung in the air and the steam swirled around her as Marcia opened the sliding door. Eamon was busy soaping himself and was slathered in bubbles.

"Let me," Marcia offered, letting her towel drop before entering and taking the soap from his hand. He leaned forward to kiss the sweetness of her lips as she lathered the soap luxuriously in her hands. Eamon inhaled sharply as Marcia rolled his balls through her foamy fingers, pulling him gently by them away from the overhead water. He watched her, heart pumping, cock stiffening, as she took the soap once more and proceeded to work it up into a mound of bubbles. Somewhere in the deep recesses of his mind, he heard the soap drop with a thud as Marcia rubbed his shaft through the froth she'd created, her hands gliding along the length, paying particular attention to the glans, diligently cleaning and caressing every part of his member. The firm slippery pressure was making him quiver with expectancy and just when he thought he'd have to give in, Marcia let go and bent for the soap, slowly licking the head of his penis on the way down. His balls jumped and tightened and he felt a surge of hot sperm begin its journey.

Marcia passed him the soap. "Your turn," she grinned up at him.

"Ye little witch," he murmured, filling his hands with bubbles. He took a firm breast in each and soaped them both thoroughly, enjoying the weight of them and her hardened nipples. Marcia's stomach flipped over as Eamon proceeded to wash her back and front at the same time. He was meticulous in his cleansing. Rubbing gently over her silken skin, his hands travelled downwards until they arrived at the intended destination. He skilfully administered to Marcia's nether regions with practiced fingers, making her whimper delightedly.

She stopped him when it became apparent that Eamon wouldn't last much longer and nor would she if they didn't call a halt now. Stepping forward, which made him move backwards she flipped the shower dial to cold and they gasped as one, as the icy water hit them chasing away the last of the bubbles and leaving them squeaky clean.

Laughing, they threw themselves on the bed, Eamon's erection already returning. Their hair was slicked back, and their eyes shone, a rosy glow on their healthy bodies. Marcia's small, feminine physique, made supple by years of self-discipline, stretched slowly in readiness, her lips parted to show even white teeth. He looked into her dilated pupils and they lost themselves in each other once more.

. . . .

Marcia drifted off to sleep. She could see the silhouette of a man whose face was turned away from her. He started to speak. Max

Greenaway's voice invaded her mind. Panic overcame her and she could feel herself struggling to warn Suzette of the danger. Why, when he was dead and buried, had he come to her in a dream? Something was not right. Then she could see Eamon standing by the sea. He was looking out into the distance as if he were waiting for someone to arrive. Her dream changed again and now she could see Suzette, her arms draped across her face. She could see that there was blood trickling from her head.

Eamon, unable to sleep, watched Marcia as she tossed and turned. He smoothed her forehead to bring her some semblance of calm and wondered what demons were plaguing her. After a few minutes, he felt her body relax, and he listened to her gentle breathing. Eamon had decided to go ahead with Carlo Gabrette's deal. With that in mind, and Marcia now peaceful, he managed to fall into a restful sleep.

....

Marcia sat in the sunshine with Roman at her side. She had awoken to find that Eamon had already gone, although he had called to say that he was on his way to the depot.

Dan and Billy joined him there. He'd got a got call from Diego, letting him know that Axel Andreas had turned up and was now at his office. The three men made their way into the building with the Belgian shepherd and locked the door behind them. As soon as they'd sat down, Axel immediately broke down and started sobbing, telling them how he hadn't wanted to take the package on his last trip to the UK but the Bulgarians had threatened to rape his wife and to slit his children's throats if he didn't follow their orders.

"I had no choice," he whimpered, pleading that he was a family man and that the work at the depot was his only means of survival.

Eamon leant forwards and Axel instantly paled at the menacing expression on his face. "This is your only warning, my friend," Eamon growled, "If ye are approached by anyone else, no matter who, then ye come straight to me." He paused to allow his words to sink in. "Otherwise the Bulgarians will be the least of your worries, I can fucking assure ye, ye caffler," he sneered.

Axel Andreas seemed to take in the message and nodded keenly. He swore on the Madonna that he would do what Eamon asked.

Eamon had a finely tuned sense of who was being straight with him and who wasn't, and looking into Axel's terrified eyes he felt sure that it was only the threats from the Bulgarians that had made him do this.

Eamon stepped away from Axel and gave him a chance to regain his composure. "Let it be known that my men and the dog will be going over lorries at random from now on. ANYONE who thinks they can keep me in the dark will be paying a heavy price, ARE YE READING ME CLEARLY?" he spat.

Axel nodded, sweating profusely, twisting his hands together nervously.

Eamon knew he had to put the pressure on the terrorised man, but he hated the way it made him feel like a bully, which was something that Eamon actually found abhorrent. He felt the man had taken enough and had learnt his lesson. "Now, I hope ye have got the full gist of me and the way I intend to run my business, so inform all your mates at my depot, that my tolerance is zero," his thumb and forefinger formed an 0 in the gibbering man's face.

Eamon stood up to his full height. He sucked air through his teeth as he studied Axel Andreas. "I am going to give ye yer job back." He paused. "I know that ye were a loyal man before their threats," Eamon said lowering his tone, letting Axel off the hook. He told Axel to go about his business and nodded to Dan to open the door for him.

Eamon hoped that the haulage company would now run smoothly with no more outside interference.

Roman watched Eamon walking across the terrace and wagged his tail in greeting. Seeing Marcia sitting in the sunshine, Eamon walked towards her. "Was something tormenting ye in your sleep last night?" he bent over her, kissing her softly. Marcia started slowly, recalling the memory that was still vivid in her mind. She remembered that it had felt like a warning of something ominous. She told Eamon as the thoughts came back to her, about how she had heard Max Greenaway's voice but had been unable to see his face, and that she'd seen Suzette with blood seeping from her head. She went on to describe the vision of Eamon in the dream, standing looking out to sea.

"It was as if you were waiting for something, but there was a feeling of danger all around you. It scared me, Eamon," she murmured. Holding his hand to her face, she went on, "It felt like a bad omen ... something awful is going to happen ... I can feel it."

Eamon gently reassured her that it had just been a bad dream, enveloping her in his arms. However, he was disturbed by her words. He knew Marcia was never wrong about these things. He kissed her again and told her that he wouldn't be long, as he had to make a phone call.

Once in his office, he locked the door and picked up the phone to call Miami. He checked his watch. It would be about 5 am there, and he knew that Carlo would be up and preparing for his morning jog.

Carlo sounded pleased to hear from Eamon. After exchanging pleasantries, Eamon calmly advised Carlo that he had decided to decline his offer. Eamon picked up the irritation in Carlo's tone; he knew he didn't like anyone to turn down his propositions.

Carlo Gabrette laughed softly, trying to convince Eamon that the huge profit was as good as his. He'd tried everything to change Eamon's mind, but Eamon was resolute, explaining that he'd decided to step back from business for a while.

He hoped that there wouldn't be any repercussions from Carlo Gabrette and that his long-standing friendship with his father Alphonso would hold him in good stead, preventing any ripples from occurring across the pond in Miami. Eamon knew that refusing a deal with the Italians wouldn't sit easy with them. He realised that they could view him as a thorn in their side. He put the phone down; his thoughts turned to Marcia's dream. He knew what her dream had meant – the vision she'd seen of him. That had been enough of a warning for him to decline dealing with Carlo Gabrette.

The land that Greg had shown Eamon had been purchased. After some small alterations, the architect's plans had been given the go-ahead. Greg had pulled out all the stops to get things moving, and, with luck, Eamon would be able to present it to Marcia as a surprise gift at their impending wedding.

....

Marcia arrived at work with Roman by her side, to find the salon buzzing.

Suzette was thrilled to see her back, although she was a little piqued by her late arrival. She smiled as she saw Marcia come through the door and asked her to join her in the staff room.

"I will keep Roman with me while you deal with your clients," Suzette said, looking pleased. "Bookings have gone through the roof now that we have added your spiritual medium services to all the hair and beauty treatments. There's no other salon that offers all of that!"

Marcia didn't feel any animosity coming from Suzette, despite her previous confrontation with Eamon and the fact that Marcia had moved in with him.

Marcia sensed that things were going well for Suzette and that she was keen to share some good news. As soon as they were alone together, Suzette spilled the beans. "Sit down, Marcia," she said, excitedly. "Greg has asked me to marry him, and we are going shopping next week for an engagement ring!"

Marcia was genuinely thrilled for her, and in the excitement of the shared news, she invited Suzette and Greg to their house at the weekend, explaining that it was a small party for a few intimate friends to celebrate *their* engagement.

As much as Suzette disliked Eamon, she was happy to accept the invitation. Suzette ran through Marcia's list of bookings. She'd arranged them so that Marcia could fit them into her part-time hours.

"I have informed all of your future clients that your fee is 200 euros per consultation," she advised, raising a hand to stop Marcia from speaking. "Each and every one of them said it was fine. I also told them that a private home visit is now 300 euros, and, once again, not one of those women batted an eye," she revealed, smiling. "Now, 50 euros of each payment will be going to the salon, if that's agreeable to you."

Marcia responded by hugging her.

Suzette continued, checking her watch, "Your first client arrives in fifteen minutes, so I'd advise you to prepare yourself and I will ring you as soon as they arrive. By the way, a man has been booked in for your second appointment – he said that he'd been given your name and mentioned that it was urgent." Suzette looked slightly more serious for a moment. "He wanted you to visit his home, but to be honest, his voice gave me the creeps," Suzette said that he'd spoken with a heavy Eastern European accent.

Marcia shrugged, not concerned by the details, commanding Roman to stay, and went to her office.

Her first client swept in with a large diamond ring on her left hand, her hands deliberately gesticulating so the dazzling jewel was in Marcia's line of vision. Marcia remarked on how beautiful the ring was as it was so obvious that the woman wanted her to notice it. Then the glamorous blonde woman went into details as to its value and the exact size of the gem. Marcia was relieved that she hadn't worn her engagement ring, whose diamond was double the size, as she would have felt uncomfortable stealing the woman's thunder.

After the initial introduction and shuffling of the tarot cards, Marcia began to lay the twenty-two major arcana cards out. She immediately sensed it was going to be one of those tarot readings where she would need to use tact. Marcia could see the woman was involved in a clandestine affair – she knew to choose her words skilfully.

Marcia began. "I see a situation, that is kept away from prying eyes, which I feel will shortly come out into the open."

The woman frowned. "Can you make it clearer, love? I'm not too savvy with words, only with maths," she added, "totting up my old man's assets," she laughed, her bright red lips practically filling the width of her face, displaying her expensive-looking veneers. Marcia tactfully spoke of a secret relationship, fully expecting the woman's denial. Marcia was surprised by her openness, however. The woman was happy to tell Marcia about her secret life. The woman went into the ins and outs of her relationship with her married lover, not leaving out any intimate detail.

Marcia felt she was hearing too much information regarding the woman's private life. She told her that she would be embroiled in a legal battle but that it would end up being favourable. She asked Marcia if her married lover would leave his wife. Marcia studied the layout and told her that he would, but there would be a price to pay.

Before Marcia had time to finish, the woman placed her hand across the cards. "I don't need to hear any more. I have my answer." She grinned, thanking her profusely.

The woman was overjoyed at the news, although she had previously paid Suzette, the woman gave Marcia a 50 euro tip and asked her if she could visit her at home in two weeks' time. Marcia told her to book in at reception; the woman assured her that she would inform all her friends about her.

Marcia wasn't judgemental. She never allowed her morals and ethics to influence her no matter what was revealed in a client's reading. Marcia had dealt with so many people over the years with various secrets – it was part and parcel of her work.

Marcia's next client wasn't due for fifteen minutes, so she popped into the salon to see if Cindy was free. Luckily, Cindy was between appointments. Marcia knew Cindy wanted to speak to her so she asked her if she wanted to join her in her office.

An excited Cindy told Marcia all about Dan and how much she loved his company. They had plans to go out that evening and he had invited her to stay over. "As you could imagine, Marcia, my overnight bag was packed immediately!" Cindy's raucous laughter filled the room. Marcia invited the pair to their engagement party and Cindy was delighted to confirm that she'd be there and that she'd ask Dan that night.

Marcia walked back into the salon to where the two flamboyant hair technicians were bent over a colour chart. She took the opportunity to invite them both to the party too, and they were ecstatic at the prospect.

"We'll have to go clothes shopping," Lloyd exclaimed and then put on his camp pose of mock indignation. "We're not going to be bloody upstaged by you women." The three of them burst out laughing.

Marcia returned to her office and a moment later Suzette rang, informing her that her next client had arrived.

The animus the man projected as he came through the door hit Marcia in the solar plexus, triggering her flight or fight response. She hadn't experienced an adrenaline rush like it since the traumatic encounter with Mario Lopez. Marcia was thankful she wasn't alone and that the Belgian shepherd, Suzette and the others were nearby.

She fought to control the nervous jumping in her stomach, as she offered him a seat opposite her at the desk. Returning to the task at hand, she slid the tarot cards towards him, fleetingly meeting his eyes that were dark brown and emotionless. Marcia asked him to shuffle them. He remained silent, observing her, as his large hands intermixed the cards and then returned them.

Marcia knew the man was studying her. He began to speak in broken English. "I have heard good things about you," he stated, telling her that he'd never had a card reading before. Marcia didn't want to make conversation with him. She wanted to complete the reading as soon as possible. She asked him in a business-like manner if he would please refrain from speaking until she had finished and then he could ask her questions if he had any.

Marcia caught his sardonic smile, which she immediately dismissed. She mentally blocked the malevolent energy that he exuded and, with deliberation, she laid each card out. She held the first card in her vision without giving anything away. She knew the connotation of the major arcana number thirteen – the *Grim Reaper*. The pregnant silence filled the small area as she placed card number sixteen, *la Maison Dieu* or the Tower, beneath it. Through years of experience, Marcia knew, even if someone had never had a tarot reading before, that these two cards never failed to cause the client unease and this man was no different. He scanned the cards through hooded eyes and shifted uneasily in his seat.

Marcia held him transfixed as she began, "You have travelled from distant shores to complete a mission," she stated. "I see mayhem, disruption and then an ending, which I feel I must advise you, will not be favourable if you continue on the pathway you are on."

Marcia was aware that her power lay in words. Her use of words could influence someone's destiny.

When she had her first experience of prescience as a young girl, she hadn't realised the "gift" she had would eventually give her so much power. Marcia's intent was only ever to give advice and guidance. But she "knew" that this man was an entirely different matter.

Marcia looked up, holding his stare, as she informed him that he was surrounded by secret activity. She didn't reveal that she could see it was linked to narcotics. She continued, telling him that the next two weeks were imperative to his safety.

He leaned forward with an unctuous smile on his thin lips as he scraped the chair back and rose to leave. "How interesting. I will give your advice some thought," he said, adding, "In my country of Romania, there are people such as you, who use witchcraft, spells and astrology, which was only legalised in 2006." He checked his watch. "I must hurry as I am running late for my next appointment." He turned as he opened the door, momentarily held her eyes, gave a sharp nod and left.

Marcia sighed with relief as he closed the door. She had had clients in the past from all walks of life but she'd never encountered anyone with such underlying hostility. She sensed he'd been mocking her. Going to the small cupboard, she took out an incense stick and holder. She lit it and the flame burned for a short while before she blew it out. It smouldered and the fragrance of sage filled the room, removing the Romanian's negative energy.

Marcia reminded herself to tell Suzette that she wouldn't accept any home visits. She would only conduct the tarot readings from the safety of the salon.

There was a knock on the door. It was Cindy, grinning. "These are from your handsome hunk, you lucky girl, I'll put them in a vase, then place them in reception to make us all envious," she laughed. Taking the large bouquet of red roses, Marcia read the message from Eamon which said, "I LOVE YOU." Marcia took in the beautiful fragrance as she texted him, "They are beautiful, I love you."

By the time Marcia had finished for the evening, she had earned over 1,400 euros from appreciative clients. It was now getting dark as she drove with Roman back to Eamon's villa. It wasn't just earning the money that gave her a warm feeling, it was the sense of independence that she was enjoying. Marcia was eager to spend the evening with Eamon.

She pulled up at Eamon's gates, punched in the entry code in and drove her car through. She noticed that Eamon's Maserati was absent. Roman joined her as she walked round to the back of the villa.

There was a coffee cup on the garden table. Marcia picked it up realising that it was cold. She felt apprehensive and couldn't make sense of it. He hadn't texted or rung her, but Marcia figured he had business to attend to. She decided to take a shower.

By the time Marcia got out of the shower, Eamon still hadn't returned and it was just after 9 pm. Marcia sensed that something was wrong. She didn't know what Eamon's business entailed and was uncertain if she should ring him. She didn't want to disturb him if he was in an important meeting.

She rang Jane instead, but it went to her answerphone. Marcia hung up and went into the garden with the ever-watchful Roman who was also waiting for his master to come home and take him for a walk. "He won't be long," Marcia said to the dog, ruffling his coat as he sat beside her.

Suddenly, her mobile phone rang – it was Jane returning her call. Jane told her that Billy had received a call from Dan saying that Eamon had rung and he wanted the pair of them to meet him at the haulage depot, as one of the lorries was on fire. It was suspected arson; Diego the manager had seen two men running from the scene.

Jane said that the call had been about 7 pm. Both women were concerned so they collectively decided to go to the depot. Jane would come to the house with Caesar. She told Marcia to bring Roman and she would be with her shortly. Marcia quickly changed into a tracksuit, grabbing the pepper spray from her bag that Eamon insisted she carry. Roman grew excited as she picked up his lead. Jane, with Caesar, pulled up in the Land Rover minutes later.

....

Dan and Billy arrived at the depot right before the burning lorry exploded. They didn't have time to wonder where their boss was as they jumped into action.

Diego the manager was shouting out orders and the yard was a hive of activity. They slowly had everything under control as Dan approached Diego asking if he'd seen Eamon. Diego scratched his head and said he couldn't understand why the boss hadn't turned up as he had previously spoken to him on the phone and told him what was happening. Eamon told him that he would be there shortly and instructed him to get the men to use every fire extinguisher in the place.

Dan and Billy, on high alert, sensed that their boss was in danger. Dan rang his number, but there was no answer.

....

As Eamon drove down the country lane on his way to the haulage depot, he slowed down on a bend, trying to avoid the speeding car coming towards him. Before Eamon had time to react, the other car sideswiped the Maserati. Eamon, unsuccessfully fighting to control the vehicle, found himself in a ditch. The passenger door was wrenched open from the outside and a shovel-like size fist slammed into the side of his head rendering Eamon unconscious.

....

Jane and Marcia arrived at the depot with the two dogs. Billy instructed Jane to take his car and for the women to return home. "One moment," he said, "I need some things from the boot of my motor." Without being seen, he removed zip ties and tape and pocketed them.

Billy was hyped up, his brain working overtime, as he drove Jane's Land Rover. "It's my bet that if they're Eastern European they'll be in the same rundown village that the others were in," he said to Dan. Adrenaline pumped through his veins as the Land Rover sped towards the village. As the vehicle approached the small bridge over the river, the tyres momentarily left the road, slamming back down on terra firma. "Bring back memories of those turban-wearing bastards, who was on our tail in Afghanistan?" Billy grinned at Dan.

"The only difference is nobody's firing at us with the AK4s," Dan replied, smiling thinly, shaking his head at Billy's driving.

There were three small, Spanish-style cottages dotted on the outskirts of the village. One was razed to the ground while the other appeared to be uninhabited. As they approached the one at the far end of the dark lane, Billy grew excited, pointing. "Look, there's the boss's car. My hunch has been proven right."

Eamon's car was parked alongside the cottage.

Keeping a safe distance away, Billy cut the engine. They stealthily moved with the dogs towards the cottage.

Looking through a window, Dan was relieved to see that Eamon was alive, although his arms and feet were tied and there was blood running down the side of his head. A big guy was brandishing a knife in Eamon's face.

Knowing that at any given moment his boss was about to lose his ear, Dan sprang into action. He wasted no time, as he rushed to the side of the house where Billy was crouched with the two dogs awaiting his command. Dan indicated to Billy to bring the dogs and follow him.

The two men watched through the back door as a smaller man ripped open Eamon's shirt and the larger man hovered over him threateningly, leaning inches from his face. They saw their boss react by bringing his head back and head butting him. Then all hell broke loose as the smaller guy brought his fist back and landed a punch in Eamon's stomach with such force that Eamon and the chair crashed backwards into the wall.

Having seen their boss take a beating, Billy and Dan took quick action. Billy gave the back door an almighty kick and both men, along with the excited dogs, stormed into the room where Eamon was being held. Billy gave the command for the dogs to attack and like two ferocious lions at a "kill" the snarling canines brought the men down by locking onto their arms, overpowering the screaming men as fangs ripped into flesh. While Dan freed Eamon, Billy was enjoying himself as he watched the spectacle. He felt in no rush to immediately call the dogs off the two terrified men who tried to no avail to protect themselves.

Billy's voice resounded, "CAESAR LEAVE," repeating the same to Roman. Both dogs stopped reluctantly and obediently returned to Billy's side. The dogs wagged their tails and Billy rewarded each one with praise. The snivelling men held their hands up in surrender.

Eamon brought his leg back and kicked each one in the groin. "Youse fucking ballbags think youse can go near her, youse cunts?" he snarled, spitting venom at the bigger of the two men.

"That prick bragged that he'd been to see Marcia for a tarot reading and told me that I was fortunate that she hadn't visited his home, as he said he would have played with her before finishing her off." Eamon's face flamed with thunderous rage as he dropped kicked the big Romanian in the face. Blood streaming from his broken nose, he said they'd leave the country, promising they'd never return to Spain.

Eamon scoffed, "That is an absolute certainty, cuntiballs. Eamon smiled caustically, his eyes were trained on them as Billy and Dan began their entertainment."

. . . .

Eamon had tried to convince Marcia that it had been a case of mistaken identity. He brushed off her fears telling her that she had nothing to worry about – the matter was over and done with.

Eamon had called his private doctor who opened his surgery late that night to stitch up his ear. It was Doctor Sagios's high fee that ensured he never asked any questions. Eamon told Marcia that the injury to his ear was worth the welcoming reception she gave him that night.

Word had reached Eamon via the depot manager Diego, that the Eastern Europeans had planned to hold him to ransom. They wanted recompense for the deaths of their relatives. He informed his men to keep their noses to the ground at all times.

Eamon briefly ran over Marcia's invitation list and asked her to add Diego and his wife Maria to it. Although the old manager wasn't in his social circle, he'd been a loyal man throughout his time with Jimmy Grant and now Eamon felt that he owed him an invitation out of respect.

Eamon had previously rung his restaurant to cater for the party at his home. He told Marcos the maître d' that he required tenderloin and filet mignon for a total of fifteen people and the finest tartiflette au reblochon for his fiancé, who was a vegetarian, and that he could use his discretion in providing the absolute best delicacies. Eamon wanted sixteen bottles of Dom Perignon and the same number of bottles of Cristal champagne. Two onsite chefs would be necessary, as well as waiters. Marcos was aware that Eamon O'Donally, who had frequented the restaurant over the years, had risen in rank to take over from Jimmy Grant and it was with great relish that he eagerly accepted the booking when Eamon phoned regarding the celebratory meal. Marcos's head was spinning with the request, but he knew if he got it right, he would move up the financial ladder.

. . . .

Greg placed his hand on Eamon's shoulder as they came through the door. Suzette smiled sheepishly and Eamon gave a curt nod in her direction. He welcomed Dom and Maureen who looked far happier than he'd seen them at their daughter Sheila's hospital bedside. They were followed shortly after by Amos Sagger and his partner Levi. Amos greeted him, passing him a small box, which Eamon immediately put securely in his safe, alongside the engagement ring.

He came out of his office as Billy, Jane and her niece Kalita, who had come from England to stay with them for the week, arrived. Marcia had insisted that they should bring her along too. Eamon heard Cindy's raucous laughter before he even opened the door. He raised his brow in surprise to see Cindy on Dan's arm as they came through into the lounge.

As flamboyant as a showman, Lloyd, one of the stylists from the salon, sporting a canary yellow suit with a multicoloured silk waistcoat and emerald green velvet shoes, made a dramatic entrance. Kieron, the other stylist, dressed in a more subtle light blue suit was on his arm. A few moments later, Eamon stepped back to allow his trusted depot manager Diego and lovely wife Maria to enter.

While everyone was being served drinks on arrival, Eamon went back into his office and took out the two blue leather boxes. Slipping them into his pocket, he headed towards the bedroom.

Eamon turned the key in the bedroom door, smiling as he ran an admiring eye over Marcia dressed in a black, off-the-shoulder Valentino dress that moulded perfectly to her form. Marcia returned his smile as he approached her.

"I wish we had a bit more private time. Look at what ye do to me," he cupped her rear pulling her into his erection. Marcia smiled softly as she gently fondled him. "Bejesus, Marcia!" he rasped. "If we were on our own, I'd tear the arse off ye." He softly bit her lip and reluctantly pulled himself away, holding her at arm's length. "I will have to give it a minute," he said, smiling, trying to control his stiff cock.

Marcia gasped when she opened the small, blue box. Her face lit up at the beauty of the large diamond and e merald earrings that matched her engagement ring. He took the ring from the box, sliding it onto her finger and then he put the earrings in her ears, smiling as she threw her arms around his neck, kissing him.

"I am going to show you my appreciation later … in ways Eamon, that I've never shown you before. You'll see just how flexible I can be." her eyes sparkled as he turned her round, patting her rear.

"Let's get this party over with … behave," Eamon playfully chastised her as he took her hand from his groin, "we have guests waiting on us."

Marcia proudly linked her arm in his. They entered the room to peals of laughter from the women as the two flamboyant stylists regaled them with risqué stories. Just then, Eamon's phone rang, glancing at the screen, he recognised the number. This was the call that he'd been apprehensive about. Excusing himself, he walked to his office and locked the door behind him.

Eamon braced himself for the onslaught, knowing that for the old man Alphonso Gabrette to call him personally it had to be serious.

"It's good to hear from you, Alphonso."

Eamon was taken aback by the tone of Alphonso's voice, which was filled with sadness.

Alphonso's next few words shocked Eamon to the core. "Though it pissed me off at the time, you did well to stay out of that deal Carlo offered you, lad. To be honest, you must have someone watching over you, as you had a lucky escape, unlike my boy who was murdered this morning."

This had been the last thing Eamon had expected to hear. Stunned, he slumped in his office chair, as the old Italian told him that Carlo had been on his habitual early morning run along the beachfront when he'd been killed in a drive-by shooting. "The burst of gunfire ensured that my boy wouldn't come back from it. Joey was driving slowly behind him when a car approached from the rear and overtook him, it all happened at lightning speed."

Eamon asked Alphonso if he knew of anyone that Carlo might have upset recently.

"I loved the boy, but my son or not, I knew he was a greedy little bastard and had upset plenty of the big players," Alphonso replied in measured tones. "I've been told that he'd worked some bad shit and there have been many who suffered as a result. You can imagine what it's been mixed with, Eamon." He went on, "Word has it that he'd offloaded a shipment of 'white' and the people he was working with were mighty pissed off with him. Carlo has tainted my name. As you know, Eamon. I'm a man of my word but the boy thought he was cleverer than me. How the fuck, did he think he'd get away with it?" Alphonso continued, "I'll have to put it right. These people want their money – that's no problem. I'd be the same if they'd done it to me." Alphonso scoffed, "I must be getting old, as I foolishly gave Carlo the benefit of the doubt hoping that he'd play it straight." Eamon knew the old Italian was chastising himself for letting Carlo take over.

Eamon told Alphonso to give his sincere condolences to his wife Marcella.

Al replied heavily, "As you can imagine, she is beside herself … but to be honest I put the blame at her door for spoiling him. She always let him have his own way, being her only boy. But look how it turned out."

Eamon sympathised, knowing Marcella doted on her only son. He knew how badly she would take the news.

Alphonso's tone took on a sharper edge. "There is another subject that you should be concerned about, son. There's a stool pigeon just across the English Channel … there are strong rumours that someone in the UK is working for the other side, many raids are going down … something's not sitting right, Eamon."

Eamon thanked him and said he was grateful for the warning. "My condolences once again, Al," he said. "I will take note of what ye said and I'll be keeping my ear to the ground. If I get any information I'll let ye know."

Eamon ran his fingers through his hair, relieved that he'd heeded Marcia's warning regarding the dream she'd had. If it hadn't been for that, he never would have stepped away from the deal with Carlo Gabrette. He drummed his fingers on his desk, as he toyed with a couple of names of people he felt couldn't be trusted – people he and Jimmy had previously dealt with in the UK. Eamon had always played his cards close to his chest and never worked with anyone outside his inner circle, however, Jimmy Grant did not operate in the same way. He had dealt with a few people that Eamon hadn't trusted, but Grant's greed had always overridden Eamon's warnings.

Eamon wasn't one to wait for the law to come calling. He would need to pull out all the stops to try to prevent this "canary" whoever he may be, from singing his name.

As Eamon locked his office door behind him, he'd decided that for tonight he would need to put his work problems on the back burner. He didn't want to spoil Marcia's special night – but tomorrow he would get the ball rolling.

. . . .

The room was full of chatter and raucous laughter as the guests chatted and joked with one another.

Marcia saw that Jane was heading her way with her niece Kalita, and, after they'd made introductions, Jane told Marcia that Kalita read tarot cards too and that she felt sure the two of them would hit it off as they had so much in common.

"Kalita has always been accurate," Jane said. "She foresaw a man coming into my life and she gave me a perfect description of Billy." The women laughed together.

"If you like, we could exchange tarot readings for one another before I return to England?" the friendly young woman asked.

"Certainly," Marcia acquiesced, smiling, thinking how she had never had someone else read her tarot cards before, and she was curious.

. . . .

Eamon stood in the cool night air with Roman at his side. He surveyed the group of people that he had gathered at his home that night. He spotted the two gay stylists, who appeared to be bickering; then the dark-haired Kieron reached out to his lover with a gentle smile and a light kiss on the lips. "That could be me and Marcia standing there, or any other couple in love," Eamon thought to himself. He had always felt repulsed at the thought of two men together. He put this largely down to his Catholic upbringing in which homosexuality was considered a mortal sin. When he was a young man, he'd seen a couple of videos of two women together. There had been one occasion in his youth when he'd had two women in his bed. His mind drifted back to that night. He'd just arrived in Victoria in Australia and on that first night, all the lads had gone out to a local bar and got completely legless. He had met two women, who had made it clear that they were up for anything. They had partied into the early hours, and the three of them had snorted cocaine. Eamon had never experienced anything like it. That was the first and last time that he experimented with the drug though. Sometimes he mused that he could be too straight-laced for his own good, but he was a product of his upbringing and preferred it that way.

Eamon felt a touch on his sleeve and came back to the moment. He turned to see Amos. He thanked him for the grand job he'd done in making Marcia's stunning ring and earrings. Marcia is extremely happy," he added.

"I am sure your lovely fiancé is well-deserving of such beautiful jewellery. I must say the precious stones complement her á la mode style of dress," Amos said, turning to look in Marcia's direction. Eamon nodded in agreement.

Amos indicated Eamon's stitched ear. "I can see that you may have had some recent problems, is there anything I can do to help?"

Eamon laughed, "No trouble, Amos. All is sorted now and should stay that way."

"You may think that I'm just a useless old queen, past my sell-by date, but I have some very influential friends, Eamon, whom I can call upon if the need arises," he smiled.

Eamon reassured Amos, "Thank ye, I will remember that, Amos. I'll see ye in the office before ye leave. I have yer money and a little extra."

Amos, smiling, gave Eamon's shoulder an appreciative pat.

The waiter announced that the meal was about to be served. Marcia had seated Cindy and Dan opposite Kieron and Lloyd, knowing that they would be bound to entertain her friends at the table. The boys' talk quickly descended into smutty banter, and the ladies, especially Cindy, were soon roaring with laughter. Cindy's cackling could be heard above everyone else's. The champagne had taken effect and she began relating hilarious stories from the salon, most of which had been kept secret from Suzette. There was no stopping her. Kieron, she told them, had managed to turn one highly valued client's hair bright green, when for some unknown reason he'd forgotten to test her new colour. They'd all thanked God that he'd been able to rectify it before the woman had sued the pants off the salon. She'd been up in arms, and Kieron had only just managed to save the day after an extra two hours of hair treatments, 200 euros of free facial treatment, and the offer of a free reading with Marcia. Cindy, tears running down her face was crying with laughter, recalling the event. Kieron had even employed all his acting skills in convincing the lady that he was going through an intense personal crisis. Cindy told them the woman had left thrilled with the results, promising to recommend The Mystique to all her friends. Suzette didn't appear amused, but when Greg put his arm around her, she relaxed and laughed along with the joke, smiling at Kieron.

The small party had been a great success. After everyone had eaten, Dom took the opportunity to ask for quiet, since he wanted to make a toast. While the waiters filled everyone's glasses in preparation, Dom spoke warmly of Eamon and Marcia, and of how they had been there for them every step of the way through their recent heartache. Everyone stood and raised their glasses, wishing Eamon and Marcia every future happiness.

Eamon rose from his seat at the head of the table. "I'd like to propose a toast as well," he beamed at Marcia. "To my beautiful fiancé," he began, "who will become my wife in six months' time. And thank youse all for coming and making tonight such a success."

Maureen, grinning from ear to ear, piped up, "I'll get everything sorted for your wedding planning. You needn't worry about a thing."

Eamon wouldn't hear of it. "Maureen!" he brought her up short, "ye have enough on your plate at the moment and it's all taken care of but thank ye all the same." Hearty congratulations were directed at Eamon and Marcia and the guests' talk resumed.

....

Later that evening, Suzette, in Greg's embrace, was standing on the terrace, taking in the peaceful solitude of the starlight sky and listening to the whispering breeze that played amongst the palm trees. Suzette felt her life was complete with Greg by her side, and her business was showing signs of becoming extremely successful. She was the happiest that she'd been in a long time. Max Greenaway was nothing but a distant memory for her. Max had been the opposite of this kind, considerate man by her side, she mused contentedly, as she kissed him.

Greg smiled, holding her close, and breathed, "I can't wait for you to be my wife and become Suzette Davidson."

. . . .

Eamon noticed Roman was alerted to something. He sat up with his ears pricked and his attention focused on something near the fence. His hackles raised, he moved quickly towards the boundary. Eamon, intrigued, followed the dog. Suddenly Roman started barking loudly, running and sniffing along the perimeter.

Dan appeared, strolling towards Eamon, sensing that something was up. "It may just be a fox – some of them are big fuckers. We get them around our place all the time," Dan suggested as they walked alongside Roman. After several moments, Roman, still alert and sniffing, had stopped barking and Eamon called the dog off. The men returned to the party.

. . . .

"Fuck," the man said quietly, adrenaline pumping, hastily retreating as he'd spotted the Belgian shepherd. He was aware of what damage the dog could do. He jumped back into his car, locking the doors, turning the key, relief washing over him at his narrow escape.

It appears things have changed since the Irishman had taken over from Jimmy Grant. Mr O'Donally will need more than the protection of a guard dog and a psychic to pre-warn him of impending problems, he mused. He hadn't been there very long outside Eamon's property as he saw what he needed to see, but when he went to leave he had alerted the dog when he'd trodden on dry twigs.

As the man drove, he smiled sardonically to himself. He was going to blow them all out of the water. He had a list of the names of many of the smug, wealthy bastards who owned luxurious homes and top-of-the-range motors, which were all paid for with "dirty" money on the Costa Blanca. Parking up, he walked through the labyrinth of streets filled with white-washed houses. The chilling pre-dawn air blowing in off the Mediterranean didn't bother him. It helped him clear his revengeful, murderous thoughts. He knew the situation he was in. He couldn't afford to commit murder but he was hell-bent on giving them a wake-up call, and he only had six days to carry out his mission. He scoffed to himself as he thought of the price he would have to pay but at least he'd have his freedom. He put the key in the door to the holiday rental. Walking into the small room, he moved to the bathroom and peered into the mirror. He hardly recognised himself. Pulling off the wig, he turned on the shower, intent on removing the fake tan he'd applied.

....

Eamon was still on edge about Roman's behaviour earlier that night. He asked Dan and Billy to come to his office for a private word. Something was telling him that it wasn't an animal that had aroused the dog's interest. Eamon informed them that there were rumblings of an informant in the UK. "Word has it that this guy is behind all the recent raids on the men on both sides of the Atlantic. I want youse both to make contact with whoever might be in the know in London to see if there are any whispers."

Dan and Billy nodded.

"My gut feeling is that there is trouble brewing. Roman sensed something tonight. Someone's sneaking around. I want youse boys to make enquiries around the bars at the beach front – see if there are any new faces or anyone asking questions. I will give youse the names of some of the owners. They'll help youse if you mention me."

The remnants of the party had been all cleared away and a stillness filled the villa. Eamon checked that all the locks were in place. This should have been the time he'd been waiting for, when he and Marcia could embrace each other, but Eamon felt weirdly detached. His head was filled with a million thoughts all colliding together and he couldn't still his mind no matter how hard he tried. He knew Marcia had showered and was waiting for him, but even the thought of her nakedness was not working on the part of his anatomy that would usually need so little by way of encouragement. He was drained mentally and emotionally.

Their engagement party had been a huge success. Marcia had looked stunning and gloriously happy all evening – she'd been the perfect hostess. He knew he'd been quiet and withdrawn later in the evening, but he hoped she'd been too busy to notice. *Jesus, she'll bloody know that something is up if I can't get a hard on,* he considered, dejectedly. He toyed with his flaccid cock, trying to conjure up images of their former lovemaking. He failed miserably. He couldn't take himself where he needed to be. There was too much rubbish in his head, crowding in, clamouring for his attention. So much was happening right now that he couldn't, wouldn't tell her about.

. . . .

By the time she had showered, it was nearly 5 am. Marcia sunk back into the pillows, the sheets cool against her back. She was deliriously happy and gently touched one of the diamond and emerald studs she had deliberately left in her ears for Eamon's benefit. She knew that being naked except for her dazzling jewellery would be a huge turn-on for him. Running her fingertips over each facet of the earrings, she marvelled over Eamon's thoughtfulness in matching them to the beautiful ring that sat proudly on her finger. A small sigh of thankfulness escaped her lips. *Where was he?* She wondered. It was so unusual for him not to follow her straight to the bedroom and she was restless for him. She put her hand down and touched herself absentmindedly, as images of Eamon sprang into her mind. She was already as horny as hell and tonight of all nights she wanted to show him how appreciative she was of his love for her. Eamon not being there was unsettling her. He had seemed distracted all evening, but she knew parties weren't really his scene. She had just put his quiet mood down to him being out of his comfort zone. She had been quite happy to let him do his own thing throughout the evening but a feeling of uneasiness was creeping over her now and she lay breathlessly still, trying to listen out for his footsteps.

As if she'd invoked him, he appeared in the doorway, blotting out what light filtered in. His mere presence caused her pulse to race and she breathed in the essence of him as he approached the bed. An electric current coursed through her, her nerves as taut as bowstrings awaiting his first touch.

He pulled her to him, her back against the hardened muscles of his stomach. He spooned her possessively, the weight of his arm across her, causing her to sink down into the mattress. She was astonished to feel his limp penis alongside her buttocks and she wriggled both cheeks suggestively against it. The coarse hairs of his crotch created friction but his cock stayed decidedly soft. Marcia was perturbed at her lack of ability to arouse it.

Eamon kissed her softly on her ear, catching his lip on her earring as he did so. "Go to sleep, Marcia," Eamon whispered in the darkness. She felt like the world had stopped spinning on its axis, so great was her shock. She remained silent and upset in his embrace until sleep overtook her.

. . . .

Eamon couldn't switch off. Pulling the sheet back, he got out of bed and glanced at the sleeping Marcia. His eyes travelled over the curves of her back and to her beautiful rear. He was tempted to return to her, but his disturbed thoughts would not allow it. He dressed and left the bedroom quietly.

Eamon walked to the gates and called Roman, who accompanied him out of the property. "Come on boy, let's have a look," he whispered to the obedient animal. The pre-dawn air was damp, but the moon cast a clear light on the landscape. An excited Roman, barking, quartered the ground. He came across the evidence that proved Eamon's intuition had been spot on. On the ground, at the far end of the fence, were footprints. They looked to him to be about a size 9 to 10 and the imprint was that of a trainer. There was broken foliage next to it, and Eamon felt sure that this would have caused a sound. "Is that what alerted ye boy?" Eamon asked Roman, ruffling his ears, praising him. He took his mobile out and zooming in, snapping pictures of the evidence.

....

The buzz of the intercom awoke Marcia at around midday. The woman said that she had a delivery of flowers. Feeling half-awake, Marcia put on a dress, slid on flip-flops and made her way to the gates with Roman walking by her side.

The delivery woman had two large bouquets of red roses in her arms. She smiled as she passed them over, asking if it was a special occasion. Marcia smiled wistfully then confirming that it was, took the flowers and went back into the villa.

Sitting down, she read the two cards that Eamon had written, "Love you always, Eamon." The other, "I will make it up to you, Eamon." Marcia's tears spilled over as she inhaled the fragrance. She'd woken to find his empty place bed at a time when they should have been entwined in each other's embrace. Marcia looked through her tears at the beautiful ring on her hand. She sensed something was troubling Eamon but knew he wouldn't confide in her. She realised last night that whatever was troubling him had affected his ability to make love to her. Marcia was at a loss to understand what problem could be so serious as to have such an impact on a man as hot-blooded as Eamon. Their lovemaking was a powerful part of their deep passion for one another. Marcia pondered on last night when he had placed the ring on her finger and how he had fought to contain his sexual desire for her. It was hard not to take it personally, yet Marcia was astute enough to know that Eamon would not have shunned her deliberately. She realised he was a complex man – but he'd had a complete shift of mood after he'd taken the phone call last night. She couldn't bear the thought that he was harbouring some knowledge so profound that it was affecting his ability to respond to her.

Marcia suddenly remembered that Jane and Kalita would be arriving shortly. She'd arranged for Kalita to give her a reading and needed to get ready. Jane had told her that she had a free day, and would be accompanying her niece.

While tidying up, the phone rang. It was Joyce, who was keen to have a final catch-up before departing for the States the next day. She warmly invited Marcia to visit them in New York any time and hoped she'd be able to return to Spain to attend their wedding. Her voice was full of excitement about her new life with her daughter Sara and her family, and she thanked Marcia for all the support that she had given her. They finished the call with warm regards to each other. Marcia found two receptacles big enough to hold all the flowers. She arranged the vast quantity of blooms and stood back to admire them. *A picture speaks a thousand words,* she thought. Eamon's apology to her was as expansive as his heart and that knowledge comforted her.

Minutes later, she hurried to have a shower in preparation for the women's arrival. After drying herself and dressing, Marcia returned to the lounge, picked up her phone from the table and noticed that she had several missed calls. The caller had withheld their number, which she thought strange, but she knew many potential clients had her business card and she didn't think too much of it. She assumed it was someone eager to book a tarot reading. She began to prepare a light salad for Jane and her niece when the phone rang once more. She leaned across the workspace, glancing at the screen of the mobile phone and saw that the caller's ID was withheld.

"Hello," Marcia answered. She felt a sense of alarm as heavy breathing came down the line. "Who is this?" she tried to sound more confident than she was feeling. Again, there was the eerie sound of rasped breathing. She clicked the phone off, slapping it onto the work surface as if it had burnt her.

Marcia returned to finish making the salad. The phone rang once more. She stared at the withheld number. Her stomach jumped. She gritted her teeth and answered, "What do you want?" she demanded, trying to control the tremor in her voice. As the heavy breathing began again, she pressed the end call button. Her heart thumping and mind reeling, she fought to regain control. Marcia knew that whoever it was intended to scare her, which began to make her feel angry. Roman's intelligent, almond-shaped eyes quizzically watched her, seeming to sense that something was amiss with his mistress.

"Thank goodness for you, my handsome boy," she said, fondly, to the ever-watchful dog. "I know that I needn't worry with you to protect me." Marcia resolved not to allow the call to unsettle her. She returned to preparing the lunch.

Jane drove her Land Rover through the gates and jumped out with her niece in tow, as Roman hurried to greet them. Marcia could see the family resemblance as the two women walked side by side. Even though Jane was fair-haired and Kalita had long, dark hair. Marcia asked them if they would like to eat before the tarot reading began, but Jane said Kalita was eager to have her tarot cards read right away. "But if you are hungry Marcia …" Jane said.

Marcia smiled. "Please…" She proffered some chairs and asked them to be seated while she went to get her cards. Marcia made herself comfortable. Passing the pack of cards to Kalita, she said, "I imagine you know what to do." Kalita briefly shuffled and returned the pack.

Marcia began to lay each card out and smiled as she perused the top line. "I see you have a son, and in the near future, you will hold a beautiful baby girl in your arms, which will make you feel happy and contented. There are changes in your residence and your husband's career, which will see him rising up the ladder in a new business venture. He will be given an unexpected opportunity within the next three months. Tell him to seize it with both hands," Marcia directed. She looked up into the beaming smile of the young woman who looked as if she had been told that she was going to win the lottery.

Thanking her profusely, Kalita asked Marcia if she would like her to "read" for her now. "I am intrigued," Marcia said, packing her cards away. Kalita took her pack of cards out of her bag and settled back in her seat before passing them to a curious Marcia.

Marcia shuffled the cards and returned them. The young woman began to take on a more serious demeanour as she began to lay the cards on the table. She looked concerned then perplexed. Marcia shifted uneasily in her chair. The young woman was making her feel apprehensive as to what she was seeing. Kalita flicked her long hair over her shoulder as she looked into Marcia's eyes. "I see you with five children, three boys and two girls."

Marcia smiled softly. The young woman was wrong, she thought. Although Marcia had one son, she didn't think she could conceive any longer. She had tried for another baby for five years after Reuben was born until her husband Andrew had died.

Kalita didn't falter as she continued, "There is a big age gap from the first boy, then in quick succession two boys who are dark and handsome, then two gorgeous redheaded girls who will always be by your side."

Marcia didn't contradict her.

Kalita looked alarmed. "I see danger around you and your man," she said to a now more attentive Marcia. "There is a man who will try to bring you both down, along with others. And I must warn you to be careful, as he seeks revenge on you both."

Kalita had Marcia's full attention. "You will leave Spain. Then after a while, you will return when the dust settles."

Marcia was aghast. "We are leaving …?"

Kalita interjected. "Not, we! You go alone, but don't worry … you will return," she smiled reassuringly.

Marcia's appetite had gone but she thanked Kalita and asked her and a subdued Jane if they would like to eat outside in the garden, to which they agreed.

Kalita was babbling excitedly, talking to Jane about her predicted baby girl and her husband's new job that Marcia had foreseen. Marcia fought the rising panic and trepidation regarding Kalita's warning to her and the situation she saw in Marcia's reading with the man who was intent on bringing her and Eamon down.

Bringing her back to the moment, her phone pinged. She looked at it, relieved to see that it was from Eamon. He would be returning after he'd wrapped up his next appointment with the solicitor and that he would be taking her out that night. She sent him five emoji love hearts in reply.

After lunch, Jane rose to leave as she said she had to feed her dogs. Jane hugged Marcia. "Please, don't look so concerned," she said to Marcia.

Marcia didn't realise her worry showed. Before Kalita went out the front door, Marcia pressed 200 euros into her hand. Kalita tried to refuse it, but Marcia was adamant and stood her ground, as the embarrassed young woman reluctantly accepted it.

Jane went to get into the driver's seat and called out to Marcia as she was returning to the front steps with Roman. "Marcia, I nearly forgot to tell you that I am planning a surprise house party for Billy's birthday in a month's time." She said that she was planning to extend the invitation to all those who'd attended Marcia's engagement celebration. "When you tell Eamon, can you ask him not to mention it to Billy? I'd like it to be a surprise."

Marcia was glad that she didn't have any bookings that day. With Kalita's words playing on her mind, she decided to swim and then work through a yoga routine; it was the one sure-fire way to help her make sense of her reading. Marcia donned a bikini, walked to the pool and entered the water, glistening in the afternoon sun. Marcia knew she was safe with the Belgian shepherd to protect her. Roman was lying in the shade, not taking his eyes from her. Her thoughts turned to the young woman's predictions. When she had said that she would have five children, she knew Kalita had it wrong, but what had thrown her was the information about the man who was seeking revenge upon her and Eamon. Marcia had recognised instantly the forthright delivery of the prediction. It was one Marcia used herself when the information she was receiving psychically was emphatically correct. A sense of disconcertion overcame her as Marcia remembered the earlier withheld phone numbers. Trying to shake off her fears, she thought maybe she was becoming paranoid.

. . . .

Dan and Billy had gone from bar to bar making enquiries, asking if any strange faces had appeared recently in the locality. They'd come to a dead end. There'd been nothing to report. The last place on their list was Michael's Irish bar. They knew that the owner was from their boss's turf in Dublin.

The two men entered the quiet bar and pulled up stools, surveying the half a dozen customers. Most looked as if they had the weight of the world on their shoulders. Michael called out that he'd be with them in a jiffy, as he was finishing chang-ing the beer barrels over. Wiping his hands on a cloth, Michael asked them what was their pleasure, and Billy asked for two halves of Guinness.

Michael put the glasses in front of them, smiling. Dan introduced himself, explaining that they worked for Eamon O'Donally and were on the lookout for any new characters that had been in the bar recently.

Michael pressed his lips together and then clicked his fingers as he remembered, "There was a shifty-looking charac-ter who," he tapped the side of his nose, "this hooter told me, smelt like trouble." "Ye know when the old instinct kicks in – that the man was up to no good."

Dan and Billy both nodded.

"This new face came in a couple of nights on the trot." Michael shook his head. "Not last night though," he added. "He'd been quiet and polite like. I couldn't fault the fella on his manners. He came out with a load of baloney, but there was some sort of agenda with him. He asked too many questions for my liking."

"What sort of questions did this guy ask?" Dan enquired.

"Well, now I think back, he asked me about Jimmy Grant, as he said he was an old associate of his and was going to pay him a visit. To be fair, boys, like I told him, I hoped he was a good deep-sea diver, as word had it that he was at the bottom of the Med. He wanted to know if Eamon O'Donally had taken over." Shock registered on Michael's face as it sunk in what he had told this guy. "Is someone bothering Eamon?" Michael asked sheepishly.

"Maybe," Dan said, asking how the guy was dressed.

Michael gave a detailed description. He'd been wearing casual clothes – shorts, T-shirt and trainers and on his inner

left arm, he'd had a tattoo. "It looked like Chinese writing …
or …," Michael gave it some more thought. "Maybe more like
Thai, thinking about it now. He hasn't been in since, though.
But give me a phone number, boys, and, if he comes in, I'll be
straight on the blower."

Dan and Billy were pleased that they'd got some sort of
a lead. Dan slipped Michael 100 euros and his phone number.
Michael asked them to pass his regards on to Eamon.

Suzette and Greg's engagement party was planned for
a couple of weeks' time. Ever the businesswoman, Suzette had
invited many of her wealthy clients. One thing she knew better
than anything was how to mix business with pleasure. Her new
salon venture had really taken off, and her clientele comprised
some of the biggest names and faces in the area.

As Suzette added many of these clients to her list of
guests, her mind drifted back to the first days of her relationship with Marcia. Their lives were barely recognisable. She
wouldn't have imagined that Marcia would now be about
to marry one of the most eligible men on the south coast of
Spain. Since Jimmy Grant's disappearance, Eamon O'Donally's
star had truly risen, she mused. Suzette was extremely fond
of Marcia, but her dislike of Eamon O'Donally was growing.
She was aware that she had to tread carefully around him. He
knew too much about how she had come by her money from
Max, which left her in a precarious position if Greg ever discovered that she had stolen the cash – even if Max deserved it.
Suzette paused, gazing up at the azure sky.

She smiled contentedly as she put such thoughts out
of her mind. How ironic, she pondered, that she and Marcia
were getting married to such wealthy men – although Suzette
classed herself as being far luckier than Marcia. It wasn't that
Eamon O'Donally didn't love Marcia – Suzette knew the man

was obsessed with her friend. But the whole time she had been married to Max Greenaway, he'd often remarked that Jimmy's right-hand man, O'Donally, was a loose cannon. Unlike, she thought, the gentle and loving Greg to whom she would be engaged shortly. After the alcohol-infused revelations of her employees the previous night at Marcia and Eamon's engagement party, she had been flabbergasted when she thought of the implications from the offended client. She could have been sued and lost everything if her staff hadn't used their initiative to placate the woman, but as Greg later pointed out to her, mistakes often happen, and she was fortunate to have such reliable and loyal staff. She relaxed contentedly on the terrace, finishing off her list of party invitations.

....

The man ducked out of sight when he'd seen the car heading towards the villa gates. He recognised the driver as he got out of the car. Suzette had come out of the villa and walked sensually towards Greg Davidson. The man watched, seething, as they embraced and Greg cupped her rear as they returned to the villa. His hands were tied at the moment but he knew that what he had in mind for the pair, would wipe the smiles off their faces. He knew that he had to bide his time, as there were other people involved that he had to answer to and even though it was choking him, he knew he had to have some degree of self-restraint. He'd already checked Greg Davidson out. He was as clean as a whistle, and no matter how much delving he'd done, he hadn't been able to dig up any dirt on him. He knew Greg Davidson had been involved with Jimmy Grant many years back and he had a suspicion that there was some sort of connection to the criminal underworld that had first put him on his feet, but there was no longer any trail to implicate the bastard. *But your woman will suffice,* he laughed caustically to himself.

He reread the gold-embossed business card advertising The Mystique beauty salon and the spiritual medium, then got in his car and headed towards the marina. He was going there on the pretence of looking to purchase a vessel. Maybe someone at the marina would know a bit more about the Irishman O'Donally and a few of the other criminals out here.

The Jamaican brothers had been working on the schooner having a refit in dry dock. They'd been feeling the effects of the Mediterranean sun as it beat down from the cloudless sky, but they were under pressure to finish the work. They were desperate for money to help finance their new club.

The man approaching in a jaunty manner called out to them, "What an amazing schooner. Does it belong to you?"

The more slightly built guy answered, shaking his head, "No man, we're getting it prepared for a refit. The owner is putting it on the market."

On the pretext of being a buyer, the man walked alongside, asking if there was anyone who was interested. The big, muscular Rastafarian's head turned around. His challenging glare held the man transfixed as he replied with some irritation, "WHY?"

The man acted nonchalantly, smiling, ignoring the black guy's projected hostility. "I don't want to waste my time if there are any potential buyers," he explained, gesturing towards the display of luxury yachts bobbing in the harbour. "There appear to be a lot of people in this area that could put up the cash." He smiled as he directed his attention to the man and introduced himself, "I'm Anthony, or Ant to my friends. I'm on the lookout for something like this. My lady wife and I are planning to sail off into the far beyond and visit many distant shores," he continued with his story, "with such a large vessel, I would require staff, if you gentlemen know of any proficient deckhands, or … people to help me on my travels."

The smaller guy seemed more receptive, extending a hand and introducing himself as Elliot. The other guy, he told him, was his brother Samuel. Samuel, disinterested, returned to scraping the hull of the boat. "If you're serious," Elliot said, "you'd be needing to dig deep, my friend. There's already someone, a guy by the name of Eamon O'Donally who is extremely interested, and, to be honest, it's whoever puts in the highest offer that will be getting this lovely lady." He indicated the schooner. "He's going to be viewing it later…"

Samuel interrupted, shouting, "Elliot, get on with your work!"

"Tally ho, boys, I won't keep you any longer," the man stated, in an affected upper-class English accent, thanking them for their time before strolling leisurely along the boardwalk back towards his car.

That was informative, he mused. It gave him an insight into Eamon O'Donally's financial position. He knew if he had more time to spare out here in Spain, he would be able to garner more evidence on O'Donally, but time was of the essence, and he would break the agreement if he wasn't back on time. The Irishman must have plenty of money to splash around if he is going to lay out a couple of million on a luxury boat. He smiled, pleased with himself, thinking of the report he would turn in at the end of the week. "It should earn me some brownie points," he chuckled to himself.

The multi-million-pound yachts were glistening in the sunshine and bobbing serenely on their moorings on the incoming tide. As he passed a magnificent vessel, he smiled, catching the eye of a young, bikini-clad girl lying on a sun lounger. "Absolutely stunning," he commented, lowering his sunglasses and making a point of taking in the girl rather than the yacht. Suddenly, a man appeared from the galley, and, hearing him speak to his daughter, directed expletives in rapid machine gun fire that saw him beat a hasty retreat.

"Well, well, well," he said, as he hurried to get out of the firing line, "one never knows who one is going to bump into," he grinned to himself as he got into his car. He had recognised the angry man from way back. He was a known "face" from his old stomping ground – Lenny Decker, from Romsey. Making a mental note to look into Decker's life out here, he chuckled, "Well, Lenny, if you're not as clean as the driven snow, that outburst of *fucking, cunt-faced bastard,* will turn out to be very unfortunate for you, my friend."

The man knew with absolute certainty that Lenny Decker had been involved in at least two armed robberies back home in the UK, and he would be very surprised if Lenny boy wasn't up to some sort of criminal shenanigans out here in Spain.

. . . .

Sitting in the restaurant, Eamon was all ears as Dan and Billy informed him about the stranger who'd been asking questions in the Irish bar. Dan described the tattoo that the guy had on

417

his inner arm, which rang bells for Eamon – particularly when Dan told him that Michael had recognised the writing as being Thai. Eamon had known a guy with a similar tattoo once, but he was dead, though strangely, the rest of the description the boys gave him fitted his description perfectly.

Eamon thought to himself that tattoos like that were commonplace back in the day and he tried to shake off the odd feeling of recognition he'd experienced. Moving the conversation on, he asked Dan and Billy if they wanted to accompany him to have a quick look at a boat he was interested in. After that, Dan and Billy planned to do a narcotic spot check with the dog at the haulage depot.

Samuel stood to his full height and smiled as he watched Eamon approach with his two sidekicks. Eamon greeted him warmly, asking if it was okay for them to look around the vessel. Samuel offered up the job to his brother while he got on with finishing his work on the hull.

Elliot's banter with Eamon had Billy and Dan in stitches; he seemed to get away with saying things to him that most other people would have got a firm slap for, but Eamon just gave him a wry smile and a comeback. Elliot also told Eamon that he would need staff to run such a big size schooner if he purchased it and he was quick to put himself and Samuel forward for the position. While they chatted and joked, Elliot let slip that he wasn't the only one who was interested in the boat, it seemed. Eamon listened with interest as he told them about the guy who'd been hanging around asking questions earlier. They said they thought that there was something suspect about the guy. "We both felt he was putting on an act, pretending to talk with an upper-class accent. Whatever his game is, it struck me he was *fishing* and not intending to buy the boat. He seemed more interested in whoever else was after it. The man, to be honest, asked too many questions for my liking and I got the feeling that he was a wrong un. Not one of us, man."

Eamon nodded, intrigued and asked him to describe him further, sensing that this latest development could be incredibly important.

When Elliot gave his description, it seemed to match that of the guy who was at Michael's bar. But when Eamon asked if the guy had any tattoos, Elliot replied that he had been wearing a long sleeve shirt.

"The man has green eyes, if that's any help. And I think that he upset Lenny Decker too. He got the full pelt of Lenny's verbal abuse after making a remark to Lenny's daughter, Lisa."

Eamon pressed his lips together and nodded. The more he heard about this guy the more agitated he became. Eamon pondered if this was the man who had the gall to walk amongst them and report his findings. He had no way to tell. "Did you notice his motor?" he asked Elliot.

"Sure man. It was a typical hired Fiat, black with a taped-up wing mirror. I noticed for sure that it was taped because it was the grey carpet type of tape. It stood out like a sore thumb amongst the flashy cars around here."

Eamon thanked him for his help and told him that he would drop by his martial arts club for a chat sometime soon. Elliot saw a business opportunity. "You're all welcome. No joining fees for you two either," he grinned, gesturing at Dan and Billy. "Bring your women along as well. If you want them to learn self-defence, then we're your men." He fished in his back pocket and passed over business cards to the three men.

Dan and Billy left to sort out the inspection at the haulage depot, while Eamon stayed longer at the marina to find out more about the mysterious man who was snooping around. His first stop was Lenny's cruiser. Lenny was quick to invite him on board when he spotted him alongside, and Eamon started quizzing him about the guy who'd upset him earlier.

Immediately, Lenny's expression changed. "I would have fucking choked the prick if he'd hung around," he told Eamon, his face turning puce with anger. "Fifteen fucking years old, Eamon, and he was stood there weighing her up like a piece of meat."

Eamon nodded to show that he understood how Lenny felt. "If Lisa hadn't been there, I would have bloody dropped him where he stood." He took several deep breaths to calm himself. If you wanted to get on Lenny's bad side the quickest route was to disrespect his beloved daughter, Eamon reflected. His friend was a little more under control now. "You know what, though, there was something familiar about him as well. I'm sure I know him from somewhere…"

Eamon could see Lenny's mind drifting as he tried unsuccessfully to pin the memory down. Having found the time to talk, the men chatted about how life was treating them Lenny brought up Jimmy Grant's mysterious disappearance "Which I might add, is no big loss, as most around here see it. He gave Eamon a disarming grin. "He upset a lot of people out here, what with not being able to keep his hands off other people's women, you know what I mean?"

Eamon nodded, not sure how much Lenny knew. "I heard through the jungle drums that you've got a new woman, Eamon." Lenny patted Eamon on the arm. "My old lady Lena hasn't stopped going on about her. Had her palm or cards read or whatever it is they do. She couldn't stop raving about how good she was – she's certainly making a name for herself out here."

Eamon smiled. He liked Lenny and his wife – they had mixed socially when Eve had been around. "Although I'm straight now, I still miss the buzz, but my old lady laid the law down. I wouldn't do anything again, miss out on my time with her and the kids, not for me mate. Give me something legit to do and I'd be your man."

Eamon didn't doubt it. He had a reputation as a solid guy. As Eamon was leaving, he gave Lenny and his wife and daughter an invitation to his wedding. Telling him that he wouldn't miss it for the world, Lenny waved Eamon off and promised that he'd get in touch if he had any recollections about the mysterious guy he'd encountered.

. . . .

Suzette's list was now complete. She was going to have the most extravagant engagement party ever. She was out to impress. Greg had bought her a stunning two-carat solitaire diamond ring, and a necklace with a one-carat diamond. Suzette was on cloud nine. It was safely secreted in her bag. She wouldn't be officially engaged until the party in two weeks' time. But she couldn't stop herself from getting it out now and then and simply admiring it. She was planning to show it off to Cindy and the boys. She was singing along to the English tunes filtering through the music system that Greg had installed in the Mercedes for her. The car cruised slowly – Suzette could feel the emotional connection with the love songs that transported her back to the special times that she spent with Greg each night. She never thought that being in love would make her feel as deliriously happy as she was now.

A small car appeared from nowhere alongside her. Before Suzette had a chance to react, the impact shunted the Mercedes into a ditch. In slow motion, the collision slammed through her body. She caught sight of the balaclava with evil green eyes peering through before she felt an excruciating pain to the side of her head.

Marcia had received a phone call from a worried sounding Cindy, who explained that she had been waiting for over an hour for Suzette to open up the salon. Marcia said she would drive over to Greg's home to see if Suzette was still at the villa, informing Cindy she would call her back and let her know. Marcia had Roman in the back of her car as she pulled up at the gates outside Greg's villa. Peering beyond the railings, she could see no sign of Suzette's car. She tried to repress the feeling that something was wrong with her friend, and she called her mobile again. Panic rising, she turned the car and headed towards the beauty salon. Marcia's intuition told her that Suzette was in trouble, much as she was reluctant to listen to it.

. . . .

Suzette's mobile phone with its perpetual ringing was grating on his nerves. He pulled over and opened the handbag. Rifling through it, he'd found no evidence of what she'd been up to – only the normal type of women's crap such as a makeup bag, a purse and the like, plus the offending phone. Angrily, he threw the bag into the undergrowth at the edge of the woods. Suddenly, as he drove away from the scene, it dawned on him that the mobile phone could have a tracker and whoever was calling would be able to trace it. He needed to make his escape post-haste before he was discovered.

. . . .

Diego rushed out of the depot to speak to Dan, who, along with Billy and Jane, were completing the lorry spot checks with

Caesar the Belgian shepherd dog. His son had called him in a panic. He had come upon a suspicious accident in a remote area known to be a run for drug dealers, and a woman looked to be seriously injured. Dan immediately offered to drive Diego to pick up his young son when he heard what had happened. Instructing Billy to carry on, Dan knew that with the fearsome dog they would be capable of dealing with any trouble should it arise.

As Dan arrived, the ambulance and the medics were in attendance. Diego, being Spanish, took over, asking if the woman would be okay. He was told that upon their arrival, she had been unconscious but her pulse rate was stable and they were taking her to the local hospital. Dan, from where he stood, was unable to recognise the woman as she was lifted into the ambulance.

After the ambulance left the scene, Diego told Dan that he had overheard the medics discussing her facial injury and they had determined it was more consistent with an attack rather than a crash injury. Dan, feeling uneasy about the situation made a mental note of the Mercedes number plates, which seemed familiar to him.

Diego's lad was upset. The policeman who remained at the scene to gather evidence was keen to speak to the boy since he was a key witness. However, he was obviously very shaken and was unable to give a coherent statement. Diego assured the policeman that he would bring him into the station later once he had had a chance to recover from the shock.

Dan's curiosity was aroused as he looked around the vehicle in the ditch on the side of the road. He saw that the only damage was to the passenger door, almost as if another vehicle had collided with it. He wrenched open the car door and looked inside, noticing that the keys were gone from the ignition. Warning bells rang. This could be a carjacking, as he saw no signs of a handbag. Things here just were not adding up to him, especially considering what the medics had discussed about the injured woman. Dan dismissed his suspicions for the moment and drove Diego and his son back to the haulage depot.

. . . .

Returning to the villa, the man removed the gloves and threw everything into a holdall. He took a quick look round to check that he had left the place clean before walking out and locking the door.

When he returned the car to the hire company at the airport, he explained apologetically that he'd hit a wall as he'd left his villa, and he was happy to pay for any necessary repairs.

There were plenty of empty seats available on the next flight out. Things appeared to be working out smoothly, and he allowed himself a smile of satisfaction as he sat in the airport lounge. No one would ever know that he had attacked the bitch. The useless old bill out here would just put it down to a car accident and would not bother chasing it up. With less than an hour to wait until departure, he treated himself to a double whisky to celebrate the completion of his mission.

. . . .

Eamon's phone had been ringing constantly. The first person to ring him had been Samuel, who'd passed on the news to him about Lenny Decker's fatal heart attack. Samuel had heard piercing screams from Lenny's boat, and Samuel and his brother had rushed over to see what was happening. Lenny's missus had arrived and had been beside herself, screaming that Lenny was dead. Eamon was shocked as he had only been speaking to him earlier.

424

Moments later, Marcia rang Eamon, apprehension in her voice, telling him that Suzette had disappeared, and she felt that something was wrong. Eamon tried to sound sympathetic but in the back of his mind, despite Marcia's suspicions, he was sure that she was just in some posh shop taking a little longer than usual. He reassured Marcia that Suzette was probably held up somewhere and would turn up soon, then asked her if she would like food ordered in and then they could shut the world out and spend time with one another.

As soon as he clicked off, his phone rang again – this time it was Dan. He passed on the news about the car accident and the woman in the Mercedes. Dan went on to say that it was the car's number plate that was bothering him – it just seemed familiar.

As Dan read it out, Eamon realised with a jolt that it belonged to Greg. "He has a pair of them," he told Dan. "Suzette drives one. I've seen it outside the beauty salon." It struck both men that the woman in the car must be Suzette. Eamon said that he'd give Greg a call to see what was happening.

Greg had given Suzette his other Mercedes as an engagement present, he told Eamon. "Why all the questions mate?" Greg was curious. Eamon told Greg what he knew about the accident, that Dan had made a note of the registration, and that it matched up with one of his.

Greg said he was going to drive to the scene of the accident to find out for certain if Suzette had been involved. Eamon had the same thing in mind and was just getting out of his car behind the ditched Mercedes as Greg pulled up behind him. Both men recognised the damaged vehicle. As Greg took in the horror of the scene, Eamon filled him in on the details that Dan had passed on. He did not reveal that Dan had told him the medic thought it was an attack.

As much as Eamon could not stand the woman, he wouldn't have wished this on her. Greg had left for the nearest hospital, which was only a few kilometres away.

Eamon decided not to tell Marcia over the phone about Suzette. Instead, he drove to the salon, as he knew she was there with Cindy. His large frame filled the doorway as he entered the salon. Lloyd smiled, directing him towards the staff room, "Marcia, Cindy and Roman are in there." Lloyd and Kieron both raised their brows in curiosity.

Eamon told Marcia about what had happened to Suzette and gave her an idea of the extent of her injuries. He had rung Greg at the hospital and told him they were on their way.

. . . .

The elderly man walked from his cottage in the woods, his faithful, old dog keeping pace with him. As they took their usual path, he stopped to listen. He could hear a phone ringing a few yards up ahead. Moving towards the sound, he bent down to see a woman's handbag, partly covered by the undergrowth. He retrieved it and looked inside. Within it, he discovered a purse containing a large amount of euros, a makeup bag and the phone that he'd heard. He unzipped the inside pocket and found a small jewellery box. When he opened the fine box, he was incredulous. Sparkling inside was the prettiest stone he had ever seen. He carefully put everything back in the bag; a beaming smile appeared on his face. All thoughts of his daily walk had been forgotten, as he clutched the bag under his arm. He turned to go back to his cottage, calling out for his old dog to follow him.

. . . .

Eamon, Marcia and Cindy were waiting for Greg to come out of the doctor's office. The young nurse had already told them that Suzette would be out of X-ray shortly. Suddenly, the door opened and Greg walked towards them. He looked as if he had aged about fifteen years. He told them in halting words what the doctor had said. She had sustained a head injury. Suzette's nose had been broken, but she seemed to have been relatively lucky, as the rest of her facial bones had remained largely intact. He did not know if there had been any brain damage. Greg had told him that he wanted her to be transferred to a private hospital five miles away as soon as possible. They sat in silence for twenty minutes before the ward doors opened and Suzette was brought out on a trolley and taken into a smaller adjacent room. The doctor accompanied her and provided them with more details. Fortunately, there was no sign of any bleeding on the brain. There was a small hairline fracture to her right cheekbone, but most of her injuries consisted of bruising and swelling, which would eventually heal. In his clinical opinion, it would be safe to transfer her after twenty-four hours under observation. Greg smiled weakly, seeming somewhat reassured, and shook the doctor's hand, thanking him.

As they stood around Suzette's bed, Greg took her hand, watching her as she attempted a smile.

Bejesus, she looks like she has been in a boxing ring, Eamon thought to himself, shocked by her appearance. Marcia looked on, holding Suzette's other hand, tears streaming down her cheeks. Suzette tried to speak, "My bag ... where is my bag?" Greg attempted to reassure her, telling her not to worry. The doctor had administered a sedative, and Suzette started feeling the effects. Her eyes closed slowly as she murmured quietly, "But ... my ring..." They were advised by the medical staff to let her sleep. As they walked out, Eamon asked Marcia and Cindy to wait for him in the car. He wanted a private word with Greg.

There was a desperate rage in Greg's voice as he spoke, "I want this bastard caught," he ranted. Eamon reassured him that they would do everything they could to find the culprit. "At some point, ye know as well as I do that the ring will be on offer and if we put our feelers out we should get a lead." Eamon had a thought. "What about her mobile phone? Has she got the tracker on, because if we find where the signal's coming from…"

Greg shook his head wearily. "We're both technophobic and only use our mobiles for the basics. What the fuck is going on Eamon? First your woman, and now mine. Is no fucking woman safe out here?"

For once Eamon had no words to offer. After a long pause, Eamon quietly suggested a plan. "Listen Greg, ye look after Suzette. I'll get Marcia to sort out the salon. Cindy will be sure to help out as well, and we'll get the wheels in motion."

Greg nodded his agreement. Putting his hand on his shoulder, Eamon left Greg with some final words, "I will get the men to speak to every man and his brother to track down the bastard who did this to Suzette, Greg." There was an air of fierce resolve between them. Eamon opened the door and left Greg in the vehicle, telling him he would be in touch.

. . . .

Marcia and Cindy arrived back at the salon. Roman who had stayed behind with the lads, wagged his tail as he greeted Marcia. Cindy, seeing that Lloyd and Kieron were busy with clients, went to the staff room to make a coffee. Marcia walked into Suzette's office and closed the door behind her. Although she felt that Suzette would pull through, she was still struggling to make sense of what had happened to her. She put her head in her hands and tried to process the recent events. Greg had said he'd suspected that the attack on Suzette had been a robbery and it seemed to him that Suzette had fought with whoever was trying to steal her bag and had sustained her injuries that way. Suddenly, something dawned on her – she had a flashback to the dream that she had told Eamon about. She had had a vision of Suzette with a serious injury to her head. She'd seen blood running down her face as Suzette had attempted to fend someone off, and she'd heard Max's voice, although she couldn't work out why Max would have been in the dream – she couldn't make sense of it at all.

. . . .

"What is occurring, Marcia? Everybody has a face like a slapped arse," Kieron asked.

Lloyd pried, "Do we have treason on the high seas? Visits from your hunky fiancé seem to always be followed by drama."

Marcia did not go into details. She passed it off as an accident that Suzette was involved in, and she explained Suzette's facial injuries to the stylists.

Aghast, Lloyd asked if there was anything they could both do. "For instance, Kieron and I could help run the salon," he said in earnest, but Marcia knew that it was more for her and Cindy's benefit as she realised the stylists were of the opinion that Suzette thought too highly of herself.

"Before you go, Lloyd, if you know of anyone that could work on reception for a while until Suzette's recovery please let me know."

Lloyd held up an assenting hand. "Leave it to Lloyd, my beautiful darling. I'll get that arranged. This ship will *not* be going down anytime soon." He flashed his expensive veneers at Marcia and shut the door behind him. Even under these trying circumstances, Marcia allowed herself a smile. She had conducted some tarot readings for them both and they were quite the pair. Kieron was insecure, thinking that Lloyd was up to no good. To be fair, when she'd looked at the tarot cards she'd seen that Lloyd did care for Kieron but he also had a roaming eye. She had become very fond of both lads and since they had become a couple, she had "seen" that they had a long and happy future together.

. . . .

Greg sat at Suzette's bedside. Her tears seemed without end, no matter how hard he tried to console her. All she seemed concerned about was the money he had spent on her ring, despite the numerous times he'd told her that it was of no consequence. He was full of gratitude, knowing the situation could have been far worse. He was relieved that she was on the mend. Greg told Suzette that he could not put a price on that. Every time he looked at her face, he could feel the white-hot rage rise in him. He would have the culprit beaten to within an inch of his life when he was found, but he didn't let on to Suzette, as he didn't want to upset her any further.

Suzette's eyes were still bloodshot. Her broken nose was hugely swollen, as was her cheek, and she could only talk in a low whisper. The doctor said that he was surprised that she had not lost any teeth. Greg had made a mental note to give a large donation to the hospital for the help they had given. They worked tirelessly and he knew it was for little pay.

It was not a patch on the private medical facility that Suzette would be going to soon, but they'd done a great job looking after her. Greg had told Suzette that the salon was running like clockwork and that Marcia and Cindy would be paying a visit later to see how she was getting on. This seemed to cheer her a little. Now that she was less sedated, he took the opportunity to reveal that she would be moved to the exclusive private hospital before the end of the night. He told her, when she fretted about her looks and her damaged features, he was going to pay a top surgeon to reset her nose.

. . . .

Marcia and Cindy had gone to visit Suzette in the hospital. They reassured her that everything with the salon was running smoothly and business was booming. The boys were working hard, and they had acquired a new receptionist who was recommended by Lloyd.

Cindy had voiced her dislike of the new woman quite clearly when she had spoken to Marcia earlier. "She's trouble," she'd confided to Marcia shortly after first meeting her. "She bleeding well loves herself. You can tell, and I know a man-eater from 100 miles away."

Marcia asked Cindy not to say anything to Suzette as it might worry her. Not one for keeping her thoughts to herself, Cindy reluctantly agreed, adding, "Mark me! Marcia, that woman is a devious bitch."

Marcia was as aware as Cindy was of the falseness of the new receptionist, but she felt that the smooth running of the salon should take priority. Rachelle's personality traits were the least of her worries – she wasn't going to be a permanent fixture in the salon anyway.

Suzette became upset as she spoke about her ordeal and the theft of her beautiful engagement ring. "I know that Greg said he will replace it, but that ring has so much significance. Greg gave me that diamond as a token of his love for me."

Marcia kept her own counsel and silently sympathised. She understood that another diamond would not replace the stolen ring. She knew how close to her heart she held the diamond and emerald engagement ring Eamon had made for her.

. . . .

Andre sat close to the fire, his loyal, old dog alongside him. In his hand he held the diamond ring. He turned it in the light, watching as it sparkled with an intense fire when the light from the flames reflected in it. The stone was like one he had seen on a television programme about the diamond mines in Botswana. Putting it down for a moment, he broke some bread and gave some of it to his hungry, old mutt, along with a piece of cheese. Andre could not read or write and his only real friend was his dog, Brisa. He had always lived a quiet life. He had devoted his time to caring for his elderly mother and father. They had seen out their days in the very same woodland cottage that Andre still lived in now. As Andre looked around the dilapidated room, he thought about the ring. He could not read the words on the items in the bag since his life had only ever really consisted of hunting and shooting in the woods with his father. His father had never believed in education, but he *had* drummed into him the importance of honesty and the sin of stealing. Andre dipped his hand into the bag and took out the leather purse inside it. He opened it and fanned the notes out into his hand. He had never seen so much money in his life, and the feel of it was alien to him. He stuffed it back into the purse and turned again to the diamond ring. He allowed himself a final thrill at the incandescent gleam of it in the light, before carefully placing it back in its box and placing the box back into the bag. With a sigh, he decided to head into the village the next day to look for some work so that he could buy himself and Brisa some food. As the light outside dimmed, Andre felt tiredness overcome him, and with the embers of the fire dying, he drifted off into sleep, joining his already slumbering animal.

Andre had knocked on every single door in the village. Most people could offer him chores to do, but none could pay him. They were all in the same boat. As he turned a corner, he came across a smallholding where a woman told him that the only people in the village who might be in a position to help him were Diego and Maria.

Andre hadn't seen Diego for many years but always thought of him as a friend as he never made fun of him as the other boys in the village had done back when they were young. On occasion, he'd gone hunting with him, which was the only thing Andre was good at. As Andre stood at the gate, he heard dogs barking. Shortly after, Diego's wife Maria answered. Maria was warm and friendly, and invited him in to tidy the yard and said that she could give him 2 euros and a bite to eat. When the time came for his lunch break, she showed Andre where to wash his hands and he gratefully took a seat at the table.

Diego came home for his lunch and stopped in his tracks when he saw Andre sitting at the table. Maria took him to one side and told him how Andre had fallen upon hard times. Andre saw Diego's face soften as he recognised him. He greeted Andre and apologised for not recognising him at first and being suspicious. He explained that there had been a violent attack on a local businesswoman not far from where Andre lived and she had her handbag stolen, which had a valuable diamond ring inside.

Andre knew he was not always the sharpest knife in the block, but he didn't have to stretch his thinking too hard to realise that the handbag they were talking about must be the very same one that was now under his chair in front of the fireplace. He would have loved to keep the sparkling ring that flashed fire when turned, but he knew that it wasn't his to keep. He hadn't known what to do with it either. He was a traditional country man and lived by the same rules as his father and his grandfather before that. He could not steal what belonged to another.

With a heavy heart and a slow voice, he told Diego that he knew where the ring was. "I wasn't going to steal the bag," he said in earnest. Diego smiled, reassuring Andre that there was a gentleman who would be incredibly pleased with him. Diego then phoned his boss, Eamon O'Donally.

Within an hour, the Englishman and Irishman were walking up to Diego's gate. After Diego had calmed the dogs and let them in, they all sat around the kitchen table. Andre felt nervous and his eyes flickering back and forth between the men and Diego. Andre felt the sweat beading on his forehead as he tried to understand the dark-haired man with the odd way of talking, who would not take his dark, intense eyes off him. Eamon instructed Diego to tell the man he was not in trouble and that they were happy that he was honest. Andre could speak some English but Diego did all the talking, explaining that Andre was a man that he'd known for years and that he lived on his own with his old dog in a rundown cottage in the woods. He said the handbag was under a chair in Andre's home. He told them what Andre had told him – how he had come across the handbag when he had heard the phone ringing as he was taking his dog for a walk.

. . . .

Greg and Eamon had followed Diego and Andre through the rundown village and into the woods towards Andre's dilapidated cottage. Their handcrafted leather shoes were somewhat the worse for wear by the time they entered Andre's dimly lit home. The old dog struggled to get to her feet when her master walked into the room, but still managed to wag her tail in pleasure at a pat on the head from him.

Greg threw a sympathetic look in Eamon's direction at the sight of the sheer poverty. There were holes in the roof and candles instead of electric lights. Andre bent down and retrieved the handbag, passing it sheepishly to Diego who gave it to Greg. When he opened it he could not believe his eyes – Suzette's Louis Vuitton bag contained everything that she said had been missing. When he opened the jewellery box, Suzette's diamond ring glinted back at him.

After a few moments, realising his good fortune, Greg pulled out his wallet and handed Andre 500 euros. Andre looked scared and unwilling to accept it, but Greg would not be refused. Andre slumped into his chair looking in amazement at more money than he had ever seen in his life, and tears began to roll slowly down his cheeks.

Greg told Diego to tell Andre that before winter set in he would get his men to fix his roof and sort out all repairs to make his cottage habitable. Greg would have done it there and then if they had not already been on a tight schedule to complete Eamon's new home. Eamon also informed Diego that Andre could take on a job at the depot washing the lorries and tidying the yard, and he could even bring his old dog with him. Even this wasn't enough for Greg, he told Eamon that he would pay his wage, and when it came to

Andre retiring, he would pay him a weekly pension until he took his last breath.

. . . .

Eamon had returned to his villa. He made himself a coffee, took it outside and pulled up a chair at the garden table. He was trying to fathom out what was puzzling him about the attack on Suzette. Why would someone inflict such violence on a woman? He could understand it if they'd robbed her, but for the attacker to have thrown the handbag away with all the cash, bank cards, and an extremely valuable diamond ring, as if it were worthless, just didn't add up to him.

What sort of assault were they looking at? It certainly wasn't a robbery, as they had first assumed, he mused. He tried to piece it all together as he sat drumming his fingers on the table. This assailant had to be someone with a personal vendetta against Suzette, but who the feck was it and, more to the point, *WHY?*

He knew Marcia had had dreams about Suzette with a head injury and blood running down her face. Eamon thought back to when Mario had accosted Marcia. If it hadn't been for her determination to fight him off, he hated to think what the prick would have done to her. *This guy won't be attacking defenceless women anymore,* Eamon thought, scathingly. But there was now someone else out there. Although Eamon knew it was mere speculation, he could not put this down to coincidence. His gut feeling was telling him there was some sort of connection and he knew that Marcia's disturbing dream had been precognitive.

He was determined that he would stop at nothing to bring the perpetrator to his knees. He was at a loss as to who it could be. However, if they'd stolen Suzette's valuables, he would have felt differently. To his way of thinking, both women were on the receiving end of some form of payback. Marcia had previously confided in him about everything that she had been embroiled in when she was coerced by Suzette into playing Max Greenaway – but that was now history. *OR WAS IT?* Eamon asked himself.

Eamon came out of his office as he heard Marcia and the dog come into the villa. He took note of how tired she looked. He knew she was under pressure with running Suzette's beauty salon and her own tarot appointments. He was concerned that she had taken on too much but knew she would not thank him for mentioning it.

He knew he was overly protective of Marcia, and it was alien for him to put those feelings on the back burner. However, he realised that if he allowed those emotions to manifest themselves he would lose what he loved most about Marcia. Her independence and spirit coupled with her intelligence and warm personality were just a few of the reasons why he had fallen in love with her in the first place. He had never felt so intensely possessive about anything or anybody, which was new, even for him. He fought to control his jealousy often. Yet Eamon knew, even though Marcia appeared peaky of late, it had not affected their alone time. Making love to her was like nothing he'd ever experienced with any other woman. Eamon knew he had no cause to doubt her love for him, but it was a continual fight to keep the green-eyed monster at bay. She smiled, putting her arms around his neck and kissed him. He smiled into her eyes as his growing arousal pressed into her.

"I will shower and then I will give you all my attention," Marcia said, teasingly nibbling his bottom lip, as he playfully slapped her rear. She pulled away and walked towards the terrace doors. He ran his eyes over her retreating curves, adjusting himself, visualising their lovemaking. He knew that they had both been caught up in all the drama, but tonight he was determined to shut the world out and enjoy her company.

. . . .

Marcia had set the mood accordingly and lit candles in the bedroom. She felt drained from the events of the last 48 hours and she wanted nothing more than to be in Eamon's arms. She wanted Eamon to be totally relaxed, so she offered him a massage. He lay face down on the bed, his large, naked frame sprawled out. Marcia took in the smooth planes of his muscular back and the curve of his buttocks sitting atop well-formed legs. She never grew tired of looking at him – how well-proportioned he was and the strength of his physique. Marcia sat astride him and settled herself in the small of his back. He felt the velvet skin between her legs make contact with his and he shifted to accommodate his trapped member growing satisfactorily under him. Marcia dribbled the oil over his upper body and began slowly kneading his knotted muscles, and then she rubbed firmly with long, deliberate strokes. She had to stretch forward and moved herself up Eamon's back, keeping her legs firmly pressed to his sides. Eyes half closed with pleasure, Eamon rolled himself onto his back to face her and she was suddenly astride his stomach. In the dim candlelight, he reminded her of a Greek god. She rubbed the remainder of the oil upwards, in firm strokes, tweaking his nipples as she reached them and felt them stiffen under her fingers. A strong presence was making itself felt against the cheeks of her behind, its blunt end decidedly damp with impatience.

As if she were a feather, Eamon lifted her by the waist and she put her hand between her legs to guide him into her.

The feel of him inside of her at last, hard and strong, coupled with his expert rhythm allowed her to get maximum enjoyment and it drove her wild. When Eamon manoeuvred her slightly so his shaft brushed against the most sensitive part of her, she lost herself totally in all-encompassing ecstasy.

Eamon's ego needed this boost. His failure to perform on the night of their engagement party was forgotten. With the utmost self-control, he took Marcia to the edge time and again. He concentrated only on pleasing her and he enjoyed hearing her ecstatic whimpering and moaning his name. The oil had left them both sleek and gleaming. In the flickering light, Marcia's shape was accentuated. Eamon devoured her with his eyes as she rode him. Her pert breasts took on a fuller look, her nipples dark in the dim light, her belly a soft curve. He adored her suppleness, the fact she was able to twist into impossible positions to aid their lovemaking had him in awe. They were like two parts of a jigsaw puzzle, locking together perfectly.

Marcia began imploring him to let her orgasm. With an iron will, he had pleasured her and she was unable to take any more. He allowed himself to release too, as Marcia shuddered through her climax. Eamon's ejaculation met with Marcia's flow and she sat in the spill of their togetherness, utterly spent. Eamon tenderly took control and laid her next to him, waiting until her breathing returned to normal. Eamon kissed her full on the mouth. The aroma of the oil mingled with their fresh sweat and the unmistakable scent of the wetness produced by their lovemaking smelt so erotic that he began to harden again. But Marcia was lost in drowsy satisfaction and was already half asleep. Eamon smiled to himself contentedly, knowing that he more than made up for the night of their engagement party.

Eamon had two things in mind. His priority was to get her to make an appointment with his private doctor to have a full medical, and his second was for her to learn self-defence. He knew Marcia ate healthily and would only seek out homeopathic treatment. Dr Sagio was an alternative medicine practitioner as well as traditional.

. . . .

Lloyd sat by Suzette's hospital bed, telling her that she'd be out soon, as she was on the mend. Suzette had always been one for keeping up her appearance and was finding it hard to deal with her facial injuries. Lloyd promised her the full treatment when she got out and was recuperating at home. He patted her hand reassuringly. However, he really didn't want her to return too soon as the salon was run less like an army camp without her there.

Lloyd smiled. "With my makeup talents, darling, you'll be back to your beautiful self straight away, so no need to fret my love," he told her brightly.

He felt a certain amount of guilt, as he hadn't actually realised how badly Suzette had been hurt, although he knew that she'd be back on her high horse, ordering everyone around again as soon as she set foot in the salon. A nurse came in with a vase for the beautiful bouquet that Lloyd had brought with him. All the staff at The Mystique had chipped in for them, even the new girl.

"The new girl Rachelle is just what you need, and the customers absolutely love her," Lloyd advised Suzette. "She's so kind and thoughtful too … even though she doesn't know you, she was so keen to pass on her warmest wishes for your recovery."

Lloyd watched Suzette's response, knowing that she loved flattery. She smiled weakly and told him that maybe she would take her on permanently if she was such an asset to the salon. This was what Lloyd wanted. He had become quite fond of, even though he sensed that some of the others at the salon did not share his enthusiasm. Still, what Lloyd wanted he usually got, one way or the other. As Lloyd left the hospital, Greg's car pulled up in the car park.

When Greg entered Suzette's hospital room, her face instantly lit up. She could see that he was carrying her Louis Vuitton handbag. Her joy was compounded when she opened it to see the jewellery box, and she squealed with sheer delight when inside she found her fabulous diamond ring. Although Greg felt over the moon at her reaction, he gently took her arm to calm her, aware that she was still in a delicate state. Suzette threw her arms around his neck and cried tears of joy.

. . . .

Eamon was determined that Marcia was taught self-defence he knew she had Roman to protect her but to give him peace of mind, he informed her of his wishes. He had spoken to Greg and his men about their women learning Muay Thai. The Jamaican brothers were at the top of their game and he suspected Marcia would become as proficient at that as she was in Hatha yoga.

He had paid a visit to Samuel and Elliot's club and he was mightily impressed as they showed him a few moves in the art of protection. They had been a font of knowledge on the subject, telling him that Muay Thai was one of the best forms of self-defence. Both Eamon and Greg had agreed. It sounded like a good idea, and once Suzette was back to full fitness, Greg wanted her to have some training with the brothers. At least then, they would be able to rest more easily, knowing that they'd be safer.

Everyone Eamon knew had been on the lookout for the guy with the Thai writing on his left arm. Eamon was not 100% sure that it was the same guy that had been outside his villa the night of his engagement party, or if it had been the same person who had attacked Suzette. He just had a nagging gut feeling that the incidents were somehow connected.

Dan and Billy had spread the word amongst the lads down at the marina. Samuel and Elliot had told Eamon that they had also put the word out amongst their associates and members they were acquainted with at the gym. There had not been any sign of the guy who'd shown an interest in the schooner. It was as if he had just disappeared. What struck Eamon as more than a coincidence was that Suzette and the Jamaican brothers had both said that this guy had green eyes. Eamon had phoned Michael at the Irish bar to see if he could jolt his memory and, bingo, Michael confirmed that the guy who had been asking questions about Eamon had the same emerald green eyes. Eamon now had the verification that this was one and the same man, and whatever this guy had set out to do, he had done it and then scarpered. Eamon would lay money on it, that his return destination would be the UK to report to the old bill.

Eamon spoke to his men about enrolling in Samuel and Elliot's Muay Thai training. They were both up for it, even though they both had kept up with weight training at home and Billy and Jane had an early morning running regime. Dan said he would ensure that Cindy would join them too. He added jokingly that with her hot-headed temperament he'd hate to think what damage she would do to someone if they accosted her once she had a few Muay Thai lessons under her belt.

"What about you, boss, aren't you going to join us?" Billy asked.

Eamon smiled. "I know my limits," he laughed, "it's not my thing. I'll stick to swimming and walking."

Eamon knew how effective the Jamaican brothers were. He'd seen their skills in action previously when Jimmy Grant had called upon their services in the past. Eamon remembered the time when there had been a group of up-and-coming thugs from Liverpool and Jimmy had done a big drugs deal with them. The plan had been that Davy Gibbs, the gang boss, start a business collaboration with Jimmy, meaning their joint venture would strengthen their footing on the Costa Blanca. Davy and his boys were based in the hills of Andalusia and he'd told Jimmy that this deal would help them to open doors in that area. Unfortunately, after a few too many drinks, Davy had made some choice remarks about his new business partner Jimmy Grant and how he intended to shaft him. It had been reported back to Jimmy and Jimmy had decided to renege on the deal, setting the cat amongst the pigeons. Davy Gibbs had sent word to Jimmy that he intended to go to war against him and knock him out of the game. Jimmy, however, had been several steps ahead of Davy Gibbs and had put the order out for the Jamaican brothers, and a couple of others as backup, to pay Gibbs an unexpected visit. Fortunately for Jimmy, he had been knocking off a woman in Davy's neck of the woods, and she had a cousin who worked for Davy's crew. Eamon had gone along with Jimmy's men, including Samuel and Elliot, that night. They had caught Davy Gibbs and his gang unawares. They had been sitting around the table at Davy's villa having a meet and a quiet drink.

Eamon had seen the Jamaican brothers in full flow. He had never seen anything quite like it. No firearms were needed, only the two lethal weapons that were the powerful Jamaicans. Samuel and Elliot wiped the floor with the lot of them. Eamon and the others stood back watching the show as the speed of feet and elbows from the expert Muay Thai trainers left their victims screaming like stuck pigs at the beating they were receiving.

Eamon smiled to himself at the memory, pleased with his decision, which would enable him to rest easier once Marcia was under their guidance. He knew he could not sit on his laurels where his freedom was concerned. He hoped that some of his contacts in the UK would be able to keep their ears to the ground about this grass who was ratting on them. He didn't fancy the guy's chances once the drums started beating throughout the counties. Eamon knew that someone somewhere would soon sniff him out, from wherever rock he was hiding under.

. . . .

Marcia walked towards Eamon. He seemed to be miles away and she sensed that he was troubled. She stood in front of him, wearing a pale blue dress with thin shoulder straps. Eamon's eyes devoured her. Marcia's face softened as he looked at her, and his hands circled her waist. He kissed her lips softly and then pulled her to him. She ran her fingers through his goatee beard as he watched her.

His voice rasped with desire as he playfully warned her, "Woman, that little dress doesn't leave much to the imagination, and if ye wants us to eat something this evening, ye had better move away from me."

As they took their seats, Eamon told her that he'd been speaking to Samuel and that he'd enrolled her at the brothers' gym. Muay Thai would help to learn the self-defence skills she needed at this time, he said.

Marcia tried her utmost to change his mind. "My life is so busy Eamon," she pleaded, "No one can come near me with Roman around."

But Eamon's mind was made up. It was a done deal. In two days-time he would take her to meet the boys and her training would begin. He caught the flicker of annoyance in her eyes when he had told her there was no debate. He took her hands in his, leaning forward. "Marcia, there is someone out there who wants to cause youse women some physical harm. Please think … is there anyone that ye or Suzette have crossed?"

Marcia felt certain in her answer. "There is no one Eamon. I have told you everything from the moment Suzette first came to me for that tarot reading."

"Ye live in my world now, Marcia. There are a lot of nasty people out there and I think that one of them has got ye in their sights."

Marcia reluctantly agreed to take up the offer of the martial arts training, though how she would fit any more into her busy days she had no idea. Eamon had ordered food in and noticed Marcia's disinterest as she picked at it. "Marcia, ye will burn yourself out if ye don't eat," he said, concerned.

"I don't have much of an appetite lately, Eamon. I think it is all these disturbing factors regarding Suzette's attack and I have been having recurring troubled dreams so not sleeping well."

Eamon put down his cutlery and gulped his wine as he watched her. "Marcia, I have booked an appointment with my doctor for you to have a full health check. I'll be with ye to ensure that whatever he advises, ye adhere to it."

445

Slowly, he reached out taking her hands in his. "Marcia, I am worried about ye. Maybe ye just need a tonic. Ye don't eat meat or much else of late. Now all I ask is that ye finish that meal, then later I will return the favour and give ye a relaxing massage."

She cocked her head, smiling. "I will look forward to it." She began to eat with more relish, which Eamon knew was only because of his insistence. He was aware that Marcia always ate healthily. The fridge was always jam-packed with what he considered rabbit food – natural yogurt and bowls of fresh fruit. The bathroom cabinet contained Chinese potions and varying organic face creams. He had met Marcia halfway and enjoyed the amazing Turkish salad she prepared, but he had not given up eating meat as she had. He'd taken to ordering his steaks and pork chops in, knowing Marcia's idea of protein was nuts and beans.

Ever since Eamon had begun his relationship with Marcia, he discovered that swimming helped him relax. He walked the dog regularly to keep himself in shape, but weight training wasn't his thing, unlike Dan and Billy. He wondered if the yoga routine Marcia practised gave her that inner calm she exuded, which certainly rubbed off on him, as she never failed to calm his inner turmoil that had plagued him throughout his life.

"That is cheating," Marcia giggled, lying face down on the bed, with Eamon astride her. His standing cock, which had been jabbing into her rear slipped between her legs as she widened them to accommodate him.

"Who said anything about playing fair," he murmured, as she took the full length of him.

. . . .

Eamon knew he couldn't undo his past. He'd realised that he couldn't keep Marcia in the dark any longer, yet he'd wanted to avoid frightening her. He had been churning it over in his mind and knew without any shadow of a doubt that after Alphonso's phone call the night of their engagement and the recent events involving the mysterious man, he had become a prime suspect. Someone would be feathering their nest nicely by targeting him and it was time to act.

"Marcia," he said quietly, as she looked up into his eyes. "I've had word that there's someone out there who wants to destroy us and I am doing all I can to prevent them from doing it, so please understand."

"Eamon," she said, alarmed. "How do you know? Are you sure?" she sat up, facing him. He silently watched her. He'd already told his brother Patrick that he was living under the threat that the long arm of the law would catch up with him because someone had turned Queen's evidence. Patrick had begged him to leave Spain and live a quiet life in County Armagh. Eamon told him that he was engaged and that in a few months he would be getting married. But if things came on top of him, he asked his brother to ensure his fiancé Marcia was safely removed from the country. He told Patrick that the law would want to confiscate his assets, but that he would set it up so that Patrick could financially take care of Marcia if the need were to arise. Patrick could not sway him to walk away from his business commitments until he had word that they were closing in on him. Eamon knew that he would need to get them all far away from Ireland once the law started delving because it would not take them long to discover where Marcia was and drag her in for questioning.

He ran his hands through her hair as she fought with the tears that were brimming in her eyes. He could not envision living his life without her. He had toyed with the idea of asking Marcia to look at the tarot cards to see if she could throw any light upon the situation. Even though he believed in her predictions, he had to admit that he thought all that mystical stuff was spooky, ever since he was a young lad. But although he was reluctant, he needed answers and he needed them post-haste.

"Marcia, would you look at the tarot cards?" he tentatively asked her.

Marcia's eyes widened.

Eamon ran his fingers through his hair nervously as he watched her with bated breath. She slowly laid each card on the dining table. He'd told her he only wanted an answer to one question. Marcia ran her eyes over the eighteen cards, settling on the scales of *la Justice* on the bottom left-hand corner and the card of *la Lune,* deception. She looked at Eamon's card *l'Amoureux,* representing his Gemini star sign, which was in the layout on the top right-hand corner. She had four cards to lay on each corner. Silently giving up thanks as she saw the card that covered his was the *le Soleil* card. She smiled as she looked at him. She gathered the twenty-two major arcana cards and packed them away.

Eamon was like a cat on a hot tin roof waiting for the answer. "For fuck's sake, woman, are ye going to tell me?"

"Eamon," she beamed "Everything indicates that you will eventually come out on top of this situation." Marcia looked as relieved as Eamon felt.

"Okay," he exhaled. "Now, put those cards away," he said, rising from the table feeling slightly more assured.

. . . .

Samuel was giving Dan, Billy and Cindy instructions when Eamon strode into the gym with Marcia. Elliot was in the middle of training with a sparring partner and he briefly looked up and nodded at them. Samuel had his back to them, but even from that angle, the physical stature of the man was impressive. Without his top on, he reminded Eamon of a Roman gladiator such was his muscular physique. He was the ultimate kickboxing machine and he looked as challenging as Eamon knew he could be. He had his dreadlocks tied back as he showed the small group his powerful roundhouse kick. He performed the axe kick with skilful expertise and Eamon knew he had made the right decision by bringing Marcia.

Elliot finished his sparring and asked Billy and Dan to follow him. Cindy stepped onto the mat with Samuel and gave her instructions. She appeared to be taking it seriously, and after being shown a few times, Samuel blocked her kick, laughing. He said it would not take her long to become proficient. Cindy walked across to watch Elliot and Dan on the mat.

Eamon sucked air through his teeth and a familiar knot formed in his stomach as he observed Samuel standing behind Marcia with his huge paw-like hands placed on her thighs, giving her direction. The man's sheer physical presence enveloped her small frame. Unconsciously, Eamon stroked his beard, fighting the desire to tear his woman away. He felt his throat constrict as Samuel turned Marcia towards him speaking into her eyes as she listened intently. Eamon was deeply disturbed. The instructor's nearness to Marcia was bringing something distinctly unwelcome in him to the fore. Samuel's brooding sexuality radiated off him like heat from a furnace and an almost primordial urge came over Eamon to take out this opponent. His rage built as Samuel lingered over placing Marcia into the correct position, his hands spending seconds longer than necessary on her body. He knew he had to get out of the club otherwise he would have caused a scene. Eamon turned on his heels without speaking to anyone. He could not, otherwise, he would have erupted. Eamon had intended to drop her at the gym and get back to business, but seeing them, he knew for sure that this would be her first and last lesson.

....

Marcia hadn't seen Eamon leave. She knew he had a busy day ahead and assumed he hadn't wanted to hang around. She thanked Samuel and told him that she was looking forward to her next session with him. She asked Cindy to drop her home. Billy and Dan were staying on, as they wanted extra training.

Samuel had advised Marcia that he should teach her on a one-to-one basis. He assured her that she would become proficient more quickly with intensive training. She felt a little uncomfortable about the idea, knowing that Eamon would probably be feeling jealous about her being in such close physical contact with Samuel. But she knew he wanted her to learn how to defend herself.

Marcia sensed that Eamon was not in a good place when she returned to the villa. He glowered broodingly as she told him how amazing the session had been. When she told him about the one-to-one lessons that Samuel had recommended he didn't reply. Eamon had given her little choice in starting martial arts under Samuel's instruction, so she felt a little irritated by his response. Instead, she cheerily kissed him on the lips, went into the bedroom, stripped off her gymwear and got into the shower. As the cool water ran over her skin, she turned her face to let the powerful jets play over her. She didn't hear Eamon as he came into the bathroom and slide the shower door open.

"What fucking reason do ye need to take a cold shower? Is it because you need to cool your desire after being in the company of that black buck?" he spat, eyes ablaze.

Marcia felt like she had been hit in the pit of her stomach, so shocking was Eamon's outburst. His accusation was totally ridiculous and she stared at him incredulously. If it had been anyone else she would have laughed at the preposterous notion, but she knew Eamon was deadly serious. Eamon turned on his heel and slammed the bedroom door behind him.

As she turned the shower off and towelled herself dry, Marcia felt all the life go out of her. She had seen in his eyes a look that she couldn't fathom and it scared her. What was wrong with the man? All she had done was what he had asked her, and now she was bearing the full brunt of his anger. How dare he treat her like that? She quickly threw a dress over her head and dried her hair. She found him sitting outside in the cool breeze.

"I want an explanation," she demanded, "How dare you treat me like that Eamon. What have I done?" Marcia's eyes raged black.

Eamon was ready with his response, "Tell me why ye felt the need of an ice-cold shower." He was glaring at her.

Marcia shook her head and moved to turn away but he was like lightning, grabbing her arm roughly and spinning her around to face him. In a second, she twisted and struck out with a diagonal knee strike with all the fury and futility she had felt building inside her over the last few days. The blow was enough to make Eamon release her. She ran. Roman looked on frantically, not knowing what was happening. Marcia snatched her bag and keys and sprinted to her car and locked the doors. She turned the key in the ignition drove out of the gates.

. . . .

Half an hour later, Eamon was on his second whisky. He walked back into the garden and looked out to sea, wondering just what was wrong with him. He was unable to control the insane jealousy over the attention that Samuel had been giving Marcia. He knew that he had fucked it up with her and that she'd done nothing wrong, but he knew that he was also incandescent with rage over Samuel's nearness to Marcia. He wasn't blind. He could see he had the hots for her and he couldn't allow her to return to the club, as he would cause a war that could get out of hand. He knew his old insecurities were coming to the fore. Eamon just did not know what to do to stop himself. He put the tumbler down and took out his phone. He punched Marcia's number in but she didn't answer. On the third try, she finally picked up.

"Please, Marcia, I want to talk to ye," he asked softly.

"Eamon I have only done what you asked me to, I didn't …"

He interjected. "Marcia, please return," he begged her.

Eamon was standing by the front door with Roman as Marcia's car pulled in. He could see that she had been crying. This was the first time he had allowed himself to get out of control with his possessiveness of her. He knew Marcia was naïve, oblivious to the Jamaican hitting on her, but he certainly wasn't. He strolled towards her with Roman alongside. "Where have ye been?" he asked quietly. She told him that she'd taken a drive further up in the hills and found an outcrop where she'd been gazing out at the sea.

He put his arm around her as they walked back together and went into the lounge. Marcia sat on the settee and

Eamon leaned back against the table opposite as he struggled with his apology. "I am sorry, Marcia; I'm not trying to make excuses for my reaction to the Jamaican coming on strong to ye. I didn't mean to take my anger out on ye. It's that black bastard that should be taught a lesson in respect for another man's woman."

"Eamon?" she started, "it was you who insisted I undertake self-defence. This makes no sense!" Eamon struggled, fighting against his emotions.

"Marcia, I watched him with ye. I know the man wants to get into your knickers. I can tell. Hear me out – Samuel has got designs on ye. It's just fucking disrespectful. If he crossed that line with ye he'd be dead, no question about it."

Marcia heard him out and when he had finished, she spoke, "Can I ask you something? What does it matter, Eamon, if Samuel has the hots for me? He may be a handsome man but so are a lot of men. There are plenty of attractive women in our circle, but how would you feel if I threw accusations at you? Do you think that I would risk one night with him or any other man when it would mean throwing away everything that we have together? Please believe me, Eamon, no man has ever satisfied me in the way that you have done. I will still want you when you're ninety years old."

He sucked air through his teeth and slowly nodded. She appeared as a child pleading her innocence. Eamon knew that feeling all too well from his own childhood. He pushed himself away from the table and moved alongside her. Marcia drew him to her and kissed him. "I will give it up if you want me to," she whispered.

"I think in that short time ye learnt enough, don't ye?" he smiled wryly, elevating his brow, returning her kiss.

Eamon said he had to make a few phone calls in his office which could not be put off. Marcia said she would swim awhile. She felt she needed the serenity of the cool water.

....

She still felt shaken by his angry outburst. She knew Eamon was a passionate man in everything he undertook and that he was a man of strong ideals. She was not in the slightest bit attracted to another man. Why would he even think she would be when she devoted herself to him? Marcia had never met a man who fulfilled her as much as Eamon did. He was an unselfish lover that had shown her heights that she had never before experienced. She never tired of him. Just the mere thought of Eamon brought on a want, a longing for his embrace. For him to think she could replace the deep love she felt for him was unimaginable to her. Marcia sensed an underlying disturbing factor in Eamon's psychological makeup but hoped with time she could help him. Marcia turned as she heard the sliding of the doors. She smiled as he held her eyes. Eamon picked up the towel, moving towards her as Marcia walked up the pool steps.

"How the hell do ye think that I can resist ye when my woman is near naked, stepping out of the pool, glistening with droplets of water," he said, through that hooded look that told her he was hers and hers Marcia moved her hand and gently fondled him.

Her fingers deftly undid his fly. In one swift movement, he picked her up in his arms and carried her into the bedroom, back kicking the door.

Marcia took his swollen cock into her opened mouth. Lightly running her tongue over his engorged glans, she began to suck hungrily on the rounded end. She felt the quivers through Eamon's buttocks. Cupping each cheek, she encouraged him closer, hearing the response form in his throat as she swallowed him a little deeper. He was so hard it was difficult for her to manoeuvre her tongue around its girth but she was practiced enough to allow more of his length to ease itself past her neat white teeth and into the depth of her throat. Her mouth flooded with saliva to enable its smooth passage. Slowly and steadily, her head held by Eamon's hands, moved backwards and forwards. She had released his behind and now had one hand encircling his balls, feeling the tightness beneath the fine hairs that dusted them. Her middle finger stretched behind, tracing a path between them and his buttocks. Her other hand held the base of his member, aiding its passage back and forth. Now and then, she would stop or increase her pace, sometimes nibbling along its length before allowing it into her mouth again.

She was aware that Eamon was finding it difficult not to hold her too forcibly. His fingers had tightened in her hair and low moans escaped his mouth. As one hand played him skilfully between his powerful thighs, her other determined the rhythm of his cock's exit and entry into her wet orifice. He exploded moments later, shuddering violently as he spent himself. Marcia held her face against Eamon's stomach, her skin warm and glistening. Eamon held her tightly to him his cock relaxing visibly as its last ebbs died away.

An hour later, they were relaxing by the pool, and Eamon suggested that he book a table for the men and their partners to join them that evening. He told her he would phone them and then ring the restaurant. Marcia agreed, happy that they had put the upset behind them. Eamon rang Dan and Billy and then spoke to Greg who agreed to join them as he said he had not eaten a decent meal since Suzette had been in hospital and he welcomed the invitation.

Jane, Billy and Kalita pulled into the marina at the same time as Greg. The group made their way to the restaurant. They all took seats around the table, which overlooked the water. With the wine poured, Billy took the opportunity to raise a toast to share some good news. "Next week, as you know, is my birthday," he started, his eyes on Jane by his side, "I would like to share the wonderful news that Jane has bought me something I've always wanted … a horse. I am now the proud owner of a magnificent black Andalusian. I couldn't have wished for anything better, apart from Jane herself, of course." He winked in Jane's direction as she smiled at him. The group raised their glasses and gave a cheer. "So that I'm not riding alone, Jane has thoughtfully bought herself her own Andalusian, but hers is grey."

Everyone laughed. It seemed that Billy and Jane were happy settling into their new life together. It was a good opportunity to catch up on recent events for the group. Greg told everyone about Suzette's excellent recovery and that he had made plans to visit Dom and Maureen while they were in Marbella. Eamon, who had arrived with Marcia just in time for Billy's toast, told the table about his plans to take Marcia away for a few days to enjoy their time together after the excitement of all the recent events.

Marcia sat next to Cindy. She hoped Cindy wouldn't mention the Muay Thai lesson in front of Eamon, as she knew it would trigger Eamon's insecurities. She had no desire to see Eamon's temper flare again.

"You look radiant, Marcia," Jane said to her.

Cindy interjected, "Come to think of it, you do have a particular glow, one that tells me that that man of yours is treating you right, as Dan does me." She squeezed his arm playfully. Eamon studied Marcia while the women talked amongst themselves, only half paying attention to what Greg was saying about Suzette's recent successful nose realignment.

Now it had been brought to his attention, Eamon was in silent agreement. Marcia's glowing good health was certainly at odds with how pale and drawn she had looked over the last week or so. He was certain that it was since they were back on good terms and he made a mental note to keep his jealousy under control in the future.

Greg and Eamon had been discussing another joint business venture that they had kept to themselves in case anyone jumped on the bandwagon and snatched the deal from under their noses. He knew that if he undertook this new enterprise he would have to be more sociable, which wasn't his thing, but it would enable him to cover his back financially. He was unsure if it would sit well with Marcia but he felt it would keep his woman more occupied and distract her from wanting to continue working at the beauty salon.

UK

Beads of sweat built up on the man's brow, as he sat in the back seat of the car. The two detectives just kept going. "We need more information on that Irish bastard … tell us what that mob in Spain are up to," one of them demanded.

It was the younger, up-and-coming detective who was putting the pressure on. "OK, you may have given us the names of a few of your associates, and we've cleaned a few big names up across the pond, but you've failed to give us fucking anything on that mob in Spain." The man was sick to death of the constant pressure they were putting him under.

"It's the woman who is warning them," he told the pair, exasperatedly raising his voice and becoming agitated.

The older detective took over, "Now listen, you prick. We struck a deal with you. We'll grant you your freedom for information on all of your contacts, and now you're telling me that some woman has the power to look into the future and is working with this fucking mob?"

The man spoke more quietly, but firmly, "She is the Irishman O'Donally's woman. She warns him to prevent him from getting his fingers burnt."

The older detective guffawed, "Your nothing but a fucking messer." He turned towards the back seat and sneered "Eamon O'Donally is fucking clean as a whistle. He doesn't do anything illegal because if he did, you pillock, we'd fucking hear of it. We cannot even have him on a speeding ticket. We know at HQ that the Irishman stepped into Jimmy Grant's shoes, but the fucking haulage business is legit, thanks to Grant's widow who's now living the high life with her daughter across the fucking pond." He paused for breath and then carried on, "Did you hear about the old villain whose name you gave us?" He laughed sarcastically. "Lenny fucking Decker … well, he's fucking dead mate, died of a massive heart attack while you were out there in Spain, so unless you want to find yourself back in the joint you'd better come up with a better fucking excuse than some bloody Mystic Meg who supposedly is working her voodoo, keeping this gang from getting their collars felt."

The detective angrily opened the car door and told him he had only a short while before they yanked the chain and pulled him back into the clink. "Now fuck off and get us something concrete to go on."

. . . .

Isabella Perez worked her magic on Chief Inspector Ross Lowe. He lay on his back as she used ice cubes and her hot tongue. He ran his fingers through the thick, dark mane that tumbled to her shoulders. Isabella Perez knew that the middle-aged chief inspector didn't have a Cuban peso worth of spark in him, but this was not the reason for her giving him the special treatment. Isabella had ridden him and whispered all the right things into his ear, but, up until a few moments ago, he had only given her a little information. She needed more. She could see that

Ross Lowe was beginning to feel knackered. Isabella had massaged him into a relaxed mood, and maybe he had let slip a few titbits while his mind had been understandably elsewhere. She feigned understanding much English, so he obviously thought it didn't matter how much he said. Pillow talk was a wonderful thing. He'd disclosed information about the Irishman Eamon O'Donally and his so-called psychic woman who was into tarot reading and voodoo and who was warning him about the law, and that's how he supposedly kept one step ahead of being locked up. Isabella was happy to offer a sympathetic ear.

"This fucking grass expects us to believe him," he told her, before falling back into silence as she continued her work.

She made sure that he was thoroughly distracted before gently continuing her coaxing. "What a fool to think he can deceive you so, who is he?" her voice was sexy and languorous. As Chief Inspector Ross Lowe divulged the name, Isabella Perez ensured that he was compensated.

Isabella phoned to say that she was on the way. Captain Thomas Harper-Watts was from a wealthy upper-class family. He had been thrown out of one of the most expensive schools in England for shagging the attractive PE teacher in the boys' toilets. He had then moved on to the English teacher. Thomas loved the seedier side of life. He had asked Isabella to work her magic on the chief inspector as a special favour to him. Isabella Perez had not stumbled across the chief inspector by chance that evening. She'd known exactly where to find him, nursing his drink in the corner of a popular wine bar. Ross had been relaxing away from the pressures of work and his nagging wife for a few precious hours. As Isabella had approached his table, his first thought had been that God must have answered his prayers. Fun with a capital F was stood there, her full mouth and glossy red lips sent messages to his groin and for the first time in many a long year, he felt arousal. She was one of the hottest women he had ever seen walk through the doors of this bar. He smiled back, and she joined him. She introduced herself and fed him the usual lines, taking no time at all to wind her fish in. In fact, within less than fifteen minutes, they were back at Isabella's place. And less than an hour after, that she had the information that Thomas had required. Isabella had a lot of time for Thomas. She enjoyed listening to his detached upper-crust voice as he answered the intercom. She also enjoyed his fabulous flat in Bayswater, riding in his Lexus Connect, and the exotic holidays that she accompanied him on. He'd explained to her about some of the work that he wanted her to help him with for an old pal, although he hadn't mentioned the name.

. . . .

Billy Mackenzie had told his boss that he had a reliable source who might be just the right person to help with the problem of discovering who it was that was making life difficult for him. Billy had contacted Captain Thomas Harper-Watts to ask him for a favour. The old-school camaraderie of the SAS code was in their blood, and however far they scattered, they knew that they could call upon one another when needed. It had not been too difficult to get in touch with Thomas Harper-Watts. He always kept the same phone number and he'd been immediately cooperative.

"Of course old pal!" he'd replied, "I know just the person to get the necessary information." He would not hear of receiving any payment either. Billy had smiled to himself. They'd ribbed Captain Thomas something rotten back in the day. With his upper-class demeanour, he'd been the target for banter, but he had taken it all on the chin, in good humour. Underneath that aristocratic exterior, however, there was a man with a backbone of steel and a real sense of fearlessness, and although he wasn't supposed to mix with the lower ranks, he was one of the boys and superior in rank alone. He had signed up for more dangerous assignments than anyone else he had known.

. . . .

Thomas was still game for most things, and so was Isabella, which was exactly why he had known she'd be up for Billy's little job. He also knew that Chief Inspector Ross Lowe was a regular at one of his favourite drinking holes where Thomas could mix with the type of people who he could converse with from the military. Even better, the barman, when asked, had revealed a few juicy nuggets about the chief inspector, who habitually sat alone in the corner. He always sat looking as if the weight of the world was on his shoulders. The barman said that he had once confided that he was getting "No life indoors". He was ripe for the picking. Straightaway, Thomas had known how to get the information that his friend Billy Mackenzie in Spain needed and he'd never doubted that Isabella wouldn't come home without the goods.

Spain

Eamon accompanied Marcia to her appointment with Doctor Sagio. He knew she took care of herself and ate healthily but he had been worried because she had gone through a spell of looking wan and feeling tired. Although she seemed to have bounced back, he didn't think they should cancel the appointment. He was there to ensure that she underwent every medical test, to give him peace of mind. Marcia had blood and urine tests, her weight was checked and they were told to return within two hours for the results. Eamon had taken her out to lunch, although Marcia had eaten little.

Eamon and Marcia entered the doctor's office. He proffered them a seat and looked down at his report. "I would like to be the first to congratulate you both on your pregnancy." He smiled at Marcia and then glanced back at the paperwork. "You will require a scan later, and given what you have told me, the baby will arrive sometime in March."

Eamon's face showed no reaction and Marcia sat rooted to the spot. The doctor held his hand out to Eamon, who, on automatic pilot, pumped it. The doctor advised Marcia to take iron supplements and to adhere to a nutritious diet, as she was at the beginning of the second trimester. He said that in his medical opinion, Marcia should sail through the pregnancy.

Marcia sobbed into Eamon's shoulder in the car. They drove home in silence, Eamon feeling shocked to the core. This was the last thing he'd expected to hear. It was a bittersweet moment to be told Marcia was going to give him a child. It should have been the happiest time of his life, but the threat of him losing his freedom at a time when they both should have been celebrating only added to the pressure. By the time they reached the villa, he had made a firm decision – even though it would be one that would tear him apart.

He wondered if someone up *there* was having a laugh at his expense. He had met Marcia and took over from Jimmy Grant and decided to go straight and put his shady past behind him, then out of the woodwork comes a "grass" that threatens his freedom, and, to top it off, the love of his life was now pregnant with his child. One thing was for certain, he mused, as he looked into Marcia's forlorn eyes. He would need to speed up the search for the toe rag. But he would need to keep Marcia out of harm's way – somewhere he knew no one would think of looking for her.

He consoled her in the only way he knew how. Showing her just how much he loved her, he caressed her and slowly made love to her. He had convinced her of his complete joy at the news of becoming a father. It was beyond his wildest dreams, he told her. He knew that Marcia had not been able to conceive previously. She had told him that it was something she had come to terms with long ago. It had come as such a shock to him knowing that Marcia was bearing him a child. Under any other circumstances, he would have been ecstatic, but he couldn't tell her how he felt about the distinct possibility that he could be torn from her and the baby. He

464

knew he had an urgent battle on his hands and it was imperative to act quickly.

Marcia writhed with intense joy as each measured
motion brought her closer to orgasm. His tongue flicked sensuously over her darkened areoles and he gently bit her nipples
as their juices began to flow. As his heartbeat was returning
to normal, he studied her. *How did I not realise it earlier?* he
thought to himself. There were changes in her body – her
breasts were fuller and there was now a gentle curve of her
abdomen where his seed was planted. Eamon kissed her as he
withdrew, knowing that this would be the last time for a while
that his woman would be able to give him so much pleasure.
He would tell her after he had made the arrangements, ensur-
ing she got on the flight because he would personally take her
to the check in at the airport.

Eamon opened the gates that evening and asked Billy
to follow him into his office. He told him to lock the door
behind him and sat at his desk as Billy sat opposite.

Billy looked pleased with himself as he informed
Eamon that his mate from the UK had given him the name of
the police informant. "This is kosher. It has come straight from
the horse's mouth, so there's no way it's not legit." Billy laughed
as he told his boss that a woman had bedded the chief inspector
who had freely given up the name in exchange for a couple of
hours of titillation.

Eamon was stunned for the second time that day as
Billy revealed the name. Eamon guffawed, shaking his head in
denial, as he stated that the chief inspector had fed this woman
a load of bollocks. "Fucking Max Greenaway had topped
himself," he said in disbelief. Greenaway's wife was informed
by the prison official and my woman was with her when the
call came through. The world and his brother know that he is

dead. "Billy, listen … the man even left a note saying that no one, not even his wife was to attend his fucking funeral!"

Billy shook his head in bewilderment. He could not understand it, because Captain Thomas Harper-Watts was one of the best there was at getting information, and Billy knew there was no way that he would have got it wrong.

Eamon tried to make sense of why the chief inspector would have pulled Max Greenaway's name out of the hat without reason. Eamon was totally perplexed by it. While still puzzling over this latest revelation, a call came through from the depot from his manager Diego. He told Billy to ring Dan and to take Jane with Caesar to check out some footage on the security camera. Diego had seen a man snooping around the lorries when he'd checked. Eamon had enough on his plate organising Marcia's speedy exit from Spain, so he told Diego he was very busy with some other business and could not make it.

Eamon reiterated what Diego had told him – that he thought it was some Spanish punk who Eamon had caught a few months back trying to steal from the cabs. He was obviously at it again. "No sweat boss, I will phone them and get right on it."

Eamon thanked him; at least he would have one problem less to deal with, knowing that they would handle the situation. He saw Billy out and then his phone rang. Eamon went to answer a call and saw that it was Samuel's number. He hadn't spoken to him since he had put a stop to Marcia's self-defence lessons. "This a late time to call!" he said, brusquely.

Samuel, ignoring his terse retort, informed him that a relative from Ilford had heard through a friend that word was circulating about the informant. Samuel said that it was believed that he was a big-time drug boss who'd struck a deal with the old bill. Samuel said that one of the prison warders at

Pentonville, working on the floor where the guy was banged up, had let it slip that this high profile prisoner, who had so much inside information regarding the names and dealings of the criminal world, had become an informant. The law agreed that they would put him under a protection programme if they gained prosecutions.

Eamon was curt with Samuel. "I'm aware of the grass but without a name that piece of information is of no use to me," he said dismissively.

"Well, the name that's on the boy's tongue in the big smoke is none other than Max Greenaway, and as you know, the Londoners never get it far wrong."

Eamon thanked him for the information. His heart skipped a beat to hear the same name mentioned twice in one day. It couldn't be just a coincidence, but Eamon would need more confirmation.

. . . .

Eamon smiled wistfully as Marcia walked up the steps from the pool. He picked the towel up and handed it to her as she came near the garden table. He did not know how long she would need to stay away from Spain or if he would be able to see his child being born – something that would have been joyful under any other circumstances.

"Why do you look so serious Eamon," she smiled, wrapping the bath towel around her and throwing her arms around his neck.

He blanched at the thought of the painful news he was about to give her. Taking her hands in his, he held her eyes. "Marcia I want ye to listen to me and then do as I ask."

Marcia reacted as if she had been stung. "Eamon you are scaring me what is…?" He put his fingers to her lips to quiet her. "I have been given the name of the informant and I have booked ye on a first-class flight this evening for Thailand, so that ye and the baby are safe. So please don't make it any harder than it already is for me."

A pallor fell across Marcia's face, as Eamon revealed Max Greenaway's name. "But I was with Suzette the morning she received the call about his death. The prison official said that Max had left a note!"

Eamon shook his head. "I've a strong feeling that it's all a get up. I have to get further confirmation but until then I can't risk your safety. I need ye to be as far away as possible. I would never forgive myself if anything happened to you and the baby."

Marcia was adamant, "No, I won't go!" she exclaimed, but Eamon held her shoulders tightly and spoke with thick ferocity, "If this IS Greenaway, he's brought down good men in Miami, and I won't rest until he's found. He knows all about ye and I'll not stand by and see the law bring ye in for questioning."

He rose to his full height. "Please go and pack a few light-weight clothes. Ye can buy what ye need in Thailand. When Aye meets ye at the airport in Bangkok, she will sort it all out for ye."

. . . .

Eamon gently prised her arms from his neck as she clung to him in the airport departures hall. He could feel the small bump pressing against him, which was his child in Marcia's belly. Promising that he would phone regularly, he resolutely turned and walked away as her tears ran in rivulets.

Eamon made it known to everyone that Marcia had left him, he did not exclude anyone, not even his men. He wasn't going to take any chances of Marcia being found and brought back if he was arrested. He told everyone who asked that they had had one too many fights and Marcia had had enough. There were whispers of disbelief and murmurings of suspicion, but, ultimately, with Marcia gone, their friends and colleagues had to take Eamon at his word.

Jane didn't think that Marcia had left Eamon. When Billy told her of the seriousness of the situation and how Eamon could lose his freedom, she realised that Eamon had probably sent her out of harm's way.

. . . .

Marcia had been booked on the Air France flight from Malaga to Paris. It was a two-hour, forty-minute flight. From there she would layover at Paris for four hours and then board an Air France flight to Bangkok. The Boeing 777 flight would take eleven hours and fifteen minutes. Eamon had booked a first-class one-way ticket. Aye and a driver would be waiting at the airport to take her to Aye's home in Jomtien – for how long, Eamon did not know.

When he knew Marcia was about to board the Air France flight in Paris, he had phoned her to reassure her and told Marcia how much he loved her and that he would contact Aye to say that she was about to board the main flight. Aye had told Eamon that she would take great care of both Marcia and his child. He thanked her and said he would transfer money to Marcia's bank account for them both.

Eamon's mind was on Marcia as he sat with Roman alongside the garden chair looking up to the starlit sky. He wondered how long he could bear to be without her. To not have Marcia's physical presence near him caused a dull ache in his heart. He sat with his hand on Roman's head, desperately needing to touch something that she had touched. If he'd let her see how broken he was by having to send her away, he would have crumpled. It was the hardest thing he had ever done in his life and he was choked with despair.

Eamon had a large whisky to help him to sleep as his mind could not switch off from worrying about Marcia. He had felt more at ease when he had spoken to her when she touched down in Bangkok. He knew she had been travelling for a total of over twenty hours, and, along with the time difference of seven hours and her pregnancy, he knew that she would be weary. Although she had a bed in first class, Eamon knew that being separated from him under stressful circumstances would ensure she wouldn't have rested. But he felt secure in the knowledge that Marcia was in the capable hands of Aye. He wouldn't need to be overly concerned about her welfare while she was in Asia.

Eamon rose the following morning, showered and, after washing the cloudy effects of the large beverage from his head with the jets on cold. He stepped back into the bedroom to dress when his phone rang. It was Billy, and Eamon told him to ring Dan and for both of them to come to his villa.

Eamon knew Billy had received a call from Thomas earlier and had been passed some more info on the "grass". He prayed that now perhaps would be the time to get things moving.

Dan and Billy sat in Eamon's office as Billy filled them in on recent developments. Captain Thomas Harper-Watts had persuaded his well-connected father, Lord Arthur, to push the chief inspector for further information. Via a contact, Lord Arthur had succeeded in passing on an invitation for the chief inspector to join him for lunch at his prestigious men-only club. Thomas's father, Lord Arthur Harper-Watts, loved the intrigue, although he had to be a little more discreet than his flamboyant son, given his reputation amongst his well-heeled associates. But he saw helping his errant son as somewhat of an adventure.

At the lunch, Lord Arthur had oiled the chief inspector with his favourite Asbach twenty-one-year-old brandy. Not only had he happily spilled the beans about the supergrass, the chief inspector eagerly agreed that his local Masonic lodge would support Lord Arthur's personal charity at their next event.

Billy said that his pal Captain Thomas had been pleased to hear that Max Greenaway's death had been feigned and had not been some false information that Isabella had pried from the chief inspector. He said he would not have wanted her to be duped after the chief had been treated to such a good time, he'd laughingly told Billy. Max Greenaway's "death" had been easy to fake. The chief inspector had boasted to a very attentive Lord Arthur.

The men took in Billy's words in silence, and Eamon felt a wave of nauseous fear hit his stomach. How much information had the low-life passed on about him and his involvement with Jimmy Grant, he wondered. Marcia had been right all along. She had told him that she couldn't understand why it was Max's voice she'd heard in her dream about Suzette being hurt.

"Max Greenaway's name needs to be out there," Eamon stated, "I'll get the ball rolling. There needs to be a large reward put on the prick's head. When we offer a half a million for the news of his whereabouts I'm sure there will be takers." Eamon's hopes began to rise as he now had confirmation and the hunt was on.

UK

Eamon called his old associate Dylan Marshall. Dylan seemed always pleased to hear from him, to catch up with what was going down. Dylan, and Shaun his younger brother, who was his sidekick, had been previously active in the drug game for years and had put a few deals Jimmy Grant's way. They'd moved to Truro in Cornwall from County Donegal many years ago. Although the brothers were from the province of Ulster, they'd left their turbulent lives behind and didn't pay too much heed to anyone's religious beliefs. They were only interested in people if they could earn from them. They lived their lives in the slow lane, below the radar, with their boys Connor and Nathan who were now running the show.

Connor was a few years younger than his cousin Nathan, who was something of a head-case, and they were into most things, gun-running, drugs and, of late, they had gone into the lucrative porn industry. "You name it, the boys were into it," Dylan stated openly to Eamon as a trusted mate. "They're also running a string of pole-dancing clubs which acts as a front for the main earner."

Eamon knew that their main earner was bringing in narcotics that passed through their hands via the local trawlers.

Dylan and Shaun had been fearsome operators in their day, "Where there's a will, there's a way," had been their whole attitude, right up until Dylan had had a stroke and Shaun had had a heart attack. They had then stepped down. They were not up for much nowadays, Dylan had told Eamon, although their lads were causing enough trouble by themselves, with Nathan recently stabbing a rival gang leader who'd been looking to try to take over their patch. Dylan reminisced with Eamon about the good times when the money had been free-flowing and life had been easier.

"Me and my Irene wanted a bit of peace after my health scare, and now, can ye fucking believe it, my Nathan's up on a fucking attempted murder rap!"

Eamon sympathised with him and then put in a word about the situation with Max Greenaway.

Dylan went ballistic. "Ye are fucking kidding me … my boy had some dealings with that fucking rat not too far back, and we heard that Greenaway topped himself, the fucking loser. Don't ye worry, lad. I will spread the cunt's name like wildfire."

Eamon told him that he had personally put a price on Max Greenaway's head for half a million.

Dylan interrupted him, "Let me tell ye, Eamon, if my old ticker was half fucking right, I would hunt the bastard down myself, money or no money." Dylan agreed to contact him as soon as any news came his way.

By the time Dylan, Shaun and their boys had finished making their phone calls, half the country knew that Max Greenaway was the grass who was putting the finger on them all. Everyone in the criminal world was now on the lookout for him. It now appeared that it would be only a matter of time now the word was out.

. . . .

Greenaway had become frustrated with the cops' constant badgering and he mouthed off. "Keep your fucking voice down!" the older detective growled at him.

The younger detective laughed, "And there's you jetting out to Spain to give your so-called widow a slap and using up your last bit of readies on paying out for an all-time Spanish loser to sort out the Irishman's woman. Do you think we don't know what you get up to when you are supposed to be working for US?" he shouted.

Max lost his rag with the cocky young bastard who sat in the passenger seat of the car.

"Why don't you get off my back!" Max spat at the young upstart, who looked to him like he'd been in the police force for about five minutes tops.

He leaned over in Max's face. "Listen to me, you prick," he scoffed, "your name, Greenaway, is being sung all over this fucking land, and with a price tag on your fucking head, I suggest you give us some decent info before we make a few phone calls and make things a bit easier for them."

Max froze. "You fucking tosser. I've told you all there is to know. It is not my problem if things have gone quiet in Spain. I gave you the fucking Irishman's woman's name and her boy's information. How was I to know that he had bolted?" Max fumed, his face turning red, all thoughts of playing the game, gone out of the window.

The older detective turned to him calmly, and in an even tone said, "Fuck off then. Let the low lives have you, you poxy excuse for a man."

Max sensed the shift of power with horror. He jerked open the car door and ran towards his bedsit.

He knew his back was against the wall and he had no one to turn to. They had used him. He had been promised a new life, money and a different ID, but stupidly he'd played it wrong and now they'd cut him loose. All he had to his name was a hundred quid, and he was in a shabby bedsit staring at a one-ring cooker. Max contemplated topping himself but for real this time.

Spain

Suzette had reeled, shocked to the core, "There is no way that Marcia would just leave without getting in touch," she told Greg. But Greg replied that there wasn't anything that they could do about it and that she just had to accept the facts as they were.

"Look, Suzette, Eamon has got on with his life. He's planning to expand his haulage business with more lorries, so don't you think that he would have said something to me if there'd been some sort of a problem?" Suzette looked unconvinced.

Greg had called in to Eamon's villa on the odd occasion and found him sitting on the terrace with his dog by his side. He'd been much quieter of late, which Greg had put down to his sadness over Marcia leaving. He had talked about the new cruiser he was buying from Lenny Decker's wife. She'd decided to sell up and go back to be with her sisters in Birmingham. Greg felt a heaviness around Eamon when he saw him and felt saddened that he and Marcia had split up. He had thought that they were meant for each other. Greg was continuing with the new build that Eamon had wanted, as he had not changed his plan. It would be ready in eight to ten weeks and Greg had been sticking to the schedule even though he could not work out

476

why Eamon would still want such a great big place to live in by himself.

....

Suzette had fully recovered and her broken nose had been reset and entirely healed. She had kept Rachelle on board since the girl had proven to be worth her weight in gold. Nothing seemed to be too much trouble, and she'd even been helping Suzette with her engagement party plans. Suzette's business had ascended to new heights, and she had taken on a new hair-stylist named Jacqueline, whose expertise matched the boys'. Lloyd and Kieron had settled on becoming engaged, much to the delight of Kieron, and planned to celebrate the occasion at Christmas. Suzette had gone along with Greg to visit Eamon and had tried everything to persuade him to come to their engagement party, more for Greg's benefit than hers.

"Greg would be really happy if you could make it," she said. Suzette could not bring herself to ask him what happened to break up his relationship with Marcia. She lived in hope that Marcia would eventually get in touch with her. To her surprise, this seemed to change Eamon's mind and he agreed to attend the party.

....

Marcia told Eamon on their next phone call, that her scan was booked for the following day. Eamon asked how she and the baby were, and Marcia told him that she was eating healthily and drinking coconut milk that Aye brought her daily from the market because Aye said it was beneficial for the growing baby. Marcia said that although she had accepted the situation and would abide by his wishes, she wanted him to have a record of how their child was growing inside of her, and Eamon agreed that she should take regular photographs of her growing bump.

Eamon felt numb when he opened the attachment. He was mesmerised. He ran his finger over the screen. The torment of seeing the full frontal naked picture of his pregnant woman who was so far from him was too much for him to bear, but he couldn't tear himself away. Eamon flicked to the next picture of Marcia's side view. Her hand rested on her extended stomach. He ran his eyes over the darkened aureoles, surrounding buds the size of cherry pips – her breasts fuller. His heart constricted knowing he could not touch her, wrap his arms around her and protect her with his own body. His breathing grew heavier as he tried to fight against the ache in his groin, his swollen cock was screaming out for release. Eamon felt as if his heart was being torn from his chest. There was nothing he wanted more than to have Marcia by his side, but her safety and that of his child were of the utmost importance. He used the age-old method and improvised – he was after all, human and had a breaking point.

. . . .

Marcia had taken regular pictures of her baby bump hoping that it would sway Eamon to bring her back home. But although Eamon had been calling her daily, reassuring her that as soon as it was safe to do so he would let her return, he had not remarked about the nude pictures she had sent him.

The nearer she got to her due date the more emotional she became. "If I stay much longer, Eamon, the baby will be born in Thailand without you," she later pleaded, sobbing.

Eamon was staunch. "Marcia, please, I beg of ye, I will bring ye home as soon as this scum is found. It's only a matter of time."

Eamon came from the shower and lay on the bed, her heartfelt cries ringing in his ears. So many times Max Greenaway had slipped the net, but Eamon knew that the grass's luck had to run out soon. Eamon picked up his phone and opened the attachment of Marcia in full bloom. His frustration spilled forth. His anger returned. He was not blaming anyone but himself for his past actions. He knew they'd all had a bite out of the cherry. Max Greenaway had been in the same league in the UK while Jimmy Grant captained Spain, but when Greenaway's luck went pear-shaped, he had not intended to go down with his ship. He aimed to drown all the subordinates and save his own skin.

. . . .

Marcia had cried herself to sleep and then awoken in the night, feeling her baby kicking. Aye had seen her light go on and walked quietly to her room. Sitting on Marcia's bed, she tenderly held her hand and wiped away her tears. "When Eamon ring me, he tell me he don't want you to have tears, Marcia. This no good for you and make Eamon's baby sad." Aye gently put a palm on Marcia's abdomen to emphasise her point.

Marcia had taken Aye with her to the ultrasound scan at the private clinic, not wanting to be alone. She had found out that she was expecting a healthy boy. Marcia and Aye had shared tears of joy. Marcia had not told Eamon the sex of the baby though. She'd wait until the birth. Marcia had tried to put it to the back of her mind that Eamon would be alone in his bed each night. The thought terrified her that another woman would put temptation in Eamon's path. The longer their separation lasted, the more it played on her mind. She knew that Eamon loved her and was solicitous about her and his baby's welfare, but she knew sex played a big role in their relationship and away from him, she wouldn't be able to fulfil Eamon's passionate desires.

. . . .

Cindy was speaking to Suzette as the dark-haired beauty Rachelle headed their way. Billy gave Dan an inconspicuous nod in her direction. Dan did not respond but took his meaning, catching sight of Cindy's angry look as the woman approached. He knew Cindy did not like her. Dan smiled to himself, knowing that Cindy, who always voiced her opinion, was never far from the truth with her assumptions. She had told him that Rachelle was a social climber and would make a play for Eamon O'Donally. It looked to Dan that Cindy was spot on the money as he observed Rachelle's eagle eye alight on his boss.

The Jamaican brothers were in attendance too and were surrounded by a group of women. Dan and Billy were aware that their boss wasn't enamoured with Samuel. They had seen that one time when Marcia had had her self-defence lesson that the Jamaican had pushed his luck, coming on strong with her, and although Eamon hadn't mentioned it, Dan knew that his boss wouldn't forget it.

A handsome, fair-haired guy who was talking to Greg and Eamon about selling them his warehouse glanced in Rachelle's direction. "I bet that would give you a couple of hours of entertainment in the sack. Pity I got my woman here with me tonight," he said grinning and then turned his back on her. As

Rachelle looked towards them she caught Eamon's eye before he turned back to continue speaking to the men.

Suzette felt she could not break away from all the potential clients who wanted to know about the special beauty treatments that her salon provided, but she noticed her receptionist Rachelle was taking an avid interest in the three men. If she kept her interest away from Greg, Suzette was not bothered but she wasn't foolish enough to think that the sexy-looking woman wouldn't try her luck, so she kept an eye on her.

. . . .

Eamon was nursing a large whisky. He ran his forefinger over his goatee beard as he pondered upon Max Greenaway's last sighting. Lord Arthur Harper-Watts had revealed that although the law had been given information about his involvement with Jimmy Grant, as Grant was now out of the running, the legal system didn't have a leg to stand on regarding making any charges stick with O'Donally. He had made numerous phone calls and had upped the money to a million pounds to whoever could get Max Greenaway sorted. So many of the big names were banged up awaiting trial, and it had made pulling strings more difficult than he had thought.

The idle chitchat had driven Eamon outside. He was missing Marcia more than ever, as she should have been on his arm right now. Her intelligent conversation and the elegant way he knew she would have dressed for this party made it all the harder to pretend he was having a good time. Lost in thought, Eamon knocked back the whisky in one gulp. He checked his watch for the time difference in Thailand. He knew that she should be sleeping now as Marcia told him that the humidity and the weight of the growing baby tired her.

Eamon had found himself sleeping less and less at night, in his cold and lonely bed.

Eamon was brought back to the here and now as he felt a hand on his arm, and looked up into the dark eyes of Rachelle. He sucked air through his teeth as he scrutinised her. Topping his drink up, he proffered her a glass.

She reached out, her fingers touching his hand that held the glass. "Can you make mine a vodka and ginger?" she purred, "that," indicating the whisky, "is for strong men like you." Eamon reached across the bar for the bottle and half-filled her glass, topping it up with her mixer of preference. Rachelle sensed he was hitting on her as she sipped her beverage, her eyes not leaving his. She shifted languorously in front of him, enjoying the attention.

"You looked lonely," she breathed seductively. "I thought that maybe you would like some company."

Eamon's mind was muddled. His groin had the familiar ache as he had been thinking of Marcia. He looked at the attractive woman's near-naked breasts. Any man could see she was offering it on a plate. The temptation was almost overwhelming. Eamon shifted uncomfortably.

Rachelle moved in closer to him and whispered seductively in his ear, "Let's leave and go back to your place. You could clearly do with the company. It's not good for a man to be on his own."

Eamon felt the whisky clouding his judgement. He wanted to rip that dress off her ... he wanted to ... But she was not Marcia. Rachelle's scarlet red lips were next to his face. Eamon jerked his head away from her and roughly grabbed her arm and pushed her away from him. His eyes were Arctic cold as he growled at her, "Get away from me! Ye couldn't walk a foot in my woman's shoes, ye whore." His scathing words tore into her.

Rachelle was angry at the rebuff, momentarily throwing her off guard. "Well," she said back at him, scoffing, "no wonder she has left your sorry arse. You obviously couldn't keep her satisfied." She spun around turning on her heels and left. Eamon had had enough. He strolled off in the direction of the villa, struggling to control his rising anger.

Suzette had observed the spectacle from a short distance, and, as Eamon made his way through the villa to his car, she knew he had been drinking. She asked Greg to take his keys and drive Eamon home, and she would follow and drive Greg back. Suzette had seen Eamon spurn Rachelle and by the angry look on his face, it dawned on her that Eamon was not interested in any other woman. Eamon's actions only served to convince Suzette that he still loved Marcia deeply.

....

It was months before the news of Max Greenaway's demise reached them. His body had turned up washed up on the banks of the River Thames with multiple stab wounds, an ear cut off and his lips superglued together. No one had put their hands up to ending Greenaway's life. Chief Inspector Ross Lowe had informed Lord Arthur Harper-Watts that someone had gotten to Max Greenaway. Lord Arthur acted appalled and later telephoned his son Thomas, who in turn phoned Billy Mackenzie, who gave his boss the happy news.

Before Eamon even had time to plan his trip to Thailand, he received a frantic phone call from Aye. There was an emergency and he needed to get there as soon as possible. He panicked, knowing Marcia was still two weeks away from her due date. Throwing clothes into a suitcase, Eamon rang Jane to organise a private jet to take him to Thailand as soon as possible.

Thailand

Marcia was eight and a half months pregnant. Her stomach and breasts were huge, and she felt like a beached whale. Her ankles were swollen to the point that she had taken to sitting with her feet in a bowl of ice water. Aye had been a great help, nursing her through her pregnancy in the intense humidity. That afternoon, Marcia had felt a sudden pain that made her wince, and within moments, the pain had returned. Aye telephoned a taxi and then hurriedly put a call through to Eamon. Marcia's third agonising cramp coincided with her arrival at the hospital.

Marcia was helped into a bed and a doctor rushed to examine her. "I think that we have a big problem," the Chinese doctor explained to Aye. The baby was the wrong way up, and he would need to try to turn it around. Marcia's agonised groans could be heard echoing throughout the clinic as the doctor pushed his hand inside her and tried to manoeuvre the baby's position. He gave her some much-needed pain relief as he continued his attempts, but the baby was not shifting. He could only hope that the baby would turn of its own accord. However, he was anxious, as the mother was older, and the baby was large, despite being not yet full-term.

Aye had run outside to find a phone, desperate to call Eamon and update him. He answered immediately and she babbled, rushing in her panic, trying to tell him in a mix of Thai and English that there was a problem with the baby, that Marcia was sick.

Eamon had to raise his voice and talk over her, just to get her to calm down. He demanded the name and address of the clinic as he was making immediate plans to come out as soon as humanly possible.

. . . .

The thought that Marcia's life was in danger shook Eamon to the core. He was beside himself with worry. Billy rushed him to the airport and as soon the jet was fuelled, Eamon was strapped into the passenger seat of the Lear jet heading to Thailand. Billy didn't know what the emergency was, but he'd never seen his boss so deathly pale or worried looking, even dealing with the most dangerous of criminals. As it roared up the runway and lifted into the clouds, Eamon said a silent prayer, just hoping that he would make it in time.

The car was waiting at U-Tapao-Rayong-Pattaya International airport, which was owned by the Royal Thai Navy, but public/military use was available, and it was only just over a forty-five-minute drive to Pattaya. As the car sped to the clinic where Marcia was struggling with a difficult labour, Eamon undid his top shirt buttons due to the heat and gave a sigh of relief as they pulled up outside of the small building.

The efficient Chinese nurse passed Eamon a gown, smiling as he struggled to put it on, his large frame not fitting its standard size. After being shown where to scrub up, he tied the mask on and followed the nurse into a room, where the whirl of an overhead fan was beating in time to the soft groans of Marcia in labour. The Chinese doctor, whose head was dripping with perspiration, palpated her large belly. The nurse was constantly mopping his brow. A feeling of helplessness washed over Eamon as the scene unfolded before him. Marcia was in agonising pain and he could do nothing to ease it for her. Her legs were elevated in stirrups as the doctor was trying to turn the baby. Marcia's face was etched in pain and misery as Eamon stepped forward and took her hand. Eamon saw the spark of recognition in her eyes, and he felt her small hand squeeze his. He was apoplectic with his need to help and, turning to the doctor, demanded that he get the baby out.

"We cannot do that here," the doctor replied, "No facilities, clinic too small."

Eamon could not believe what he was hearing. "Do something, and do it now!" he commanded.

"I will need to make an incision," he said, as Eamon nodded in agreement. He gripped Marcia's hand as the doctor reached for a scalpel and made an incision, ignoring Marcia's cries. Quickly, the doctor's hand went inside of her. "All's good," he breathed with relief, without looking away from his task at hand. With the other hand, he pushed hard, helping the baby move into the birth canal.

Eamon could only watch in fascination as Marcia's stomach heaved. "Baby good now, baby on way," the doctor told Eamon, beaming.

"Now you push … now stop," he ordered, guiding Marcia through her contractions. "Now push big, one last time."

Eamon marvelled as he watched the crown of thick black hair appear, then the screwed-up features, miniature of his own. Eamon could not take in that he was now the father of this beautiful child that was his son. He fought with his emotions as he cut the baby's umbilical cord. The baby cried as the nurse placed him across Marcia's chest so that she could feed him. The tiny mouth searched noisily. Marcia was oblivious to the pain as the doctor carefully stitched the incision that had been necessary for her beautiful baby to be born.

Eamon kissed her face lovingly, running his fingers across her cheek. He was so proud of her, he thought he would burst, and relief flooded through him.

Spain

Marcia was thrilled with their luxurious new home. Eamon had left nothing out – pride of place was a beautiful swimming pool. There had not been time to furnish the nursery but Marcia knew that Eamon had placed a call to Jane who got straight on it. He had given her carte blanche to order everything that was needed. The baby furnishing shop in Alicante said they would make the delivery the following day.

Marcia called Suzette at the salon and told her to come over. Suzette sounded ecstatic to hear from Marcia but stunned to find out that she now had a babe in arms. She instantly forgave her for not contacting her when she explained the reason for her long absence.

Jane had not been the least bit surprised about Marcia's return to Spain with a baby. Over lunch together Jane laughingly reminded Marcia of Kalita's prediction about her having five children. Marcia thought it had been a fluke that she had fallen pregnant after thinking that she was infertile after Reuben. Her firstborn had been constantly on her mind since she had given birth to Eamon's son. It seemed a lifetime ago that she had brought her eldest son into the world and her raging hormones meant thinking of him brought tears to her eyes.

"I knew that you and Eamon would be reunited," Jane remarked, "and seeing how happy you are now with this beautiful baby makes all the stress of you having to leave worthwhile."

Jane picked up the baby, who Eamon had named Niall, and rocked him as she spoke. "What about you, Jane?" Marcia enquired. "Motherhood would suit you."

"To be honest, Billy and I have discussed the subject, but he doesn't want to share me," she laughed.

Marcia knew Eamon wanted another child. She could not fault the way he'd taken to fatherhood, being overly protective of Niall, he had invited his ex-sister-in-law Aye to live with them to help take care of the baby. Jane was fussing over him like a mother hen, much to the chagrin of Aye, who had taken on the role of the baby's nanny.

. . . .

Both Eamon and Marcia were thrilled when she fell pregnant again only six weeks after the birth of Niall. Quinn was born ten and half months later making them a family of four.

Five years later

Eamon stood on the balcony, watching his two sons Niall and Quinn in the pool with their mother. The ever-watchful Aye was hovering, trying to coax them out to have their lunch and then an afternoon nap. Eamon could not deny that his two sons were handsome, so dark in looks, their complexion deepened by the Spanish sunshine. With their coal-black hair and Eamon's features, no one could argue that he hadn't sired them. Niall would be five years old soon and his brother Quinn ten and a half months behind him, both had boundless energy.

"Quiet child," Eamon commanded softly but firmly. Niall struggled and cried when his mother lifted him out of the water to Aye, who was standing with the towels to dry them. In comparison, Quinn held his mother's hand and was led quietly to the waiting Aye. Niall, as young as he was, knew that his father's words, though gently spoken, were to be obeyed. Eamon knew that when he was not at home, Niall had his mother twisted around his little fingers, and he despaired at the boy's strong will. Quinn, in contrast, was a gentle boy with more of Marcia's disposition. Eamon had taken note of his elder son's jealous streak and, on occasion, he had had to chastise Niall for hurting his brother. *How could I sire two boys so close in age that have such different personalities?* he mused. He watched Marcia swim on her own, now that the boys were under the charge of Aye.

He observed her lithe body as she rose from the water to walk up the steps. She looked no different to when he had first seen her emerge from the pool steps at Jimmy Grant's villa. He felt himself stir as the ache in his groin grew, his eyes stayed fixated on her as she leaned forward to pick up a towel. He wanted her now just as much as he had back then. She smiled as she dried herself walking towards him. Eamon took her hand and walked with her towards the privacy of their bedroom, with the cool white-opaque majolica tiles that he had laid on every floor in the beautiful villa.

The heat surged through his body as he unclipped her bikini top. His hand moved slowly down across her mound, his fingers moved deeper into the wet warmth. He quickly removed his clothing.

Marcia took his deep penetration with a low moan of pleasure, her legs on his shoulders. He was as physically close to her as he could be and loved looking down on her from that angle. Her soft breasts spread freely, her nipples chafed from her wet bikini top, standing proud. He opened her with his fingers and rubbed gently, enhancing her gratification, cock thrusting just below. She grasped handfuls of the bedding on either side of her, opening and closing her fingers in time to Eamon's thrusts, and her hair flew wildly around her face.

The satisfaction she gave him was unsurpassed. He could not begin to imagine that they wouldn't always be like this, and, yet, he knew he was going to be responsible for shattering the bliss that was their life together. His decision was made, and he knew he would have to tell her shortly.

Eamon could not complain about being neglected in the bedroom – Marcia time and again, lovingly gave him release as she knelt before him. Eamon's fingers and mouth had given Marcia fulfilment in return. But when Niall was six weeks old and Marcia had finished breastfeeding the baby that night, their restraints broke. Unable to control their passion after their abstinence, they could not get enough of one another. Marcia had fallen pregnant again straight away. He had noticed the changes in Marcia before the doctor had confirmed it.

Their only worry had been that Marcia would have another difficult labour, but their second son arrived safely and easily. They had married when she was four-months pregnant with Quinn. He had come into the world far easier than his brother had. They both wanted a large family but since her last pregnancy, try as they might, Marcia did not conceive again. The doctor had told them that there was no reason other than her biological clock, as Marcia was now forty-one.

Eamon discovered the fulfilment that fatherhood gave him, but as the boys grew older so did his concern for their safety.

Eamon smiled at the memory of Marcia breastfeeding Niall in her wedding dress in the hotel room after their wedding ceremony. Marcia looked radiant and as contented as he was. He could not have loved her more than he did at that moment. He was completely gratified by his life as a proud father and loving husband. Eamon had agreed to Marcia having some independence, allowing her to return to her work two days a week at The Mystique beauty salon. She was only able to do this as Aye had willingly given her life up in Thailand to come to live with them while her daughter Stephanie was away at university. As loyal as ever, Aye stepped in to help with their growing family.

Eamon looked at his youngest son sleeping peacefully, and, as he stood over him, Quinn sleepily opened his eyes and then closed them. Both boy's eyes were the same shade as their parents', deep chocolate.

Eamon lovingly placed a kiss on top of Quinn's head, "God bless ye son," he said quietly and wondered how long he would be able to keep his precious children safe. He opened the door to his eldest son's bedroom and repeated the procedure, as was his ritual, "God bless ye son," he said to Niall and closed the door. He knew he always lived with the threat of the net closing in on him. So many of his associates were now behind bars. Eamon had laid low in Spain throughout the time Max Greenaway was pointing the finger. He had managed to disconnect himself from the criminal world. He had fingers in varying pies with Greg, and his businesses were all legitimate. His priority was his family, their welfare and safety.

On arrival to collect Marcia from work, Eamon pulled himself up with a jolt. He had just noticed Marcia standing outside the salon talking to a young man who was carrying a briefcase, and a feeling he hadn't experienced for a long time hit him in the solar plexus. Maybe he had become complacent by having Marcia all to himself for the last few years. Their family life had been full-on – he had spent as much time as he could with his growing boys, and having Aye living with them meant he and Marcia had been able to have plenty of free time together. He sat rooted to the spot as the young man put his hand on Marcia's arm and let it linger a moment too long in Eamon's estimation. He could feel his bile rising and fought desperately to contain his rage. Marcia had not moved away and she appeared relaxed with the physical contact. The first pangs of doubt took root. He knew Marcia was attractive to men – he had seen them glance her way when she was on his arm, but as he watched his wife laughing gaily with this handsome male, Eve's betrayal with Jimmy Grant came to the forefront of his mind. The thought of Marcia with another man ripped him apart, even though he knew how stupid he was being.

Marcia smiled as she got into the car. She reached across and put her arms around his neck and kissed him. "Where are you taking me, my handsome husband?"

"Wait and see," he smiled back at her without mentioning what he had seen, as he fired up the engine.

. . . .

Eamon heard through his contacts that Chief Inspector Ross Lowe had spilt some more vital information. A couple of large brandies and the comfortable environs of Lord Arthur Harper-Watts's club had been all that was required. The previous reassuring news was that they had not managed to get anything on Eamon and had put away the file. He realised then just how fortunate he had been by paying heed to Marcia's warnings. If he had gone ahead with the deal that last time with Carlo Gabrette, Alphonso's son, the Columbians would have come after him, and if they hadn't succeeded, the law certainly would have. He knew that in the past, Jimmy Grant had let Max Greenaway in on deals and then the bastard had turned Queen's evidence. But Greenaway had come unstuck, as someone got to him and put paid to his singing once and for all.

Eamon had been told what Billy's buddy Captain Thomas in London had found out. Chief Inspector Ross Lowe had related to Lord Arthur, that it was their understanding at HQ that although Jimmy Grant's body was never found, it was assumed that he had been murdered and that it was highly likely that it had been gang-related. This, he said, was just as well, since if Jimmy Grant had not been gotten rid of, he would have been doing a twenty-five-year stretch in prison. But Eamon thought with Grant out of the way, they had not had one iota of proof of his connection. Eamon knew the law were unsure what else was happening in Spain, or if anything at all was going down. The chief inspector even knew the names of Eamon's sons, Lord Arthur reiterated to his son Captain Thomas. His father said the information came from the chief inspector who, being rather inebriated, was slurring his speech, while casting a worried look around the hushed club, apologising for his colourful language. Lord Arthur said to his son that he had waved away the chief inspector's concerns. He was more than happy with the information that he had gleaned from him, as was Thomas. Billy told Eamon that

Lord Arthur's plan at their next tête-à-tête was to lean on the chief inspector regarding another informant that Eamon was interested in, as "whispers" came to his ears about someone on Eamon's turf being active and Eamon wanted a name.

. . . .

Aye had proved her worth. Eamon and Marcia regarded her as one of the family. She had lived with them since the birth of Niall and was like a mother hen with the two boys. Eamon knew Aye treated Niall and Quinn equally, but he had taken note that she was aware of his eldest son's jealous streak towards his brother. He had heard her reprimand Niall, even though she never used English when she spoke to them, but Eamon understood chastisement in any tongue. Eamon did not relish having to break the news to Aye, but he had no choice and hoped she would comprehend the situation. Aye knew all about the threat that Eamon lived under. She had been married to the Australian, Graham, whose involvement with Max Greenaway and narcotics had seen him being murdered as she slept alongside him.

It was blatantly obvious to Eamon that Niall was envious of the attention that the younger boy received from his mother. Eamon knew that he would have to keep his eldest boy on a tight rein. He thought that there was an almost cruel streak running through Niall, which Eamon had struggled to admit to himself, but there was no denying that it shone imperceptibly in his young dark eyes at times. For Eamon, there was almost a sense of recognition – he knew all about the passionate and intense emotions that Niall was experiencing, and he pondered if he had passed his tumultuous feelings to his eldest child. However, Eamon hadn't experienced jealousy over his sibling Patrick. He had felt only a strong protective bond and it made him feel uneasy that Niall was showing signs that he would be capable of hurting Quinn.

However, Eamon, being a man who did not miss anything that went on under his roof, would endeavour to teach his son that he would have to be more tolerant. Eamon realised that Quinn, on the other hand, was much more like his mother. He was soft and warm, always wanting to please. Eamon wanted his sons to have the best education that his money could buy, far away from the influence of the world they lived in. He had given it a lot of thought and decided that sending his sons to boarding school would be the best way forward. He envisaged them growing up as educated gentlemen. His worst fear was for them to follow the same path as he had and become embroiled in the criminal underworld. Breaking the news to Marcia and Aye would not be easy, but he hoped that both women would understand that he only wanted what was best for his sons. Eamon had checked out a prestigious school in Barcelona and other areas. Uppermost in his mind was the need to have his boys protected. He would have thought differently if he had girls; they would have been less likely to follow in his footsteps, but he was determined that his boys were not going to end up like him.

Eamon had his sons baptised into the Catholic faith. Father Miguel was the Catholic priest from their local village and had conducted Eamon and Marcia's marriage. It had been necessary for Marcia to put to one side her own spiritual beliefs, and she had attended weekly confessions before taking their vows.

....

Father Miguel had reassured Marcia over the guilt she felt regarding not being able to give Eamon more children. He told her she must leave it in God's hands.

Marcia had noticed the changes in Eamon as the boys grew up, he had become more resolute in his opinions, and when he informed her that both Niall and Quinn would be attending a top boarding school in Barcelona, Marcia was devastated. She reeled, shocked to the core as Eamon revealed his plans. Both boys would leave for school shortly. No amount of pleading moved Eamon. Marcia cried inconsolably when she realised she could not sway him. For the first time, she had not been able to reason with him and she felt immense hurt. Eamon tried to make her see his point of view, that their sons would be in a safe environment in such a prestigious school. Aye had accepted the situation. She told Eamon she understood and was happy to remain living with them, as they both needed looking after and she would be their housekeeper.

Marcia accompanied Quinn as she had done previously when Niall was enrolled at the school months earlier. But whereas Niall had stoically accepted the situation, Quinn was entirely different. Eamon drove them to the boarding school; Marcia had clung on to her youngest son and as the time got nearer, she fought against the rising panic that at any given moment Quinn would be lost to her. She had put on a brave front, but her fortitude was gradually crumbling as her husband's Maserati drove through the imposing gates behind which her boys would be locked away for the next twelve years.

Marcia did not know how she could withstand the feelings of desperation; her mind was screaming. Quinn, unlike his brother, had cried, clinging tightly to his mother, as Eamon gently released his grip. Marcia silently cried out that she had not betrayed him, as he turned his small head in her direction and his father took command. She watched numbly as Eamon spoke to the young boy firmly, telling him that he had no choice and he had to learn, as his brother had, that mummy and daddy were not deserting them. The boy pleaded with tears streaming down his face. Eamon marched Quinn towards the huge building and a feeling of desolation gripped Marcia's heart. She saw Eamon walk back down the steps without her baby boy. She was battling against the same feeling of separation that she had experienced when she'd lost her firstborn son Reuben. Now history was repeating itself and there was nothing she could do about it. A shadow of darkness began to engulf her, slowly dragging her to the depths of despair. She desperately tried fighting her way out of it, but Marcia knew that this time she could not reach the light. As Eamon took his seat in the car and started the engine, Marcia turned to look at the imposing building. She could find no words to say to the man who she had loved more than life itself, but who was responsible for creating the huge hole in her heart she now felt.

....

Later that evening, Eamon had tried to reach out to her. He wanted to console her and make her understand that although luck had been on his side so far, he didn't want to take any risks what with someone close to home who had started to cause unrest. He tried to explain that his past could catch up with him and he could not have their sons growing up in that environment. For the first time, Marcia had turned her back on him and quietly cried. Her soul aching for her boys.

Marcia would not speak to him and the first cracks in their relationship began to appear as Eamon gave up trying to make her see it from his point of view.

Eamon could see the light had gone out of Marcia and he was concerned. Crestfallen, he had wanted to take her in his arms and make love to her, to make things right. Marcia barely responded to his persistent advances. She could not bring herself to enjoy what had always been such a huge part of their relationship. Her body became a traitor and her mind would not engage. Marcia went through the motions, but their mechanical sex left Eamon feeling dispirited and empty. Eamon resignedly rolled off her and Marcia turned her back on him.

Eamon sighed and slid out of bed. He put on a robe and walked out into the cool night air. He stared out towards the writhing sea in the distance and looked up at the new moon reflected across the bay. He silently prayed that Marcia would soon realise that once the boys settled into their new routine that they would be happy.

. . . .

Marcia was about to get her life back, but not in the way she wanted it. She had to fight against a constant rising panic that was telling her to flee. It went against her nature to wallow in misery, and she was determined that she would not allow life to kick her back down. She had risen from the depths before, and she was resolute in her desire to resolve this conflict in her mind. The next morning she had driven to Suzette's beauty salon. She had devoted the last few years to Eamon, and she felt that he had betrayed her by separating her from the children that she loved.

Suzette was thrilled to see her friend back in circulation and had rushed to put the advertisements out for Marcia's availability to take bookings. She told Suzette that her sons were in boarding school and she was free to make a new life for herself. Suzette was secretly pleased, Eamon O'Donally not being one of her favourite people. She was delighted to have her friend back full time.

Marcia put on a brave face as she sat in Suzette's salon having her hair coloured and restyled by Lloyd. Marcia looked at her reflection in the mirror. She told Lloyd that she loved her new, brighter red look. All the staff and the new receptionist Carla, who had replaced Rachelle, whistled and applauded as Lloyd span her around in the chair.

"Now, book yourself in with me tomorrow morning, darling," Lloyd told her, "I will be giving you the works in the beauty room, lovely lady." Laughing, as Lloyd sashayed across to reception, Carla booked her in for a facial treatment and a session of micro-blading.

Cindy told Marcia that she attended Elliot's gym three nights a week and asked Marcia to join her. Marcia agreed and, during her lunch hour, she went shopping and purchased the latest gym wear. She decided to reinvent herself and splashed out on dresses in a style that she would not have worn in the past.

. . . .

Eamon had been deeply hurt when Marcia rejected him. He had hoped that night when he began to make love to her, that she would have succumbed, but she just lay there, unresponsive. He knew how badly she was taking it that the boys were at boarding school, but he was adamant. Eamon would let her have her way in almost anything else but not this.

He concluded that his wife was playing games with him as he hid his shock at her dramatic new look. She had changed her hair colour and her skin was glowing. He took note of the shorter hemline and had got wind of her rejoining the Jamaican brothers' gym. Most evenings now, she left the salon and set off to the gym rather than returning home. Eamon was disturbed and angry at this change in her but could not think of how to put a stop to it. The last thing he wanted was to push her further away from him by insisting she curtailed her newfound freedom. He wished she could understand how imperative it was that he protect their sons, but she had become unreachable, and he felt desperate with the situation.

Marcia had returned to their beautiful yet quiet, empty-feeling home. Eamon's car was not there again. Each night over the last two weeks, he had gone out. Marcia had awoken in the early hours to the sound of Eamon stumbling around. She knew he was drinking heavily. She deeply regretted that their relationship had turned out this way. When she took in the fragrance of perfume on his shirts that he'd thrown in the washing machine, her anger rose. She knew that he was a man with powerful sexual needs, but she could not believe that he would be so insensitive to her feelings that he'd turned to other women already.

. . . .

Suzette excitedly told Marcia about the plans that Greg and Eamon had to open a nightclub. They had missed the boat on the previous sale, but the new owner had grown tired of the commitment and offered the club to Greg. The contracts, she said, had already been signed, and Greg was planning the required renovations as they intended to make it the biggest draw on the Costa Blanca. She was also at pains to tell Marcia that a young woman had been sniffing around Eamon recently, and in her opinion, Marcia should not continue to turn away from him if she did not want to lose him to another woman.

Suzette informed Marcia that Greg's source had told him that this woman who had her sights set on Eamon was named Robyn and that she had a reputation for getting what she wanted. She owned an upmarket boutique in town.

Although Marcia was looking radiant, Suzette was not fooled. "Listen, Marcia, please stop making yourself more unhappy," she said, for the umpteenth time that afternoon. Suzette threw her arms around Marcia as she started to sob, telling her friend how much she missed her children, and how it had driven a wedge between her and Eamon. Suzette reassured her, "Please Marcia, Niall and Quinn are in the best place, away from any harm and the trouble there might be here. Please dry your tears and go and get your man back before it is too late because I cannot bear to see you like this."

"Suzette, you don't have children and you don't know what it's like to have them taken from you. It is like you have lost your soul."

"Please, Marcia," Suzette implored, "bare your soul to Eamon. He will understand."

Marcia's eyes looked vacant, "Don't you think I haven't tried, Suzie? Eamon will not have his sons brought up in the environment we live in and that was his final word on the subject."

Marcia stood in front of the full-length mirror looking at her reflection. The black dress fitted her like a second skin. It was not her usual style but nothing about her new life was usual anymore. She was aware that she looked as if she was dressing for male attention. She intended to show her husband she was not going to sit back and take his disinterest in her feelings any longer. Marcia got into her car and set off towards the seafront.

Marcia pulled up alongside her husband's Maserati, which was parked up outside the Irish bar. She reapplied her lipstick and adjusted her short dress. As she stepped through the door, she was aware that heads were turning her way. One of the men in a group at a table whistled his approval. She pulled up a stool and ordered a vodka and ginger ale from the barman.

"Please let me get that for you," a voice came from behind. Marcia saw it was the guy who had whistled at her, pulling up a stool beside her. She had not looked around but knew Eamon was in the bar. Suddenly, Marcia felt uncertain about what she was doing and declined his offer, even though she thought he was rather handsome. But the man was persistent. "Maybe you and I could see a bit more of one another. I have a place nearby if you would like a little …"

The guy was suddenly lifted by his shoulders and thrown unceremoniously to the ground. "Get the fuck away from her ye toe rag."

The guy's friends rushed in and helped him up, then they hastily left the bar. Irish Michael said, "Steady there, Eamon lad."

"She's my wife!" he growled, without taking his eyes from Marcia. She glared back at him. Eamon shook his head in dismay. "Come outside Marcia, I don't want to make a show of it."

"Eamon…" a woman called out to him from the back booth. Marcia's head spun round to see the attractive woman wearing a low-cut top, staring at her.

"Your TART is calling you, and as far as I'm concerned, she's welcome to you." Marcia turned on her heels and walked out with her head held high but with her heart shattered.

Marcia could not see the road clearly as the mascara, blending with her tears, flowed without restraint. Her sorrow at losing her sons and the knowledge that her relationship with

Eamon was over, had made up her mind. Marcia knew she could not stay, as strong as she was, she knew that she couldn't cope with the physical pain that gripped her heart. To stay would only be a constant reminder of her once fortuitous life.

Marcia felt she did not have the strength to go on with this crazy life as it spiralled out of control. Eamon had taken everything she'd lived for. She thought he was clearly sleeping with other women and drinking heavily. She decided she would book a one-way ticket out of this place. Marcia neither knew nor cared where her destiny would take her, all she wanted was to release the feelings of utter despair. For the sake of her sanity, she had to flee to distant shores far away from her anguish.

. . . .

Eamon failed to return home that night. He had stayed on at the Irish bar to try to drown the demons that were plaguing him.

Irish Michael sat with him behind locked doors until the dawn's rays began to break through the Mediterranean sky. Being a barman for many years made Michael a good listener. He sat through the long hours before dawn as Eamon told him about his life – his brutal childhood at the hands of a drunken father, Eve's betrayal with Jimmy.

"…Then I read in her secret little book how she wanted Jimmy Grant's baby, after telling me she couldn't conceive, so that got me searching cupboards and her chest of drawers, where I discovered packets of contraceptive pills. The whore had even lied to me about that," he slurred. "Ye couldn't believe how painful it was Michael."

Eamon went to pick his glass up and missed, banging his hand on the table. "I didn't have a fucking clue," he rambled, then slumped across the table in a drunken stupor.

When he awoke, bleary-eyed, Michael had some words for him before he put his pal in a taxi. "Now take a bit of advice. I want ye to sit your woman down and talk to her, to explain about your early life, and the fears about your boys' future, Eamon."

Eamon was quick to respond, "How the fuck can I reveal to the woman that I love, that I have all these fucking hang ups?" he asked Michael, incredulously.

Michael counselled him, "Talk to her," he urged, "Don't be a fool, don't throw a good woman away, believe me, they are hard to find."

. . . .

Marcia searched the internet and, after finding what she wanted, she made her booking.

She had packed a small travel case with light clothing and photographs of her sons. The large shoulder bag she chose to take held everything else she required. She took out the bank card for the account that Eamon transferred money to. She did not want his money. She placed the bank card on the bedside cabinet. She removed her diamond and emerald engagement ring, along with her wedding band and she placed them alongside it. She had not slept and was now feeling nauseous and exhausted. She remembered that she had not eaten for at least twenty-four hours. She would eat and then get some sleep on the long-haul flight that would take her thousands of miles away from all her heartache. Marcia hugged and patted Roman, who watched her expectantly, as he hadn't been for his nightly walk. It would be a wrench leaving the faithful dog behind too, but she knew Eamon would take care of him. She shut the front door and walked in a trance-like state out of the villa gates and got into the waiting taxi. Marcia couldn't tell any of her friends she was leaving. She felt she could trust Jane, but it would be unfair to involve her because of Billy who was close to Eamon. She had never felt so alone in her life.

Marcia broke out of her reverie. They were asking all passengers to board in the departure lounge at the Paris airport. She had booked business class to ensure that she could get some rest and she joined the queue along with the other priority passengers.

Marcia was crying inside as she sat in the window seat of the Air France plane. The flight attendant checked to ensure her seatbelt was clipped in. The loud roar of the powerful engines filled her ears as the aircraft began to move along the runway. She looked out and sent a silent prayer out to her sons, for them to be protected. The surge of power took the aircraft up into the sky. As it began to ascend, Eamon's face rose before her. She held him in her vision and closed her eyes, fighting back the tears. How could the happiness that she had shared with him be swept away by their lack of communication when their relationship had been built on their mutual dependence on one another, she thought, sadly. Marcia did not know how she was going to endure her pain.

The young flight attendant placed her hand gently on Marcia's shoulder asking her if she was all right and passed her a menu. Marcia smiled thinly, thanking her. She had not realised they had reached cruising level. She placed an order for an avocado and mixed bean salad with a bottle of mineral water, thinking she must eat, knowing how taxing the long journey would be.

. . . .

Eamon stumbled towards the front door of the villa; he tried a few times with the key but kept missing. He could hear Roman whining behind the door. On the fourth attempt, he practically fell into the room to see a startled Roman, who appeared nervous by his master's actions. Eamon ruffled his coat as he steadied himself and tried to make sense of the quietude that greeted him. His befuddled mind knew Marcia was at home. Her car was parked out front. Eamon called to her as he went through the lounge and headed for their bedroom. The hollowness of what should have been a happy family home echoed in Eamon's ears.

He slumped down on the bed and stared in disbelief at Marcia's engagement and wedding rings that she had left behind. He knew that she had gone, that he had pushed her too far.

Eamon lay in the foetal position with his hands covering his face, as the seven-year-old child within the man released a plaintive cry with the pain of his loss.

Acknowledgements

I am indebted to the following people. My sister-in-law Jane Whiteley. Thank-you for being my mentor throughout. To my editor Kerry Boettcher for your hard work and patience. My daughter Serena, son Stacey and niece Carly. Dear friends Karina, Clark, Deonne and Nicky for walking with me every day, (also for the numerous healthy breakfasts). Tina Jopling, Cindy, Lesley, Helen, thank you all for your encouragement.

Printed in Great Britain
by Amazon

74376699R00292